BURIED IN THE HEART

M. E. HARRINGTON

BALBOA.
PRESS

A DIVISION OF HAY HOUSE

Balboa Press books may be ordered through booksellers or by contacting:

Balboa Press
A Division of Hay House
1663 Liberty Drive
Bloomington, IN 47403
www.balboapress.com
1-(877) 407-4847

Because of the dynamic nature of the Internet, any web addresses or links contained in this book may have changed since publication and may no longer be valid. The views expressed in this work are solely those of the author and do not necessarily reflect the views of the publisher, and the publisher hereby disclaims any responsibility for them.

The author of this book does not dispense medical advice or prescribe the use of any technique as a form of treatment for physical, emotional, or medical problems without the advice of a physician, either directly or indirectly. The intent of the author is only to offer information of a general nature to help you in your quest for emotional and spiritual well-being. In the event you use any of the information in this book for yourself, which is your constitutional right, the author and the publisher assume no responsibility for your actions.

Any people depicted in stock imagery provided by Thinkstock are models, and such images are being used for illustrative purposes only.
Certain stock imagery © Thinkstock.

ISBN: 978-1-4525-3633-0 (sc)
ISBN: 978-1-4525-3632-3 (hc)
ISBN: 978-1-4525-3657-6 (e)

Library of Congress Control Number: 2011910736

Printed in the United States of America
Balboa Press rev. date: 7/27/2011

PROLOGUE

Tunbridge Wells, England, 1920

Albert Sanders sat at his desk, watching the rain fall steadily outside his window. The blank sheet of paper beneath his idle pen was stark testimony to the difficulty he was having writing the farewell letter to his family. To the rest of the world, he was simply going on an extended business trip to India, but even though he had not said otherwise to his wife Elizabeth, she seemed to know that this trip was not all that it appeared to be. He wanted to write a letter that would explain what he was doing and why. He just hadn't realized how difficult it would be. But write it he must, because he did not want his family to worry like they had the last time.

He laid the pen down and sat back in his chair as he thought back to the day in 1898 when, hungry and cold, he had stumbled into a cave in the French Pyrenees and his life had been changed forever. His left index finger gently rubbed the black onyx stone of the ring on the third finger of his right hand. He looked down at the only physical remnant of his adventure. The ring and the five years he'd "lost" while living in the caves beneath the mountains reassured him that the whole episode had been more than a vivid dream.

To the world he had vanished completely, leaving his family and friends to worry, then grieve, over his disappearance. They grieved for five years when, just as suddenly as he had disappeared, he reappeared, walking into the French village of Eylie wearing the same clothes he'd been wearing the day he vanished. When he discovered the date was June 5, 1903, he was dumbfounded. He had been within the mountains for five years!

He traveled to Toulouse where he sent a telegram to his brother John and then waited for his reply. It came the next day, and John arrived three days later. John was the only person to ever hear the true story of where he had been for those five years. John especially felt that it was best to not repeat the story to anyone for he feared that everyone would think his brother was delusional.

Upon his return to England, he said that he'd fallen into a crevasse while searching for botanical specimens on slopes above the village of Eylie. In the fall he'd hit his head then suffered from amnesia for five years. He was relieved when everyone believed him and did not press him for details. At first, many had treated him as if he were an odd zoo specimen. He came to understand that the unknown or unexplained weighed heavily on the minds of most people. For the first few years after his return, he would hear of some new fable being whispered about him or where he had been. But three years after his return, he married a well-respected, steady girl and then fathered two children. Slowly the stories about his disappearance faded.

Seventeen years had passed since his reappearance, and he knew it was time for him to return to the life he had known during the lost years. It was time to return to the Pyrenees. The war that was supposed to end all wars was finally over and he was heartsick with grief over the loss of John and so many friends. He hungered for the peace he had known while in the caves. His fingertip ran over the cool, black onyx stone and felt the finely carved lines on its face—the lines of a map that would help him find his way back to the cave.

He looked down at the blank paper and pulled his thoughts back to the task at hand. After a moment's hesitation, he reached for the pen, dunked it in the crystal inkwell, and began to write. When he finished, he removed the ring and slipped it into the envelope with the letter. He knew he didn't need it to find his way back.

CHAPTER ONE

Seattle, Washington, May 1, 1994

Danny slid the house key into the lock, pulled the door toward her, and then released the dead bolt. As the door swung open, she stepped over the mail that lay scattered on the floor. Taking a quick glance down, she scanned the assorted envelopes and then bent down to retrieve the one piece of mail that did not appear to be junk. There was no return address listed, but she noticed that the postmark was from Los Angeles. Intrigued, she nudged the door shut with her foot and then walked into the living room, ripping into the envelope as she went. Reading the brief letter within caused her to stop in her tracks. With a scowl, she crumpled the letter into a ball and flung it at the wall. Stalking to the telephone, she picked up the receiver and punched in the number for her brother's house in France. After three rings with no response, she thought about the time difference between Seattle and the French village of Foix and realized that it was nearly midnight there. Her realization was interrupted by her brother's voice.

"Oui?"

"Allo, Philippe. C'est Danielle ici. Je m'excuse pour l'huere. Est ce que tu est au lit?"

"Non, non, pas au lit. Je fais de la peinture. Qu'est-ce qui se passe? Ca va?"

"Oui, oui, ca va." She paused for a second and then went on. "Well, no, actually at this exact moment, things are not fine."

1

Philippe was used to his sister's habit of switching from one language to another, so he switched also. "What's up?"

"I just received a letter from Austin Taylor, you know, the lawyer?"

"Yes. I remember him."

"He wrote to tell me that Pembroke never did the required 500 hours of community service." The bitterness in her voice betrayed her disdain for the light sentence handed down to the wealthy and influential industrialist, Avery Pembroke. "Austin wants to know if we want to take him back to court. He says that, even though it's been nearly ten years, we have a solid case against him. What do you think?"

Philippe paused for a moment before responding, knowing that his answer would not be what his sister wanted to hear. "Danielle, I think it's time to let it go."

Danny couldn't believe her ears. "Philippe! That drunk killed our parents, obviously paid someone off to get such a ridiculously light sentence, and then didn't even do the time! How can you suggest that we let him go?"

"He is a lonely, embittered old man, Danielle. All he has is his money, and you managed to relieve him of a good portion of that when you sued him after the trial. My point is that Maman and Papa are dead and taking Pembroke to court to make him do 500 hours of community service is not going to bring them back. Let it go."

Danny shook her head in wordless response to his advice. "I don't know if I can do that, Philippe."

"You asked for my advice, and I've told you what I think, but I know you well enough to know you'll follow your own impulses."

A ghost of a smile touched Danny's lips as she heard the wise, older-brother tone come into Philippe's voice. He was always so calm and even tempered while her passionate temper flared and waned like a geyser in Yellowstone Park. Not for the first time did she envy her brother's equilibrium. "I promise to think about your advice and not act rashly."

"I think that's a good idea. Let me know what you decide."

"I will. Thanks Philippe. Sorry to have interrupted your painting."

"Don't worry about it. I needed a break."

"Oh! I almost forgot! I've landed a job assignment in London, so perhaps I'll pop over for a visit."

"That would be great. Do you know when you might be coming? Sophie and Claire are going to Paris in June to see Sophie's mother."

Danny's brow creased. "Probably in late June. I'll let you know for sure as soon as I know."

"Okay."

"Well, I've got to go. I have to break the news to Stephen that I'm going to London for the job."

"He's not going to like that, is he?"

"No. My traveling has become a source of irritation for him."

"Good luck."

"Thanks, bro. Tell Sophie I said hi."

"I will."

Danny hung up the phone. Although she felt better than when she placed the call, she still felt agitated because of the letter. She wanted to be calm and centered when she told Stephen about the assignment, so she decided to do an aikido exercise designed to calm the heart and mind. She stood very still, feet apart, and began to breathe slowly in and out. She began the graceful, fluid movements of the routine, and a familiar sense of peace descended upon her. When she finished, she felt refreshed and ready to face Stephen.

On her way to his house, she detoured to Pike Place Market to buy some food, thinking that preparing a good dinner would soften him up for what he was sure to take as bad news. She shook her head, amazed that two people could have such divergent reactions to the same news.

She would have bribed, begged, or badgered for this assignment had she known it was available. But the senior editor of *Music on the Move* had called to tell her that the job was hers if she wanted it. If she wanted it! Of course she wanted it! When the editor went on to say that the band had specifically requested that she do the interview, she could hardly believe her ears. The Mystic Celts had not done a personal interview in years, so this qualified as a high-profile assignment. She was determined to do it.

She parked her car then walked down the steep hill to the market which overlooked Puget Sound. She paused to watch a ferry ease away from its dock, moving smoothly over the sparkling water. She grinned at the office workers who had come outside to soak up the sun and take in the view of the snow-capped Olympic Mountains. As she entered the cool shadows of the market, brightly colored photographs, fabrics, and works of art lined the walkway, and she felt her cheery mood returning. She'd make a great dinner and then tell Stephen about the assignment. She felt sure that he would understand how important it was to her.

After buying the ingredients for Stephen's favorite dinner, she left the market and drove to his house. Letting herself in, she carried the groceries to the kitchen. The house was quiet as she had expected, since Stephen wasn't due home from work for at least an hour and a half. The time would give her a chance to get dinner ready while she figured out the best way to tell him about the assignment. She nodded her head as she mentally worked through the evening. They would sit down to a nice leisurely dinner, drink the fine wine she had purchased, and then, when he was good and relaxed, she would tell him.

She opened the bottle of red wine, poured herself a glass, and then began sorting through the groceries. As she finished arranging them for easy access while she cooked, she heard the front door open. Stephen was home early from work.

"Merde!" She muttered the French curse as she heard the door close.

Danny walked to the kitchen door and watched as Stephen draped his coat over the back of the couch before turning toward the kitchen. Seeing her in the doorway, he smiled as he came toward her.

"What a nice surprise!" He brushed his lips lightly against hers. "After the rotten day I've had, your car in the driveway was a sight for sore eyes."

Danny smiled. "My plans changed, so I thought I'd surprise you by making you a nice dinner." She pointed into the kitchen at the food on the counter.

Stephen looked in at the ingredients sitting on the counter and then looked at her apologetically. "I hate to tell you this, but I'm not in the least bit hungry. I had a late, long, and very grueling lunch with a client."

She moved to the wine bottle, not letting him see her disappointment. "In that case, how 'bout I pour you a glass of wine?"

"I was thinking of something a bit stronger," he said as he pulled a bottle of Johnny Walker Red out of a cupboard. He put a couple of ice cubes into a glass and then poured three fingers of the scotch over the ice. "I have truly just had the day from hell," he said after taking a swig from the glass. He took her hand and pulled her toward him. "The only good thing that happened today, besides the very nice surprise of your presence here now, is that I found the perfect place for us to stay when we go to Oregon in June."

Danny swallowed and gave him a bleak smile. In her excitement over the assignment, she had completely forgotten about their plans to go to the Oregon coast at the beginning of June. "Oh brother," was all she could say to him. Nothing was unfolding as she had envisioned. No dinner, no softening him up before telling him that she would be in London for the first three weeks in June.

"What's the matter? I thought you'd be happy about that."

Danny disengaged her hand and moved to where she'd left her glass of wine. She took a big drink, swallowed, and then took a deep breath. "I've accepted an assignment to interview the Mystic Celts for the August edition of *Music on the Move*. In fact, the band specifically requested that I do the interview." She checked his face to see if that made a favorable impression on him. It didn't.

"Christ. The day from hell continues." He loosened his tie and unbuttoned his collar button as he leaned against the counter and thought about what she'd said. "I suppose this means you'll have to go to Los Angeles again?" The flat tone in his voice almost made her wince. It told her that they were about to have another discussion about her job and the travel it required.

"Danny, I don't know if I can take much more of this traveling job of yours. Why can't you get a writing job that allows you to stay in Seattle? The music scene here is booming. You could write about all the new bands coming on the scene here."

"Stephen, we've had this discussion too many times in the past two years. I love my job. I'm a freelance writer and photographer, which means I go where the stories are. I did a series last year on the Seattle music scene and, as I recall, you complained then that you hardly ever saw me because I worked out of my own house."

"There's plenty of room for you to work here. The whole bottom floor of the house could be your studio. It gets plenty of natural light, and you love the view of the mountains." He paused and then added, "At least then I'd get to see you on a more regular basis."

"Stephen, you know that I have erratic work habits." She paced a few steps away from him and then tuned to face him. "I work all hours of the day and night. I need solitude when I work—no distractions. Besides, this is *your* house, your pride and joy. I'd always be aware that it's *your* house, *your* space."

"I've said I'd be willing to sell this house and find another one with you, if you'd just say the word. A house that would be *our* house." His gaze was solemn as he looked at her standing on the other side of the kitchen. His voice was quiet when he spoke. "Danny, I've said it before—I want to marry you and live like normal people. As things are now, I never know from one day to the next if you'll be around for dinner or off gallivanting around the world. This new assignment, for example. How long will you be in LA?"

She nibbled on her bottom lip. "Well, it's not in LA. The band's other condition, besides the one that I do the interview, was that it take place in London. And I need to be there by June first." Sensing his displeasure, she rushed on. "The job will take two or three weeks, and then I figured I'd stay for a couple of weeks at the River Windrush cottage I told you about. If it's available, that is."

"So you're completely tossing off our plans for Oregon in June?" He made no attempt to disguise his irritation.

"Well, why don't you join me at the cottage after I've finished the assignment? The English countryside instead of the Oregon coast? What do you say?"

"I can't just pick up and go at the drop of a hat. I'm in the middle of a very important project."

"This isn't 'the drop of a hat.' It's not until the middle of June, which is over a month away. Besides, you've already planned to take time off for the trip to Oregon." She paced back and forth in front of him, ticking off the schedule on her fingers. "I expect I'll be done with the assignment by the second week of June, third week at the latest. You could fly to London, I'd pick you up, and we could drive directly to the cottage. We could have our little vacation in England instead of Oregon." She stopped pacing. "What do you think?"

Stephen looked at her in silence for a few moments and then slightly shook his head. "Danny, this isn't about vacations. It's about your unwillingness to commit to our relationship."

"Oh, right. Here we go again." She flung her arms out in frustration. "I have to give up my job that I love to demonstrate my commitment to this relationship. Why is it that I have to give up so much so you can feel secure? Why do I feel like I'm the only one who has to compromise here?"

"I have made adjustments in my life to make room for this relationship," he protested. "Don't make it sound like I haven't made compromises."

"You gave up the things you were ready to give up. You told me you were tired of the jet-setting, man-about-town routine and were ready to settle down."

"I didn't realize I was tired of that life until I met you, Danny. I don't want to just settle down. I want to settle down with you. Please don't go to London." The tone in his voice caught at her heart, and she was glad that she couldn't see his face clearly in the fading light. She knew from past similar discussions that an expression of love mingled with sadness was there. Part of her wished she could say what he wanted to hear, say the words that would clear the sadness from his handsome face. But to tell him she would give up this interview was something she just could not do. She had to do this interview.

"You're asking too much from me. It would be like me asking you to stop designing downtown skyscrapers and work on low-rent housing. You work where your heart is, and so do I. A high-profile band has asked for me to write about them because they like my style. Not only that, they are also one of my favorite bands, and I feel honored that they asked for me. I do not want to turn this down. Please don't ask me to."

Stephen flipped a switch and three recessed lights came on. The evening gloom receded from the kitchen. "We always come to the same place, don't we?" He sounded tired. He massaged his forehead in a way that told her he had a headache. His hand fell away from his face, and he squared his shoulders as if he'd made a decision. "The same crossroad we reach whenever we talk about the future of our relationship. I want to go in one direction, and you don't seem to want to go that way with me. Perhaps it's time we went our separate ways."

"Do you really mean that?" She scanned his face. "Yes, I think you do." Her voice became tight and cool. "I'll get my things together." She turned and left the kitchen, making for the spiral staircase that led to the second floor and Stephen's bedroom.

Stephen followed her to the stairs and caught her arm before she started up the steps. Danny stopped and slowly turned to him, her body tense. He pulled her into his arms. "Oh, no, you don't. You're not going to get out of this that easily. You know I don't really want us to go our separate ways. I'm the guy who wants to marry you, remember?"

His arms felt strong and sure around her, and she could hear the steady rhythm of his heartbeat as they stood together. The beat and the warmth of his embrace calmed her. She relaxed against him, which he took as a good sign.

"I love you, Danny. Please don't go to London. I've got a bad feeling about this one."

She stiffened and pulled away from him, the sense of calm vanishing as her temper flared. "I have a very good feeling about this job. It's an opportunity I don't want to pass up." She stepped back from him and regained a measure of calm. "I do love you, Stephen. I just don't understand why I have to give up this job to prove it. You've got to love me for who I am, not who you think I could be if I changed. That's not how love works."

She walked back into the living room and then turned to him. "Listen, I'm not thinking clearly right now. Can we talk about this when I get back?" She tried to read the expression on his face, but the dim lighting left his face completely in shadow.

"Danny, I'm ready to move on to the next phase of this relationship. Relationships are supposed to grow and change—good ones are, anyway. I need to know why you don't want this one to move beyond its current status. Now, I've told you what I want. You need to figure out what you want." He moved toward her, paused, and then added, "We could be very happy together if you would just let it happen." He brushed past her on his way back to the kitchen. She heard him make another scotch as she went upstairs to get a few of the things that she kept at his house that she'd need on her trip. When she came down, he was standing at the living room window, his back to her as he watched the sun set behind the Olympics. He didn't say a word when she said she was leaving. She stood for a moment near the door, watching his back, and then turned and left the house.

CHAPTER TWO

Esher, Surrey, England mid-May 1994

Sebastian Sanders sat with his back to his desk and looked out of his office window at the fog that completely obscured the ancient cemetery across the street from his antique shop. The fog made the glass a better mirror than window, so he scrutinized the reflection staring back at him. He knew he was considered handsome, looking much younger than his sixty-three years. He kept his five-foot-ten-inch body in good shape and bought suits that were cut to enhance his trim physique. The suits were always black or charcoal gray, colors which he had been told complemented his silvering hair and blue eyes. In spite of the financial reversals he had experienced of late, he always dressed the part of the successful businessman. He noticed a strand of hair out of place and smoothed it into place as the voice of his shop assistant squawked over the intercom.

"Excuse me, Mr. Sanders?"

He turned around to his desk and pressed the intercom button. "Yes, Groundwater, what is it?" he replied, not bothering to hide his irritation at the interruption.

"It's Lady Evans, sir. She's on the phone."

Sebastian sat up and straightened his already straight tie. Lady Althea Evens was one of his best and most loyal clients, and while her demands sometimes tried his patience, he never let it show. "Alright. Put her through." His voice oozed smooth charm as he greeted her.

"Good morning, Althea. How may I help you?"

"Hello, Sebastian. I hope I'm not interrupting?"

"Not at all. Your calls are always welcome. Are you calling about the Kraak porcelain?"

"Oh, Sebastian, I do so hate to be such a bother, but I've decided not to buy the Kraak piece. I just don't think it will look right with the other Chinese porcelains."

The smile froze on Sebastian's face, but his voice did not betray his discomfort. "But, Althea, they'll look marvelous together. I know what you have in your collection—you've bought most of the pieces through me—so I know that this Kraak will be a very nice addition."

"Yes, yes, I know, Sebastian, you've told me all this before. I just wish you would have checked with me before you bought it."

"Althea, years ago you gave me carte blanche to buy pieces as they came on the market. It was your responsibility to tell me that you changed your mind about that arrangement."

"I am sorry, Sebastian, but I just don't feel like buying it right now."

Sebastian grimaced, keeping his lips firmly pressed together lest he say something he would later regret. A moment of silence ensued as he composed a lie. "I am honor-bound to tell you that I have another client interested in buying the bowl."

"That's wonderful, darling! I feel much better about not buying it. Now I really must be going."

"In the future, I'll make sure to check with you before I buy a piece." He sounded more nonchalant then he felt and was glad that his voice did not betray his anger.

"Thank you, Sebastian."

"Good-bye, Althea." The receiver went down with a bang. "Damn!" he whispered. His fist clenched and unclenched, and his eyes blazed with anger. "Damn!" he thundered as his clenched fist came down hard on his desk top.

Of all his clients, Sebastian had truly believed that Althea would stand by him in these troubled times. And of them all, he thought she would believe that he had not known that the Sevres porcelain he'd sold to the American was a forgery. A very good forgery, but a forgery all the same. A grim smile came to his lips. In this case, it was probably just as damaging to his business that he unknowingly sold the forgery since his clients now doubted his ability to discern the real thing from a copy. Althea was probably making an appointment right now with one of his rivals to have her porcelains appraised. This thought galled him so much that he stood up from his desk and began to pace his office, trying to unwind the coil of angry tension twisting in his stomach.

For twelve years, Lady Evans had spent a goodly portion of her considerable fortune at Sanders Enterprises indulging her passion for Chinese porcelains. Her patronage and extended connections had turned Sebastian's burgeoning business into one of the most prosperous antique shops in southwest England. But if she was withdrawing her patronage, he knew that his profit margin would shrink considerably, and that thought chilled the flame of anger that the phone call had ignited. He stopped in front of his window and looked out at the grave markers he could now see through the thinning fog.

In the past year, he had watched his finances slowly thin from thoughtlessly secure to frighteningly unstable. The woman he'd married for her money had died leaving nearly all of it to charity. Two weeks after that shock, he got the news about the forged Sevres and business had been abysmal ever since. His vision of living out his life in the lap of luxury was becoming dimmer with each passing day.

But a small ray of light flickered in the dim future he perceived and, as he sat back down at his desk, he smiled. After a year of searching, his private detective had located his grandfather's long lost onyx ring. The ring had been an important prop in his father's bedtime stories about the secret treasure cave that grandfather Albert had discovered in the Pyrenees. Sebastian would hold the ring as his father wove fantastic stories about the magic cave, the vast treasure and the special map on the ring. He was convinced that, once he had it in his possession, the map etched on the onyx stone would lead him to a treasure buried in the Pyrenees. That treasure would end his financial worries forever.

His manicured fingers drummed the carved wooden box sitting before him on the desk. On impulse, he opened the box and pulled out two pieces of paper. The top paper was an old telegram that still bore the marks of having been crumpled into a ball years before. Sebastian gently smoothed the paper and read the short message from his grandfather Albert.

6 June 1903

John,

Know this will come as a shock, but am in Toulouse STOP Have made an amazing discovery in the mountains STOP Please meet me as soon as possible STOP Will wait here for your response STOP
Albert

When Sebastian finished reading it, he slid the other piece of paper on top of the telegram. The yellowing paper crackled with age as he carefully unfolded it. His grandfather's faded, spidery handwriting wove its familiar spell as he read the letter addressed to his grandmother.

18 April 1920

Dearest Elizabeth,

I do not have to tell you that this is the hardest letter I have ever had to write. I can see in your eyes that you know there is more to this trip to India than I have told you, and you are right.

You have never asked any questions about my disappearance before we met, but you must have guessed that the stories I have told Henry and Amelia about the secret cave allude to those "lost" years. The cave exists, is as real as you or I, and the stories I have told our children are but dim reflections of the wonders

I beheld while I was there. And now I must return. You may think me a coward for not being able to live with the grief I feel over the loss of John and so many other friends, but you have always been stronger than me— more equipped to confront and live in this mad world. Yes, I do feel a coward for not telling you face to face that I am leaving, returning to the life I knew in the mountains.

I have done everything possible to ensure that you will live comfortably, free from financial worries. The solicitor will be able to help you with any questions you may have about your finances.

I hope one day you will be able to forgive me for leaving. I can only hope that you will never forget that I love you very much and that only a deep longing that was planted in my heart before I met you could induce me to leave you now.

You will always be in my heart.
Albert

Aside from the bedtime stories, Sebastian had heard many unusual stories about his grandfather and had always thought of him as a very mysterious man. Since he had found the letter and telegram a year and a half ago, he had wracked his brain to remember every story he had heard about him. Stories he had thought were silly tales began to make sense as he read and re-read the papers. His grandfather had found a fabulous treasure, and the ring would show him where it was hidden.

His research of the area revealed that the Pyrenees were riddled with caves and that finding the treasure cave without the map would be like trying to find a needle in a haystack. His need to recover the ring brought to mind the woman who now owned it. Why his father had let the ring out of his possession, he would probably never know. But now that he had rediscovered its whereabouts, he was determined to get it back.

Sebastian did not begrudge the money he had spent on the private detective who found Ms. Davis. In fact, he had thought the ring was hopelessly lost to him, so the service performed by the detective bordered on the miraculous as far as he was concerned. Following a few scant clues found in his father's journal, private detective Benton had found Danielle Davis.

She was the daughter of a dead and, in Sebastian's opinion, highly overrated photographer. His success had made her a member of the new-money set, and if there was one thing that Sebastian despised more than Americans, it was people of the new-money set. That she was both made her particularly undesirable in his eyes and someone whom he would, under other circumstances, most certainly have avoided. But when Benton reported she had the ring, Sebastian decided to fly to Seattle to try to buy it from her.

He had followed her to Pike Place Market and innocently engaged her in a conversation. He remarked on the unusual ring she wore, saying it reminded him very much of a ring his father used to own. When he asked if she would sell it, she refused, claiming the ring had sentimental value and vowed she would never sell it. He could feel her suspicions rising as he tried to persuade her to sell so, when someone distracted her attention, he melted back into the crowd. Nearly three weeks had passed since that encounter, during which time he had almost resolved to let it go. But the call from Althea had convinced him that she was withdrawing her patronage, and his future as a successful antiques dealer was in jeopardy. He was now determined to do whatever was necessary to reclaim the ring.

His mind made up that he had nothing to lose and very much to gain, Sebastian picked up the telephone receiver and placed a call to Benton. Sebastian had one more job for him.

CHAPTER THREE

Late May 1994

The steward looked over his list of passengers, thankful for the light load they were carrying from Atlanta to Jacksonville, Florida. List in hand, he began his walk down the aisle making sure everyone was ready for take-off. As he neared the end of the plane and the last passenger, he saw in her the familiar signs of someone who does not like to fly. He hesitated for a moment before speaking and searched the manifest for her name. When he looked back at her, he found himself looking into eyes that were as blue as the Caribbean Sea on a sunny day. The woman's left eyebrow, black as pitch against her creamy skin, arched into a silent question as she looked up at him.

"Hello, Ms. Davis. My name is Richard. Can I get you anything before we take off? A magazine or newspaper, perhaps?"

"You wouldn't happen to have some gum, would you? I forgot to buy some before getting on the plane."

He reached into his pocket and pulled out a pack of sugarless gum, studying her as he extended a piece.

"Thanks," she said as she unwrapped the package.

"I've found that gently rolling the head from shoulder to shoulder loosens tight neck muscles."

Danny looked up at him in surprise and rewarded his concern with a smile. "Is it that obvious?"

Richard grinned in return, pleased that he had been able to coax a smile from her. "I'm very familiar with the signs. Seriously, gently roll your head so that your chin moves from shoulder to shoulder and that will help relieve the tension."

"Thanks. I'll give it a try."

He nodded and left to make final preparations for takeoff, leaving Danny to her thoughts.

The cabin lights dimmed and the jet backed away from the gate. Danny ran her fingers through her neatly cut, short, black hair then down to her neck, massaging it in a vain effort to relieve the tense muscles. She then followed the steward's suggestion, gently stretching her neck muscles as her chin moved from her left shoulder to her right shoulder.

As far as she could remember, flying had always made her uneasy. It wasn't really the flying itself, it was taking off and landing that made the muscles in her neck and shoulders bunch up. She always felt as if she were participating in a game of Russian roulette each time a jet revved up to take off or when the landing gear went down. Not one given to fatalistic thoughts, she wondered where this particular preoccupation had come from. *Probably some nasty past-life experience*, she thought with a grim smile and a shake of her head. She took a deep breath and looked out the window, deciding it was time to think about something else.

Twilight gathered as the jet sat on the runway. Danny marveled at how the light from the setting sun was softened into tints of mauve and blue by the thick, humid, air. All sharp edges were smudged by the humidity and by the heat waves rising off the tarmac. Such heat and humidity at the end of May was a sure indicator that Atlanta was going to have a scorching summer.

From Jacksonville, she'd rent a car and drive north to Jekyll Island to visit with her cousins who lived on the Georgia coastal island, having accepted their long-standing invitation the day after her fight with Stephen. She planned to use the time to relax with her cousins, do some more prep work on the Mystic Celts interview, and maybe even figure out her feelings about Stephen. The jet began its run down the tarmac, and Danny was pushed back into her seat. She closed her eyes and concentrated on chewing and swallowing as the nose of the jet rose into the evening sky.

When the jet reached cruising altitude, Danny relaxed and sipped some mineral water as her thoughts wandered back to Stephen, wondering why things had to be so complicated. One part of her thought that she was crazy not to accept Stephen's proposal. But another part of her was not sure, and she would not, could not, say yes until that doubt was dispelled. She wished she could ask her parents for guidance. But they were dead, and she knew she'd have to figure this one out on her own.

She felt a distinct sense of relief knowing that she would not have to find a solution to this dilemma for at least a couple of weeks but then felt a little guilty for feeling so relieved. Rather than indulge either feeling, she turned her thoughts to the approaching interview. She was excited by the prospect of interviewing the members of the reclusive Mystic Celts, especially their lead singer, Geremy Hawker. She had met him once before, years ago, and wanted to see how her memory compared with current reality.

She pulled the meager information she had been able to find on the band out of her briefcase along with her laptop computer. She had found information from the late sixties before the band's aversion to publicity set in, but aside from the standard press releases about albums and concert tours, recent information on the band and its members was scant. She had heard rumors that Geremy Hawker was a ladies man, but hadn't heard any gossip circulating about the other band members. The guys were very low profile. She read over the information one more time, turned on the computer, and began to type possible story angles as the jet made its way to Jacksonville.

Later that night, Danny stood on the moon-washed beach and knew she was exactly where she wanted to be. She could hear her cousins laughing and splashing in the surf as they moved away from her down the beach. She stood at the water's edge looking out at the inky ocean and the full moon that hung low in the midnight-blue sky. Its light made a white trail on the water's surface, a trail that lapped at Danny's feet with the gentle surf. She just stood there in a tee shirt and shorts, her arms out away from her sides, and enjoyed the warm ocean breeze as it blew around and through her. How marvelous it felt to be caressed by the breeze rather than chilled by it. She wanted to wrap the soft breeze around her like a cloak and walk the white path that the moon had laid down for her, away from all the tension and chill that she had left behind in Seattle. She had felt so weighed down with cares, but the breeze pushed and tugged at them until they slipped away from her like balloons on the night breeze. As she stood there, she realized how good her life was at that moment. She was with people she loved, the weather was warm and beautiful, and she would soon leave for London where she would interview the members of one of the most popular rock-and-roll bands on the music scene. So what if her personal life was a bit of a mess? Professionally, things couldn't be better.

—

Sebastian Sanders was in a foul mood. Over the past week, he had left three messages for Benton and had heard nothing in return. He was considering firing him when his private phone began to ring.

"Mr. Sanders? This is Benton. Sorry for the delay in getting back to you."

"Yes. I was beginning to think I would have to hire someone else," Sebastian replied arrogantly.

"No need for that, Mr. Sanders." Benton did not seem ruffled by the arrogant tone. "Your messages about the girl and the ring were clear and detailed so I got right to work. Didn't want to waste your time or money, as it were."

Sebastian was somewhat mollified by the explanation. "Are you calling to tell me that you have good news?"

"I think my information falls into the good news category, Mr. Sanders, but I'll let you decide. First of all, she's not in Seattle."

"What the hell do you mean she's not there?" Anger cut through Sebastian's arrogant tone.

"Just what I said. She's not here. When I called her house, a woman with an English accent answered the phone and informed me that Ms. Davis begins an assignment in London tomorrow. She also gave me the number where Ms. Davis can be reached." He reeled off the London telephone number.

"In London? Now that's convenient," Sebastian commented coolly while writing down the number.

"I thought you'd think so."

"Did you receive the fax with the drawing of the ring?"

"Yes."

"Fine. I want you to see if the ring is in her house. If you find it, I'll double the fee I promised you."

"I'll call you when it's done."

Sebastian cradled the phone and thought about what he'd heard. He had not received the information he wanted; nevertheless, he was much closer to reaching his objective than he dared hope possible. Benton's information that Danielle Davis was coming to London was a sign that his luck was changing at last. Of course, the best scenario would be for Benton to find the ring in her Seattle home, but since Sebastian had seen her wearing it, he was fairly sure it was with her in London. He was relieved to know that he would probably not have to keep his promise to pay Benton the increased fee.

His hand slid back over the cradled receiver. While Benton looked for the ring in Seattle, he'd find out where she was staying in London. He punched in the number for his warehouse on the other side of Esher. The warehouse foreman, Jackie Hansen, would know how to find Danielle Davis. In their former career as burglars, Jackie and his partner Chas Maloney had acquired a detailed knowledge of London and a list of contacts that was as extensive as it was varied. That list and the phone number from Benton was all they would need to identify her London address.

CHAPTER FOUR

June 1, 1994

After Danny finished setting up her photographic equipment, she looked around her friend Jasmine's London flat. The main room was large with hardwood floors and white plaster walls. It had three narrow, floor-to-ceiling windows that looked from the second story onto Cornwall Gardens in South Kensington. The windows allowed a profusion of soft light into the living room which was why she converted a corner of the room into a studio. The kitchen was in the corner opposite the windows and was separated from the main room by a five-foot-long breakfast bar. A hallway between the kitchen and the dining area led to the bathroom, the master bedroom, and a small guest bedroom. The dining area opposite the kitchen was small, having room enough for only a wooden table and four chairs. A short bookshelf was built into the wall behind the table and held a collection of cookbooks and novels. The flat was one of four in the building, so it was smaller than her house, but it was cozy and conveniently located near the heart of London.

Danny sat down in one of the living room chairs and, as she sipped on her cup of tea, sent a silent prayer of thanks to Jasmine. They had an arrangement to trade homes, if possible, whenever one had to be in the other's city. Jasmine was a much sought-after studio singer and musician and had received offers to work in Seattle. When Danny called to see if they could trade, Jasmine was happy to oblige.

Danny finished her tea and glanced at her watch. It was eight thirty, and Geremy Hawker wasn't due until ten thirty. She decided she had enough time to run to Annie's market and be back before he arrived. She didn't know why the band members wanted to be interviewed one at a time since most bands are more comfortable with a group interview. But it was fine with her since it meant she would have Geremy Hawker all to herself for a few hours. She slipped on her running shoes, grabbed one of Jasmine's canvas shopping bags, and headed out the door and down the stairs to the first floor landing.

As she came out the front door, her eye was caught by a man standing on the sidewalk across the street, facing her building. She paused long enough to get a good look at him. He was wearing a white Panama suit with a bright blue shirt and red tie. In the morning light with the new green leaves on the trees, he was a bright splash of color. He appeared to be people-watching and seemed oblivious to the picture he created. She was tempted to go back inside for her camera and ask him to pose for her. It was a Kodachrome moment begging to be captured. Then she remembered the time and decided that the shopping was more important than the photograph. The Kodak Company would have to get by without her help today. She ran down the four steps to the sidewalk and headed for the Underground unaware of the signal that passed between the Kodachrome man and his partner in a nearby car. After getting an answering wave, the Kodachrome man followed Danny to the Underground.

—

The owner of the fresh fruits and vegetables market looked up when she heard the bell over the door. Her face brightened when she saw Danny coming into the store. "Ello, luv. Been a while since I've seen your face 'round 'ere. Where've you been keeping yourself? Been back to the colonies, 'ave you?"

"Hello, Annie. It's so good to see you again." Danny gave Annie a big hug and then held her back at arm's length. "How are your knees? Have you been taking care of them like I told you?" she asked in mock sternness. Annie had arthritis in her knees, so Danny had sent her an herbal-tea blend to help reduce the swelling and pain along with some other health-care instructions.

"Yes, doctor. I've been doing just like you told me. Look 'ere, I even bought a chair for be'ind the counter." Danny looked behind the counter as directed and saw that Annie had followed her recommendation. "My knees 'ave been just fine since you told me 'ow to 'elp them. And you, 'ow are your knees?"

Danny laughed and looked down at her legs. "They are just fine. I stopped running, and they don't bother me anymore. I do miss running, though. I guess I just needed a mother to tell me to take better care of myself." She smiled at the woman who had befriended her during that first visit to London. Annie had told her she looked like a little lost girl when she had ducked out of the rain into her store six years ago. Danny *had* been lost and soaked to the skin in the sudden downpour. Annie had given her a cup of hot tea, a towel, and had invited her to stay until the rain stopped. They'd been good friends ever since.

"What can I get for you today, dearie?"

"That depends on what you've got."

"Well, it's still early for many fruits, but the tomatoes from Jacob's are very good—'e knows 'ow to make things grow, that man does, even out of season. The strawberries are very tasty, and so are the oranges. The mushrooms came in fresh this morning, and the lettuces are out of my own garden so they're nice and fresh, too. And, of course, your favorite chocolate!" A loud rapping came from the back of the store. "Get what you need and call me when you're ready. I need to let the delivery man in." Annie made her way slowly to the back door. "Stop pounding!" she yelled. "I'm coming!"

Danny smiled as she watched Annie retreat. She loved this little corner store. It was out of her way to come here, but on top of being her surrogate mother, Annie had a wonderful selection of fresh fruits and vegetables. Most of the produce was bought from local farmers, and the rest came from other common market countries. She was looking at the fruit bins in the front window when she noticed the Kodachrome man across the street. He was watching the store when he saw her looking at him. He immediately turned and started walking away. *How odd*, she thought, as she watched him walk down the street and out of sight.

"This is your lucky day, Danny."

Danny turned from the window and saw Annie coming toward her carrying a large bucket of bearded irises. She forgot all about the Kodachrome man when she saw the flowers. Annie knew how much she loved flowers, and these were one of her favorites.

"Oh, Annie, they're beautiful! I've filled my bag with goodies, so I'm ready to pay you and be on my way. I've got an interview to do this morning." She looked at her watch. "Yikes! Where did the time go?" Annie wrapped the flowers and added up Danny's purchases. Danny paid the bill and promised to come back soon for a long chat. She kissed Annie good-bye and dashed out the door. Since she was running late, she decided to catch a taxi back to the flat, but much to her chagrin, no taxis were in sight. She walked quickly to the Underground and hoped the train would be there when she arrived at the platform. As she dashed down the steps, she caught a flash of white out of the corner of her eye. Thinking it was the Kodachrome man, she turned to get a better look, but saw a woman in a white raincoat instead. As she hurried down to her platform, she couldn't shake the feeling that she was being followed. The train stood waiting, doors open and inviting. She boarded, took a seat, and did not notice the Kodachrome man as he jumped into the car behind hers just as the doors were closing.

She hurried up the steps and out of the Glouster Road Tube station carrying the groceries in one hand and the flowers wrapped in newspaper in the other. She looked back over her shoulder to see if the Kodachrome man was anywhere in sight. When she didn't see him, she figured that her imagination had gotten the better of her. Why would anyone want to follow her? Anyway, she was late so she picked up her pace and prayed that Geremy Hawker wasn't the punctual type. As she approached the building, she stuck the flowers into the bag and reached into her jeans pocket for her keys.

A burly man burst out of the front door of her building, jumped down the stairs, and knocked her over as he rushed past. She landed hard on the pavement. The shopping bag hit the ground and toppled over while the flowers skittered across the sidewalk before stopping a few feet away from her. She sat speechless and watched as two tomatoes rolled out of the bag and into the gutter.

"What the hell?" she finally asked of no one in particular.

She slowly got to her feet, rubbing her sore bottom, as she watched the man who had knocked her over run down the street.

"Are you alright?" a man asked as he handed her the tomatoes.

Still a little dazed, she looked down at the proffered tomatoes and took them. "Yes, I think so." She picked up the overturned bag and put the tomatoes back into it. Then she looked around as she straightened back up. "Thanks for asking. I thought the British were mild mannered …" Her sentence trailed off when she noticed that the man was no longer there. "Brother. What a strange morning." Danny grabbed the bag of groceries, picked up the flowers, and stuck them back in the bag before proceeding slowly up the steps. When she reached the outer door, she noticed that the lock was damaged. Feeling uneasy, she shut the door behind her and made for the stairs.

She was relieved that Geremy Hawker hadn't arrived, because she wanted to change her clothes and make herself more presentable for the interview. She came to the second floor landing and was moving down the short hallway when she realized that the door to the flat was slightly ajar. She could also see that the lock had been forced. Moving quietly to the door, she reached out and gently pushed it open.

A tall, blond-haired man neatly dressed in a charcoal-gray blazer and black slacks stood in the center of the room surveying the wrecked flat, his back to the door. Even from behind, she recognized him immediately as Geremy Hawker. Her first thought as she looked at the back of his head was that she would not be able to make herself more presentable. The thought had barely registered when she noticed the flat.

"What the hell?" She whispered to herself as she stood frozen in the doorway, her fingertips still resting lightly on the door.

Geremy Hawker turned around, a puzzled expression softening the chiseled features of his handsome face. His expression cleared when he saw her, but his response was momentarily forgotten as his sapphire-blue eyes met and locked with hers. They both just stared, she because of her confusion over the scene before her, and he because he didn't know what to say to the unknown woman who stood in the doorway. For a moment, he wondered if he had come into the wrong flat, but then didn't care if it meant he had a chance to make the acquaintance of the beautiful woman standing before him. He realized he was staring and that the silence was beginning to feel awkward. She didn't appear inclined to break it, so he cleared his throat and addressed her in the velvety voice recognized by millions around the world.

"The door was open so I came in, and I found it like this. I have an appointment with Danny Davis. This is his flat, isn't it?"

Danny's fingertips slid down the door and her hand dropped to her side before she walked slowly to the kitchen where she set the bag of groceries on the counter. She felt stunned as she looked at the mess that spread out before her. Furniture cushions were scattered around the room, pictures were hanging at crazy angles, and her studio lights, camera, and backdrop cloth were in a heap in the corner. In the dining room, books littered the floor in front of the bookshelf.

"Excuse me? Is this the flat of Mr. Davis?" His voice expressed concern as he took in her shocked expression.

The tone more than the words snapped Danny back to reality. "What? Oh, yes, I mean. How do you do, Mr. Hawker?" She stuck her hand out as she walked across the room to him. "My name is Danielle Davis, but I go by 'Danny'."

He took her hand and looked at her in surprise. "You're Danny Davis?" His voice echoed the look of surprise on his face. That Danny Davis would turn out to be a woman was absolutely the last thing he expected. His other hand came up and enclosed her hand in his.

As they stood there with Danny's hand sandwiched between his, she was conscious of the warmth of his touch, the strength of his fingers, the softness of his palms, and the roughness of the calluses on his fingertips. His eyes bored into hers, and she felt strangely breathless.

Sensing that she was succumbing to his charisma, he leaned closer to her and, with a smile, asked, "Are your tomatoes alright?"

She let out a breath and laughed, relieved that the spell was broken. She gently pulled her hand from his hold. "So you're the tomato retriever. Well, that's one mystery man identified." She moved away from him and walked through the living room. "But, yes, to answer your question, the tomatoes did survive the collision. They fared much better than the flat, that's for sure." She nudged a couch cushion with her toe.

"Your flat is a mess!"

"That's what we in America would call an understatement." She stood in the center of the room and shook her head in disbelief. "Actually, though, it's not mine. The flat belongs to Jasmine Baker. Do you know her? She's a studio musician and singer." She began moving around the living room again, resisting the urge to pick things up.

"I know the name, though I've never worked with her." Geremy watched her as she moved around the room. He smiled as he imagined the expressions on the faces of the other band members when he would later tell them that Danny Davis was definitely not the balding, overweight man they had joked about.

None of them had wanted to do the interview. It had been their manager's idea, and he had set up everything. Since the band was set to go on tour in September, he had thought the article would be good publicity. They all agreed, but no one volunteered to do the interview. They had decided that one of them would go for the initial interview to suss out the interviewer and determine if contact with the rest of the band was necessary. They ended up drawing straws to decide who would go. Geremy had pulled the short straw so had lost, or so he had thought at the time. As he watched Danny Davis, he found himself reconsidering his assessment of the situation. This might not be so bad, after all.

"Is there anything I can do? I'll ring the police if you'd like."

Danny was so intent on assessing the damage to her things and the flat that she had practically forgotten that Geremy was there.

"Oh, uh, yeah. Yes, that would be great. Thanks." She had a puzzled look on her face.

"Where's the phone?"

She pointed. "It's over there on the table next to the breakfast bar." She looked around the living room. "Something strange is going on here."

Geremy had the phone in his hand, but the handset stopped in midair as he turned to look at Danny. "What do you mean?"

"Well, the place is a mess, but I don't think anything is missing. I mean, there's some valuable electronics in here. Stuff that's easy to carry, but none of it is gone. I'll check the bedroom while you call the police."

She came out of the hallway as he was hanging up the phone. "The police are on their way. Did you discover anything missing?"

"Not as far as I can tell. The rooms look like they've had a thorough going through, so it's hard for me to be sure. Listen, I'm sorry about all this. Would it be possible for you to come back this afternoon, after I've spoken to the police and straightened things up?"

Geremy looked at his watch and pursed his lips. "Yeah, I can come back later." He looked at her thoughtfully. He did not have anything scheduled for the day, but even if he had he knew he would have changed his plans. He enjoyed few things more than being in the company of a beautiful woman with whom he could play the seducer. "Let's see," he said, looking back at his watch, "It's ten forty five now. How about if I come back at half past one?"

"That would be great," she said as she walked with him to the door. "Thanks for being so flexible. I'm really sorry about the delay."

"Sometimes things don't work out the way we planned." As he reached the door he turned to her. "I'll see you at half one."

Danny closed the door behind him and leaned against it. "Whew! When they were giving out pheromones he must have received a double dose!" She gave a slight shake of her head as she thought about the rumors that he was a ladies man. In spite of that knowledge, she could already tell that she was vulnerable to his charms.

She walked slowly to the kitchen to put the groceries away and pondered her first impressions of Geremy Hawker. Well, not really her first impressions. She had gotten those the first time she'd met him when she was eight years old. Her father had taken her and Philippe to a Mystic Celts concert in Los Angeles in 1968, and they had met the band after the show. She remembered Geremy Hawker as being cute, soft-spoken, and polite. Maturity and experience had turned the cute, soft-spoken boy into a handsome, self-assured, and very charismatic man.

All the band members had been very nice to her and Philippe that night, but Geremy had made a real effort to talk to them and answer their questions. They, of course, had been awestruck and a little shy at first, but Geremy had asked them a few questions and before long they were asking him all about life as a rock star. Then Philippe had gone to talk to the drummer, Miles Jensen, and Geremy had taken her hand and showed her around the stage. She'd had a bit of a crush on him ever since.

—

"You were supposed to get in and out cleanly." Sebastian told the men through clenched teeth. "That means, no one sees you, and no one knows you were ever there." The restraint which had kept his teeth clenched and voice at a normal decibel evaporated, and his anger exploded. "Instead, you knock the Davis woman down as you leave the building. Now the police are there poking around. And to top it all off, you didn't find the ring!"

The two men stood quietly as Sebastian yelled at them. When he appeared to be finished, the man who had knocked Danny over spoke up, somewhat defensively. "It was a quick search, so I knocked a few things over."

"You moron, you weren't supposed to knock *her* over."

"Jackie didn't signal she was back until she was almost at the door. I had to get out fast. Anyway, the ring isn't in there. I'm sure of it."

"Benton didn't find it in Seattle, either. She must be wearing it, so you'll have to go back and get it from her."

Jackie and Chas looked at each other, both faces showing concern although neither said anything to Sebastian. Professional burglars for most of their adult lives, they tried very hard not to encounter their targets. Breaking into a house in broad daylight was unusual enough for them, but making face-to-face contact in order to steal something was totally contrary to their usual methods.

Sebastian did not notice the exchange between the two men but carried on with his instructions. "Try not to make it obvious that you are after the ring. I don't want her to make any associations between this theft and my offer to buy the ring a few weeks ago. That said, it might be best if you drug her first and, since the police have been nosing about, get her away from the flat before you search her. And I want it done today. I don't know how long she's in London, so I want this taken care of immediately."

The men exchanged looks again. Tight time lines with little advance planning also went against their grain, but Sanders was paying good money for this job so Jackie shrugged and Chas nodded, non-verbal signals between them that indicated acceptance of the job.

"And one last thing. Don't let her see your faces. If that happens, you'll have to kill her, and I'd rather you didn't have to do that. Too messy." Sebastian paused and glared at them. "Well? Go!"

As Chas and Jackie walked down the hall to the back stairs, Chas asked, "You ever kidnapped anyone before?"

"No," came Jackie's clipped response.

"Me neither." Chas fell silent as they reached the top of the stairs. Jackie proceeded down ahead of him. "But how hard can it be? She's not very big, and I still have some of that chloroform we used on the guard at the Abercrombie estate. It knocked him out long enough for us to that job. We should be done with her in less time then it took us to do that job." He fell silent again when they reached the back door. They stepped out into the bright sunshine and went straight to their car.

"You ever killed anyone before?" Chas asked conversationally.

"No." Jackie answered tersely.

"Well, it won't come to that. We'll get the ring, and she'll never know what this whole thing was about."

Jackie just grunted, and both fell quiet as they drove back to Sander's antiques warehouse. Jackie was busy working out how they would grab the girl, and Chas left him to his thoughts.

As they entered the small, sparsely furnished warehouse office that served as a base of operation for the legal as well as illegal activities they performed for Mr. Sanders, Chas plopped down into a chair covered in tattered fabric, which groaned and squeaked under his weight. "What did you work out for this one? How we gonna do it?"

" What did you do with the chloroform?"

" It's in the cabinet over there." Chas pointed to the gray metal, double-door cabinet in the corner of office.

Jackie nodded. "We'll do it today. We know the territory, and the sooner we get this over with the better." He went behind the olive-green metal desk and sat down. "The car needs petrol. You go fill it up while I work out where we can take her when we search her."

Chas struggled out of the chair and left Jackie looking over a map of the greater London area. Before Chas reached the side door leading out to the car park, the huge receiving area door began to roll up. A shipment was coming in. The truck driver saw Chas and hailed him. "Chas! Good to see you. Can you help me unload the truck? Tommy called in sick, and I just about broke my back loading the things into the truck."

"Sure, Roger, I'll help you unload." He took off his jacket and rolled up his sleeves, thinking he'd fill the car up after he helped Roger.

CHAPTER FIVE

Danny put the groceries away and filled the electric kettle with water for tea. She had just turned the kettle on when the doorbell rang. She opened the door part way and found two men standing in the hall.

The man in front spoke first. "Ms. Davis?" He had a gravelly voice and piercing gray eyes that Danny sensed missed very little. He was about the same height as Danny but, unlike her lean figure, he was slightly overweight. He wore a beige, calf-length raincoat over a rumpled gray suit. His hair was thinning on top, and he looked tired. His sidekick was a different story. Looking fit and trim in his police uniform, he stood a couple inches taller than the man in front, had thick brown hair, brown eyes, and a square jaw.

"Yes?"

"I'm Sergeant Earling, and this is P.C. McCafferty. You reported a burglary, I believe."

Too much fat and not enough exercise in this man's routine, Danny thought. *Probably smokes, too.* She opened the door all the way and motioned them to enter. "As you can see, someone made a bit of a mess in here. Strangely enough, though, nothing appears to be missing." As Sergeant Earling passed, she caught a whiff of stale cigarettes. She smiled. She loved being right. Sherlock Holmes would have been proud of her.

"Ah, you're from North America. US or Canada?"

"US. Seattle, to be specific."

"Are you here on holiday?" The three of them stood just inside the door while Earling and McCafferty obtained the preliminary information before investigating the crime scene. McCafferty scanned the room and wrote his observations in a small, black notebook. Earling asked the questions and committed her answers to his own notebook.

"No. I'm here on a job assignment. I'm a freelance writer and am here to do an interview article for the magazine *Music on the Move.*"

"I see. Have you touched anything in here?"

"Not a thing. I've seen enough movies to know not to touch anything at the scene of a crime." The water came to a boil, and Danny heard the kettle click off. She went to prepare the tea while McCafferty began to take photographs of the front and back rooms.

"Do you have any idea why someone would want to do this?" Earling asked.

Danny put a bag of Earl Grey tea into a small teapot before pouring the hot water. "No, sir, I don't. This flat belongs to a friend of mine, Jasmine Baker, so it's hard to say if this was directed at me, at her, or if it was just a random hit. It's just kind of strange that someone would do so much damage and then not take anything. There's plenty of small, easy-to-carry equipment to steal."

"Have you seen any suspicious people hanging around since you've been here?"

Danny poured a cup of tea. "Would you gentlemen care for a cup of tea?"

Earling answered for them both. "No, thank you. Have you seen anything suspicious?"

"Well, when I approached the building, a large man came bolting down the steps and knocked me down. When I saw the flat, I wondered if there was a connection. And there was the Kodachrome man."

"The Kodachrome man?" Earling asked. McCafferty, who had just starting dusting for prints, stopped and looked at Earling and then at Danny.

"That's what I call him. Kodachrome is a high-color resolution slide film made by the Kodak Company, very good for bright color pictures. Anyway, he was standing outside the building when I went out this morning. He was wearing a white Panama suit with a bright blue shirt and red tie. I almost came back to get my camera to take a photograph of him. I thought I could sell it to Kodak as a promotional picture. I didn't have much time to get to the market, so I decided against taking the photo. But then, when I was in Annie's Market on Portobello Road, I saw him again and could have sworn he was watching the store. When he saw me looking at him, he walked away, and I didn't see him again. I probably wouldn't have even noticed him if he hadn't been wearing such bright colors. He was a photographer's dream—like I said—a Kodachrome man."

Earling and McCafferty exchanged looks. "Too bad you didn't follow that urge and take a picture of him. From the descriptions you've given, these two guys may be a team we've come across before. They are thieves, but breaking and entering in broad daylight and then not taking anything is not their usual style. Your 'Kodachrome' man sounds like Jackie Hansen and the big guy could be his partner Chas Maloney."

"Do I have anything to worry about with these two guys? Like, are they dangerous?"

"Not usually. Like most burglars, they prefer as little contact with their victims as possible. But if you do see them again, please call me. Here's my card."

Danny took the card and placed it next to the phone, noticing for the first time that the message light was flashing on the answering machine. She set her mug of tea down on top of the card before turning back to Earling and McCafferty.

McCafferty had finished photographing and dusting for prints and was putting his equipment away as Earling finished his questions. "There's nothing more we can do here. I'll call you if anything comes up. Just remember to keep your eyes open and call if you see anything suspicious."

She closed the door after them and leaned against it. She'd have to get the door fixed, but at least the dead bolt still worked. She didn't bother throwing it because she expected Geremy any minute.

Chas and Jackie were sitting in their car in front of Danny's building discussing the options on how to get into the building and then out with the drugged woman when Jackie noticed movement at the door. "Christ!" he said as he slid down in his seat. "Get down, you idiot! It's Earling."

Chas had a little more trouble sliding down because the steering wheel jammed into his stomach. Then he reached down to the seat-adjustment knob, pulled it, and the seat-back went down.

Jackie peered over the dashboard and watched as the policemen drove away from the building. "Okay, all clear. I think we should go in like we own the place, quietly go upstairs, and suss out the situation. If the building is quiet and she is alone, we grab her. If it doesn't feel good, we leave and figure out another approach."

Chas shook his head. "Why don't we wait until it gets dark? Working during the daylight makes me nervous."

"Me, too. But we can't wait. She may not plan to stay there tonight or someone may come to stay with her. Anything. I say we move now and get it over with."

"Okay. Hand me the bottle of chloroform. It's in the glove box."

The bottle of chloroform and a white rag created a bulge in Chas's jacket pocket as the two men walked slowly to the front door. The street was quiet. Jackie walked up the outside stairs ahead of Chas and smiled at the still-broken door lock. He walked in with Chas close on his heels. They went up the stairs slowly, tuning in to the sounds in the building. All was quiet; even their footsteps were muffled by the thick carpet on the stairs.

Danny had just finished listening to a message from Jasmine when she heard a noise behind her. She was turning around as a cloth went over her nose and mouth. She smelled an acrid scent, struggled, and then went limp in the arms of her assailant. The mug of tea that she'd been holding crashed to the floor.

Geremy pulled his sporty, silver Jaguar up to the curb a few doors down from Danny's building and looked at his watch. He was fifteen minutes early and was looking at the building, wondering if he should go on up to the flat when he saw two men come out the front door with Danny between them. Her head was lolling and her feet were dragging. One man, short and thin, opened the back door of an older, somewhat battered, red sedan while the other, much taller and stockier, supported Danny and maneuvered her onto the seat. When the big guy released her, she fell over and out of sight. He tucked her legs into the car and closed the back door. Then he opened the front door and slid in behind the wheel while the smaller man quickly looked around to see if anyone was watching them. He seemed to relax when he realized that the street was quiet and no one appeared to be watching. Chas started the engine as Jackie jumped into the car. The screech of the tires as the car pulled away from the curb betrayed that they were in a hurry to get away from the building.

Before he was even aware of what he was doing, Geremy started his car and began to follow them. Something strange was going on, and it was apparent that the men did not have good intentions toward Danny. He'd call the police later if necessary. For now, he'd just follow them and find out where they were taking her.

"Jackie, why don't you go ahead and check her out now while we're driving? If we're lucky, we'll find the ring and be able to dump her before she comes to."

"Listen, Chas, I'm not turning around. Riding backward, even for a minute, makes me sick. Besides, she's out cold and will stay that way until after we are long gone. I saw how much juice you put on the cloth. We'll be at the deserted warehouse before she comes to. We'll search her proper then."

"Just check her hands. A gold ring with an onyx stone should be easy to spot."

"I'm not turning around. I'll look for it when we get to the warehouse."

Danny lay very still on the backseat. She was groggy and her lips and nose burned, but she was far from being out cold. She had managed to hold her breath when the cloth went over her nose and mouth, but had still gotten a pretty good sniff of the chloroform. She caught snatches of their conversation, but it didn't make much sense to her foggy brain. She decided that she would just relax and wait for her mind to clear. She had to fight the urge to adjust her position even though she could feel her left arm and leg falling asleep beneath her. She wanted them to think that she was out cold. It might give her time to figure out what the hell was going on.

Geremy followed the red sedan at a discrete distance as it zigzagged through London, but he made sure to keep a car between them in case they were watching their back. "What am I doing?" he said out loud. "These men could be professional killers. I should pull over and call the police." Then he reminded himself that if he pulled over he wouldn't know where they were taking her. As he followed the sedan, he re-considered his aversion to cell phones. One certainly would be handy right now. He smiled as he thought of an advert for the cellular phone company, "You never can tell when you might be following kidnappers. A cell phone would allow you to call the police and avoid personal danger."

The thought of personal danger wiped the smile from his face. "What am I doing?" he asked himself again. "I don't know anything about this woman. She could be a drug dealer or something. She is in the music business, after all." A little voice in his head reminded him that he was in the music business, too, and he wasn't a drug dealer. "Good point," he responded to the little voice.

When the kidnappers took the A40, heading northwest toward Oxford, Geremy continued to follow them. They had been driving for about twenty minutes when, much to Geremy's surprise, the red sedan pulled into a petrol station. He saw his chance to call the police and then continue to follow the sedan, if necessary.

Jackie glared at Chas. "What do you mean, 'We need petrol'? You were supposed to fill the car up before we left."

Chas winced. "I know! A shipment came in and Roger needed help unloading so I helped. Then I forgot about filling the car." He pulled the car up to the pump and cut the engine. Without another word, he got out and began to fill the tank. Jackie got out, slammed the car door, and walked to the toilets as he fumed about the stupidity of some people.

Despite her best effort to remain awake, Danny had dozed off but the loud bang of the closing door jarred her back to consciousness. Her head was pounding, but the car had stopped, and she could tell that neither man was in the car. She couldn't quite tell what was happening, but something told her it was time to act. She opened one eye a fraction of an inch to see if the men were in sight. Suddenly, the right-rear car door opened, and a finger poked her in the thigh. It happened so quickly she didn't have time to react.

"Still out cold. Good." Chas closed the door and went to pay for the petrol. The car was quiet.

Come on, Danny, move it. Now's your chance. Move it! She made her right arm cooperate and was moving her hand toward the door handle when the door was flung open. Her arm froze in midair.

"Danny? Are you alright?" The question was so softly spoken that she didn't recognize the voice. "It's Geremy Hawker."

"Geremy?" Squinting against the light, she lifted her head to get a look at him. "What are you doing here?"

"Later. Let's go. Can you walk? We need to get out of here." She heard the urgency in his voice. He helped her sit up and slide her legs around so she could stand.

"My left side is asleep and my right knee is stiff, so I'll need some help getting up." Geremy reached in and helped her out of the car. She tried to take a step with her numb leg, but the knee buckled. She grabbed the side of the car for support, but not before she went down hard on her knee. She gasped in pain. Geremy, feeling the moments slip by, quickly reached down to help her. He didn't see the piece of metal molding bent out from the car body as he reached for her, but he felt the sharp pain as it jammed into the palm of his right hand.

"Damn!" he said as he jerked his hand away. He grabbed Danny's left arm with his left hand, helped her up and away from the car, and slid his right arm around her waist to support her as they moved toward his car. "Come on, my car is over there on the other side of that lorry." Danny's left leg began to tingle and then hurt as the circulation improved. She winced in pain and was grateful for the support of Geremy's arm. "Jeez. How long was I in that car? My leg feels like it's just been reattached to my body." Geremy leaned her against his car then opened the door for her. "Get in quickly and stay down." He helped her into the front seat and put the seat all the way back so she could recline in a straight position. As he pulled his hand away, she saw the blood dripping from the palm.

"Your hand!" She started to sit up, but winced at the pain the movement caused in her head.

Geremy pointed at her. "Stay down. We can take care of my hand as soon as we get away from here. Just stay down."

She was more than happy to oblige. The pounding in her head made her feel sick. Keeping still made the nausea subside.

Geremy walked around the car and slid in behind the wheel. He looked at his palm and decided the cut wasn't deep enough to warrant stitches, but it was still damn painful. He reached over to the glove box, opened it, pulled out a soiled strip of cloth, and wrapped it around his hand. He then started the car and inched it forward far enough to see the sedan at the pump. A moment passed before he saw the big man come out from the cashier, opening a candy bar as he walked toward the sedan.

Chas was nearly to the car when Jackie came out from the toilet. When he reached the car, Chas casually glanced into it and nearly choked when he saw that Danny was gone. Throwing the half-eaten candy on the ground, he swung around and started yelling at Jackie.

"They've discovered you're gone. The big bloke is jumping up and down and yelling at the little bloke. They're starting to look around for you. Stay down now, time for us to exit stage left." The Jaguar pulled slowly away from the lorry and out into the flow of traffic.

—

Sergeant Earling stood looking down at the broken mug and the spilled tea. He had received a call from the Mrs. Willson, the resident building manageress, an hour ago asking him to come immediately. The manageress, who lived on the first floor of the building, said that there was a problem at Jasmine Baker's flat. When he heard the name, he told the caller he'd be there in thirty minutes.

"Thank you for coming so quickly. First, discovering that the building's front door lock was damaged and then finding Jasmine's place in such a state has left me very upset. I've always prided myself on how secure this building is. We've not had a burglary since I became manageress ten years ago."

Earling looked at the small woman who stood fidgeting in the doorway. He had the impression that she was uneasy about coming into the flat. She looked to be in her mid-fifties and had brown hair with touches of gray at the temples. She had a soft melodious voice that he wouldn't have matched with the frail woman who stood wringing her hands in the doorway.

"I was checking the building as I do every day when I noticed that Jasmine's door was open a crack. I went to look more closely and saw that the lock was broken. I pushed against the door and was about to call out to the American woman who is visiting when I saw the room. You won't be surprised to hear that I was speechless. I walked in and, recovering my voice, called out to Ms. Davis, but received no answer. I decided I'd better ring the police, because I could tell something terrible had happened. When I got to the phone, I saw your card, so I called you. Can you tell me what's going on?

"Ms. Davis rang us this morning to report the break-in. I left the card for her to use in case she saw anyone suspicious hanging around. Looks like whoever ransacked the place came back."

"Why do you say that?"

"She was drinking tea out of this mug while we were here." He crouched down and picked up one of the jagged pieces. "Now it's broken on the floor with the tea spilled. I'd say she was overpowered probably soon after we left." Earling was looking around the area to see if any other clues were evident. When he saw that there was a message on the answering machine, he pressed the play button.

"Hello, Danny? Are you there? It's Jasmine. I've got bad news and good news, kiddo. Someone broke into your house, but the good news is that I don't think they took anything. In fact, I don't think

I would have even noticed that anyone had been here if the bed hadn't been mussed. You know me, the neat freak. Well, the quilt on the bed was off-kilter, and I knew I hadn't left it that way. Then I started noticing other things that were slightly off-kilter, too. I can't tell for sure if everything is still here, but your camera equipment is still here as are your stereo, television, and computer. I called the police and reported it. I'll let you know what comes of it. Call me when you have a chance. Bye now, love."

Hearing that Danny's house in the United States had also been broken into did little to tell which one of the women was the target. "Did you see anything unusual today, Mrs. Willson? Any strangers hanging about?"

"No, but a man, saying he was from the phone company, rang to tell me that I had to come down to the central office on the other side of town to straighten out a billing mix-up. When I went, no one down there knew what I was talking about. I ended up being gone from a little before nine until one thirty or so. When I returned, I made my daily building check and found the door. Then I rang you."

"Someone wanted you out of the way while they did the job. This appears to have been a carefully planned job. Did Ms. Baker leave you a number where she could be reached? "

"Yes, she did. I have it downstairs."

He walked back to where she stood. "Do you have a key for the dead bolt?"

"Yes, I do."

"May I have it? I want to lock the place up for now, but I may need to come back in the next day or so."

"She pulled a small key ring out of her pocket, removed one of the keys, and handed it to him. As they left the flat, Earling locked the door before following Mrs. Willson to her flat, where he waited in the hall as she retrieved the number for Ms. Baker. "Thank you, Mrs. Willson," he said as she handed him the number. "Keep your eyes open. The men may be back." Mrs. Willson watched until the outer door closed behind him and then closed and locked her own door before calling a locksmith.

—

McCafferty looked up when he heard the office door slam. Earling walked over to him and sat on the edge of his desk. "I've just been back to Ms. Davis's flat. The resident manageress rang to report a problem. When I arrived, everything looked as it had when we were there, except for two interesting differences. Ms. Davis was not there, and the mug she had been drinking out of was smashed on the floor."

McCafferty chewed on the end of his pencil as Earling spoke. He took it out of his mouth and gave his report. "The lab is in the process of comparing the prints we lifted in the flat against our records. So far, nothing."

"Well, I've got the telephone number for the owner of the flat, a Ms. Jasmine Baker. I'll ring her to find out if she's heard from Ms. Davis. In the meantime, keep on the lab. Tell them to check the prints against Chas Maloney and Jackie Hansen."

"They're doing that now."

"Good. Start doing a background check on Ms. Davis and Ms. Baker. They're both in the music business, so we may be dealing with drugs. Drugs aren't the usual bailiwick of Hansen and Maloney, but then neither is kidnapping. Keep me posted."

Earling went into his office to ring up Jasmine Baker. He looked at his watch and made the time change calculation. "Let's see, if it's 3:30 p.m. here that means it's 7:30 a.m. in Seattle." He picked up the receiver and dialed the number.

CHAPTER SIX

The countryside flew past as Geremy sped down the road, still heading northwest toward Oxford. "It's clear now. You can put the seat back up if you'd like."

Danny found the adjustment knob and pulled it. The seat back popped up, and Danny felt as if she'd left her brain on the small seat behind her. "Oh, my head. If you wanted to get me alone, you really didn't have to resort to such drastic measures, you know." She leaned back against the headrest and put her hand over her eyes. "My kingdom for a pair of sunglasses." The mid-afternoon sun went behind a cloud, and she sighed in relief. "Thanks for turning off the sun." Rain began to spatter against the windshield. Danny peeked through her fingers and saw that sunshine would probably not be an issue for the rest of the day.

Geremy turned on the wipers. "So, who were those guys? Are you in some kind of trouble?"

"I have no idea who those guys are." Her hand fell away from her eyes, and she looked over at Geremy. "If I am in some trouble, I don't know about it. I really don't know what's going on."

"Could they have thought they were taking the owner of the flat? You know, mistook you for her?"

"I don't know." She paused, thinking back on the events of the day. "No, I don't think so. Just before those thugs grabbed me, I heard a message from Jasmine. She called from Seattle to say that someone had been through my house. Someone has gone to a lot of trouble for some reason, so I've got to believe they know who it was they were kidnapping. Since Jasmine has nut-brown skin and thick, wavy, dark-brown hair down to her waist, it would be hard to mistake me for her." She turned to look out the window at the passing scenery. "Where are we, anyway? How long was I in their car?"

"You were in their car for about thirty minutes. They were heading northwest, so I've just kept on in the same direction. We're already over halfway to a cottage I own on the other side of Oxford, so I'm taking you there, if that's alright with you." He glanced over at her and then back at the road. "London doesn't seem particularly friendly to you right now."

She watched him as he drove, his eyes on the road. "Why are you doing this? You hardly know me. I could be a drug dealer for all you know."

He had to smile at her saying exactly what had crossed his mind. "Are you a drug dealer?"

"No."

"I thought not." He took his eyes off the road long enough to look into her eyes. "Your eyes are too clear and honest." He flashed a winning smile before returning his attention to the road. "No. Those are definitely not the eyes of a criminal."

Danny felt a twinge inside her chest when their eyes locked and for no reason she could identify, she felt apprehensive. She looked at Geremy's profile and dismissed the feeling, putting it down to the crazy day she'd been having. She laid her head against the headrest and closed her burning eyes. "Right now they feel like very bloodshot eyes."

They fell silent, letting the hum of the speeding car and the slap of the wipers fill the space between them. Danny was the first to break the silence. "You still haven't answered the 'why' part of my question."

"The best I can do is to say that I felt compelled to follow. So I did. Not much of an answer is it?"

Danny closed her eyes. No, it wasn't much of an answer, but she was glad he had followed them because she didn't know if she would have been able to get away on her own. She felt better now than she had when he helped her get away, but she still felt ill from the chloroform.

"How much longer 'til we reach your cottage?"

"Not much longer."

Twenty minutes later, they turned off the main road onto a country lane. After a couple of miles, Geremy turned right and the car proceeded slowly down a narrow, gravel lane. Branches from the trees on either side created a canopy lending to the sensation that they were in a tunnel. With the sky so dark and the tree branches overhead, it could have been night, but Danny knew it was still late afternoon.

"Looks like we're in for a good storm," she said as she watched the trees sway. When the car came out from under the trees, the rain hit the car in gusts and the headlights illuminated the driving rain and the ground a few feet in front of the car. She could see the vague outline of the cottage through the trees when Geremy stopped the car and cut the engine.

He got out and came around to open Danny's door before heading up the stone pathway to the cottage's small, covered porch. Danny got out, stomped her legs to make sure they were back to normal, and was relieved to find that they felt fine. Then she turned a slow circle, taking in her surroundings. Though the falling rain and gloomy light prevented her from seeing things clearly, the place felt familiar. *I think this is—* She shook her head before completing the thought. It couldn't be. She felt her shirt begin to stick to her back and goose bumps rise on her arms. The temperature was falling fast. The first wave of shivers told her it was time to get out of the weather.

Geremy watched her as she stood in the rain. The shirt that had been baggy when dry was now soaked and molded to her slender figure. He found it difficult to take his eyes off her. As she began to make her way toward the cottage, he turned his attention to his keys, trying to find the one that fit the door. In the fading light, he was having a hard time finding it and began to wonder if it was on his other key chain.

Danny came onto the small porch, brushed past Geremy and went to the door. As Geremy watched, she stood on tiptoe and retrieved the key from its hiding place. She unlocked the door, flicked the switch for the inside light, and gestured a silent invitation for him to enter.

Geremy ducked through the doorway and cast a quizzical look at Danny. "Mind telling me how you knew where the spare key to my cottage was hidden?"

She closed the door behind him. "All in good time, all in good time. Sit down and let me have a look at your hand." She walked to the bathroom medicine cabinet and found some iodine, gauze, and tape. Fully prepared to tend the cut, she returned to the table.

Geremy sat down at the table as directed, but was feeling a little bewildered as he watched Danny move around his house as if she owned the place. She put the items on the table, sat down, and held out her hand. "Let me see your hand."

"Are you a doctor as well as a journalist, Ms. Davis?"

"No, but I have taken lots of first-aid classes, Mr. Hawker." She wiggled her fingers impatiently. "Let me see your hand."

He brought his arm up to the table and laid his right hand palm up in hers. Danny gently unwound the grimy makeshift bandage and dropped it on the floor as she wrinkled her nose in disgust. She tilted his hand to the left and then to the right to get a good look at the cut. It started as a scratch just below his ring finger and ended as a deep gouge in the fleshy part of the palm below the thumb. It was not a pretty sight, but the major vein that runs into the thumb had not been cut, so it was not as serious as it might have been. Stitches would not be necessary. The blood had stopped flowing and clotting had started.

"Will I live?"

"Yes. Well, I think so, anyway. The cut won't require stitches, but the bandage you chose may have given you blood poisoning." A look of concern came over Geremy's face, and she felt bad for teasing him. "Just kidding," she said with a grin. She soaked some gauze with the iodine and began dabbing the cut. Geremy flinched. "Sorry, but I want to make sure the cut is clean."

To take his mind off what she was doing, she told him how she knew about the key. "I can't believe this is your cottage. It's not the type of place I would picture a rock star owning." She poured more iodine on the gauze and dabbed the cut once again for good measure while she continued to talk. "I knew where the spare key was because I've rented this place twice before. I actually have booked it for two weeks at the end of June. Small world, huh?"

"You've stayed here before? But, how?"

"You knew that the cabin was being rented out, didn't you?"

"Well, yes, of course."

She sat up straight and looked at him, his hand momentarily forgotten. "I met your real estate agent at a London party about four years ago. We started talking and got around to our professions. I told her I was a writer and she told me she sold real estate. I asked her if she could recommend a rental agency, because I wanted to rent a vacation house for a couple of weeks before I went back to the States. Turned out, she knew just the place. She had a client who had a cottage that he allowed to be rented when he wasn't using it. She would not tell me the name of the owner, as she wanted to respect his privacy. Worried that renters might take a souvenir if they discovered that he was a well-known rock star, I suppose. I arrived, and it was love at first sight. Just the kind of quiet simple place I was looking for."

Danny unwound a clean piece of gauze and wrapped it twice around Geremy's hand before taping down the end. He examined her work and moved his thumb to check for mobility. "Thanks. It feels much better."

"Good. You can make dinner while I take a shower. I'm feeling a little chilled."

"Right." He stood up and paused as he looked down at her. "Would you like me to find you some dry clothes?"

"Sure. If you have something to spare, that would be great."

While Geremy was in the master bedroom, Danny opened the woodstove and found that a fire was laid and ready to light. She adjusted the knobs to allow for maximum ventilation, lit a match, and was crouched in front of the stove ready to apply the match when Geremy returned from the bedroom.

"Oh, wait a second. You've got to open three air passageways before you light the fire."

Danny touched the match to the paper, stood up, and gave him a knowing smile. "I know." She threw the match into the fire before closing the stove door. A glass panel in the door let the light of the fire shine into the cabin.

"Oh, right." He shook his head and shrugged his shoulders. "Small world." He held out some clothes for her to try. "As requested, a change of clothes for milady. Not much of a selection, but I hope you'll find something to suit you."

She took the clothes, looked at them and then at him with a puzzled expression. "Wherever did you find these? I don't recall seeing any clothes around here when I've visited."

"The closet in the master bedroom has a false back. I keep personal items in there in case I'm in the area and want to drop in."

"Good thing." She held up the small pile. "Thanks. I'll be out in a few." She started for the bathroom, but had only taken a few steps when Geremy's voice stopped her.

"One more thing before you disappear. It's about dinner."

"Yes?"

"Well, I haven't been here since Christmas, so we may not have much of a selection. In fact, the selection is no selection. If I remember correctly, there's some pasta, a couple of jars of red sauce, a few tins of tomatoes, and some biscuits."

"As a matter of fact, pasta and red sauce happens to one of my favorite meals. You wouldn't happen to have a bottle of red wine hiding around here, would you?"

He gave her a smile and nodded his head. "As a matter of fact, I do. I'll change into something more comfortable and then I'll get started on dinner." In the bedroom, he exchanged his blazer, slacks, and shirt for a pair of faded jeans that were ripped at the knees and a black tee shirt. He walked barefoot to the kitchen to make the promised dinner.

Danny stood beneath the stream of hot water, letting the warmth seep into her, and felt the last traces of the chloroform headache melt away. When she turned to let the water soak the front of her body, her right knee began to sting. Remembering the fall she had taken at the gas station, she bent down to inspect the damage. As she did so, her necklace fell forward, and she saw the ring dangling from the gold chain. She looked past it to her knee and then back at the ring. Straightening up, she grabbed it and held it before her eyes. The gold ring with the onyx stone. The ring the men in the car had described.

—

"A drugged woman does not just disappear into thin air. Either she was not drugged enough or someone took her out of the car." The calm tone with which Sebastian Sanders spoke to Jackie and Chas put them both on guard. Sanders often said that things are most calm right before the storm. They both knew the storm was about to hit them hard.

He walked around his desk and stood in front of the men. "You morons!" he roared. "How could you have let her get away?" He slammed his hand down on the desk. They watched him struggle to regain his composure. "This was supposed to be a quick job with no one to have a clue about what happened. She was supposed to wake up in a strange place without a clue as to how she got there, and I was supposed to have the ring in my possession by now. Instead, you lost the girl, I do not have the ring, and the police probably have a very good description of you by now." He walked back to the chair behind his desk and sat down. He rested his elbows on the arms and brought his fingertips together in a point just under his chin. Jackie and Chas knew better than to disturb him.

"As I see it, she must have gotten away on her own and then found a ride away from the station. But where the hell did she go? You say you searched all around the station?" He paused long enough to glare at them as he gave the word "station" extra emphasis.

"Yes, sir. We looked everywhere," Chas responded. "We even looked out on the road for her. She disappeared into thin air. But I don't think she saw us. She never saw us coming when I knocked her out, and she was lying on the backseat the whole time she was in the car."

"We can't take that chance, now can we, Chas? We have to assume that the police are looking for you two and your car. Where is it, by the way?"

"Jackie parked it in your private garage in back. I pulled the garage doors closed before we came up."

"Good. Leave it there for the time being. I'll take care of it. As for you two, get out of the country tonight. I want you to go to France and keep an eye on her brother, Philippe. She may go there because of this business. That'll get you out of the country and keep you out of trouble. Call me when you get set up in Foix so I know where to reach you. I'll keep tabs on things here."

They stood there, not knowing if the meeting was over.

"Well? Why are you still here? Get going!" When the door closed behind them, Sebastian pressed a button on his desk. Almost immediately, the other door to his office opened, and a young man with dark hair and olive skin entered. "Diego, I have a job for you. I want you to go to this address and watch the building." He handed him a piece of paper and a photograph. "If you see this woman, call me immediately. You may have to keep watch through the night, so make sure you don't fall asleep. Call me if she's not there by eight tomorrow morning, and I'll decide how to proceed."

Diego nodded as he took the picture. He examined it briefly and left without saying a word.

—

Earling hung up the phone and called to McCafferty. "Any news from the lab?"

McCafferty closed the door behind him after entering Earling's office and sat down in a chair next to the door. "They called while you were on the phone. They found one thumb print belonging to Chas Maloney."

"Got him!"

"I put the word out to pick him up for questioning, but no luck so far."

"What's the game, here? Either he or Hansen calls the building manager with a cock-and-bull story to get her out of the building. Then Chas goes into the flat—in broad daylight—where a visiting American is staying, ransacks the place, and then doesn't nick anything. They apparently return after we leave and take her by force out of the building. No one sees a thing."

"What did Ms. Baker have to say?"

"She confirmed that Ms. Davis's house had been burgled, but the intruder had been much neater than the intruder in her flat. She was very concerned to hear about the break-in to her place and asked if Ms. Davis was alright. I told her that she appeared to be missing. Ms. Baker said she hadn't heard from her. I asked her if she knew any reason why someone would want to abduct Ms. Davis. At first, she couldn't think of any, but then she told me that Danielle Davis is the daughter of none other than Liam Davis, the photographer. She wondered if someone had kidnapped her for a ransom."

"Who would they contact to make a ransom demand?"

"She has a brother somewhere in France, but Ms. Baker couldn't remember where he lives. The whole thing doesn't make sense, though. Maloney and Hansen are burglars. Kidnapping is not in their usual line of work. If they did take her, they must be working for someone." Earling leaned back in his chair and turned the events over in his head, trying to find the key to it all. He brought his chair back down with a thump. "We've got a number of things to track down. As I see it, we need to find her brother, Philippe Davis. I'll leave that to you. When you find him, ask if he's heard from her or the kidnappers. Try not to alarm him since we are not absolutely sure she's in danger. We also need to find out who Chas and Jackie are working for. You say you've got people out looking for Maloney?" McCafferty nodded. "See if anyone on the street knows if they're working for someone. If so, who? That may help us figure out what they're after. I'll call Jefferson at the Times and ask him to run a brief story on her disappearance. If she's not in trouble, hopefully she'll see the article and call us. That's it. Let's get to work."

CHAPTER SEVEN

When Danny came out of the bathroom, she saw that Geremy had cut the overhead light in favor of a small table lamp in the living room and two candles on the dining room table. The soft lighting was complemented by faint strains of Mozart floating through the air. She listened to the music as she watched the shadows cast by the fire flicker around the room. The cottage was already warm from the heat of the stove, and the taste buds at the back of her tongue tingled as she savored the aroma of tomato sauce coming from the kitchen.

She stood in the bathroom doorway taking in the simple beauty of the cottage. She guessed that it was probably two or three hundred years old, but she could also tell that someone had remodeled in more recent times. The beauty of the remodel job was that, aside from the obvious improvements to the plumbing and wiring, it wasn't easy to tell where the original structure ended and the improvements began. The walls and floors of the living room, dining room, and the short hallway to her right that led to the master bedroom were covered with aged-wood paneling the color of cognac. The ceiling was white plaster striped with exposed, dark, wood beams. Big windows in the living room and dining room kept the rooms bright during the day and at night, and the soft lights brought out the warm, rosy-orange tones of the paneling, which created a snug and inviting atmosphere.

Right now, the warmth coming from the woodstove felt very inviting. She was tempted to curl up in one of the two large chairs that flanked the stove and soak up the warmth, but her nose reminded her that her host was busy making dinner and that she might lend a hand.

She walked around the breakfast bar that separated the dining area from the kitchen. This bar, like the one in Jasmine's flat, allowed people to talk to someone in the small kitchen while staying out of the way of the cook. She stood just outside the circle of light that flooded the semi-darkness of the dining room, fluffed her damp hair with her fingers, and watched Geremy as he prepared dinner. He was unaware of her, so she took the opportunity to get a good look at him. As he leaned forward to taste the red sauce, his layered, shoulder-length hair slightly obscured his face. All she could see of his profile was his perfectly straight nose.

She guessed he was around six feet three inches with broad shoulders that tapered down to a narrow waist. No paunch on this man. She decided he was definitely easy on the eyes. He turned and took a step in her direction but then stopped in his tracks as she stepped into the light.

"It smells great, maestro."

Geremy whistled softly as he looked at her. "I bet you even look good in a burlap sack." His eyes traveled up and down admiring the sight of her in one of his flannel shirts and a pair of woolen socks. The shirttails came almost down to her knees, but the slit up the side revealed a firm and shapely thigh. Then he noticed the scar running down the outside of her right leg. He whistled again. "That's one hell of a scar. How'd you get it?"

He felt something in her change, almost like she withdrew from him. She ignored the question by changing the subject. "I need to call the police."

Geremy shook his head. "I already tried. The phone is dead. These windy storms usually knock it out, sometimes for days at a time."

She nodded slowly. "Then I guess I'll set the table."

"Good idea. The dishes ..." Danny had already pulled two dishes from the cupboard and was moving toward the table. "You know, it's the oddest feeling to be in my own house with a practical stranger who seems to know the house as well as I do. It's quite unnerving."

"I know what you mean. I feel like you've intruded into *my* space. I've always been here by myself, so this feels odd to me, too. It's funny to think we feel the same way about the same house when we hardly know each other." She pulled some flatware out of one drawer and napkins out of another. She placed them on the table and turned to examine the bottle of red wine Geremy had retrieved from somewhere. "Shall I open it?" she asked as she held the bottle up.

"Yes, please. The hand is a little tender for me to do it, but I do want to put some in the sauce. Have to doctor this stuff up, ya know?"

She nodded as she opened the bottle. After handing it to him, she retrieved two wine glasses. Geremy poured a shot into the sauce and handed the bottle back to her. She half-filled each glass and handed one to him. Holding hers up, she made a toast. "Here's to a more normal tomorrow." Their glasses clinked and they each took a sip.

Danny took her glass and the bottle from the glare of the kitchen to the semi-darkness of the table. "The scar is a memento of an accident I was in a few years ago. A drunk driver ignored a red light and plowed into my parents' car. They were killed instantly. I decided not to die, but was in physical therapy for almost a year afterwards."

"I'm sorry." He didn't know what else to say. He settled for the first thing that came to his mind. "Is that where you learned your skills as a doctor?"

"Some of them. Plus, I was studying sports medicine before the accident. I was in school on an athletic scholarship." She became quiet and took a sip of wine. "So that's how I got the wicked scar."

No one except Philippe knew how devastated she had been by the accident. She tasted the bitterness that congealed at the back of her throat whenever she thought about Avery Pembroke. After killing her parents, he had stumbled away from the wreck with only a few scratches. She took a big drink of wine in an attempt to wash away the bitter taste.

They were both quiet, deep in their own thoughts. Mozart's fortieth symphony played as rain beat against the roof and a tree branch tapped on one of the windows at the back of the cottage.

Geremy broke into her thoughts with welcome news. "Dinner is served. If you bring the plates over, I will load them up."

Danny snapped back to the present and brought the plates over to him, setting them down on the tile counter next to the stove. He placed a pile of pasta in the center of each plate and spooned sauce over the top. "Sorry that this is all I have to offer. I didn't tell Martha I was coming."

"Martha?"

"A friend of mine who keeps an eye on the house and gets it ready whenever I or a renter will be using it."

"That explains why it's always stocked with essentials when I arrive. I thought little fairies tended the house—food in the cupboards, well-tended flower beds, sheets on the bed."

He handed her one of the plates. "Nope, just Martha. She fits more into the angel category."

Danny took her plate and sat down at the table. "Man, I'm starving. Don't mind me while I inhale this fine dinner. It really does smell delicious."

Geremy brought his plate of pasta over to the table and chuckled as he sat down opposite her. "At this point, you'd probably say that about boiled shoe leather, but I'll take all the praise you want to give me."

All conversation ceased while they ate. "I must admit that I'm very hungry, too. Rescuing damsels in distress works up an appetite!"

"Geremy, thank you so very much for helping me. I was in pretty bad shape when you opened that door. I don't know if I could have gotten away without your help."

He was touched by the soft sincerity in her voice. "You are quite welcome," he responded softly. He raised his glass to her and took a drink. "I just wish we knew why they abducted you."

"Oh my God! How could I have forgotten? The smell of food drove all else from my mind, I guess." She pulled the gold chain and the ring out from under the shirt. "I think they were after this." She held the ring up for him to see.

"What makes you think they were after that?"

"They thought I was unconscious in the car so they spoke candidly. I was groggy, but I heard one of them describe a gold and onyx ring. This is the only one of those that I own."

He put his fork down. "May I see it?"

"Sure." She slid the chain over her head and handed it to him.

Geremy got up to turn on the overhead light. Danny squinted in the sudden brightness.

"Sorry." He sat back down and looked more closely at the ring. "No offense, but this hardly looks worth kidnapping someone over."

The ring consisted of a large square of onyx set into gold with scrollwork etched on either side of the stone. Tiny diamond chips were embedded in the scrollwork, and one small diamond was set into a squiggly line that cut across the face of the stone. The gold band was thin and slightly bent.

"No offense taken. Its value to me is purely sentimental. In fact, I thought the stone was cracked the first time I saw it. When I was a teenager, I found it in my mother's jewelry box. As it looked like a man's ring and since I had never seen her wear it, I asked her where it had come from. She told me that during the Second World War she was a member of the French Resistance. My mother was French, by the way, and she grew up in Foix, near the Pyrenees, but spent most of the war living in Lyon. She paused in her narration to drink some wine and eat more of her dinner before continuing the story.

"She said that the ring was given to her by a British navigator who had been injured when his plane was damaged on landing. He and another man got away from the plane before it exploded, but the navigator broke his arm in the process so he had to be hidden until his arm was good enough to travel. Mother and my Uncle Marcel hid him in a secret room in their house in Lyon. I guess Mother spent a good deal of time with him so when he was well enough to travel, he asked her to go with him to England. She said he had fallen in love with her. She told him she couldn't leave, that she still had work to do in Lyon. When they parted, he gave her the ring, told her it was quite valuable, and that he would return for her and the ring as soon as he could."

"Sounds like a story that could only come out of a war."

"I thought so, too." Danny took a sip of wine and thought about how softly her mother had spoken when she recounted the story. It dawned on her that her mother might have been in love with the Englishman. "At first, she thought it kind of strange that he never came back for the ring, because he had been quite insistent that it was very valuable. Then, a few years later, she heard that he had died before the end of the war, so she put the ring away and forgot about it. Thirty years later, I dug it out of her jewelry box." She twirled some pasta around her fork but forgot about the food as she finished the story. "I used to tease her about this secret lover. She said he was no secret. My father was the other man who got off the plane so knew all about the Englishman. I was never quite able to figure out what an American was doing in a Royal Air Force plane over France, but I think he might have been taking pictures of enemy positions when the plane was shot down."

Geremy alternated between eating and examining the ring as Danny told the story. He saw something on the left side of the ring near the stone that he thought was a nick, but then saw that it was a notch of some kind. He put his fork down and pressed his fingernail into the notch. He was startled when the stone popped up.

"What the—?" Danny leaned forward to get a better look at the ring.

"Didn't you know about this?"

"No. I don't suppose I ever looked at it that closely."

They both looked at the back of the stone and found another line, only this one had a much more dramatic peak-and-valley configuration. The diamond embedded in the top showed through to the backside of the stone and was situated just off center of the middle peak. The gold face on which the stone rested was covered with small, neatly written words. Danny took the ring and looked closely at the script.

"I don't recognize this language. Do you?" She handed the ring back to Geremy.

"No. Maybe it's Gaelic?"

"Could be, I suppose. What about the lines? What do you make of them?"

"Before I saw the line on the back I thought it was just some abstract design. But the way the diamond shows through on both sides makes me think it's some kind of map or something, and the diamond is marking a spot."

"Marking a spot? The line on the front could be a river. What do you think?"

"Maybe. But what's the line on the back? It looks like a mountain range. A river and a mountain range? Like the beginning of a river that springs from some mountains?" Geremy leaned back in his chair and rubbed his eyes with his good hand.

"Tired?"

"Yes. It's been a long day."

"Yeah, my brain is feeling pretty foggy. Why don't we let the little mystery rest while we finish the wonderful dinner you made?"

Geremy gave a slight smile as he laid the ring down on the table and noticed that Danny's plate was nearly empty. "There's more pasta and sauce, if you're still hungry. Would you care for more?"

"Thanks, but what's left on my plate will take care of me. I will have some more wine, though." She poured herself half a glass before setting the bottle near Geremy's plate.

"Do you keep a supply of wine in the hidden closet, also?"

"Just a few bottles of red for surprise special occasions. This one has actually been in there for about three years."

"It's splendid." She swirled the wine around in her glass, sniffed the bouquet, and took a drink. "This vineyard is one of my favorites. They produce a superior cabernet."

"Sounds like you know a bit about wines."

She nodded and shrugged. "It's in my blood. My grandfather was a wine merchant, so my mother passed her knowledge of wine on to my brother and me."

They sat and talked about the best and worst wines they had tasted as well as the circumstances surrounding the tasting. Geremy told of a particularly embarrassing incident wherein he spilled his glass of very expensive cabernet onto the very expensive dress of a baroness sitting next to him at the dinner table. Danny chuckled as he described the expression on the face of the baroness as she jumped up from the table and ran out of the room. "Needless to say, I would have crawled into a hole had one been available," Geremy said as he poured the last of the wine into his glass and held the empty bottle up. "Would milady care for more wine? There are four more bottles in the hidden closet."

Danny shook her head. "No, thank you. I've had enough." She was warm, her stomach was full, and her brain felt a little fuzzy.

"Then I propose we adjourn to the living room."

Danny went over to the stove, opened the door, and added a chunk of wood to the fire. Then she stood with her back to the stove and watched Geremy as he cleared the table and took the dishes into the kitchen. "And how did you come to be at a dinner party sitting next to a baroness?"

He came back into the dining room, turned off the overhead light and blew out the candles. "My father, the influential banker, had friends in high places. I was usually excused from attending the more formal dinners, but father wanted everyone present to meet the baroness." He turned out the overhead lights and came to the couch that faced the stove. When he sat down, he reached over and turned off the small table lamp so that the fire that shone through the glass was now the only source of light. It was enough for Danny to see the slight grin on his face. "It was a few years before my father asked me to attend another important dinner."

"How old were you when you baptized the baroness?"

"Sixteen. I'm sure I did it on purpose, even if only subconsciously. I found the dinners dreadfully dull. I was more interested in perfecting my guitar playing than sitting around talking to the square older generation."

She moved toward him. "Mind if I share the couch with you?"

"Please do."

She eased herself into the big pillows in the corner opposite him. She sighed as she stretched her legs out, her feet just barely touching his thigh. "What a lovely and very long couch. Now that I've seen the owner, I know why it's so long!"

"I wanted a couch long enough to allow me to lie down. I had this one custom made." Conversation ceased as Geremy settled into his corner of the couch, stretched out his legs, and watched the fire. He noticed for the first time that the music had ended, and now the house was quiet except for the crackle and pop of the fire and the sound of the rain against the house. He suddenly felt very tired. Closing his eyes and resting his head against the back of the couch, he thought back over the long day.

All he could seem to remember was Danny, standing in the doorway of the flat, the fingertips of her hand lightly resting on the door, her eyes wide as she took in the scene before her. The sensation he'd felt when he saw her for the first time—a current, almost like electricity—rippled through him. The feeling was akin to recognition, as if some part of him was insisting that he knew her, but he felt sure that they had never met before today.

A distant memory fluttered at the edge of his mind of a similar feeling he'd felt for another woman years ago. He found the comparison unsettling, because the woman had disappeared from his life without a trace, leaving him bewildered and brokenhearted. An image of the other woman flitted through his brain, bringing with it a trace of pain. He grimaced and shoved the image out of his mind, willing the melancholy that always accompanied the memory of her face to go with it.

Danny stirred, and he turned to gaze at the source of these new feelings. He looked across at her and realized that she had fallen asleep. The light and shadows from the fire played over her face, lending animation to her still features. She looked so soft and vulnerable as she lay there, very unlike the self-assured woman he had spent the day with. He felt very drawn to her, and he wondered why.

"Danny, have we ever met before?"

Danny shifted and mumbled something, but he couldn't make it out. Drowsiness settled on him as he watched her sleep, and he knew it was time for him to go to bed. He thought about waking Danny, but decided against it. He knew from experience that the couch was very comfortable. He went to the linen closet for a blanket to put over her, came back, and tucked her in. He stood looking down at Danny, a puzzled expression on his face. After a second's hesitation, he bent down and, brushing her hair back, kissed her lightly on the forehead. He straightened and wondered once again about the strong feelings he felt for this stranger asleep on his couch. Then, as if realizing that his feelings were moving into an area he was not willing to explore, he turned abruptly from the couch, went to the stove to stoke the fire, and made his way through the darkness to his room and bed.

A few hours later Danny, woke with a start, her heart beating from a dream. She was cold and disoriented as she looked around. The fire had burned down to glowing embers. *Great. I fell asleep on the couch again,* she thought sleepily. *I've got to quit doing this.* She slowly stood and stumbled back to the bedroom, made her way to the bed, pulled back the covers, and crawled in. She was asleep before her head hit the pillow.

—

The sun streamed through the bedroom windows, and Danny woke up and smiled. She loved waking up in this house. It meant she was on vacation. She stretched her whole body, her arms over her head. As they came down, her left arm brushed against the body next to her. Her arm jerked away, and she sat bolt upright in the bed. Geremy's warm, sleepy smile greeted her when she looked down.

"Good morning, milady."

Danny looked down at her body and was relieved to see that, contrary to her usual custom, she had clothes on, but when Geremy shifted, she could see his bare chest. She couldn't tell if the rest of him was bare or not. Then she remembered waking up on the couch the night before and coming into bed.

"I am so sorry. I was half asleep when I came to bed and forgot you were here. This is where I usually sleep when I stay here." Her words tumbled out in a nervous stream as she slid out of the bed.

He rolled over and propped himself up on his elbow, his head resting on his hand. "No need to apologize. I rather enjoy seeing the face of a beautiful woman first thing in the morning. I just want to know if anything fun happened while I was asleep?"

All nervousness was forgotten as she grabbed a pillow and thumped him. Geremy laughed and rolled away from her attack. "If it did, then we're both guilty of necrophilia since we were both practically dead with fatigue." She threw the pillow at him as she left the room. "Out of bed, lazy bones. Time to solve the great mystery."

Geremy stretched. "Nope. Not until after breakfast. What are you making?"

Danny poked her head back into the room. "What am *I* making? Aren't you the host here?" She left again to put on her own clothes.

"Good point." He eased himself out of bed and put on his robe. He walked to the kitchen where he saw dirty dishes in the sink and on the stove. "Oh, my, look at all these dishes and me with an injured hand."

Danny came up behind him and surveyed the scene. "Oh, brother. Okay, okay. I'll do the dishes. That's fair enough."

He tossed her a dish towel as he left the kitchen and went back to his room to get dressed.

—

Sebastian Sanders sat at the table of his house in Esher, enjoying a quiet and leisurely breakfast while he read the *Times*. His peaceful morning was disturbed when he saw a small article about Danielle Davis. The coffee cup he was bringing to his mouth reversed course and went down on the table with a bang as he brought the paper closer to his face. The article, in the lower-right corner of the front page, reported that Danielle Davis, daughter of the well-known photographer Liam Davis, had disappeared. She had last been seen by police at around twelve thirty in the afternoon the day before when she had reported a break-in where she was staying. When police were called back to the scene by the building manageress, evidence suggested that she had been removed from the premises by force. She had not been seen since. Anyone with information was instructed to call Sergeant Earling. His number was listed after his name.

Sebastian lowered the paper slowly to the table, perplexed. Where was she? He had felt sure that she had gone straight to the police when she had escaped Chas and Jackie. It appeared that she had not, and Diego had checked in to say that she had not shown up at the flat. He was glad to have sent Chas and Jackie to her brother's, since she was probably on her way to his house even now. He went to the phone to call them at their hotel in Foix. When Jackie picked up the receiver, Sebastian didn't identify himself. He went straight into his instructions.

"Jackie, the girl is still missing. The police don't appear to know where she is. You sure she hasn't arrived at the house?"

"We have been watching the house in shifts since we arrived yesterday evening. If she had arrived, we'd know it."

"Good. Keep watching, but keep a low profile."

"Yes, sir."

"If she hasn't arrived by day after tomorrow, proceed with the plan to abduct her brother. She'll turn over the ring if we have him. Have you worked out how you'll do it?"

"We don't know enough about his routine yet to have worked it out. We will be ready by day after tomorrow."

"Good. Call me if she arrives. I want to be there when you move in. Remember, if she doesn't arrive, grab him, and we'll go from there. I'll call if I hear of any new developments." He hung up without saying good-bye.

Jackie hung up the receiver and walked to the window that overlooked the town square. They had rented adjoining rooms in this hotel because it was close to the Davis house and the cafe he frequented every morning. Jackie drank his coffee as he wondered once again why the ring was so important to Sanders.

He and Chas had been working for Sanders for almost a year. When Sanders had approached them with the offer of working for him in his warehouse and as estate consultants, they had accepted. They were both ready for a change from the burglary and fencing operation they had been running. More and more houses had electronic security systems making the jobs more difficult, and the police had begun to ask around about them. They were becoming too well-known. So when Sanders offered them the job, they quietly shut down the fencing operation and went to work for him.

The job was to their liking. From the looks of it, Sanders did very well as an estate sales agent. Of course, Jackie suspected that he must have some other operations on the side or why would he hire a couple of burglars? Then this ring thing had come up. Sanders had told them to track down the girl and to get the ring from her. All this effort for a small, gold ring with an onyx stone. Jackie was certainly curious about the ring and why it was so important. Sanders hadn't told them anything other than to get the ring and to avoid killing the girl, if at all possible. Jackie knew that he had never murdered anyone, but he suspected that Chas had before they met. In any case, neither of them was comfortable with the idea of killing.

Jackie shook his head, set down his coffee cup, and looked at his watch. Nine a.m. He would relieve Chas at noon. In the meantime, he would walk around town to get the layout memorized, just in case they did need to kidnap Davis. He wanted to know the options for leaving town. He put on the jacket to his Panama suit and left.

CHAPTER EIGHT

Danny placed the last dish in the rack to dry as Geremy came into the kitchen, wearing the same faded jeans and tee shirt he'd had on the night before. He came up behind her and looked over her shoulder at the empty sink.

"Your timing is impeccable. I just finished the last dish." She turned her head and was surprised to find his face even with hers. He smiled as he looked into her eyes. A tingle passed through her as she thought of kissing those lips.

"It's a talent I have perfected," he said softly.

Knowing that she had to move away from him before she lost her resolve, she took a step to the side. "So, what's for breakfast?"

Geremy, enjoying the disconcerting effect he was having on her, began to look through the cupboards. Lack of dairy products reduced his options. Then he found what he was looking for—a box of powdered milk. "Ah, the options are limitless."

She looked from the box of powdered milk to Geremy and then back at the box, a skeptical expression on her face. "I'll get out of your way, maestro. I need to stretch my legs. I'm going for a quick walk while you make breakfast."

"Alright. I should have something put together in twenty or thirty minutes."

Danny stepped out the front door and began her walk down the sun-dappled lane. As she went, her thoughts moved over the past few weeks and the strange turns her life had taken. She realized with a twinge of guilt that she hadn't thought about Stephen once since her arrival in London four days ago. And since she'd met Geremy, he was constantly in her thoughts. That she was attracted to him was beyond question, but the trace of apprehension she felt when he looked into her eyes tempered the attraction. She stopped in the middle of the lane and shook her head to clear it. *Danny*, she thought to herself. *Get a grip. Not only are you already in a relationship, but you learned the hard way that getting involved with interview subjects is bad business.*

She was nearing the main road when a white mini-van turned onto the lane. Danny stood aside to let it pass. Instead of passing her, it came to a stop and an older woman with snowy white hair and rosy cheeks hopped out.

"Hello?" The proper English accent and tone made the word more of a question than a greeting as she looked Danny over.

"Hello."

"Are you at the cottage?"

Danny did not enjoy being questioned by the stranger, so she replied with a question of her own. "Who are you?"

The woman's eyes narrowed slightly. "I'm Martha. And who might you be?"

Danny relaxed and smiled. "Hello, Martha. I'm Danny Davis. And yes, I'm at the cottage. With Geremy."

Martha smiled back. "You've stayed at the cottage before, haven't you?"

"Yes, a couple of times."

"I didn't know you knew Geremy."

"We met yesterday."

"You just met yesterday? And he brought you to the cottage?"

"Yes." Martha looked so amazed that Danny felt the need to explain further. "We had a strange day yesterday, and he thought it best we come here rather than go back to London."

Martha stood looking at Danny as if looking at something miraculous. "Imagine that. I can't remember the last time he brought a woman here."

"Uh, well, it's nothing like that. I'm writing an article on the Mystic Celts. I'm interviewing Geremy for the article. We're working together."

"Call it what you like, lass, but he doesn't bring just anyone here. In fact, he hardly ever brings anyone at all to the cottage. My, my, my." She beamed at Danny for another moment, shaking her head in amazement. Then, as if realizing that she didn't have all day to chat, she turned to the van, motioning for Danny to follow her. "I saw the lights from the cabin last night, but when I tried to call, the phone was dead. I thought I'd better come over and check on things before I go in to work." She opened the van's sliding side door and pulled a wicker basket to the edge of the opening. She lifted the lid to show Danny the contents. "When Geremy shows up out of the blue, he usually forgets to bring decent food. I brought a few things, just in case. Fortunately, yesterday was market day." She moved the items around as she called them out. "Milk, eggs, butter, some scones and fruit pastries I made this morning, apples and strawberries, asparagus, mushrooms, broccoli, four trout fillets, and a bottle of white wine." She paused and looked up at Danny. "How long will you two be here?"

Danny was flabbergasted at the amount of food in the basket. "I don't really know. A day or two more, I suppose."

"Well, this should hold you over for a few days." She shut the lid, picked up the basket, and handed it to Danny.

"Aren't you coming to see Geremy?" Danny asked as she took the heavy basket. Feeling its weight, she gained new respect for Martha.

"No time. I have to get to the restaurant. Can you manage the basket alright?"

"Yes, it'll be a good workout for my arms," Danny replied with a chuckle.

"Tell Geremy I told him he'd better hurry and feed you. You need some more meat on your bones."

Danny grinned back at her, but didn't dare release a hand to respond to Martha's farewell wave.

Martha stood for a moment more watching Danny walk down the lane. *Imagine that,* she thought to herself. *A woman, after all these years. Davey's going to love this.* She shook her head in wonder as she got back into the van.

Danny was smiling as she thought about what Martha had said. *So he hasn't had a woman here in years.* She was surprised at how happy that bit of information made her feel.

Geremy watched from the porch as Danny huffed toward him with the heavy basket. He met her halfway up the stone path and took the basket. "Something tells me you met Martha."

Danny was happy to relinquish her hold on the basket. "She came to check on things because she saw the lights last night. She brought the food in case you'd forgotten to bring any."

He laughed. "She'd have sent food even I'd told her I'd brought plenty. She's always telling me that I need to eat more. 'You're too thin, Geremy. It's not healthy,' " he said in very good imitation of Martha.

Danny laughed. "She told me to tell you that you'd better feed me because I need meat on my bones. I didn't tell her that I eat more than anyone I know."

They got into the kitchen and began to unpack the basket. Danny was amazed at the selection. She pulled an apple pastry out of a bag and took a bite before hopping up onto the kitchen counter.

"This is great. With these pastries and fresh fruit, you won't have to cook our breakfast." She looked at the box of powdered milk, wrinkled her nose, and added, "So you can put that away."

"Are you not a fan of the twentieth-century miracle known as powdered milk?"

"I am not a fan of milk in general, so when I was a kid my mother thought she'd try the powdered variety." She shuddered and wrinkled her nose again. "The tactic was unsuccessful. I detest the stuff." In an effort to banish the memory, she took another bite of the pastry, savoring the spices, apples, and flaky crust. "Does Martha usually keep this kind of gourmet food around her house?"

"She and her husband own a small but outstanding restaurant just up the road in Bourton-on-the-Water. Martha makes the baked goods herself, and Dave does most of the rest of the cooking." He put the vegetables and fish into the refrigerator. With a smile, he held up the bottle of white Bordeaux wine for Danny to see. "Good old Martha. Always thinks of everything!" The wine followed the other things into the refrigerator. He straightened up and looked around the kitchen to make sure everything was put away. He saw the tea pot and remembered the tea he had brewed. "Would you care for some tea?"

"Yes. Thank you. Have you known them for a long time?"

Geremy got a cup out and poured some tea. "Milk?"

"No, thanks."

He handed the cup to her, poured some milk into his tea, and put the milk in the fridge. "I've known them all my life. Martha and Dave are my second parents."

"So you've owned this cottage for a long time?"

"My parents bought it right after the war. They said they needed a peaceful place after all the noise and destruction. It was my summer home all through my childhood."

"Do you have any brothers or sisters?"

"One older brother, Graeme. He lives just outside London. He's a banker like my dad was. Followed in Dad's footsteps, as it were. I, on the other hand, fall into the black-sheep category. My brother is still not sure if he considers my chosen profession as very respectable."

He paused to pour himself some tea, topped off Danny's cup, and reached for an apple pastry. "This is all off the record, isn't it? You won't put any of this in your article?"

"No. But that reminds me. I haven't done a very good job of interviewing you for the article. I'll need to get to work on that pretty quick. Also, do you think it will be possible for me to talk to the other band members?"

"Yes. I'm sure that can be arranged."

"In the meantime, do you mind if we work a little on the ring mystery? We can do some of the interview work this afternoon, if that's okay with you."

"To be honest, I was hoping you'd say that. I'd much rather solve a mystery than do an interview."

"Do you have a map of Great Britain around here?"

"Not in the house, but there's one in my car. Why?"

"Well, we've discussed the possibility that these lines represent geographical features. The soldier who gave the ring to my mother was English, so I was thinking we should take a look at a map of Britain to see if any of the lines match."

"Great idea. I'll go get it."

Within minutes, Geremy brought the map in and unfolded it on the table, smoothing the creases as he went. "As I see it, there are three mysteries to solve about the ring: the line on the front of the stone, the line on the back, and the writing. I'm not very good with languages, so I'd prefer to work on the lines, if you don't mind."

"Sounds good. I'm pretty good with languages. Can you get me some paper and a pen so I can transcribe the script? I'll enlarge the words so I can see them better."

"Paper and pen coming right up. Are you very good at drawing?"

"I do alright. Why?"

"A larger rendition of the lines would be easier to work with, too. Do you think you can replicate them exactly?"

Danny looked at the lines. "Looks easy enough." She set to work copying the lines and script while Geremy put scones, another fruit pastry, and strawberries on a plate for them to eat while they worked. He filled a pitcher with water and got two glasses out of the cupboard. He put the food and water on the table as Danny finished drawing. "Here you go, Dr. Livingston. Start exploring. Mind if I put on some music?"

"Go right ahead." Geremy filled a glass with water, sat down at the table with his half-eaten apple pastry, and began comparing the lines Danny had drawn with rivers on the map.

Danny put two CDs on the carousel before choosing one of the living room chairs as her work station.

Two hours passed as they worked quietly on their respective projects. The last song on the last CD finished before Geremy stood up and stretched. "I've had no luck whatsoever. How are you doing?"

"Not much better. Aspects of the language seem familiar, but I'm mostly guessing."

"As I worked on the lines, I began to wonder how old the ring is. If the front line does represent a river, the river itself may have changed course and may no longer resemble the line on the ring."

"Oh, brother. I hadn't thought of that." She stood up and stretched,. "I need a walk. Why don't we take one, and I'll start on the interview. The fresh air will clear our brains."

Geremy agreed and led the way out the kitchen door to the backyard. "Come on. I'll take you to my favorite spot." He walked down the sloping lawn toward the river which was situated about fifty yards behind the house. "But first, look at this." He stopped by the river's edge and pointed out a recently added feature to the river. "Have you been here since this was created?" Danny looked in the direction he was pointing and saw what looked like a natural swimming pool close to the bank.

"No, I don't think so. When did that happen?"

"Last year, the river gouged it out while depositing rocks, branches and sand in the middle of the stream. It's almost six feet deep in the middle. The current runs through it very quickly so you can swim in place and get a great workout without ending up a mile downstream. I have enjoyed it but don't know how long it will last. Another big storm could wipe it out. "

They stood for a moment admiring the pool before Geremy turned to his left and cut into the woods, motioning for her to follow. For a second, Danny thought they were embarking on a backwoods trek. Then she noticed the path. It was narrow and so overgrown that only someone who knew it was there could have found it. They walked single file downstream, following the path which mimicked the course of the meandering river.

Geremy looked back to make sure Danny was still following. "Sorry. Looks like I should have brought a machete! Actually, I don't particularly want the path to be obvious to people who don't already know about it. It leads to a spot that is special to me."

Danny nodded, but said nothing. She and Philippe had a secret spot near the family house in Foix, so she understood the sentiment.

She was rolling up the sleeves of the flannel shirt she was wearing over her tee shirt when she ran into Geremy, who had stopped walking. She looked around at the spot and decided it wouldn't have qualified as special in her book.

"This is it?"

"No, no. It's on the island, and we have to row over. I just don't see the boat. Wait here while I check the bushes." Geremy disappeared for less then a minute and then reappeared dragging a small rowboat behind him.

"I know this will not sound very gallant, but can you row us over? It's not very far, and we can use the current to get us there, but my palm is still tender." He held up his right hand as if to remind her that it was injured.

"Sure, no problem. Just point us in the right direction."

"Right." Geremy rolled up his pant legs, and Danny noticed for the first time that he was barefoot. They slid the boat into the river, and Geremy held it while Danny climbed in and put the oars into the oar locks. When she was ready, Geremy pushed off and climbed in.

Danny pulled on the oars and felt the river current push the boat to the center of the stream. A few strokes later, the boat scraped the beach pebbles of the small island in the middle of the River Windrush.

Geremy hopped out as Danny took the oars out of the locks and laid them in the bottom of the boat. He pulled the boat up so she could get out without getting her feet wet. Then together they pulled the boat all the way out of the river and into the trees.

"It's just through here," Geremy said as he pushed back some branches and walked into a small clearing.

Danny stepped into the clearing and immediately felt the wonderful presence of the spot. A steady breeze was blowing causing the trees to sway and rustle, but the late spring sun was warm enough for her to take the flannel shirt off and enjoy the feel of the sun on her skin. Yes, a very beautiful spot.

"Do you mind if we walk while we talk? I'm afraid if I sit down here I'll forget to get any work done."

"Sure. I understand. This place will cast a spell on you if you stay still for too long," he said with a knowing grin.

"I believe you," she said quietly as she looked around the sunny clearing. "Now. To work." They began to walk slowly around the perimeter of the clearing. "First off, I'm sure you've done plenty of interviews, but I want to give you an idea of how I work. If I had my camera, I'd take pictures while we talked, but those will have to wait. I like to think of an interview as a conversation, so I don't take notes—it's too distracting. I rely on my memory. As part of the interview agreement, your manager will see the draft before it goes to print."

Geremy kicked a stone, keeping it in motion as they walked. "Good. As you may have noticed, none of us are too crazy about doing interviews. In fact, we drew straws to decide who would do this one."

"What? My editor told me that the band had specifically requested that I do this article because you guys liked my style."

"Our manager Dennis set everything up. I don't know if I've ever even read any of your work."

"And here I thought that one of my favorite bands had asked for me only to find out it was your manager." She took over kicking the stone. "Well, it's nice to know I've got a fan somewhere in the organization."

"One of your favorite bands? The Celts are one of your favorite bands?" He stopped walking.

Danny was concentrating on keeping the stone moving, so did not notice that Geremy was no longer beside her. When she looked up to respond, he wasn't there. She turned around. "What's the matter?"

"Danny, have we ever met before?"

She smiled and nodded slowly.

"I knew it!"

"I was eight years old."

"What!?"

"I was eight years old. It was in Los Angeles in 1968. My father had taken my brother and me backstage after a concert. That's when we met."

"Eight years old." He looked so crushed that Danny wanted to laugh.

"Your father? Who's your father?"

"Liam Davis."

"Liam Davis, the photographer?"

"The very same."

"Do you look like him?"

"Not really. I take after my mother. Why are you asking me all these questions? I'm supposed to be interviewing you."

"You'll think I'm crazy, but I feel like I've met you before. It's as if I know you. I thought if you looked like your father, that might explain it. John Dearing, the keyboard player, is a great fan of your father's and has a photograph in his house of the two of them. I thought perhaps I was making an association."

"It was John who invited dad backstage. Dad admired him very much, too. But, no, I look like my mother. Philippe, on the other hand, is the spitting image of my father, except for the eyes, of course. Philippe's eyes are hazel, not brown like dad's ." She started walking again, took a few steps, stopped, and looked back at Geremy with a smile on her face. "Looks like we've got another mystery to solve. But for now, the interview!"

She waited until Geremy came even with her before she began her questions, walking slowly by his side. "The band made its mark in the sixties by putting Celtic myths to music, with most of the songs written by you. Can you tell me what inspired you to write songs based on Celtic myths?"

"First of all, while I penned many of the songs, every member of the band made a significant contribution to the final product. John's understanding of music combined with an understanding of my vision for the songs gave them the 'mystic' quality that set them apart from other rock songs. As for the songs, well, the myths themselves are full of passion, passages, love and hope, sorrow and death. Pretty inspirational stuff." He paused. "Well, *I* found the topics inspirational, in any case." Geremy smiled and winked at her before continuing.

"The ideas for the songs themselves came out of my fascination for the myths. I started reading them as a child, and I never seemed able to get enough of them. Then, when I was twelve, I saw Elvis Presley on the television, and I was hooked. I wanted to play the guitar and make rock and roll music. Since I had a notebook full of verse relating to the myths, putting them to music seemed the logical thing to do." He looked at Danny as if expecting her to respond. When she didn't say anything, he continued. "It was a double-edged sword for me, though. While the verse had been very easy to write, the music was harder for me to develop. I had very specific ideas about how I wanted it to sound, but had a devil of a time bringing it out. In the process, though, I did figure out how to play the guitar."

Danny smiled at the understatement. Geremy was considered one of the best guitar players in rock and roll, but she let it pass without comment.

He continued, not noticing her smile. "Then, when I was sixteen, I met John, who was nineteen and very talented. When I heard his music, it clicked. I could hear my words to his music. It was one of the strangest experiences I've ever had."

They had gone halfway around the clearing and had reached a large solitary rock. As Geremy stopped walking to lean against it, his narrative ceased also. Danny could tell he was reliving the moment. His eyes were half-closed, and he was smiling slightly. The late afternoon sun was on his face, deepening the blue of his eyes and making his hair look like spun gold. The effect made him look much younger than his forty-six years and so illuminated his beauty that she caught her breath. The carefully constructed mask of the charmer momentarily fell away and was replaced by an expression that was so open and unguarded, she felt as if she were invading his privacy. She forced herself to look away from him and out into the clearing. After a few moments, Geremy shook his head as if waking from a dream. "Sorry. I faded out on you."

"No problem."

"Anyway, John thought we should form a band. He and Miles had worked together in a band called The Deserters, so John called Miles, asking if he wanted to get another band together. Miles said yes. We put the word out that we needed a bass player and Neil Fairgraves answered the call. The rest is history."

They began walking again. "After the first five albums, you moved away from the myths and started writing more standard lyrics. Can you tell me about the change in the direction?"

"Well, as you may imagine, after five albums, I had reached a burn-out level. All of us had, actually, so we took a break and pursued other projects. John and Miles traveled to exotic places, and Neil went to his house in Scotland to help his wife plant trees in the Highlands."

"What did you do?" Danny watched as his mouth became a thin line and the muscles in his jaw tensed. His eyes became slits, and he looked down at the ground causing his hair to fall forward and obscure his face from her gaze.

"I wandered." He said it with a degree of finality that told her he would say no more about that subject.

"So what brought the band back together with such different types of songs? You wrote more standard rock-and-roll and love songs while John's and Miles's songs still had the mystical feeling, but the lyrics were more thought provoking. Neil's love songs seem to be the only thing that stayed pretty much the same through the break. What brought you back?"

Geremy laughed. "That's no big mystery. We are very good friends! We had taken a break and felt rejuvenated and ready to make music again. We had lots of new ideas and wanted to play with each other again."

"There was a rumor that you guys had a falling out. Any truth to that?"

"People always say things like that when a band takes a break. That someone's ego got too big or whatever. I think people need that kind of drama in their lives. They find it too boring to consider that we just needed to take a break. So, no, in a nutshell, there was no falling out."

"You are set to go on tour this year. Do you have any new material to play for your fans?"

"We've been working on some new songs, but we haven't decided if we'll play any of them. Probably not."

They had walked completely around the clearing when Danny noticed that the wind had picked up and clouds completely obscured the sun. She put the flannel shirt back on as she looked at the darkening sky. "Looks like a good time to head back. I don't want to get caught in the rain again. Plus I need to transcribe what we talked about while it's still fresh in my mind."

CHAPTER NINE

Peter McCafferty stood in the doorway of his boss's office holding a cup of coffee, watching Earling work. They had worked together for almost five years, and Peter was used to Tim Earling's workacholic nature. "Did you ever get out for lunch?" Earling kept working as he replied, "No, not yet. I'll go in a bit."

McCafferty looked at his watch. "Don't bother, it's tea time."

"Damn." He leaned back in his chair and rubbed his eyes. "Have you heard anything about Chas and Jackie?"

"Word on the street is that Maloney and Hansen have left town, but no one seems to know where they went."

"Have you found the brother?"

"He lives in Foix, France. I've called his number, but no answer yet. I've got Emerson working on it."

"Sit down." He motioned Peter into the battered, fake-leather chair by the door. "I've been trying to figure out why Maloney and Hansen are working out of their league." He got up and walked over to the large blackboard attached to one wall of his office. He liked visuals when he was working out a problem and liked the large format the board provided. He wrote only a few words by each number as he listed the facts.

"The facts as we know them are, we are notified of the break-in, we discover that Ms. Davis is an American on assignment, she's in the music business, the flat is owned by another woman in the music business, the flat was searched, but nothing was nicked, and

Hansen and Maloney appear to be involved in some manner. We are called back to the flat by the building manager, who tells us that she received a prank phone call which removed her from the premises during the break-in. And now it appears that Ms. Davis has been removed from the flat by force. She has not been seen since we left her at twelve forty five yesterday afternoon." Earling turned to McCafferty holding the chalk out to him. "Put down what you've learned."

McCafferty took the chalk and set his coffee down on the corner of Earling's desk. Turning to the board, he put a line down the middle of it and started his own list. " Danielle Davis is the daughter of Liam and Marguerite Davis. She was born April 10, 1960, in Foix, France. She has one older brother. Family moved to California in 1967. Parents were killed in a car crash in 1985. She is a graduate of University of California, Los Angeles. She lives in Seattle, Washington, and has been working as a freelance writer for music publications for six years. She has no police record of any kind." He turned and shot a crooked smile at Earling before saying, "Couldn't even find any traffic infractions." He reached for his coffee, took a drink, and continued.

" Ms. Baker is a British citizen, born August 18, 1958, in London to Richard and Constance Baker, who emigrated from Barbados in 1956. Father's a retired music professor, mother gives private piano lessons. Ms. Baker has been in the music business as a studio musician and back-up singer for fifteen years. She inherited the residence, has lived there for five years, has no police record, and is a charter member of Musicians Against Drug Abuse." He looked over his shoulder at Earling, who shrugged his shoulders.

"Involvement in an anti-drug group doesn't prove much these days. It's fashionable."

"I've seen no evidence of illegal drug activity."

"Do we know anything about Philippe Davis?"

"An artist, painter. His paintings are in galleries in Europe and the United States. No illegal activity from him either. Very clean family."

"So what are Chas and Jackie up to?" A knock at the door interrupted their discussion. A young man opened the door and addressed McCafferty.

"I've got Mr. Davis on the phone, sir."

"Excellent." He turned to Earling. "Hopefully, he can shed some light on this mystery." He left Earling pondering Maloney and Hansen's motives.

—

The phone was ringing as Danny and Geremy came back to the cottage from their walk. "Aha! The phone line is repaired!" Geremy went in to retrieve the handset. Danny followed him in far enough to pick up a pad of paper and a pen. When she'd found them, she went back out to the patio. She wanted to make notes about their discussion and jot down some thoughts.

Geremy activated the handset. "Hello?"

"Geremy! It's Miles. Are you alright?"

"Yes, of course. Shouldn't I be?"

"Did you make the interview with that reporter?"

"Yes. Well, sort of. Why?"

"So you know the reporter is a woman and not a man as we all thought?"

"So I found out when I arrived."

"Well, she's disappeared and the police think she's been kidnapped. Turns out she's the daughter of Liam Davis, the photographer. So you saw her that morning?"

"Yes, but someone had just ransacked her place, so I left while she talked to the police. I came back to do the interview, but ran into some trouble. The long and short of it is that she is here with me."

"She's with you? At the cottage?" Miles did not bother to hide his surprise.

"Yes. Listen, Miles, do me a favor, will you?"

"Name it."

"Hold on a second." He called out to Danny. "Danny, do you remember the name of the policeman you spoke to?"

"Um. Let's see. Yes, his name is Sergeant Earling."

"Miles? Danny says she spoke to someone named Sergeant Earling."

" 'Danny,' is it?"

Geremy ignored the question and the tone in Miles's voice. "Can you find out his number for me and ring me here when you get it?"

"Sergeant Earling, did you say? His name and number are listed in the article. Do you have a pen?"

Geremy took down the number Miles gave him. "Thank you. Danny will call him to let him know she's alright."

"Will you please tell me what's going on?"

"Some men did try to kidnap her, but I managed to get her away from them when they left her unattended. I figured it was safest to bring her here, but I hadn't thought of the possibility that she would be missed. I'll let her know in case she has to call someone to let them know she's alright. I'll call you tomorrow."

"Fine. I'm looking forward to meeting her."

"Good. She wants to meet you, too."

"She does?"

"Of course, she does. She wants to interview you for the article."

"Oh, right. Call me when you get back."

"Yep. Cheers." He turned the phone off. Leaning out the door, he found Danny sitting in one of the wooden patio chairs with the hand holding the pen lying idle on the pad on her lap as she watched ominous clouds move across the sky. He could smell the promise of rain in the air. He stayed in the doorway, leaning against the door jamb.

"That was Miles. Sounds like you've been missed. Miles said that the newspapers list you as possibly kidnapped. He gave me the telephone number for Earling. Perhaps you should call him to let him know all is well with you. Also, any loved ones who may be concerned about your disappearance? Your brother or a boyfriend, perhaps?"

Danny stood up. "Gosh! I didn't even think about people missing me! I'd better make some calls." She heard him fishing for information, but since she wasn't sure what to say about Stephen, she let it pass without comment. She had to call Philippe and Jasmine. She didn't think that Stephen would have heard anything, but she'd ask Jasmine to call him, just in case. She did not want to talk to him. She felt guilty; he'd been so far from her thoughts, and her feelings for Geremy were growing almost by the minute. No, she'd ask Jasmine to call him.

"I'll get started on supper." Geremy went back into the kitchen and passed the phone to Danny.

"Thanks." She went out to the patio. Geremy watched her pace as she spoke to whomever it was that she had called. He felt quite the dunce for not even thinking that she might be involved with someone, but it really hadn't crossed his mind until Miles said that she been reported missing. How could he have been so stupid? He was surprised to realize that he felt a twinge of jealousy. He pulled a pot out of the cupboard and banged it on the counter.

Danny came back in and set the phone down. "It was Jasmine who told the police that my father is Liam Davis. That's probably how they hit on the kidnapping idea. Philippe had just hung up from talking to P.C. McCafferty, the officer who came to the flat with Sergeant Earling, when I called. He was very relieved to hear from me, as you might expect. Sergeant Earling was also glad to hear from me, and he wants to talk to me and you, too."

"Me?"

"Yes. The presence of the rescuer of the damsel in distress is required," she said with a smile. "He wanted us to come by his office this evening, but I told him that would not be possible. Actually, I think he was relieved to hear it. He sounded tired. I told him we'd be by tomorrow morning. Do you mind?"

"No. I was thinking it was time we returned."

"Oh," she said softly. Danny realized that she didn't really want to leave.

"Did you call your boyfriend?" Danny was surprised to hear the bite in his voice, but a little relieved also. She hadn't mistaken that he was attracted to her.

"'Boyfriend' is not exactly the term I would use to describe the man with whom I'm currently involved, but, no, I didn't call Stephen. I asked Jasmine to call him. He was not happy with my decision to do this job. He told me that he had a bad feeling about my coming to London, so we parted on strained terms."

"Seems like he was right, about your coming to London, I mean. Your trip has been rather dangerous so far."

Something told Danny that Stephen had not been referring to the physical dangers that she had experienced. She didn't know how he knew it, but she felt sure that he'd had a premonition that if she came to London, something would happen that would ensure that she would not marry him. And he was right. The feelings she was experiencing for Geremy were enough to tell her that she could not marry Stephen. The finality behind that realization brought her feelings of both sadness and relief. It wasn't what Stephen wanted to hear, but she knew it was the right answer for her.

She watched Geremy, wondering how it would feel to be kissed by him. Her skin tingled to think of his calloused fingertips caressing her body. He looked up and caught her staring at him. Feeling as if she'd been caught with her hand in the cookie jar, she flushed. In an effort to cover her discomfort, she moved into the kitchen.

"Why don't you let me take over? You made supper last night, and I'm a pretty good cook. My mother was French, after all."

"Say no more. The kitchen is all yours." He bowed and removed himself to the other side of the breakfast bar where he sat down on one of the two stools. He watched her for a moment in silence before asking, "Is there anything I can do to help?"

She didn't hesitate to respond. "Set the table, open a bottle of white wine, pour me a glass, and talk to me while I cook."

Geremy did as directed and then sat back down at the bar and watched her as she worked. Her familiarity with his kitchen still felt weird, but natural, too. Very odd, indeed.

He sat twirling the stem of his wine glass between his fingers. "How long have you been writing?"

"In general or for the music business?"

"In general."

She answered as she continued to work on the meal. "I started as soon as I learned how to write. Mom used to say that I'd walk around and talk to the neighbors and then make up stories from what they told me. When I learned to write, I committed them to paper."

"No wonder your style feels so natural. You've been interviewing since you were a child! What led you to focus on athletics instead of writing when you went to university?"

"Addiction," she said with a smile. "When I was fourteen, I was taller than everyone in my class and very skinny. Not the greatest combination when moving through that awkward age," she said with a laugh. "One day, on a whim, I tried out for the school track team and discovered a latent, natural talent for running. The long, skinny legs were good for something!" She placed a handful of cut mushrooms onto a plate and turned to him. "From the moment I won my first race, I was hooked. The exhilaration of physical competition against a clock, an old record, or someone else was like nothing I had ever experienced. The challenge was there every day. There was always something to beat. I became addicted, not only to the joy of running and winning, but to the acceptance that I felt from my classmates. I wasn't the tall, skinny, quiet girl in the class anymore. I was the track star. I beat a lot of people and records during my career and thought for sure that I was destined to win an Olympic gold medal."

"But the wreck changed all that?"

Danny turned back to the stove, quiet as she unwrapped the fish fillets. Avoiding his question, she asked, "Is broiled fish and sautéed vegetables alright with you? Martha gave us lots of vegetables, so I thought I'd skip the carbohydrates."

When he didn't answer immediately, she looked over at him. Geremy's eyes were narrow as he looked at her, almost as if he were taking her measure. "That will be fine. When did the accident happen?"

She put the fish into the oven. "A little over ten years ago."

Geremy was surprised. He thought it would have been more recent. Then he thought about the pain he'd been carrying for more than twenty years and knew that he was the last person who should be surprised at how long pain can last. At least Danny knew that her parents were dead. He saw that knowing the fate of a loved one didn't always mean that the pain would be lessened.

"I am always amazed at the paths we take to get where we're going. Do you like what you do for a living?" Danny walked over, refilled her glass, took a sip and faced him from the other side of the bar. "I love it. I can't imagine doing anything else for a living. I wish I hadn't taken such a painful path to find my true calling, though." Leaving her wine glass on the bar she moved back to the oven to check the fish.

"What do you mean?"

"I did a lot of writing while I was recovering from the accident. It kept me from going insane and helped me understand how much I really loved to write."

"Why music and not sports?"

"At first, it was too sad to just write about things I was no longer able to do. Then I became involved with a musician and turned my talent to writing about musical happenings." She returned to the bar and her glass of wine."How about you? Do you ever get tired of playing the same songs over and over again?"

"You'd think so, wouldn't you? But, no, I don't. Well, maybe just a little by the end of a tour. Interestingly enough, though, the songs take on new meaning as the years go by. I know what I was thinking when I wrote them or when we recorded them, but the words apply to things in my life now. The world still needs more love and understanding. That's what most of our songs are about."

"The love songs take on new meanings? They always sounded so specific, to me. Like you are singing to someone in particular." It was her turn to fish.

Geremy examined the glass he was twirling, watching the wine move around within it. "They were then. Now they are just songs that the fans like to hear. When you write a song that people like, it becomes part of their lives and you, as the performer, lose some of the ownership in it. The songs mean something to them, so you play it more for them and their meanings and memories. Not for yours."

"I never thought of it that way, but it makes sense." She sniffed the savory aromas that filled the air. " I do believe that dinner is ready!"

They ate in silence for a while. Then Geremy paused and looked at Danny.

She looked over at him. "Something wrong with the food?"

"No. It's very good," he replied in a distracted voice. "It's just … do you remember that I said you seem familiar to me?"

Danny nodded. "Yes. But other than that time when I was eight, we've never spoken to each other."

"Could we have crossed paths somewhere else? You're in the music business, maybe at a party or something? This will drive me crazy unless I figure it out."

"I took some pictures when the Celts played at the Gorge in Washington. A friend gave me a backstage pass on the condition that the band had all rights to the photos. Unfortunately, I didn't realize that the meter on the camera was malfunctioning, so the pictures were too light. I tossed them. Maybe you saw me there."

"Maybe, but that doesn't ring a bell." He moved more of the mushrooms across his plate and then looked at her with a curious expression. "Have you ever wondered how many times you cross someone's path before you finally meet them?"

She shook her head as she chewed on some asparagus and then swallowed. "No. But I've got to believe that you meet when the time is right."

"Then that means that this is the 'right' time for you and I?"

Danny opened and then closed her mouth without speaking. His question had caught her by surprise, and she didn't know what to say.

CHAPTER TEN

Earling rubbed his eyes and leaned back in his chair. The call from Ms. Davis had been a relief, but he was most relieved when she said she wouldn't be able to talk to him until tomorrow. He was tired and needed to step back from the case. She was safe at the house of a friend, whom she would not identify. He'd meet the mystery friend tomorrow when they came by the station. For now, he was glad to go home, see his wife, and forget about the case for a few hours.

He looked over at the blackboard one last time before leaving for the night. The brother had not been able to shed any light on what was going on. He had assured them that, whatever it was, it would have nothing do with illegal drugs. He said she had never shown any interest whatsoever in drugs. Earling shook his head as he walked to the door. Perhaps Ms. Davis had something new to tell them. He'd find out tomorrow morning. He hit the light switch and headed for home.

—

Geremy gave a contented sigh as he pushed his empty plate away. "That was delicious. Your mother was a good teacher."

Danny nodded and stood up from the table. "Both of my parents loved to cook, so I got a double dose of good cooking genes." She took their plates to the sink and called back to him over her shoulder. "Guess what, maestro? Your turn to do the dishes."

He held up his hand. "What about my injury?"

Danny walked back to the table and gave Geremy an unsympathetic look. "Let me take a look at it." She sat down and motioned for him to put his hand on the table. She unwrapped the gauze. "Lookin' good, maestro. In fact, I'm sure the soapy water will be good for it."

"Slave driver."

"Hardly." She strolled over and picked up the dish towel. "No self-respecting slave driver would dry."

It seemed to her that the kitchen had become smaller as they worked because she noticed that no matter how she moved, she touched Geremy. Not that she minded. In fact, she was enjoying it and was disappointed at how quickly the dishes were finished.

"So, how does the hand feel?" She took his hand to look at the cut again.

"I'm in agony."

He said it with such soft urgency that she quickly looked up at him to see if he was serious. His lips were smiling, but it did not reach his eyes, which were almost sad as he looked into hers.

She felt the twinge again and, releasing his hand, took a step backward. She found it hard to maintain her composure when he looked at her like that. Her cheeks grew warm, and she looked away. "Do you want me to wrap it again?"

"Yes. That would be nice." He found any touch from her very nice. She went to get the gauze and tape, but when she came back to the kitchen, Geremy wasn't there. She heard a door slam in his bedroom and turned to see him coming out with a guitar.

She looked at the guitar, mildly surprised. "Let me guess. The hidden closet?"

He gave a slight nod. "I keep this guitar here in case I need to work something out. I've got a few ideas rambling around in my head. Do you mind?"

"Not at all! Do you want me to wrap your hand before or after?"

"Now, please." He sat down at the table and held his hand out for her to wrap. Watching her work, he said, "You'd have made a good doctor."

She laughed. "I've been told that my bedside manner could use some improvement. When Stephen sprained his ankle running last year, I lost patience with him after two short days. He told me it was good I had decided against doctoring."

"Stephen is your, uh, what's the term these days? Partner?"

"Yes, I think that's the term these days."

"Been together long?"

"Three years."

"What's he like?"

"What do you mean? What does he do for a living?"

"Yeah. Do for a living, how old, what's he like?" He was trying to get a bead on the competition.

"Stephen is a very successful architect. He's forty-four years old, brilliant, charming, very handsome, moves with ease through Seattle's upper-crust society, and is a very nice man."

"Will you marry this god among men?" he asked, not quite able to keep the sarcastic tone out of his voice.

"That's certainly a question on his mind." Danny taped the gauze strip down to the back of his hand. "There you go, maestro. That should hold your hand together while you play." She took the leftover gauze and tape to the bathroom, leaving Geremy to stare after her and wonder.

He picked up his guitar and tuned it as a light rain began to fall. Danny poured a glass of wine and adjusted one of the living room chairs so she could watch the gray twilight engulf the woods outside the front window. Sweet strains of music floated through the air from Geremy's guitar, and she felt more content then she had felt in a very long time.

Next morning, Danny woke at dawn, alone in one of the twin beds in the upstairs bedroom. She felt pent up and knew she needed to do some serious exercise. Between not having a good workout recently and having to keep her attraction to Geremy in check, she felt like a taut rubber band. She lay in bed thinking about her options. She needed a total body workout. Running was always an option. She had a pair of shoes she could run in, but wasn't too thrilled at the prospect of running in her only pair of jeans and tee shirt. This would be her third day wearing them, and they were beginning to feel pretty grungy. A good run in them would take them out of her range of acceptability for wearing, even for grunge. Geremy probably had something, but she didn't feel like waking him to find out.

She sat up in bed and looked out the window and through the trees to the river. She watched the gray, morning light glint off the surface of the river. She snapped her fingers. She could go swimming in the river pool. It would be much better for her right leg than running, and it didn't require any special equipment, just the water and her body. The spot was secluded, so swimming nude was not an issue.

At the river's edge, she paused and looked at the water. The air was cool and a veil of clouds screened the newly risen sun. Not her favorite weather for a dip in a river swollen with cold spring rain, but it would have to do. She went through a stretching routine she used before her weekly judo class, warming up her muscles so they wouldn't cramp in the cold water. When she was finished, she peeled off her clothes and waded into the pool. Damn, it was cold!

She dove into the water and began to swim against the current. It was rushing and, for the first few minutes, she kept getting pushed to the end of the pool where the water escaped through a narrow channel. Enjoying the challenge of the river current, she dove into it, swam her way to the center of the pool, and kept herself there. She swam the crawl and was soon into a rhythm. As the shock of the cold wore off, she felt her muscles respond to the challenge. She loved the feel of the water on her skin and the strength of her body as she kept herself in place against the current.

After fifteen minutes, she began to feel the pent-up tension leave her body, and after thirty minutes, she'd had enough. She waded out of the pool and plopped down on the towel she had placed on the sandy bank. She laid on the ground, breathing deeply, enjoying the feel of the adrenalin pumping through her system, the cool air on her wet skin, and the goosebumps that passed over her skin in waves. Her whole body was tingling.

Geremy stood at his bedroom window watching her swim. She swam in place as if her survival was dependent upon it, unswerving and determined. He considered going down and joining her, but decided against it. He didn't think he'd be able to resist the urge to caress her naked body, and he knew that once he touched her, he'd want much more than just a touch. When she walked out of the water, he thought of the water sirens mentioned in so many myths. Many a man would willingly respond to the call of Danielle Davis. She had the slender, well-toned body of a dedicated athlete, and moved with a precise grace that made him think of a black panther easing through the jungle.

As she lay down on the beach, he knew he'd made the right decision not to join her. Even from this distance, he felt a stirring as he watched her. He turned from the window and went to take a shower.

Geremy was in the living room wearing his robe and towel-drying his hair when Danny came in from her swim. Her cheeks were rosy, and she was full of energy. " Wow, you're right! The current running through that pool makes for a wonderful workout!"

"You went swimming?

She nooded.

"You eally should be careful swimming in the river." His tone was very serious.

"I'm an excellent swimmer," she said with a touch of annoyance.

"All the more reason to be careful. It always goes for the strong swimmers." He was very earnest as he looked at her.

"What are you talking about?"

"The river creature. Hasn't anyone warned you about it? It's really best to swim after the sun is fully risen since dawn and dusk are the times it's most likely to catch the unwary swimmer." His expression was as serious as she had ever seen it. For a moment he had her. Then she saw him purse his lips in an effort to keep from smiling, and she started laughing at her own gullibility. Geremy couldn't hold his serious expression in the face of her laughter.

"You almost had me there," she said before cracking up again. "For a half-second, anyway." Tears sprang to her eyes from laughter.

Geremy doubled over with laughter, putting his hands on his knees for support. "You should have seen the look on your face," he managed to choke out between bursts of laughter. "I had you for more than half a second, though, admit it!" He straightened and wiped a tear from his eye. "I haven't played that trick on anyone in years." He continued to chuckle as he looked at her. She was standing in front of him with a big grin on her face. A tear was on her cheek, and he reached out to wipe it away. When his thumb touched her cheek, they both felt the spark of electricity run between them, and their smiles faded. He laid his hand against her cheek and slid it into her damp hair and behind her head. He drew her to him and kissed her gently on the lips.

Danny moved into his arms without a thought. She could see nothing except his eyes, feel nothing but the touch of his hand on her face. Before she realized it, his lips were on hers, and she was responding to his kiss. She felt the full length of his body pressed against hers as he held her tight with one arm around her back, one hand behind her head. She went up on tiptoe to kiss him more deeply as he moved his hand from her head and encircled her with both his arms.

Then Danny realized what was happening. She pushed away from him and, as he loosened his embrace, she stumbled back and into the couch.

"I'm sorry." Her hand went to her lips, which were tingling from the kiss. "This is not a good idea. It's not good for the interview." She was trembling from the emotions and desire that his kiss had sparked in her.

"What?" He wasn't sure he'd heard her correctly. "Did you say it's not good for the *interview?!*"

"Listen." She walked away from him, turned around, and came back. "It's not unusual for people involved in an interview to feel like they are attracted to each other. In fact, it happens all the time."

He stiffened. "It may happen to you all the time, but I can assure you this is not how I usually behave in an interview situation."

"I'm sorry. I didn't mean it that way. It's just that interviews can lend an aura of artificial intimacy to a relationship and, if acted upon, can impair the objectivity of the interviewer." She hated how impersonal she sounded, which she knew sprang from her jangled emotions.

All Geremy knew was that she had gone cold on him. "I see. Well." He squinted as he looked at her and his tone had turned quite chilly. "If you'll excuse, I'll change so we can be on our way." He turned and went to his room, struggling to make sense of his feelings.

When he had first met her, he was immediately attracted to her and decided straightaway that he wanted to charm her into his bed. But just then, when he touched her cheek and looked into her eyes, he forgot all preconceived ideas of seduction. He felt as if the floor had opened up under his feet and that she held the lifeline that would keep him from being swallowed up. Then, when she pulled away and questioned his motivation, he thought she had seen through him. While he could rationalize that he had never before seduced an interviewer, he also knew that was more because none had struck his fancy rather than out of some respect for the integrity of the interview or the interviewer. He was feeling at a loss as he tried to figure out what had just happened between them.

Danny watched him retreat into his bedroom, unaware of his confusion. "Oh, brother." She hit her forehead with the palm of her hand as she walked into the bathroom. She stopped in front of the mirror and looked at herself. "Great way to handle a sticky situation, Danny. Why not just throw some cold water on the guy?" She held onto the sink for support and continued to stare at her reflection. She still felt shaken by her immediate and overwhelming response to his kiss and was wondering what had come over her. Her mind had gone blank when he laid his hand against her cheek, so much so that she couldn't actually remember moving into his embrace. Her effort to remember the sequence was interrupted by the sound of the kitchen door slamming. She knew she had to give him a better explanation.

She followed his path out the kitchen door, but he was nowhere in sight. Her instincts told her he was on his way to the island. When she caught up with him, he was staring at it, his back to her. She noticed that the jeans and tee shirt were gone and that he was once again wearing the clothes he'd had on when they arrived at the cottage. She looked past him to the island. Mist swirled around it, causing it to appear and then disappear from view.

Not sure how to begin her explanation of why she had pushed him away she chose a safer subject. "Your island looks like Avalon today," she said quietly. She didn't like the wall that had grown between them and was afraid he was not going to acknowledge her presence. The tension she hadn't realized she was holding in her shoulders eased when he replied, though he did not look at her as he spoke.

"When we were children, Graeme and I used to play Camelot games. Of course, he was King Arthur since he was the oldest and I was Lancelot."

"Ah, now I understand. The rescuer of damsels in distress."

He smiled slightly. "You've caught me. When we'd come to the island, my brother and I pretended that we were coming to Avalon. One of my songs was about the Avalon adventures we invented."

Danny nodded as Geremy softly sang a passage from the song.
'When we arrive
the mist hides it from our eyes.
We cross over the stream
as if in a dream
to the island in the mist.'
"*Island in the Mist.* It's one of my favorites. Is it usually misty?" Danny asked softly.

"That seems to be the way I remember it most, with a mist swirling around it." He turned from the island. "We'd better get back if we want to get to London before lunch." He started to move past her, but she caught his arm. Geremy stopped and looked down at her, his expression wary.

"Geremy, I need to explain something. I didn't do a very good job of it earlier." She paused for a moment, searching for the right words. "When I first started interviewing celebrities, I was pretty naïve. The second man I interviewed was a rock star, who shall remain nameless. We hit it off beautifully and ended up making love. I thought he really cared for me, but I found out very soon after the article was published that he was only interested in having a favorable article printed. Turns out, he tries to seduce any and all members of the press, male and female. Thankfully, that incident has turned out to be the interviewing exception rather than the rule, but it still made me aware of the emotional pitfalls that can develop during an interview. I promised myself that I would not allow myself to become involved with the people I interview, especially during the interview."

"Do you think I kissed you so you'd write a nice article about the Celts?"

She looked into his eyes and saw that the wary expression was gone, but the troubled look that replaced it was almost as hard to bear. "No. But I'm asking that we maintain a professional relationship until I finish this job."

It wasn't until he had asked her the question that Geremy understood what had happened back in the cottage. In that moment, when he had touched her cheek, he had felt a stirring at the very core of his being. Now, as he stood looking at her, he realized that he was in love with her. Just like that. "And after the article is written? Will you return immediately to …" He paused. "Seattle?" He didn't have to say it, but she knew he was asking about Stephen.

"I plan to stay at the cottage for two weeks after I send the article off to the magazine. After that, who knows?"

"Fair enough," he said with a bit of a smile. "Come on. Let's eat some breakfast before we go back to London."

CHAPTER ELEVEN

Jackie sat in the cafe across the street from the cafe that Philippe Davis visited every morning. From his vantage point, he could see both the cafe and Davis's house. He had been on surveillance duty since six this morning, and it was now five minutes to noon. His six-hour shift was nearly up, and Chas was due to relieve him for the next shift. They were on day three of the surveillance of Davis's house in an attempt to discover his routines, and they only had one more day before they had to act. Trying to identify a routine in such a short time was always a difficult proposition. In their days as burglars, they had watched a potential target for at least a week, and more often two, before finalizing plans on how to pull off the heist. Having only four days to identify a way to kidnap someone made both of them a little nervous. The woman had proven to be relatively easy to snatch, and yet they had still failed to pull it off.

Davis's apparent habit of going to the corner cafe for his mid-morning coffee was the only thing they had been able to classify as a routine. He would stay for an hour or two, reading the paper and talking to other cafe inhabitants. For the rest of the day, he demonstrated a decided lack of routine. If the woman didn't show up by tomorrow night, they'd have to act on what they had observed in the past few days and the opportunities were slim.

Chas walked into the cafe as Jackie was considering the options. "Anything exciting happen this morning?" Chas asked facetiously as he sat down at the table. The six-hour watching shifts were tremendously boring, but at least he was able to do the more interesting research during his off hours.

Jackie looked at him with an irritated expression. "No. Except for the trip to the cafe, he has remained in the house all morning."

"Well, while you were resting here all morning, I got some real work done."

Jackie shot him a dark look, but held his tongue.

Unable to provoke his partner into a retort, Chas proceeded to tell Jackie what he had found out. "While he was out getting his morning coffee, I got a good look at the house. I guess you saw me go to the door to ask for directions. No one answered when I knocked, so I took a look around." Chas quit talking. A couple of seconds passed before Jackie took his eyes off the house and looked at Chas.

"So? What did you see?"

Chas grinned. "Just checking to see if you were still listening. No security whatsoever. No dogs, no electronics. The door was even unlocked." Chas looked quite pleased with himself.

Jackie yawned, stood up, and stretched. "Your turn. I'll be back at six."

"Well, you could at least say 'good work' or something."

Jackie was walking away from the table when he stopped and looked back at Chas. "Or something." He ignored the scowl Chas cast at him.

—

Danny stood at the only window in Earling's office, looking down on the traffic that moved sluggishly along Earls Court Road. Geremy was sitting on the couch reading the facts written on the blackboard. They had arrived a little over an hour ago and had filled Earling and McCafferty in on the abduction. Then a call came in for Earling. He took it, listened for a minute, hung up the phone, and signaled McCafferty to follow him as he left the office.

"Danny?"

She turned from the window. "Yes?"

Pointing at the board, Geremy said, "It would appear that they have some concerns that you may be involved in the illegal drug trade."

"What?!" She looked at the numbered facts on the board. "Oh, right. I'm in the music business, so I must be into drugs. You considered it a possibility, too, as I recall. Should I just tell them to look into my eyes so they can see how clear and honest they are?"

"I don't think they'd consider that as proof."

"Right. I guess it didn't help my case that my rescuer turned out to be—oh no!—in the music business. The cards are stacked against me." She laughed and pointed to fact number two on the right side of the board. "They are even wondering about Jasmine. They are barking up the wrong tree there." She sat down next to him. "I wish they'd come back so we can get out of here. If I have to keep these clothes on much longer, I'll break out in hives. Which reminds me, why don't you have a washing machine at your cottage?"

"Never seemed necessary."

"What did your mother do when you were a kid?"

"She went to Martha's. Now that I think about it, mum probably enjoyed the excuse to get away from us and visit with Martha. So I'm used to the cottage not having a washer." They fell silent, listening to the muffled sounds of ringing telephones and muted voices that drifted through the walls from the common area outside Earling's office.

"Danny, why didn't you tell them about the ring?"

She pursed her lips, got up from the couch, and leaned against Earling's desk. "I don't know. It didn't seem necessary. They think, or at least I was under the impression they thought, I was snatched for a ransom. Now I understand that they think I might be involved in some drug business. As long as they thought it was for a ransom and I knew they were wrong, I didn't see any point in telling them about the ring."

"Danny, they are trying to help you. You need to tell them everything."

She nodded her head and shrugged. "You're right. I'll tell them." She stopped talking when she saw through the glass in the door that

Earling and McCafferty were approaching. As Earling opened the door, Danny went back to the couch and sat down.

"Sorry to keep you waiting. We thought we had found Hansen and Maloney, but our contact was mistaken." Earling took his seat behind the desk while McCafferty closed the door and leaned against it.

"Sergeant Earling, I don't think those men kidnapped me for ransom." Why did she feel as if Earling wasn't surprised at her statement? He leaned forward as if waiting for a confession. "I don't mean to disappoint you," she jerked her right thumb at the board, "but it wasn't for drugs or anything illegal. At least, I don't think it's anything illegal." She pulled the chain out from under her shirt and showed Earling the ring. "When the men in the car thought I was knocked out, they discussed their mission—to get this ring from me."

"Why didn't you mention this before?"

"It didn't seem necessary."

"May I see it?" She took the chain from around her neck and handed it to him. Earling examined the ring "Do you know why they want it?"

"I thought I heard them say something about a boss, but I'm not sure."

"A boss? Did they happen to mention a name?" Earling sounded exasperated.

"If they did, I didn't catch it."

"Ms. Davis, in the future will you please let us determine the importance of the information? Now, do you have any idea why their boss wants this?"

"No, sir, I don't." She then told them what she knew about the ring. "I don't think the ring itself is very valuable, but Geremy, ah, Mr. Hawker and I think that the stone is a map and the line represents a river." She leaned forward and popped the stone up. "We haven't figured out the line on the back of the stone or what the writing says, but we think the men want the ring for the map."

"It doesn't look worth kidnapping someone over. You say your mother received it from an unidentified man during the war?"

"Yes."

"It's been a while, but if it's alright with you, I'd like to get some photographs of it so we can run a check on it. Probably won't get anything, but it's worth a try. We should be able to figure out the writing, anyway."

"Well, I know for sure that it's not French, Spanish, Italian, or German, so you don't need to bother checking it against those four."

"You are familiar with those languages as well as English?" Earling asked her.

"Yes. My mother was French, but spoke Spanish and Italian as well as English. My father was multilingual also."

Earling nodded and held the ring out toward McCafferty. "Take this to the lab so they can get some good pictures of it."

Geremy leaned over toward Danny and whispered in her ear, "I think it's safe to say you're more then 'pretty good' with languages." He straightened up as Danny smiled and shrugged her shoulders.

"Now, Ms. Davis. What are your plans?"

Danny furrowed her brow. "What do you mean?"

"Where are you staying, how long will you stay in England, what are your plans?"

"My first plan is to change into some clean clothes. I plan to do that at the flat, clean the place up, and then finish the interview. Then I plan to take a brief vacation before returning to the United States."

"I don't think it's a good idea for you to stay at Ms. Baker's. We don't know where Hansen and Maloney are, so I want you to stay someplace else."

"May I at least go straighten up the place? If Jasmine comes back and her house is a mess, she won't be happy with me." Only Danny knew what an understatement this was. Jasmine would possibly become physically ill if she saw her flat in such a state of disrepair. 'A place for everything and everything in its place' was embroidered and hung in a frame in the living room. At least, she hoped it still hung in the living room.

Earling sat back in his chair, considering her request. "You can go in to tidy the place up and retrieve your belongings, but I don't want you to stay there any longer than necessary and certainly not alone."

Geremy perked up. "I'll stay and then she can come with me to the band's house in Richmond. She can stay there as long as she needs." He looked from Earling to Danny. They remained silent. He couldn't read Danny's reaction to his suggestion.

"Thanks for offering to babysit, but I can't believe these guys would be stupid enough to try the same thing twice. As for the house, frankly, I think it's best if I stay at a hotel."

Earling felt an undercurrent running between them, but he couldn't identify its source. He was happy that Hawker had volunteered an alternative place for her to stay. He didn't want her left alone, and she was less likely to be bothered if she was at Hawker's house. Independent women made his job more difficult than need be. Oh well, he couldn't force her to stay with Hawker.

"You can stay where you choose, but I do not want you to be alone at the flat. Just call me when you know where you'll be staying. I want to be able to get in touch with you if we find out anything about the ring or if we discover who is behind the troubles you've been experiencing."

McCafferty came back with the ring and gave it to Danny. She looked at Earling. "May we go now?"

He nodded. "Just call and tell me the name of the hotel you choose."

As they stepped into the elevator that would take them down to the ground floor, Danny looked at Geremy, trying to read his thoughts. She sensed that her decision to stay at a hotel bothered him. "Thanks for offering to let me stay at your place. It was kind of you."

He looked at her and nodded, but said nothing.

"I like to be in a space of my own choosing when I work. I have erratic work habits, staying up late, sleeping in, that sort of thing. So I prefer to be where I know I'm not impinging on someone else. Or they on me."

"I understand. It's much the same with me. I get inspired at all times of the day and night. It does cause some strife for housemates. My wife certainly didn't appreciate it."

"Your wife?" Her brow creased.

"I was married for a while in the mid-seventies. It didn't work out."

From his office window, Earling watched as the pair left the building.

"Do you think she told us everything she knows?" McCafferty asked.

"I knew she was holding something back before we left the office. But I think she's told us everything she knows. I don't know if we'll get anything on the ring, but we have to check. This thing still doesn't make much sense."

—

Sebastian Sanders walked quickly to his desk and picked up the receiver to his private phone. "Yes?"

"It's Diego. She's back, but a man is with her. What do you want me to do?"

The line was silent as Sanders considered the question. Then Diego heard the instructions he had expected. "Keep an eye on the building, and call me if the man leaves and she stays. If they leave together, follow them and call me with an update."

—

Geremy looked around the flat, a frown on his face. "Danny, are you sure you won't reconsider and stay at the house? No one is there right now, and it's quite big. Big enough for four grown men, in case we all needed to stay there at the same time."

"You don't live in London?"

"Good Lord, no! My house is in Devon, near Exeter. I can only take London in small doses. What do you say?"

Danny shook her head. She needed some space to sort out her feelings, and she knew that would be much easier if Geremy was not around. "Thank you, but I've decided to stay at the Grosvenor House."

"Grosvenor's? They usually require advance reservations."

She gave him a quirky smile. "I have friends in high places."

"Ah. They are helpful in these types of emergencies. So there's no persuading you?"

Danny shook her head. "Listen, I'll be perfectly honest with you. I need some time alone. Mrs. Willson said she'd help me clean up, and I can call a cab when I'm done. So it would be most helpful for me if you didn't wait around."

"Earling said he didn't want you to be here alone."

"You heard Mrs. Willson say she'd be up to help me straighten up the place so I won't be alone. Besides, I just can't believe that these guys would return to the scene of their crime. All crooks know that's bad luck."

"I don't think Earling had Mrs. Willson in mind when he suggested you not be alone."

"I'll be alright. I'll call you in the morning so we can set up a time to meet and finish the interview. Is there any chance that any of the other guys can meet with us?"

"Miles wants to join in. He lives just outside of London, so he'll be there. But a word of warning, he may try to talk about your father rather than himself and the band. Neil lives in Scotland, so I don't think he'll make it. I don't know where John is but, like Miles, when he hears that the interviewer is the daughter of Liam Davis, I'd be very surprised if he didn't show up. But I have to find him first, so I'll take care of those details tonight."

"Thanks. I owe you. And about my father. I usually don't reveal my parentage for the very reason that people often forget who is interviewing whom and start asking me about him."

"I'll remind them that we are the ones being interviewed, not you." He stood there for a moment looking at her and then realized it was time he left. "Call me in the morning?"

"Yes. Thanks again, Geremy. I don't know what I would have done if you hadn't been there. You've been more than kind."

He took her hands in his. "It was my pleasure," he said softly before he leaned down and kissed her lightly on the lips. "Really." He looked at her for a moment more and then, releasing her hands, turned and left the flat.

Kind, my eye, he thought to himself as he walked down the stairs. He recognized that his motives now were purely mercenary. He simply wanted to be near her as he tried to figure out his feelings. The fact that she seemed wary brought a wry grin to his face as he thought of all the women who were all too eager to be with him. As he left the building, he found himself wondering if he was drawn to her because she was wary.

As soon as Diego saw the tall, blond man get into his car and drive away, he called Sebastian. "He's left, and she is still there. What do you want me to do?"

Sebastian only thought for a moment before speaking. He wanted that ring! "Do you have something you can use to cover your face?"

Diego looked into the glove box and pulled out a ski mask. "Yes."

"The woman has a gold ring with an onyx stone that belongs to me. I want you to get it. I'm sure she is wearing it. Be very careful. If, when you get into the building, you don't think it's safe, withdraw and call me again."

Diego hung up the cellular phone and slipped out of his car, gloves on and mask in hand. He crossed the street slowly while considering his options for getting into the building. He paused on the sidewalk at the base of the stairs and lit a cigarette, stalling for time without looking suspicious. He was estimating how fast he could pick the lock when a man walking toward him turned and went up the stairs. Diego heard the buzzer and then the click as the door unlocked and the man entered. He crushed the cigarette beneath his shoe before slipping unnoticed through the slowly closing door. He then stood quietly in a shadow, waiting as the man disappeared up the stairs. He waited for another second, listening to the sounds in the building, before creeping silently up the stairs to Danny's flat.

Danny had been standing in the center of the living room when Geremy left. For the first few minutes, she was unable to decide where to begin the cleaning job. Then her eyes passed over her Nikon camera lying on top of the backdrop cloth. Thinking that her camera equipment was as good a place as any to start, she walked over and picked up the Nikon. She turned it on and checked the auto focus, meter, and flash. She had loaded the camera with black-and-white film in preparation for the interview with Geremy, so she shot off a couple of frames to make sure that the auto advance was still working. She was relieved to discover that the camera was undamaged.

She was just about to set it down when she heard someone come in the door. The hair on the back of her neck stood up as she recalled the last time she had been in the flat and had heard a noise behind her. Turning slowly, she saw a tall man wearing a ski mask closing the door behind him. Then she saw the knife in his hand.

"Oh, brother," was all she could say. The flat was definitely loosing its charm. She felt the weight of the camera in her hand and thanked God that she had not turned anything off. She knew that the flash had recharged so that at least one picture would have the flash. She just hoped the police would check the camera for the evidence when they found her dead body.

The man was advancing slowly toward her as he twirled the knife in his right hand. "All I want is the onyx ring. Give it to me, and I won't hurt you." He had a soft, Spanish accent. He was five feet away from Danny when she pulled the camera up and started shooting. Her action surprised him, and the flash blinded him for a second. Danny began to back away from him as she continued to shoot the roll of twenty-four frames. The last frame was shot just as her foot caught on the protruding leg of an overturned table, and she went down. She lost her grip on the camera; it bounced off a couch cushion before landing on the floor.

The spots began to clear from Diego's eyes, and he saw Danny on the floor. He smiled. "Where's the ring?" he asked as he advanced toward her, the knife twirling in his hand again.

Danny scrambled up from the floor and kicked the debris away from her feet while keeping her eyes on the man. She didn't want to trip again. She cleared her mind of all thoughts as her judo instructor had taught her and assumed the defense potion. She pushed the fear from her mind.

The man hesitated for a moment and then sneered at her. "Think I'm going to fall for that old trick?" He was a couple inches taller than her and at least seventy pounds heavier. He was confident he could take her down even if she really did know martial arts.

Danny kept her expression cold and unrevealing, but didn't say a word. She knew she had an advantage over him. He didn't know that she'd been practicing judo and aikido for nine years. Plus, since he used a weapon, he probably relied heavily on his prowess with it. If she could disarm him, she hoped his confidence would waver. She was moving slowly to her right, keeping away from the knife in his right hand. She slid her feet in order to move anything on the floor out of her way as she moved, all the while maintaining eye contact with him.

Diego hadn't considered that a female might not be afraid of him. Fear in his quarry, male or female, had always been one of his best weapons. Her apparent lack of fear and steady gaze were unnerving. Her foot hit something hard, and she looked down to see what it was. When she did so, he lunged.

Danny knew exactly what she was doing. She figured if she broke eye contact, he'd move, and he did. He led with his right hand, the blade of the knife flashing as it moved through the air toward her left arm. Danny leaned to her right and turned and chopped at his right arm, catching him just above the wrist. A sharp pain shot up his arm, and he dropped the knife. His momentum carried him further forward, and Danny leaned a little further to her right so she was out of his way until he was even with her. Then she stuck her left foot out to trip him while she shoved her left elbow into his back, using gravity more than strength to send him sprawling to the floor. He slid across the floor until his head slammed against the wall beneath the window. It was an elementary series of moves and had taken less than thirty seconds to complete. She was looking down at the intruder and feeling pretty good about her ability when she heard a crunching noise by the door. She whirled around, thinking not to be taken off guard again.

Mrs. Willson jumped at Danny's sudden move and defensive posture. She looked from Danny to the masked man lying on the floor and then back at Danny.

"Oh, Mrs. Willson. It's you."

"Yes, I came up— Oh, look out!"

The man jumped up from the floor and shoved Danny hard. Her feet came an inch off the ground before she went crashing to the floor. The man dashed for the door and, pushing Mrs. Willson out of his way, bolted through it. Mrs. Willson bumped against the wall next to the door and slowly slid down the wall until she came to a rest on the floor, dazed but unharmed.

Danny rolled over and groaned. "That's what I get for being cocky." She raised herself to all fours before getting slowly to her feet. She knew she'd have a bruise or two by which to remember this little episode. She was making sure that Mrs. Willson was alright when Geremy burst into the room.

"Are you alright?" He was out of breath.

"Yes. I think we're okay. Aren't we, Mrs. Willson?" She helped Mrs. Willson into one of the living room chairs and was turning to Geremy when her knees gave out. All the fear she had been holding at bay broke through, and she felt herself begin to sink to the floor. Geremy caught her and pulled her into an embrace. She leaned against his chest, felt the strength of his body, and let her body relax. He felt her shudder and tightened his grip.

Danny pushed away and looked up at him with a lopsided grin and tears in her eyes. "I've reconsidered. Can I stay at your house?" She made an effort to laugh, but the tears spilled out and down her cheeks instead.

He pulled her back into his arms. "For as long as you like."

Mrs. Willson stood up from the chair and cleared her throat. "Shouldn't we ring the police?"

Geremy loosened his hold on Danny as she sniffed and pulled away from him. "Yes, Mrs. Willson, you're right. I'll call Sergeant Earling. I'm sure he'll be overjoyed to hear from me." She walked to the phone and looked back over her shoulder at Mrs. Willson. "Would you mind making some tea?"

"That's just what I was about to suggest," she replied, happy to have something to do. She went into the kitchen, began making tea, and decided they all needed something to eat as well. Geremy began putting the cushions back on the furniture. He picked up Danny's camera and set it on the bar while she rang Earling.

Danny listened to the ringing on the line and was surprised at the relief she felt when Earling answered the phone.

"Hello, Sergeant Earling. It's Danny Davis. I've just had another run-in but with a different goon. Can you come over to the flat? I think I got a picture of this one." She paused, listening to his response. "Great. We'll be here." She hung up the phone. "He'll be here in twenty minutes or so."

She picked up the camera and activated the film rewinder. The whir of the camera mechanism filled the air as each person worked in silence. When the camera was finished rewinding, she popped the back of the camera, removed the roll of film, and placed both it and the camera on the bar. Then she turned and looked around the room for the knife the goon had dropped. She saw the hilt sticking out from under the drop cloth. She went to where the knife lay and, using the hem of her tee shirt, picked it up and took it to the kitchen. She found a paper bag in one of the kitchen drawers, put the knife in the bag, and laid it next to the roll of film.

As she tucked her shirt back in, she surveyed the room with an air of determination. Geremy had finished with the furniture, and he and Mrs. Willson were returning a few stray books to the bookshelves behind the dining room table. It felt good to see the flat returning to some semblance of order. The hot-water pot clicked off, so Mrs. Willson left the rest of the books to Geremy while she finished making tea and sandwiches.

Danny went to her photographic equipment and started packing it up. Since she was going to Geremy's apartment, she wouldn't be using the studio she had set up for pictures. She'd just use the Nikon and improvise. She was folding the black backdrop cloth when Earling came into the flat.

Earling took in the scene, seeing the flat in its more normal state. Danny looked up from her folding job and saw him standing in the doorway. "Hello, Sergeant Earling. Thanks for coming. I'm afraid I'm becoming a bit of a pest." She motioned to the couch. "Please come in and sit down."

He removed his coat and draped it over the back of the couch. He then pulled his notebook out of his jacket pocket and sat down. "Tell me what happened."

"Not much to say. Geremy left around two o'clock, and Mrs. Willson had not yet arrived, so I was here by myself." She held up her hands as if to shield herself from the heat of Earling's glare. "I know, I know, you were totally right." Her hands fell back to her sides. "Anyway, I heard something behind me, so I turned around and saw a man wearing a black ski mask standing by the door. He said he wanted the ring. As he came toward me, I started taking pictures but then I dropped the camera and fell down. When I got up, he lunged. I know judo, so I disarmed him and knocked him down."

Earling's eyebrows went up in surprise. "Judo?"

Danny gave a slight shrug of her shoulders. "It was part of a physical therapy program I was in after being injured in a car wreck a few years ago. I liked it, so I kept it up after the therapy sessions ended."

"Good thing."

"Yeah, this is the first time I've used it in an actual self-defense situation." She shook her head, slightly amazed at how easily the moves had come to her. Years of practice had paid off. "Anyway, Mrs. Willson came in, and the goon jumped up and knocked us both down on his way out the door." She went to the bar and got the roll of film and the bag holding the knife. "Here's the film and the knife. I used my tee shirt to pick up the knife so I wouldn't smudge any prints that may be on it."

Earling took the film and put it in his pocket. He opened the bag, quickly looked at the knife, closed the bag, and set it on the couch beside him.

Mrs. Willson brought over a tray of tea and finger sandwiches and set it on the table in front of the couch. She poured everyone a cup and then sat down in one of the two living room chairs and sipped her tea.

"Food! Mrs. Willson you're wonderful! I didn't even realize I was hungry. Thank you." Danny reached for a sandwich and took a bite as Earling began to question Mrs. Willson.

"Please tell me what you saw, Mrs. Willson."

"I came into the room just as Ms. Davis was chopping at the man's arm. When she did that, he dropped the knife. Then she moved out of the way as he kept moving toward her. She poked him in the back with her elbow and he went down and crashed into the wall. I thought he'd been knocked senseless. Then Ms. Davis jumped around and gave me quite a fright because I thought she was going to attack me. When she saw it was me, she relaxed. But then the man jumped up, pushed her real hard knocking her down, shoved me out of the way, and ran out the door."

Looking at Danny, Earling asked, "Can you give me a description of the man?"

"Well, like I said, he had a mask on, but he was around six feet tall, maybe two hundred pounds, and he was dressed completely in black." She paused, thinking back to the encounter to make sure she had given all the details she could remember. "Oh! And he spoke English with a Spanish accent."

"Can you add anything to that, Mrs. Willson?"

"I didn't get a good look at him because everything happened so quickly."

"What brought you back to the flat, Mr. Hawker?"

"I came back to see if Danny wanted to have dinner with me this evening. As I came up the outside stairs, a man rushed out the door and down the steps. He didn't have a mask on, but I still didn't get much of a look at him, other than he was dark and in a hurry. With all the crazy things going on around here, I was concerned that he may have been up to no good, so I ran up here to make sure Danny was alright."

Earling stood up from the couch, picked up his coat and put his notebook into his breast pocket as he looked over at Danny. "Have you decided where you'll be staying?"

"After we finish here, I'll go to stay at Mr. Hawker's house for the remainder of my stay in London."

Earling was glad to hear it. "When you leave here, watch to see if anyone follows you. I don't think that our Spanish friend stayed in the area, but keep your eyes open just the same. Be careful." To Geremy, he added, "Where do you live, Mr. Hawker?"

"The house is in Richmond on Royston Road."

"May I have the telephone number?"

He pulled out the notebook, wrote down the number, and returned it to his pocket. "Thank you. I'll call as soon as I have some news." He paused and looked at each person one by one. "Please have an uneventful evening."

Mrs. Willson and Geremy were finishing in the living room and kitchen while Danny straightened the back rooms and packed her things. She set her briefcase, a medium-sized suitcase and a small case filled with camera equipment next to the door.

Seeing her things by the door Geremy asked, "Are you ready to go?"

"Yep."

CHAPTER TWELVE

Jackie was wakened from a deep sleep by the ringing phone. Groggy, he picked up the receiver. "Yes?" The sleep fog lifted when he heard Sebastian Sanders's voice.

As was typical with Sebastian, he didn't waste any time with platitudes. "The girl is still in London. You will probably have to move on the brother."

"What happened?"

"Diego was watching her flat when she showed up with a man. When the man left, Diego moved in on her. He tried to get the ring, but someone interrupted him, so he had to get out without it."

Jackie could hear the exasperation in Sanders's voice. He knew that Sanders had expected that getting the ring would be easy, at least much easier than had so far been the case. Repeated efforts and repeated failures made each succeeding attempt that much more difficult. Jackie thought about asking why the ring was so damn important, but his thoughts on the matter were cut short.

"The girl and the police now know what all this is about, that someone wants the ring."

"Where is the girl now?"

"I don't know. That idiot Diego didn't stay in the area long enough to watch her next move. He panicked and drove away from the building. He called me to tell me what had happened and that he was getting out of town. Damn fool! I'll send someone over to make sure she's not still at the flat, just in case." He paused for a second and then said, more to himself then to Jackie, "One thing is still in our favor, though. They don't know why the ring is important."

Jackie saw the opening he was looking for. "Why *is* the ring so important?"

Silence greeted his question. Then Sanders answered. "The ring was my grandfather's and is a treasured family heirloom." Jackie knew this was only half the reason, but Sanders was obviously not willing to divulge more. Jackie was a patient man. He'd find out sooner or later. "Have you identified a way to get the brother?"

"We have been watching him, but so far we've not seen him exhibit much of a routine. Chas looked the house over and did not see any type of security system. If the girl does not show up, we expect to move tomorrow night."

"Well, we may be able to influence her decision there. Make your presence more obvious so that he knows about you. If they talk and he tells her someone is asking around about him, it may induce her to go to France. If she doesn't, proceed with the kidnapping. And don't bungle it."

Jackie bristled at the reminder of their failed first attempt. "We are burglars, Mr. Sanders. Kidnapping is not our usual line, but we are fast learners. If we have to take him, we'll do it right."

"Good. Call me tomorrow."

—

Geremy maneuvered the Jaguar through a black wrought-iron gate and onto a narrow, brick car park in front of the band's house in Richmond. Danny examined the house as she got out of the car and was quite taken by the unusual style of the detached, four-story, red-brick building. The ground floor was three steps below street level. A second-story porch ran along the front of the house, creating a covered patio for the ground level. The porch had a black wrought-iron railing that was matched by black iron grills enclosing the lower half of all the front-facing windows, which had white-painted trim and were flanked by white shutters. Danny was reminded of the houses in the French Quarter of New Orleans.

She strolled to the left side of the ground floor and then went down the three steps, joining Geremy at the front door. As he unlocked the two dead bolts, she slid to her right and peered through a ground-level window. She could see through to the windows at the back of the room, but saw only the silhouettes of the plants and furniture within the room. The door opened, and she followed Geremy into the foyer. She was curious and had no idea what to expect. She smiled, impressed by what she saw.

Geremy put down her bags and laughed when he saw her expression. "We 'ad one o' them interior designers do it up proper," he said in a perfect cockney accent.

They were standing just inside the door on a terra-cotta tile floor. To their right, a carved, wooden screen extended from floor to ceiling, slightly obscuring the small kitchenette that occupied the space on the other side of the screen. The living room that spread out before them was spacious and furnished with casual though comfortable-looking chairs and a couch. The warmth of the earth tones that dominated the color scheme was cooled by the greens of the plants, which stood grouped around the back windows. A break in the plants allowed access to a pair of French doors that opened out onto a balcony, which in turn looked out over the park that sloped away from the back of the house. Geremy had not turned on any lights, so the late afternoon light filtering through the trees in the park cast long, cool shadows into the room. Danny gave him a sardonic smile. "Pretty nice digs for a man who doesn't live in London."

"Well, technically this is not London, even though it does seem more like it every year." He shrugged. "It's a nice home away from home when I am in London. Plus, it's handy when emergencies crop up." He winked at her and put his hand under her elbow and guided her into the room. "Come on. I'll show you the rest of the house."

The cream-colored carpet of the first floor continued up the stairs to the second floor where Danny found herself on a landing looking into the second-floor living area. Geremy led her from the landing through the arched opening. To her immediate left, she saw another archway through which she had a partial view of the tile floor and glass-front cabinets of the main kitchen. To her right was another, though smaller, living room. He led her through the kitchen to the dining room and completed a full circle which brought them back to the far side of the living room.

Like the room on the ground floor, windows on the back wall provided plenty of natural light and plants sat in clusters around them. The cream carpet covered this floor also, but brighter shades of blue, rust, and teal covered the furniture. Unlike the bare walls of the first floor, a multitude of nature and band photographs covered the creamy, plaster walls.

Hardly allowing her a chance to catch her breath, Geremy lead her back to the landing and then on up the stairs to the third floor. Danny followed him, her curiosity piqued once again at the prospect of seeing the bedrooms. Geremy spoke over his shoulder as they went up. "You can take whichever room you like. If you don't like either one of the rooms on this floor, I'll show you the other two on the top floor."

"Fair enough. Which room is whose?"

"Oh, no. You have to guess."

At the top of the stairs, Geremy proceeded down the hall toward the back of the house and opened a door on the left. Danny followed him into the room. Longer than wide, the two windows on the back and side walls gave the room a feeling of spaciousness. Colors in the room were varying shades of green and beige, and the inside wall was covered with wallpaper with a bamboo forest design. The other three walls were painted a pale shade of green. The furniture was sturdy-looking oak except for a bent-cane rocking chair situated by the back windows. Balinese masks hung on the wall opposite the door while carved wooden Balinese birds hung in two of the corners. A large futon on a platform with built-in end tables stood to her left against the far wall. She walked over to the bureau that stood against the inside wall and noticed a picture of the Dalai Lama sitting on top of it.

When she was ready, Geremy took her to the room across the hall. The first thing she noticed was the dark hardwood floor, which had small royal blue and crimson Persian rugs scattered over it. This room also had a rocking chair by the back windows, though it was an antique style that matched the other furniture in the room. She stepped over to the chair, sat down, and surveyed the room from her seat. The antique furniture was stained a warm shade of brown and the creamy plaster walls were dotted with maps framed in wood the same shade as the furniture. She turned her gaze out the window to the tree tops which filled the view. She looked over to Geremy who leaned against the door jamb, arms folded across his chest. "No need to look further, maestro. I'll take this room, if that's all right."

A mischievous light came to his eyes as he grinned at her. "It's fine with me. This is my room, and I'd be happy to share it with you."

Her eyebrows went up, and she gave him a resigned smile as she stood up from the rocker. "Ah, it's your room. That figures. Well, I'll take the bamboo room then. Interviewer impartiality, remember?" She slid past him and started back down the hall. "I'll just go get my bags."

"I have yet another item to add to my list of why I don't like interviews," Geremy muttered as he watched her retreat down the stairs.

She returned with bags in hand and came upon Geremy just as he was putting the receiver down on the hallway phone. "You've chosen Miles's room. Thought I'd give him a call and make sure that's okay with him."

"And it's alright?"

"He was pleased and honored that you chose his room. So, yes, it's alright."

She proceeded into the bamboo room, depositing her bags just inside the door before she returned to Geremy.

"Do you mind if I call my brother? I want to let him know where I am."

"Of course. You can use this phone or the one downstairs in the kitchen. I'm going down to check the food supplies." He started down the stairs with Danny on his heels. He pointed to the cordless phone on the counter. Picking up the receiver, she retired to the living room and dialed Philippe's number. She listened to the ringing and willed him to answer the phone. He picked up. "Allo, Philippe. Commet ca va?"

"Danielle! Ca va bien! Et toi? Qu'est qui passe?"

"Tout va bien, maintenant, but, I, uh, had a little more trouble."

"Do you mean beyond the 'little trouble' you've already told me about?"

"Yes."

"What happened?" She clearly heard the concern in his voice.

"I think everything is alright now." She proceeded to fill him in on what had happened since she spoke to him from the cottage. "I'm in a house that the Mystic Celts own in Richmond. Here's the number." She read the number off the phone and he repeated it back to her.

"Are you safe there?"

Only Danny could appreciate the double entendre of the question as she thought about the growing attraction between herself and Geremy. But Philippe was referring to the goons.

"Yes, I think I'll be fine here, and I don't think we were followed."

"You think someone was watching Jasmine's?"

"It's possible. We didn't want to take any chances."

"Danielle, this is all getting out of hand. Why don't you come here until this thing settles down?"

"I've got to finish this interview."

"Your safety is more important than a damn interview, Danielle."

"I got the message. I'll be very careful. And you be careful, too."

"I thought they were after the ring Maman gave you."

"They are, but who knows? They may try something with you in order to get it from me."

"Have you figured out why the ring is so important?"

"It's still a mystery. The police are doing a background check on it to see if it's a long-lost treasure or something." She paused. "So, have you noticed anything unusual lately?"

He slipped into his Darth Vader imitation. "Do you mean have I felt a disturbance in the force?"

Danny laughed, as she always did at his impersonations. "Yes."

Philippe's voice became serious. "Actually, I have. This may explain it. I have had the sensation that someone is watching me, but I haven't paid much attention to it. I figured it was just my imagination."

Danny's brow creased. The possibility that the men might try something with Philippe caused a knot to form in her stomach. "You'll be very careful, won't you? Are Sophie and Claire still in Paris?" Worrying about Philippe was bad enough without having to worry about his wife and daughter, too.

"Yes. I plan to join them in a few days. Marie is having a party for Sophie to celebrate her opening in a gallery on Rue des Beaux Arts. She wants to show off her daughter to all her friends."

"That's wonderful! Why didn't you tell me that Sophie had a show coming up?"

"It's all been rather fast. Sophie took two small sculptures with her when she and Claire went to visit her family last week. The owner of Chez Bernard liked the pieces so much that he wants to include her work in a show he's doing next month."

"Oh, good, it's not until next month! May I come to the opening?"

"I'm sure that Sophie would be disappointed if you did not attend."

"I wouldn't dream of missing it. But back to the business at hand. I don't like the idea of your being there by yourself. Why don't you ask Francois and Fabrice to come stay with you?" Their twin cousins were ten years younger than Danny, but they were big and strong. Plus they adored Philippe. "It would make me feel better if you did."

"I'm not exactly alone here, but I'll call them."

"Thanks. I have to go now, but I'll call you tomorrow, just to check in."

"Good. Be careful, okay?"

"Okay. Talk to you tomorrow. Je t'embrasse, cher."

She hung up and went back to the kitchen to find Geremy.

"Did you reach your brother?"

"Yes. He's up to date on the latest developments. How goes the search for food?"

"Not as bleak as the cottage, but I think we should go out to eat."

"That sounds like a very good idea, but I really want to take a bath and change out of these clothes."

"I'll show you where everything is." He caught her arm and walked back upstairs, directing her to the huge bathroom situated above the kitchen. The bathroom had a closet for linens and towels, which he opened for her inspection. "Towels are here as are some bath products. Feel free to use whatever you like." He looked around the bathroom, considering if there was anything else he needed to tell her. Finding nothing, he went to the door and said, "I think that's everything, so I'll leave you to your bath, milady. I'm going to change my clothes as well and then I'll be downstairs."

"Thanks. I won't be long."

Danny stood by the door and scanned the bathroom. It was a luxurious affair with light-blue tiles laced with streaks of gold covering the floor and walls. Two long, narrow, stained-glass windows of peacocks in varying shades of blue and green faced each other as they filtered the light that came in from the front of the house. A double sink was to her right and a shower was in the far-left corner. But Danny's eyes were drawn to the large, marble bathtub to the left of the shower. She could hardly wait to take her clothes off and get in.

Wasting no time, she started the water running into the tub and went down the hall to Miles's room to get some bath gel out of her bag. Returning to the bathroom, she poured the gel under the running water, and the air was instantly filled with the scent of lavender. She peeled off her clothes, letting them fall in a heap on the floor. She stepped gingerly into the hot water and sighed as she sat down and let the scented water cover her.

CHAPTER THIRTEEN

McCafferty dropped a photo envelope on Earling's desk. "These are the photos that Ms. Davis took. Most are dark or blurry, but she got a couple that I think you'll find very interesting."

Earling slid the black-and-white photographs out of the envelope and laughed when he saw the top one. He quickly flipped through the others before coming back to the first. In spite of the ski mask, he knew the identity of the assailant. "Ortega? This gets stranger with every new clue."

"I thought you'd think so. And the lab confirmed that the knife has two clear prints that belong to Diego Ortega."

"At least he's up to the tricks we expect from him, unlike Hansen and Maloney. Do we know who he's been working for lately?"

"He was hired as a security guard for Sanders Enterprises, an estate sales management firm."

"Estate sales? Now we're getting somewhere. Has Records found anything on the ring?"

"None nor anything matching its description as being stolen or reported missing. The guys are still looking, going back as far as they can. It's taking them a while, because Records is in the process of computerizing the files so information dating back to 1950 is on the computer. But before that, the information is still on paper and film."

"What about the script?"

"Hold on a second." He left the office and went to his own desk. He returned with a piece of paper which he placed in front of Earling. "It's Basque. That's the translation."

Earling read the translation. "Basque?" He walked to the blackboard and erased the information he'd written yesterday. "So now we have some new information to consider." He picked up the chalk and wrote brief bullets of information as he spoke. "Whoever is behind this is after the ring. The ring was given to Mrs. Davis by a British soldier in France during the Second World War. Ms. Davis thinks that the ring is a map of some kind. The writing is in Basque." He paused as he looked over what he had written and then began writing again. "Diego Ortega has come into the picture. Last we knew, he was working for Sanders Enterprises, a company that specializes in estate sales." He stepped back, looked at the board, and then at McCafferty. "Have I missed anything?"

"I don't think so."

Earling walked back to his desk. "I want you to look into Sanders Enterprises. Find out if it's all above board, or if they've ever been involved in anything illegal." McCafferty nodded as he went out the door and back to his desk.

—

Geremy changed out of the clothes he had worn to Danny's the day before yesterday and into a loose-fitting, blue, cotton shirt, khaki slacks, and a black leather belt to finish the ensemble. He stood in front of the open door of the closet looking at shoes as he rolled up his sleeves. When both sleeves were done, he shook his head at the shoes, closed the closet door and went barefoot to the living room.

As he entered the living room, he had a thought which made him stop in the doorway. He retraced the steps to his room, noticing the scent of lavender as he passed the bathroom. In his room, he went to the maps on the wall and began to examine them. He removed two from their wall hooks and took them back to the living room where he began to examine them more closely. Sitting at a desk by the windows, he was so engrossed in his task that he did not hear Danny come into the room.

She paused in the doorway looking at him, wondering what he was doing. The late afternoon sunshine came through the window and glinted off the glass of the framed maps. Of more interest to her was the halo of golden light that shone around Geremy's head. She immediately saw its photographic potential, so she slipped out of the room without a sound and went to get her camera. She just hoped he'd stay still for a few more minutes.

When she returned, he hadn't moved, and the lighting had improved so that the halo had tinges of violet as well as gold. She was able to get two pictures before he looked up and then she took two more of him looking at her. She didn't really have time to register what she had captured with the second set, but felt sure that the first set was perfect. She walked over to the desk, held up the camera, and said, "I hope you don't mind, but I couldn't resist. The effect was perfect."

"No, I don't mind. Well, as long as you don't go out and sell them to the general public."

Danny shook her head as she set the camera on the desk. "No, sir, that's not part of the job. No picture selling to the general public."

Geremy leaned back in his chair and looked at her, a gentle smile playing about his mouth. "You look lovely."

"Thank you. It's not very fancy, but it's the only dress I have with me." It was a simple cornflower- blue dress of clingy, cotton jersey that accentuated her trim figure. The dress was hemmed above the knee, had long sleeves of the same clingy fabric, and a scoop neck. A slender, silver chain graced her neck and another larger silver chain was wound twice around her waist. On her feet, she wore black sandals. It pleased her that Geremy obviously appreciated what he saw.

She leaned over the desk and looked at the maps. "So. What are you doing?"

Geremy explained that he was comparing lines. "Since we don't know how old the ring is, I thought I'd compare an old map with a new map to see if any of the rivers have dramatically changed course in the past sixty years."

Danny saw the date of the top map printed in the corner and looked back at Geremy. "Where did you get a map from 1936?"

"I collect maps."

"No kidding?"

"No kidding."

"Any reason in particular or just for the fun of it?"

"The old ones because they relate to the myths, the newer ones just for the fun of it," he said with a grin. "I started collecting them when I was a teenager because I wanted to know the location of the places mentioned in the myths. Then I just became interested in the stories the maps themselves told about the history of these islands. I have a few here, but most of my collection is at my house in Devon."

"Your collection?"

"I've been buying maps of these islands for years, so it has become a collection. In fact, historians, geographers, and cartographers make appointments to study the maps I own."

"No kidding?"

He smiled again. "No kidding."

"You're just full of surprises, aren't you?"

"I try."

She looked back down at the map. "So, what's the verdict?"

"As far as I can tell, none of the lines from the ring match the 1936 map either."

Danny sat down on the corner of the desk, dangling her left leg over the edge. "This angle keeps bringing us to a dead end. I think we need to rethink the whole problem. What do you think?"

At that exact moment, Geremy was thinking about the leg swinging back in forth in front of him, wondering if it felt as smooth as it looked and was resisting the urge to reach out and find out firsthand. He decided not to share that particular thought. Instead, he took his eyes off her leg and looked down at the soiled bandage that was wrapped around his right hand. Danny followed his gaze. He was spared from responding to her question by her exclamation.

"Good grief! Look at that bandage. The cut probably doesn't need a bandage any more, but that one has to come off, in any case."

She stood up from the desk and took his hand, bending over to get a better look at it. "Come on," she gave his bandaged hand a small tug, "come over here so I can see what I'm doing." She walked over to the sofa and sat down. Geremy walked over, sat down beside her, and gave her his hand.

"Let's see how this cut is healing." She pulled at the tape and unwound the gauze bandage. Geremy watched her ministrations with a bemused expression on his face. "How does it look, doctor?"

"It's healing very well." She leaned forward and turned the palm toward the light. The scab was a very dark crimson and the edges were a healthy, red color. She lightly pressed the edge of the cut and watched as the spot first turned white then red as the blood returned to the area. Then she ran her fingertip softly down the length of the wound.

Geremy leaned closer to her and breathed in the soft scent of lavender. "So my career as a guitar player isn't over?" His voice was soft and low against her ear. The warmth of his breath on her ear sent a shiver through her.

Her hair brushed lightly against his jaw as she looked up at him. She looked serious and, dropping her voice, imitated a very stuffy doctor she had known during her recovery. "Your hand will be tender for a week or so, but I don't think the cut will hinder your playing. But I do recommend rest and relaxation and no funny business."

She was so close that he could see the all the flecks of color that made her eyes so intensely blue and the tiny freckles that were lightly dusted across her nose and cheekbones. They looked into each others eyes, and the outside world disappeared. Geremy was moving forward to kiss her slightly parted, inviting lips when he heard a noise at the door.

Miles Jensen cleared his throat.

"Hello? Hope I'm not interrupting anything."

"Miles!" Geremy stood up and held up his hand. "Danny was just checking my hand."

"Your hand, was it?" Miles's merry brown eyes twinkled as he grinned at his friend. He was about Danny's height with a wiry frame that exuded vitality and energy. That vitality was reflected in the brightly colored Hawaiian shirt he wore tucked into blue jeans. The leather sandals on his feet completed an outfit that conveyed the image of a fun-loving, carefree man. If his brown hair had not been so streaked with silver, Danny would have sworn that he was her age, not fifteen years her senior. He sparkled with life.

Geremy strode over to Miles and laughingly pulled him into the room. "Yes, my hand. And remind me later to talk to you about your timing."

Danny stood up as Geremy brought Miles over to the sofa. Geremy flexed his hand as he looked at Danny. "What is your prognosis, doctor?"

"You'll live, and you don't need another bandage."

Miles looked from Geremy to Danny. "What happened to your hand?"

Geremy held his right hand up for Miles to see. "Cut it."

"Bloody hell! Can you play?"

"Not to worry. It's not that serious. I played the guitar at the cottage. It was tender, but not unbearable. Besides, the tour doesn't begin for three months. I'm sure it will be completely healed by then." Miles took Geremy's hand in order to get a good look at the cut.

Danny had been standing a little behind Geremy, listening to their exchange and watching the easy, affectionate manner between the two men.

Miles looked up from Geremy's hand and saw Danny standing quietly. "And now, my forgetful friend, will you please introduce me to your doctor?"

Geremy turned in embarrassment to Danny. "I am so very sorry." He turned back to Miles and provided a formal introduction. "Miles, Danny Davis. Danny, Miles Jensen." They shook hands as Miles slowly shook his head. "You look very different from the last time we met," he said with a smile and a wink.

Danny was surprised. "The last time we met?"

"Yes. Years ago, after one of our concerts. I remember meeting your father for the first time. He had brought you and your brother backstage with him."

"You have a very good memory!"

"Actually, I didn't put it all together until I discovered your identity. Then I remembered meeting you and your brother. I remember him better than you, though."

Danny nodded. "Yes, he was much more interested in the drums than I was. I spent most of my time talking to Geremy."

Geremy snapped his fingers. "I remember now. You were a very quiet and earnest little girl." He got that faraway look in his eyes again, then refocused on Danny. "That seems an eternity ago." Danny nodded in agreement. "Twenty-six years."

Geremy broke eye contact with her and turned to Miles. "We're going out for dinner. Want to join us?"

"Sounds great. Allison is out with the girls, so I'm a free man."

"Good. I'll make the reservation at The River Terrace."

As Geremy turned to go to the phone in the kitchen, Miles took Danny by the elbow and directed her back to the sofa. "There's something I've always been curious about regarding the series of photographs your father took of Mount Everest …"

Geremy was stepping into the kitchen when he became aware of what Miles was saying. He stopped and, turning back, interrupted Miles in mid-question. "By the way, Miles, please do not bombard Danny with questions about her father. She is here to interview you, not answer questions about him." He looked at Danny and winked before leaving the room.

Miles gave Geremy a puzzled look and turned to Danny with a sheepish expression. "I guess people are always asking you about him?"

Danny laughed. "Always! But I'll be more than happy to answer your questions, if I can, after we finish the interview. Work before pleasure."

"Ah, you're a shrewd girl. Dangling a tantalizing reward to reluctant interview subjects. You drive a hard bargain, but I agree."

"Are you a reluctant interview subject?"

"In a word, yes. I like to entertain people with music, but don't think that gives them the right to know everything about my personal life."

Danny nodded as she looked at Miles, carefully choosing the words that would best describe what she hoped to come away with at the end of the interview. "I am most interested in your perspectives on the course that music has taken over the past twenty-five years and how the Celts have managed to stay in the pop-music stream. I think the readers are interested in a personal angle that relates to musical events in your life so, hopefully, we can give them a little of the personal angle without infringing on your privacy." She paused, smiling at him, "That's what I want to write about, anyway."

Miles relaxed into the couch. "That sounds fine. I know Neil will be especially glad to hear that."

Neil was the author of some of the groups most poignant love songs. Danny had always wondered about what had happened to him to cause him to write so many songs about heartbreak.

"Don't worry. I won't ask him who broke his heart."

"Broke his heart?"

"Yes. Well, lots of fans wonder about the source of all his sad love songs."

Miles creased his brow as he looked at her. Suddenly, his face broke into a smile and then he began to laugh. "No, that's not why he'll be glad you'll not pry into personal matters." He chuckled a little more and said, "No woman ever broke his heart or, at least, no more than usual." He couldn't seem to stop chuckling as he let her in on a little secret. "Neil is a voracious reader of romance novels. That's where he gets the ideas for his love songs. He has a house in Scotland that he shares with his wife of twenty years and their four children. He holes up there with his books and writes the songs when he's not helping Julie with the trees, that is."

Danny shook her head in disbelief and then began to laugh, too. "His secret is safe with me, but it certainly will put me in a different frame of mind the next time I hear one of his songs. I am relieved, though, to hear that his life has not been as sad as I had thought!"

"No. He is a happily married man. He just doesn't like the fans having any idea whatsoever about where he lives. That's a concern for all of us."

"So that has made all of you reluctant to do interviews?"

"It's the main reason." He paused and then continued, "When we first hit it big years ago, we weren't quite prepared for the fan attention. We were just some blokes doing something we loved. The shift from anonymity to fame happened almost overnight. Suddenly, everyone wanted to know all about us. We all had to move at least once to get away from fans who thought they had every right to invade our privacy because they liked our music. Neil, being the handsome writer of those sad love songs, received more attention from female fans than the rest of us, so he felt particularly overexposed. Now that things have settled down, we all want to make sure they stay settled, so we closely guard our privacy."

Miles broke off when he heard Geremy's footsteps. The phone began to ring, and they heard Geremy answer it. After a few minutes, he came back into the living room carrying the handset, which he laid on the end table.

"That was Earling calling about the ring. As far as they can tell, it was never reported stolen."

"Were they able to decipher the writing?" Danny asked.

Geremy pulled a chair over to the sofa, and she could see the excitement in his face. "Yes." He held a piece of paper up for her to see and then pulled it back so he could read it to them. "It's Basque and says, 'Three peaks guard the plain. In the heart of the middle, find the cave of the blue light, there but not there, in plain view but hidden, eternal haven to seekers of the flowering heart.' "

Danny looked perplexed. "Wow. That sounds like one of Gollum's riddles. May I see it?" Geremy passed the written text to her. "The language is Basque?"

Geremy nodded his head.

"Oh great map collector, do you have a map of France?"

Geremy went to a bookshelf and pulled out a world atlas. He fingered through the maps as he walked back to the sofa where he sat down between Danny and Miles so they could all look at the map together. Danny pointed to the western Pyrenees. "This is where the Basque's live." Then she moved her finger east across the map stopping at Foix. "This is the home of my mother's family where Philippe now lives."

Miles could no longer contain his curiosity. "What are you two talking about?"

"Sorry, Miles. I guess we got carried away." Looking back at Danny, Geremy asked, "Will you show him the ring?"

Danny pulled the ring off her index finger and handed it to Miles. "This whole crazy thing started on the day that Geremy came for the interview."

"Right. Geremy told me you'd had some trouble, but he had helped you out. The paper said it was possible you'd been kidnapped."

"Two men did try to kidnap me, and Geremy helped me get away from them. They wanted the ring. Now we're trying to figure out why anyone would go to such lengths to get such an ordinary-looking ring."

Geremy picked up the story. "We went to the police this morning, told them about the ring, and they did a trace on it. Sergeant Earling called, and you've already heard what he said."

"But where did the ring come from?"

"A British soldier gave it to my mother during the Second World War. Beyond that, I don't know anything else about it." She gave Miles a mischievous grin. "But the mystery has us intrigued. The more we find out about the ring, the more mysterious the whole thing becomes."

Geremy had been looking at the map as Danny spoke. Suddenly he pulled it closer to get a better look. "Wait a minute. Look here!" He pointed to the mountainous border between France and Spain.

Danny looked where he was pointing. Since she had not been working with the lines, she did not see what he saw. She looked up at him and shook her head slightly. "Sorry. What?"

Geremy went to the desk and picked up the paper that had the enlarged lines on it. When he laid it on the map near the spot he'd been pointing to, she saw what he saw. "That's it!" she exclaimed.

The line on the front of the ring was identical to a small segment of the borderline on the map. "And look! There are three peaks on that segment of the line, Mt. Rouch, Mt. Valier, and pic de Mauberme." She looked back to the paper and saw that the second drawing had three peaks, with the middle being the shortest of the three. She took the ring from Miles and saw the tiny diamond sparkling on the front line. Its placement on the line matched the location of Mt. Valier on the map. She popped the stone and saw that, on the back side, the diamond was positioned just above center right of the middle peak. The heart of the mountain.

Visibly excited, Danny stood up and began to pace. "Well, now we know what the maps depict, but we still don't know why it's so important to those men." She stopped pacing and looked at Geremy and Miles. "Like I said, the more we know, the more mysterious this thing becomes. Why would anyone go to so much trouble to make a map to the middle of a mountain in the Pyrenees?"

Geremy shook his head. "Still more, why would someone go to such drastic lengths to recover the ring?"

As Danny stood looking at the two men, the photographer in her recognized the quality of the picture waiting to be taken. They were sitting side by side on the couch, both were wearing brightly colored shirts, and both had very animated expressions on their faces. As they continued to talk, Danny retrieved her camera from the desk and casually walked back to the couch.

Miles, caught up in the excitement of the mystery, was posing his own solution to the mystery. "Maybe it leads to the treasures of the Knights Templar."

The flash from the camera went off just as he finished his sentence. Miles looked at her with a startled expression.

"Sorry. You know, the job? It was too good to pass up." She sat down, camera in hand, in the chair Geremy had pulled over earlier. "Fair warning: I'll probably take some more. If you don't mind?" She directed the question to Miles.

"No. Not at all. I had just forgotten that you were here because of the interview, so the flash took me by surprise." He blinked a couple of times before asking, "Now, where was I?"

"The Knights Templar," Geremy reminded him.

"Right! Well, I read a book that suggests that the Knights Templar had a massive treasure and that some of it may be secreted in the Pyrenees."

"Yes, that's right! I remember hearing the stories when I was a kid," Danny said.

Geremy still looked mystified. "What stories?"

Miles brought him up to speed. "I know you're familiar with the Knights Templar."

Geremy nodded. "Of course."

"And that they were supposedly dedicated to protecting the Holy Grail? They have always been closely associated with Grail stories."

Geremy nodded again.

"Well, they also supposedly had a huge fortune, a treasure if you will, and some contend that, when the Order was destroyed, this treasure was buried, interestingly enough, in the very region you're looking at on the map." Miles paused for dramatic effect. "But the treasure has never been found."

Geremy looked at the map and nodded. "As strange as this whole thing has been, that could be a plausible explanation."

Danny grinned. She felt the adrenalin start to pump through her system as she contemplated the prospect of doing the unexpected. "Let's go find out!"

Both men looked at her with surprised expressions. Geremy was the first to speak. "Don't you have a deadline for your magazine?"

The light left Danny's face, and her heart slowed down as reality reared its ugly head. "Yes. In the excitement of the moment, I forgot about that." She paused as she thought about the deadline. Slowly, the smile returned to her face. "The article isn't due until the end of June so I think I can take a little time to check this out.. We know where the maps lead, and we have the script deciphered. We could go over and give it a try to see if we can solve the mystery. If we haven't figured it out by the middle of June, we can return to England, and I'll finish the article." She looked from Geremy to Miles, trying to gauge their interest in her suggestion. Looking at Geremy, she said, "I'm curious, and I know you are, too. What do you say?"

Danny's quick leap from talking about the mystery to suggesting they go investigate it had caught him by surprise and he needed a minute to gather his thoughts. Instead of answering her question he stood up and asked one of his own, "Anyone care for a beer?"

"A beer would be great," Danny agreed.

Geremy nodded. " Miles?"

"Yeah, sounds good."

As stood to go get the beers, Danny noticed that he was once again barefoot.

A question she'd meant to ask earlier diverted from her thoughts of the proposed adventure. "Do you not like to wear shoes?" she asked as she looked from his feet to his face.

Geremy looked down at his feet and wiggled his toes. "Not if I can help it."

"That is no understatement," Miles chimed in. "He used to perform barefoot."

"Yes, and I paid for that, didn't I?" He sat down on the arm of the sofa, the drinks momentarily forgotten as he told the story that convinced him that shoes were a good idea onstage. "At one of our early concerts, one of the spotlights had broken prior to our arrival and somehow a large piece of glass was missed by the bloke who cleaned up the debris. The glass was a smoky color and blended right in with the stage floor. How I managed to avoid it during the whole concert will always be a mystery, since I was moving all over the place while I played. When the concert ended and we were taking our bows, I stepped on it hard. I proceeded to fall down, which created quite a stir as I recall! Most people in the audience thought I was stoned or something. All I knew was that my foot was on fire. I was rolling around on the stage with my foot in the air." He was laughing as he spoke. Danny took another picture of him.

Miles also began to laugh and picked up the story as Geremy went to fetch the beers. "We were trying to figure out what was going on when I caught a glimpse of his foot, which had a big piece of glass embedded in it. It looked quite gruesome, blood all over his foot, and dripping onto the stage." Danny got another one of the two of them together.

Geremy returned with the opened bottles of beer and resumed the story as he handed them off to Danny and Miles. "Miles and John picked me up and rushed me to hospital where I received fifteen stitches. I've never gone barefoot onstage since. Otherwise, I prefer to go barefoot whenever possible."

"You said that, when you fell down after cutting your foot, everyone thought you were stoned. Were you?"

Geremy gave her a hard stare. "By the end of the show, I was just high on the adrenalin of performing, but I had smoked some grass before the show. We partook regularly back in those days."

"And now?"

"No, I don't do that stuff anymore. Well, not very often, anyway." He glanced at Miles, who grinned back at him, and then continued. "We were all avid participants in the drug scene back then. It was part of the whole rock-and-roll scene. So when I fell down, everyone naturally surmised that I was stoned."

"Did it bother you that people put you in that category?"

Miles broke in with a laugh. "It increased our popularity, if you can believe it. When people heard that he had fallen down because he'd stepped on a piece of glass, they were disappointed. Drugs were more glorified then, especially the psychedelics."

"I remember the concert I went to when I was eight. It was quite a visual experience. Mystic Celt concerts were as famous for their visuals as for the music. Were you keying into the psychedelic drugs the fans were taking when you developed the stage shows?"

Geremy answered this one. "We were trying to create through color and form some of the images we saw when we played the music. We wanted to share those impressions with the audience, but I certainly didn't even consider the altered state of the audience when we were putting the shows together. Did you, Miles?"

"Not at first. I just wanted to participate in a show that people would remember for a long time." He grinned at Danny. "Glad to hear you still remember a concert we put on twenty-six years ago! John always said that a show should be a total experience—a treat for the eyes as well as the ears. We all had similar thoughts on the matter. After the first few shows, the word got out that our shows were made for psychedelics. That was not our original intention, but that's how they came to be perceived."

"The shows today don't have as much visual stimulation. Why the change?"

Geremy's expression showed both respect and humor as he looked at Danny. She was interviewing them. He wondered if Miles was aware of it. "Change is good for the soul. We've changed, the audience has changed, times have changed. Back in those days, rock-and-roll concerts were still so new everyone wanted to be over the top. We wanted to pull out all the stops. Plus, you've got to remember that audio systems have improved a thousand-fold since 1968. We can present the music in a way that requires little visual embellishment."

Miles picked up when Geremy paused. "We were trying to present a state of mind. It's hard to explain. There was so much turmoil and change in the air. Drugs, the war in Viet Nam, women's liberation, racial tension. We wanted to give people an experience that was beautiful and would lift them above the turmoil, if only for a few hours."

"What about today? There's still a lot of turmoil in the air, but the concerts have very little visual diversions, even when you play the older songs."

Miles nodded his head as he responded. "Yes, that's true, but like Geremy says, we can amaze people with sounds that we were not able to achieve in the old days." He shrugged his shoulders and added, "We sell-out every gig, so I think that the fans don't mind the change." The twinkle returned to his eyes. "Plus, we can still rock and roll with the best of them!"

Danny thought back to all the Celts concerts she'd been to and knew he spoke the truth. There was a feeling of love in the air at a Celts concert that she didn't feel at other concerts. The fans loved the music and didn't seem to miss the visual extravaganzas that had been the hallmark of a Celts concert in the past. The people came to hear the music. "What's the biggest difference between today's audiences and the audiences of the sixties and early seventies?"

The men looked at each other. Miles held out his hand to Geremy, signaling him to go ahead. "It's funny you should ask, because we were just discussing that last week. For one thing, the audiences of today have people of all ages. People that heard us in the beginning are still in the audience now. In the early days, the audience was very young, like us. I guess you could say we've grown up together." Geremy looked at Miles who picked up the cue.

"And the audiences seem to listen more and better than in the past. Maybe it's because they're not as drugged as they used to be, I don't know. They seem more tuned-in to the music."

"That's not to say that we didn't thoroughly enjoy and appreciate the early audiences." Geremy added. "They were experiencing a different aspect of our creativity, and the energy at those concerts was very powerful. The energy at concerts today is just as powerful, just more sublime."

Danny turned to Miles. "Will this tour have any visual special effects?"

Miles gave her a devilish grin, his eyes sparkling. "We've got a few tricks up our sleeve, but we'd prefer not to divulge them before the tour. Suffice it to say, we'll have more than we've had in the past ten years, but not as much as we had in the beginning."

Danny's next question was interrupted by the ringing of the phone.

Geremy picked up the handset. He greeted the caller, paused a moment, and then extended the phone to Danny. "It's your brother."

Danny set the mug and her camera down on the end table, took the handset, and walked over to the window. She looked out at the deepening twilight that pressed against the window and had a feeling of foreboding.

"Philippe?"

"Danielle, I'm sorry to bother you, but Pierre Valmont called from his house next door to tell me that a couple of men had been asking questions about me. One of them wears a white suit and the other is much bigger."

"That sounds like the men who kidnapped me." She spoke quietly, but both Miles and Geremy noticed the change in her voice. Their conversation ceased.

"Philippe, did you call Francois and Fabrice?" Her voice took on a sharp edge.

"I called the house, but they are in Nice."

Danny felt her stomach clutch. "Please be very careful, Philippe. They want the ring. I guess they think that if they threaten you, I'll give it to them. And they're right. I'll be there tomorrow afternoon."

"Why would you come here?"

"Because I have the ring! I can't give it to them if I'm not there."

"I don't know, Danielle. This doesn't sound like a good idea to me."

"I'll be there tomorrow afternoon. In the meantime, please be careful. The police here said they didn't know if these men are dangerous, but they were willing to kidnap me."

"Alright, I'll be careful. I'll even lock the doors and windows."

"Thank you. I'll see you tomorrow." She turned the phone off and laid it on the table as she sat back down. Her face was pale and drawn.

"Danny? What's wrong?" Geremy asked as he reached out to cover her hand with his.

"Philippe said that two men matching the description of the goons who jumped me have been asking questions about him. I've got to go to Foix and give them the ring before they try something with Philippe. When it was only me they were bothering, I could deal with it, but I don't want them to try anything with Philippe." She gave them a strained smile.

"I'm going with you," Geremy said.

"Thank you, but this may be more dangerous than the little expedition we were just talking about."

"Be that as it may, I'm going. You can't expect me to come this far and then sit back while you find out by yourself what this is all about." He paused as he caught and held her gaze. "Besides, I want to go," he said softly. He squeezed her hand.

Danny looked back at him and was more relieved than she cared to admit. Her expression brightened. She looked at Miles. "How about you? Ready for an adventure?"

Miles looked at her and for a moment was tempted to say yes. Then he remembered that he had a wife at home who might not think too kindly of him trotting off to have an adventure with a beautiful woman. "I must decline your most tempting offer." Then looking at Geremy, he said, "I will stay behind and explain to everyone why you are not at the rehearsals we have scheduled in June."

Geremy's brow creased. "Ah, yes. I, too, have forgotten my responsibilities in the excitement of the moment." He fell silent and considered his options. Danny watched him closely, fearing that he would decide not to go. His face cleared, and he spoke to Miles. "We have already gone through the playlist twice, and it's not as if I don't know the songs. The June rehearsals are as much for logistics as for music, so if you guys work it out, I'll go along with your decisions."

Miles nodded his agreement as Danny let out the breath she didn't realize she was holding. Geremy looked at her and asked, "Which airport should we fly into?"

"That depends on flight schedules."

"Not necessarily. We could charter a flight. The band employs a pilot for use during concert tours. I can call him and see if he or someone he knows can fly us over."

"That would be great! The airport at Toulouse would be the most convenient, and we can rent a car there so Philippe won't have to pick us up."

Geremy retrieved the telephone handset and went to find his personal phone book. "Shouldn't take but a minute, if he's home, that is."

Though it took more than a minute, Geremy returned successful. "We have a plane to Toulouse, booked to depart at ten a.m. How's that for service?" He half-sat, half-leaned against the sofa arm.

Danny shook her head as she looked at him. "You are amazing," she said softly.

He grinned. "I'm very glad you think so."

Miles cleared his throat. They looked and saw him reading his watch. "Is it time for dinner yet? All this mush is making me hungry."

Geremy laughed at his friend and gently nudged him with his foot. "You're always hungry! But, yes, now that you mention it, it is about time we left."

Danny stood up. "I'll go get my things."

Geremy stood up with her, his eyes following her as she left the room. Miles watched his friend and whistled.

"Well, well, well. Now that's a look I haven't seen on your face in a very long time, my friend, but I do approve!"

Geremy's expression became more reserved as he turned to Miles, but he did not respond.

"She's caught your fancy, then?"

Geremy paused before speaking. Then a slight smile played about the corners of his mouth. "Practically from the first moment I laid eyes on her. It was like the proverbial bolt of lightning that came out of nowhere."

Miles stood up next to Geremy and set the empty beer bottle on an end table. "This is a story I want to hear from the beginning. You need to get some shoes on, so let's go to your room, and you can tell me all about it."

Geremy told Miles the story while first looking for and then putting on his socks and shoes. He finished the story as he tied the second shoe. He sat on the edge of his bed and cast a bewildered look at Miles who was sitting cross-legged on the floor in front of him. "Can you believe it? After all these years and all the women I've known, I had just about decided I was immune to love. Then *wham!* She walks through the door."

Miles looked sympathetically at his friend. "Any idea how she feels about you?"

Geremy thought about the kiss they had shared that morning, how she had melted into him and responded to his kiss. He nodded slowly. "Yes, I think she likes me." He paused before adding, "But she has reservations."

"I'd say that's good thinking on her part. She must know something about your track record." Miles looked at Geremy, his eyes daring him to respond. Geremy ignored the dare, so Miles went on. "Besides, she's here to do a job."

"That may be the case while she is in England, but we're about to go to France for personal reasons." He looked at Miles with a speculative look on his face that Miles wasn't sure he liked. "Then she's on her own time so, as far as I'm concerned, all former agreements are off."

"Hmm. Right. Well, just don't forget to let her know that you've changed the rules, okay?" Geremy started to respond, but Miles held up both hands in a placating gesture. "I'm just reminding you to keep everything in the open." Geremy closed his mouth as Miles got up from the floor. He held a hand out to Geremy. "Come on, let's go. I really am hungry."

They found Danny waiting for them in the living room, phone in hand. "I'm calling Earling's office in the hopes that he has an answering machine or service so I can let him know that we are going to my brother's and why."

Geremy nodded. "That makes sense."

"Damn. Nothing. Just ringing. Haven't they entered the age of technology?" She asked as she put the receiver back onto the base. "I'll try again before we leave in the morning."

Miles hooked his arm in hers and directed her toward the door. "Let's go eat." Geremy followed them out the door. Since it was such a beautiful evening, they opted to walk to the restaurant.

Twenty minutes later, they were seated at a table on the terrace of The River Terrace restaurant overlooking the section of the Thames that flowed through Richmond. As they waited to place their orders, they watched people strolling along the riverbank path enjoying the balmy summer night. When they had ordered, Danny noticed that they had all ordered vegetarian meals.

"Are you two vegetarians?"

"I eat white meat sometimes, but not very often," Miles answered as he looked to Geremy.

"I eat fish, but no other type of meat. Why do you ask?"

Danny shrugged. "I guess I always think of rock-and-rollers as being decadent. The ones I know tend to be more into sex, drugs, meat, sugar and rock and roll, of course."

Miles laughed. "You should have seen us twenty-five years ago! Age has a way of mellowing the wild side of most people. If it makes you feel better, I do smoke cigarettes."

"Are the other guys vegetarians, also?"

"John is a strict vegetarian. Neil thinks all vegetarians are crazy and professes to eat beef every day."

The waiter interrupted their conversation to pour from the bottle of white wine that Danny and Geremy had ordered with dinner. He then set a draft of ale in front of Miles.

She took a sip of her wine and said, "I guess it shouldn't be such a surprise, because so many people are going vegetarian these days."

"John has been a vegetarian as long as I've known him, so he was way ahead of the trend," Geremy said with a smile. "Miles and I went off meat for the most part in 1973."

"Why?"

"Before we went onstage for what turned out to be our last show before we took the break, we ate some meat that had gone bad."

"It still turns my stomach to think about that night," Miles said with a grimace. "We had been touring for eight months, so our energy was down to begin with. We had been working on sound checks and other stuff all day, so we had all forgotten to eat much. Two hours before the show, we ordered out for some Chinese food and were so hungry and preoccupied about the show that we just wolfed it down. John, of course, was the only one who didn't eat the tainted food. To this day, I still cannot eat Chinese food."

"So what happened?"

"About three quarters of the way into the show, Miles, Neil, and I started feeling pretty bad. John told me later that he glanced over at me at one point and thought I looked pretty green, but thought it was just the lighting." Geremy chuckled at the memory. "Then he noticed that both Miles and Neil were very pale and that all three of us were sweating profusely. He began to suspect that something was wrong."

The story was interrupted by the arrival of their meals. Danny looked at her pasta primavera with renewed appreciation for her vegetarian preferences.

Miles took a bite of his stuffed eggplant and resumed the story. "We managed to make it offstage before we all, well, you know," he waved his fork in the air in front of him in an effort to communicate that they had thrown-up without verbalizing the indelicate details.

Danny swallowed the bite she had just taken and nodded that she caught his drift. He continued.

"We were able to go back on and do one encore, but the show was undoubtedly the worst one we've ever done. Then, about two in the morning, John called an ambulance to take us to hospital where we had our stomachs pumped. Once again, rumors flew about the drug problems we were all experiencing."

Geremy nodded in agreement. "At the time, we hadn't really talked about taking a break from recording. But when we made the announcement a few months later, the press said it had been obvious from our last show that there was trouble in paradise. The truth of the matter was that we were very tired and wanted to pursue some other interests. The food poisoning was like a physical manifestation of how sick we were of the grind."

"So you and Miles went off meat, but the experience didn't faze Neil?"

"Well, Miles eats meat on occasion, but Neil said that was the only time in all the years of eating meat that he'd become sick, so he figured those were still good odds."

"I didn't eat meat for a number of years after the food poisoning, but in the past few years I've eaten it from time to time."

"Geremy said that you and John traveled to exotic places after the band took the break. Where'd you go?"

Miles eyes narrowed as he looked at Geremy. "Talking about me behind my back, are you?"

Geremy smiled. "I told Danny that you and John had gone traveling for a couple of years, nothing more."

"And did you tell her what you were up to then?"

The smile faded as he looked across the table at Miles. "Not exactly."

Danny could feel some tension between the two men, which made her all the more curious to know what it was about. She remembered how uncommunicative Geremy had become when she asked what he had done after the band took the break, but her thoughts on that subject were diverted by Miles's laughter.

"Fair enough. I'll tell what John and I did, but I'll leave you to tell her about your adventures. Or should I say misadventures?"

Miles seemed to be poking good fun at his friend, but Danny could tell that Geremy did not find the subject amusing. In fact, she sensed that he had become quite withdrawn.

"The trip was John's idea. He wanted both Geremy and me to go over to India, Tibet, and Nepal with him, but Geremy wasn't in the mood." Geremy glared at Miles, but didn't say anything. Danny was beginning to feel uncomfortable with the exchanges between the two men. Miles, sensing Danny's discomfort and Geremy's real displeasure, realized that his jokes were missing the mark. He cleared his throat before continuing.

"John was a great student of the world's religions. You may recall that eastern religion and music became very popular in the late sixties?"

"Sure. My father took the pictures of Everest in 1966, and the trip had a big effect on him. I don't know exactly what happened, but he began to meditate every day." She gave a little giggle. "When I was seven, I asked Maman why Papa needed medication every day. I was afraid he was dying or something. She couldn't keep from laughing even though I was quite serious. But she set me straight and, after a while, meditation was just another part of the daily routine." A sad look came over her face, and she looked over at Miles. "I had forgotten about that," she said quietly.

Miles nodded sympathetically. "I think John met your father soon after the Everest pictures were published."

"Probably. Those were the photographs that made Papa famous. Our lives changed dramatically after they were published."

"Well, they certainly impressed John! He was already into eastern religions and philosophies, and he had a favorite from that series that he focused on as he went into meditation. Anyway, he always had books on the East laying around his flat or with him on tour. During one of the tours, I was just about out of my mind with boredom, so I asked John if he had something I could read. He tossed me a little book called *Life and Teaching of the Masters of the Far East, Volume One*. It was a great retelling of an expedition some Americans took to India and Tibet in the late 1800s. When I finished it, I passed it on to Geremy. I must say that our late night conversations, as we went from gig to gig, changed dramatically after we started reading John's books." He grinned at Geremy. "Do you remember the conversations we had, Ger?"

"I'll never forget them. Those are some of my fondest memories. We'd be high on the adrenalin from just finishing a show, smoke some grass, and have some great conversations about life, God, the universe, reincarnation, you name it."

"What about Neil?"

Geremy chuckled. "Being a firm member of the Church of Scotland, Neil wasn't interested in Eastern philosophy. Besides, that's about the time he discovered romance novels and was hooked. We kidded him about the books at first, but then he started writing those amazing love songs that are now so popular. The kidding stopped when the first song inspired by one of the books went to number one in the US, Great Britain, and Europe." Geremy smiled at the memory as he toyed with his wine glass.

The waiter came to clear their plates and asked if they'd care for dessert. Danny ordered crème brulee, Miles ordered chocolate cake and coffee, but Geremy passed. Miles waited until the waiter had returned with the dessert before he resumed the story.

"Now, where was I?" he asked just before putting a piece of cake into his mouth. Before anyone could remind him, he had rediscovered the trail of his thoughts about the trip. "Oh yes. I was very curious about the people and places described in the Masters' books, so when John suggested we go, I didn't hesitate to say yes. Geremy, on the other hand, said he wasn't up for it." He paused and looked at Geremy. "I often consider how very different life would have been if you'd gone with us."

Geremy abruptly backed his chair away from the table and stood up. "I've got some things I want to take care of, so I'm going to head back to the house. I'll see you back there." Without waiting for a reply, he strode from the restaurant leaving a surprised Danny and Miles at the table.

Danny looked from Geremy's retreating figure to Miles. "What happened?"

"Sorry, I should have quit poking at him. Sometimes he can take it, and sometimes he can't. I'm not always good at reading the signals."

"Should we go after him?"

"No. When he's in this mood, it's best to leave him alone. He'll probably be fine by the time we get back to the house."

"What was the poking about?"

"John and I really wanted Geremy to go with us because he was depressed. We were worried at what he might do if he was left to himself."

"Why was he depressed?"

"A woman he'd be in love with was killed while we were on our first tour, and five years later, he was still grieving for her. To be perfectly honest, we were worried he might kill himself, but short of kidnapping him, we couldn't make him go with us. So we went and had some incredible spiritual as well as musical experiences, and Neil was left to keep an eye on Geremy. We returned to England eighteen months later and found that, six months after we had left, Geremy married a woman he'd known for less than a month." He took another bite of cake and washed it down with some coffee.

"Sometimes it only takes a moment to fall in love," Danny said softly.

Miles nodded emphatically. "I know, and I wouldn't have minded if she'd been right for him. But she didn't care for him as much as she cared for the lifestyle she was able to lead because she was married to him. She and I took an instant disliking to each other and, as a result, Geremy's and my friendship was sorely tested. She saw the rift developing and worked very hard to widen it, whispering in Geremy's ear that I was jealous of him and didn't want to see him happy." He fell quiet as he stabbed the last bit of cake on the plate.

"How did it all get sorted out?"

"He found out the hard way who his real friends were," he said matter-of-factly as he slipped the cake into his mouth. "And he found out some things about her that really shook him up. He came by my house to talk and ended up staying for a couple of days while he sorted out his feelings. When he left, he went straight to his solicitor and began divorce proceedings."

"How long were they married?"

"Three years. The divorce was not nice and took about another year to sort out."

"If it's all water under the bridge, why does he still get so riled up about it?"

A look a speculation came over Miles face as he regarded her. "I'm only guessing, but I think he's having feelings he hasn't felt in a long time, and it's making him somewhat touchy."

"Somewhat?" Danny muttered.

Miles flagged the waiter and asked for the bill. "I think it's time we returned to the brooding prince and see what he's up to."

CHAPTER FOURTEEN

Earling drank his morning coffee as he stood looking out his office window at the hustle and bustle on the street below. The streams of people rushing around reminded him of ants scurrying to their anthills. He caught sight of McCafferty cross the street in front of the station but then lost sight of him as he entered the building.

Earling finished his cup of coffee as he turned back to the work on his desk. He had arrived at the station earlier than usual, because he wanted to complete some paper work before he and McCafferty paid a visit to Mr. Sebastian Sanders, recent employer of Diego Ortega. While it was possible that Ortega had been acting on his own, they had not been able to find him, so they would talk to Sanders to see if he knew anything about Ortega's activities.

McCafferty walked into Earling's office and was not surprised to see his boss hard at work. "What time do you want to go see Sanders?"

Earling looked up at the big man. "Good morning, Peter," was all he said before looking back down at his desk.

McCafferty smiled. "Good morning, Tim." He moved into the office and sat down on the couch. He let the silence stand for a few minutes before posing the question again.

Earling looked at his watch and then at McCafferty. "Where did you say his office is located?"

"Esher."

"Were you able to find anything on the company or Mr. Sanders? Any illegal or suspicious activity?"

"A preliminary search revealed nothing on either the company or Mr. Sanders."

"Have you called him to let him know we want to pay him a visit?"

"I tried last evening as soon as I had the number, but no one answered. I'll try again in a few minutes."

"I've got a few things to clear up before we go, but they shouldn't take more then an hour. After that, I'll be ready to go."

McCafferty started to leave, but was stopped by Earling's voice. "Have we heard anything more on Hansen and Maloney?"

"No. They appear to have vanished into thin air."

"Alright then. Try to get an appointment with Sanders, the earlier the better, and let me know the time." Earling looked at his watch again. "It's eight twenty. See if you can get us in there around ten. Please close the door on your way out."

"Right," was all McCafferty said before leaving. Upon returning to his desk, he discovered that a message had come in while he was talking to Earling. One of his informants had come through with an interesting bit of information. He smiled as he walked back to Earling's office.

Earling looked up when he heard the light tapping on his door. When he saw it was Peter, he motioned him to enter.

"I just received some interesting information," he said as he walked over to Earling's desk. He laid the written message down on the desk. "It appears that about a year ago, Hansen and Maloney joined the ranks of those employed by Sanders Enterprises."

Earling read the message. "Is this source reliable?"

"Hasn't been wrong yet. When I put the word out that we wanted to talk to Hansen and Maloney, we had not yet made any connection to Sanders Enterprises, so none of my contacts knew of the relevance of this information."

Earling handed the message back to Peter. "It would appear that our visit to Mr. Sanders is taking on greater importance by the minute."

Peter took the message back, nodding in agreement. "Considering the connections we've identified, do you think it would be better if we made an unannounced visit?"

Earling squinted. "Yes, I think that would be a good idea. I'll be finished with this paperwork in a few minutes and then I'll be ready to go."

Fifteen minutes later, he was at Peter's desk ready to pay a visit to Mr. Sebastian Sanders at Sanders Enterprises. As they left, neither one noticed that one of the ringing phones they could hear was coming from Tim Earling's office.

Danny was getting more than a little irritated as she listened to the endless ringing. Just as she was about to hang up, she heard a click and then a woman's voice asking how she could direct the call.

"I have been ringing the office of Sergeant Earling. Do you know if he is in?"

"His schedule indicates that he is in the office today, but circumstances can change. May I give him a message?"

"Yes. Please tell him that Danny Davis has gone to her brother's in Foix, that's F-O-I-X, France. The two men are there, and I am going to give them the ring." She paused to give the woman time to write it all down. "Can you read that back to me, please?"

The woman did as requested and asked, "Sergeant Earling will understand this?"

"Yes, he will. Thank you." She hung up and joined Geremy in the foyer. "Let's go, maestro. I left a message for Earling."

"Very good, milady," he said in a grandiose manner as he swept his arm toward the door and pointed to the taxi in front of the house. "Our carriage awaits."

—

McCafferty had to drive around the block before finding a parking space on High Street in Esher, just around the corner from Sanders's showroom and office on Church Street. They walked the block and a half to the small showroom and stood outside the building long enough to observe that the facade was well-kept and that a new coat of white paint had recently been applied. The immaculate exterior coupled with the expensive furniture displayed in the large, front windows effectively communicated that this was a store for the wealthy.

When they entered, a buzzer notified the shop assistant that possible clients had arrived. Mr. Groundwater hurried from the back room, but slowed his pace when he saw Earling, instantly assuming from his attire that he was either lost or a door-to-door salesman.

"May I help you?" he asked in a patronizing tone.

Earling stepped forward and displayed his identification. "Sergeant Earling to see Mr. Sanders. Is he available?" The clerk looked past him and noticed McCafferty, in uniform, who had just let a low whistle escape when he saw the price of a chair in the middle of the shop. "He's in his office, but I believe he's busy. Please wait here while I call him." He turned on his heel and returned to the back room.

Sanders blanched when Groundwater rang to inform him that a Sergeant Earling was in the shop and wanted to talk to him. For a split second, he considered saying he was not available but then, almost as quickly, reconsidered.

"Wait five minutes and then bring them up." When Groundwater showed them in, Sanders greeted them at the door, composed, polite, and curious as to what had brought them to Sanders Enterprises.

"Good morning, Mr Sanders. I'm Sergeant Earling, and this is Police Constable McCafferty. Sorry to barge in like this, but we have a few questions. It shouldn't take long."

"Well, I am rather busy right now, but I can spare a few minutes. How can I help you?" he asked as he motioned them to the two chairs in front of his desk. As they took the offered chairs, he walked around the desk and sat down in his chair.

As was their custom, Earling asked the questions while McCafferty watched. "Mr. Sanders, what exactly is the nature of your business?"

"As the sign outside indicates, I handle estate liquidations," Sanders replied smoothly.

"What does that entail, exactly?"

"Usually someone dies and other members of the family decide to sell off the property of the deceased." He paused and leaned forward, resting his elbows on the desktop. "What, exactly, is this about?"

Earling ignored the question and leaned forward in his chair. "Do you handle all types of property? Furniture, rugs, china, jewelry?"

Sanders gave Earling one of his most disarming smiles. "I handle the larger estate items, such as the furniture and rugs, and, on occasion, I buy porcelains, but the smaller items like china and jewelry are handled by an associate of mine. Now, will you please tell me what this is about?"

"So you do not concern yourself with jewelry?"

"As I have already explained, my expertise is in furnishings, not jewelry," Sanders replied curtly.

Earling leaned back in his chair. "We are hoping that you will be able to give us some information about some men who we have reason to believe work for your company."

Sanders looked convincingly perplexed. "I will certainly help you in any way that I can. For whom are you looking?"

McCafferty pulled out three pictures from his inner breast pocket, leaned forward, and placed them on Sebastian's desk. "These are the men. Do you recognize them?"

Sebastian took his time carefully examining each picture, a look of focused concentration on his face. "Well, this is interesting."

"How so, sir?" Peter asked.

"All three of these men have been recently discharged for not showing up for their work shifts."

"Is that so? When exactly did you release them?" Earling was once again asking the questions.

Sebastian looked off into the distance. "Let's see. I believe it was last week for these two," he held up the photos of Hansen and Maloney, "and just yesterday for this man," he held up the photo of Ortega.

"In what capacity did they work for you, Mr. Sanders?"

"They worked as security guards at my warehouse just outside of town." He reached for the phone. "Hold on a moment, and I'll have Mr. Groundwater pull their personnel files so that you can see the exact information."

Earling nodded.

After a moment's hesitation, Sanders spoke into the phone. "George, would you pull the personnel files of Mr. Hansen, Mr. Maloney, and Mr. Ortega and bring them up to me?" Another brief hesitation and then he hung up.

"Mr. Sanders, do you make a habit of hiring known criminals?" Earling asked casually.

"They are hard workers, Sergeant. If they keep their noses clean, I do not concern myself with their past mistakes. Everyone should be allowed to put their past behind them."

Earling was not convinced by the little speech. "Very noble of you, Mr. Sanders, but these men have not kept their noses clean."

"And as I have indicated, they no longer work for me."

"When they were in your employ did they work together?"

"How do you mean?"

"Did they share the same shift at the warehouse?"

"It's possible, but I'm not sure. I do not make up the schedules. That's done by my warehouse manager."

"May we speak to him?"

"You could, if *she* were available. Unfortunately, she's on holiday. Schedules and the log of exact hours worked are placed in the employee file at the end of each pay period, though." As if on cue, Groundwater walked in with the requested files. Without a word, he handed them to Sebastian and then left the office. After a quick perusal, Sebastian extracted the pertinent information from each file, which he then turned over to Earling.

"May I see the whole file?"

"Personnel files are confidential, Sergeant. Unless you have a court order, of course."

Earling's eyes narrowed, but he said nothing. He instead turned his attention to the information Sanders had supplied.

"It would appear that these men did share shifts, so it's possible they are working together."

"Sergeant, will you please tell me what this is all about?"

Earling handed the papers over to McCafferty. "We just want to talk to these three about some occurrences in the South Kensington area in the past few days. A woman has been assaulted, and we believe these men have been involved."

"Do you think that's why they haven't shown up for work?"

"I wouldn't know, sir. But if they should return, you will give us a ring, won't you? Here's my card."

Sebastian took the card, nodding emphatically. "You may rest assured that if they return to work, I will call you immediately!"

Earling and McCafferty stood up in unison. "Then we'll be on our way." Earling stuck out his hand. "Thank you for your time." Sanders shook his hand and then McCafferty's, who handed the personnel papers back as they shook hands.

After they left, Sebastian sat back down in his chair, a cold and remote expression on his face.

Earling waited until they were outside before initiating a discussion about the interview. He was curious to hear what Peter had seen. Over the years, they had worked out a system that they both found quite effective: Earling asked the questions while McCafferty studied the subject and the environment. Peter had a keen sense of observation, so their arrangement maximized his effectiveness.

"What did you notice?" Earling asked as they walked back to High Street.

"That he was nervous, though he covered it very well."

"Lots of people have that reaction to unexpected visits from the police."

"When he saw the photos, he acted like he was only vaguely familiar with the men. Yet when he buzzed George, he called them by name without a moment's hesitation."

Earling nodded. "I noticed that, too."

"Some of the entries on Ortega's time sheets had been erased and re-entered or covered with corrector fluid so that a new date could be written in. It could be coincidence, but it still looked suspicious to me."

"To me, also. Anything else?"

"Something is not right about the office. It's all very posh as you'd expect it to be, but something wasn't right about it. I can't put my finger on it right now, but it'll come to me. I need to let it perc. In the meantime, I want to dig a little deeper into Sanders and his business. After all, how many estate liquidators do you know that would hire former burglars and fences to guard their merchandise? Not to mention a thug like Ortega?"

Earling chuckled as they approached the car. "I need some coffee." He pointed to a French bistro at the end of the block. "Let's stop in there, get some coffee, and see if we can do anything to get your brain to perc faster."

McCafferty smiled at the pun that Earling did not seem to notice he'd made. He slipped the car keys back into his pocket and followed Earling into the bistro.

CHAPTER FIFTEEN

By the time they arrived at Philippe's house, Danny felt like a zombie. She had not slept well the night before, tossing and turning as she tried to ignore the almost overwhelming urge to go to Geremy's bed. More than once, she had decided to throw professional restraint to the wind and had gotten as far as her own door before reigning herself in and returning to her own bed. Despite her desire, she felt that now was not the right time to act upon it.

When she and Miles had returned to the house, she went to her room to work on the article while some ideas were still fresh in her mind. She came downstairs an hour later and found Geremy in the living room, listening to the stereo as he sat writing at the desk. When he looked up as she came into the room, she saw that the dark mood that had descended on him during dinner still clung to him.

"I came down to say goodnight." She looked around. "Where's Miles?"

"He left soon after you went upstairs. He didn't want to bother you, so he asked me to tell you goodnight." He stood up from the desk and came over to her. "Would like a cup of tea before you go to bed?"

"No, thank you. I'm pretty tired, so I'll just go on up."

He leaned down, kissed her lightly on the cheek, and wished her sweet dreams before he returned to the desk and his work.

She stood by the doorway and watched him for a moment. He had withdrawn into himself, and she now felt a little awkward in his presence. She started to ask him if he wanted to talk about whatever it was that was troubling him but then changed her mind. They were in that limbo of the developing relationship where they knew each other well enough to sense emotional currents, but not well enough to pose as a confidante when those currents became turbulent. She retreated to her bed and had a relatively sleepless night. The closest she came to the sweet dreams Geremy had wished her were the maddening images of him as she had seen him, bare-chested, the first morning at the cottage. By morning, she was exhausted. By the time they reached Philippe's, she was in the zombie zone.

"I apologize for deserting you as soon as we arrive, but if I don't get some sleep, I'll drop."

Geremy, who looked like he hadn't slept too well either, gave her an understanding look. "Did you not sleep well on Miles's futon?"

She ignored the slightly mocking tone of his voice and looked past him to her brother. "Thanks Philippe. I should be down in a couple of hours."

Philippe watched Danielle retreat up the stairs and then shifted his gaze to Geremy. He could not see Geremy's face clearly because it was turned away from him, his eyes still following Danielle. Philippe had to admit he was intensely curious about him since Danielle had never shown any inclination to bring outsiders to this house. Geremy turned, and Philippe smiled when he saw the look on his face. That look and the fact that Danielle had brought Geremy to the house told him that love was in the air. He, being a good Frenchman, was more than willing to help the romance along any way he could. He picked up Geremy's bag and proceeded up to the second floor. "Come on. I'll show you to your room."

Geremy took in the house as they went up to his bedroom. From the outside, it looked like a typical French country house with its whitewashed walls and window boxes exploding with red geraniums and electric blue lobelia. A line of trees separated the house from the lane in front of it. When they had arrived, Danny turned the rental car off the lane onto a narrow driveway, which she followed to a small, cobbled courtyard behind the house where she parked. The house itself served as a very effective shield for the courtyard and the garden behind it. Geremy had gotten out of the car and turned in amazement to take in the profusion of plants and flowers that burst out from every available spot. Philippe came out to greet them and, upon seeing Geremy's expression, had smiled and said, "My wife likes flowers."

Once inside, Geremy had taken an immediate liking to the house. As in most old houses, the rooms were spacious with high ceilings and hardwood floors. As he and Philippe walked up the stairs, he saw photographs of Danny and Philippe and what must be other family members hanging on the wall. He made a mental note to get a better look at them later.

When they entered what was to be his bedroom, he couldn't help but smile as he took in the hardwood floor strewn with oriental rugs, the large mahogany bed, and the matching wardrobe and bureau. He almost felt like he was at home.

"This was my parent's room. Neither of us felt right taking it after they died, so we made it into a guest room." He walked to the bed and set Geremy's bag down on it before moving over to and opening a door next to the bed. "This is the water closet. You'll find towels in the wardrobe. Now, I'll leave you to get sorted out. I'll be downstairs making some coffee, if you'd care to join me."

"Yes, I would, thanks. I'll be down in a few minutes."

Geremy could smell the coffee brewing as he started downstairs, but he paused on the stairs to look at the photographs displayed on the wall. There didn't appear to be any order to the arrangement of photos as he moved from a picture of Danny as a young girl to one of her as a teenager, from a color photo of other people to a black-and-white photo of Philippe, who took very much after his father, Liam Davis. Philippe had his father's tall though slender build, square jaw, and dark, wavy hair. One picture caught and held Geremy's eye, a black-and-white that he at first thought was Danny but then realized that the photo was too old for the subject to be her. Then he saw that the woman's features were slightly more delicate than Danny's. The face was oval like Danny's, but Danny's jaw was stronger and her mouth more full than the woman's in the photograph. Geremy placed his hand over the bottom portion of the photograph leaving the top half exposed and felt he could have been looking at a picture of Danny. The eyes were the same shape, and even in a black-and-white photo, Geremy guessed they were the same arresting shade of blue.

"That was our mother," Philippe said from the bottom of the stairs. "But you probably already figured that out since Danielle looks so much like her."

"For an instant, I thought it *was* Danny."

"That photo was taken at their wedding in 1946." He came halfway up the stairs to stand beside Geremy and look at the photo. "This is my favorite picture of my mother. She looks so radiant and peaceful." He gazed at it for a moment before going back toward the kitchen. "Coffee's ready."

Geremy followed him but then paused to look at the photographs in the hall outside the kitchen.

"Do you take milk or sugar?" Philippe called from the kitchen.

"Milk, please." Philippe came out of the kitchen carrying a cup of coffee which he handed to Geremy. "Thanks. Are you a photographer as well?" Geremy gestured at the wall with his cup.

"No. Most of these are my father's. The rest are Danielle's. I'm the painter in the family like my mother."

"Do you always call your sister 'Danielle'?"

"Yes. I prefer it." He went back into the kitchen, and Geremy followed him. "When we moved to California, she wanted to be more American, so she told everyone to call her Danny, but I always preferred Danielle. In fact, the French side of the family calls her Danielle and the American side calls her Danny." He poured himself a cup of coffee and invited Geremy to sit at the table.

"It's interesting that Danny looks like your mother and you look like your father, and yet, she's a photographer like your father and you're a painter like your mother."

Philippe brought his cup and a small pitcher of milk to the table. "Yes, I am my mother's son." He went back to the kitchen for the coffee pot which he brought to the table.

"Is that why you live in France rather than the US?"

Philippe slid into the seat opposite Geremy. "Yes. Well, that and the fact that Sophie said she wouldn't marry me unless I promised to stay here," he said with a laugh. "Actually, though, I have always preferred France to the States. I was not at all happy when we moved to California. We came back here for holidays, of course, but that was hardly enough for me. I moved back as soon as I could. Then, when our parents were killed, Danielle took the house in California, which she then sold, and I became the owner of this one. It's been in my mother's family for a little over a hundred years, and I'm very attached to it."

"I can see why. It's a lovely house." Since Philippe had touched on the subject and Geremy was curious about the accident, he veered the conversation in that direction. "Danny told me how your parents died. It's still very hard for her to talk about."

"It was a very bad time for her," Philippe said softly as he looked into his coffee cup. "For both of us, really." He looked back at Geremy. "How much did she tell you?"

"That it happened ten years ago, that a drunk driver ran a red light, that your parents were killed instantly, and that she was in physical therapy for a year."

"She probably said it just like that, too. She's not one to talk about herself and especially not about that time in her life. It left her very emotionally scarred."

"Would you mind telling me about it?"

"There's not much to tell. The drunk driver plowed into the car and pushed it into oncoming traffic. The bastard walked away, or rather stumbled away, with a few scratches. Our parents were killed by the head-on collision."

"What happened to Danny?"

"She was in the backseat, so she was pinned down by the front seat. When they cut her out, she was unconscious and then was in a coma for a week. She was in very bad shape. When I saw her in the hospital all bandaged up, tubes going in every direction, and machinery monitoring her vital signs, I was so scared. I had to identify my parents, but somehow seeing her like that was more terrible. They were dead, and I was so afraid that she would die, too." He stopped speaking for a moment and shook his head as if to clear it of the memory. "The doctors said it was a miracle that she survived. They also said that she was likely to have difficulty walking, if she was able to walk at all." A ghost of a smile touched his lips. "It was obvious that they did not know my sister."

"What do you mean?"

"Danielle has a will of iron. She can and will do anything she sets her mind to and nothing motivates her more than someone telling her she can't do something. When the doctors told her that she might not be able to walk again she became determined to prove them wrong. Plus, it gave her something to take her mind off her grief." He paused to take a drink of coffee. "Anyway, that determination and the fact that as a triathlete she was in excellent physical condition helped her to an almost complete recovery. Four months after the wreck, she was walking with the help of a cane. On the first anniversary of the wreck, she had her last therapy session. Her right knee bothers her on occasion, but otherwise she's in good shape."

"And the man who caused the whole thing wasn't even hurt?"

Philippe snorted. "His being so drunk was a major reason he wasn't seriously injured. Most injuries in wrecks are caused by muscles tensing right before the wreck occurs. He was so drunk that his body was like a bowl of Jell-O."

"Did he go to jail?"

Philippe sighed and shook his head. "Not even one day. His driver's license was suspended, he got a three-month jail sentence, which was suspended because he had no previous record, and he was required to do five hundred hours of community service. We've recently learned that he didn't even do that part of his sentence."

"Good Lord!"

Philippe nodded. "Needless to say, we were pretty upset that he got such a light sentence, so we did some research on the man to find out more about him. Turned out, he was a big industrialist with companies located almost exclusively in developing countries where he can pay low wages and trash the environment. We discovered that he was very rich and, as you may expect, had friends in high places. Danny saw him as a living, breathing Scrooge. Definitely not one of the good guys."

He topped off his coffee cup and offered more to Geremy, who declined. Philippe took a drink and smiled as he continued the story. "So Danielle sued him. You know, get him where it hurt: his wallet. She was right, too. When confronted with the possibility of a jury hearing about how he had killed Liam Davis, his wife, and nearly his daughter, he offered Danielle a pot of money to settle out of court. She agreed, but her price was ten million dollars. He balked at first, but ended up paying it all."

"Ten million dollars?" Geremy whistled. "So she's a wealthy woman," he said as he wondered if she had been kidnapped for money after all.

"We are both very well-off thanks to Dad's work, but she didn't do it for the money. She wanted him to hurt from a loss and figured that paying out ten million would do it. She said he cried when he agreed to her terms. Then she took the money and gave it all away to charity. That had been her intention all along, to give back to society some of what he'd taken. She gave it to food banks, homeless shelters, environmental organizations, those sorts of places. And she created a scholarship in our parents name at UCLA for fine arts students." The ringing phone interrupted Philippe. "Excuse me."

Geremy was still sitting at the table finishing his coffee when Philippe returned.

"That was my aunt Marie. The word is out that Danielle is here, so everyone is coming over for dinner. Prepare yourself for the third degree, my friend."

"The 'third degree'?"

"The family will be very curious about the man that Danielle has finally brought home."

"What about Stephen? Hasn't he been here?"

"No. In fact, Marie thought you were him when I mentioned that Danielle had arrived with a friend. I told her otherwise, but some of the family may not get the word, so don't be surprised if they think you are him."

The way Philippe kept saying 'the family' made Geremy a little uneasy, as if he were about to face a gauntlet. "How many people are we talking about here?"

"Not too many. Let's see," he paused as he mentally calculated a number. "Around fifteen or twenty, I guess." He grinned. "But don't worry. They are a very friendly crowd." He took a big gulp from his coffee cup and added, "But a crowd they are, and I need to make some food and drink arrangements. Marie said everyone would bring food, but I am in charge of drinks, some of the food, and," he looked at his watch, "time is not on my side." He turned to Geremy. "I've got to go on a buying trip. Care to join me?"

"Yes. I'd like to stretch my legs." They finished their coffee and left for the market.

—

Jackie jumped when Sanders answered the phone with an angry 'Yes?'. Jackie recovered and gave the good news to his boss.

"The girl showed up, just like you thought she would."

"When?"

"About an hour ago. She showed up with the blond guy who, by the way, is Geremy Hawker, the lead singer for a band called the Mystic Celts. Anyway, he and the brother just left the house. Chas is following them. Do you want me to move in and get the ring from the girl? I think she's alone in the house."

"No! I'll be there as soon as I can, so wait until I get there. Just keep watching them. We can decide how to proceed after I arrive."

Sanders hung up the phone and found that the anger he felt before the call was now gone. The police may be a little too close for comfort, but he hoped he had set them on a wild-goose chase with the doctored work schedules for Ortega. The police will concentrate on the activities of the individuals with the known criminal records and leave him to find his treasure.

He found it particularly convenient that the family lived so close to the Pyrenees. Perhaps the section of the mountains he was interested in was near Foix? Maybe that was why his father had left the ring with the mother in the first place. Had he planned to return to the Pyrenees and search again for the treasure? Perhaps the woman was just an added incentive to return? He would never know. For now, he must prepare for the journey. He picked up the phone, rang his travel agent, and ordered a ticket to Toulouse, France. That done, he made a list of the hiking equipment he would need for his trip to find the cave. From the moment he had rediscovered the existence of the ring, he knew that he would find the cave and the treasure. He knew it!

—

When Danny came down from her nap, feeling refreshed and looking cool and comfortable in a pink, cotton dress she'd found in her closet, she came upon Geremy examining the photographs lining the stairway wall.

Hearing a sound above him, he looked up at her. "Good afternoon, Sleeping Beauty. Who was the lucky fellow that wakened you with a kiss?"

"The wind." She came halfway down the stairs to stand next to him and look at the pictures. "You know, I haven't looked at these pictures in years. They've been here so long I kind of forgot about them." Her eyes moved over the pictures, giggling at some and almost embarrassed at others. She pointed at one black-and-white. "This is Philippe and me at our special place. If we have time, I'll take you there."

"I'd like that."

Her eyes kept moving over the pictures. "Here! Dad took this one at the Mystic Celts concert in 1968. Look, there's John and Miles talking in the background."

Geremy looked closely at the small, color photo he had not noticed before. "So it is." He pulled away from it and pointed to another. "This is the one I find most fascinating," he said as he drew her attention the picture of her mother that had caught his eye earlier.

A slow smile came to Danny's lips as she looked at the picture and saw the expression on her mother's face. "I don't think I've ever seen this one before. Philippe," she called downstairs. When he arrived at the bottom of the stairs, she pointed to the picture.

"Philippe, I don't remember this photo of Maman. Where did you get it?"

"I found it in a photo album of Marie's. She took the picture at their wedding. Papa is just outside of the frame, talking to Maman." He paused to take a long look at the photo. "It's a beautiful picture, isn't it?"

"So that's how she looked on her wedding day. And she was still looking at him like that over twenty years later."

"I hope Sophie looks at me like that twenty years from now!"

Danny laughed as she went down to her brother. She threw her arms around him and gave him a hug. "But how could she not, my most charming, lovable brother?"

He returned her hug, lifting her off the ground in the process. "You're biased."

He set her down, and she stood beside him, her arm around his waist. "So what have I missed since I've been asleep? Did you tell Geremy embarrassing stories about my childhood?" They looked up at Geremy, who was watching them from the stairs.

Philippe winked at Geremy. "Everyone I could remember, little sister."

Geremy came down the steps. "Yes, but I promise to keep them to myself on pain of torture."

Philippe jerked his head toward the kitchen. "Speaking of Geremy's torture, it may occur sooner than he realizes."

"What do you mean?" Danny asked as she walked into the kitchen. Then, seeing all the drinks and the assortment of food, she stopped. "Oh, no! You don't mean …?" She looked at Philippe, a horrified expression distorting her face. "Not *the family*??"

Geremy felt even more uneasy than he had before about the approaching party.

Danny turned from Philippe to Geremy in time to see the doubt move over Geremy's face, and she giggled. "I'm just kidding, Geremy." Seeing that he was not quite convinced, she added in her most convincing voice, "Really."

"He's probably dubious because I gave him the same routine."

She went over and placed her hand on his arm and looked into his eyes, a serious expression on her face. "Really. They will be curious about you, so they will give you the twenty-question routine, but they are wonderful people. I mean, they are related to *us*." She went and stood next to Philippe, both of them striking a serious pose.

He had to laugh at their silly expressions. "Well, if it gets too tough, I'll use one of you as a shield."

"Fair enough," Philippe said with a nod. "But, to the task at hand. Louise said she would come over to help get things set up, but we can get started."

"Wait." Danny held her hands up. "Before we do anything, I need to talk about the men who have been asking questions about you, since that is the primary reason we are here."

"Sounds like a good idea, sis." He went to the table and wordlessly invited them to join him.

"Tell me what you know about them," Danny said as they sat down.

"Since I became aware of them, I've been doing a little investigation of my own. I think there are only two of them—I already told you what they look like—and they take turns sitting at the Tout le Monde cafe, walking around town, or hanging out at Hotel Le Lys where they have booked two rooms." Noticing their intrigued expressions, he shrugged and added, "It's a small town, and I know practically everyone in it."

"Well, I've got what they want." She laid her left hand, palm down on the table, clearly displaying the ring on her index finger. "How do we get it to them before they do something to us?"

Philippe shrugged. "Why not just deliver it to their hotel or to the cafe? One of them is there at the same time every morning. You don't even have to deliver it yourself. You can send someone else over with it."

Danny thought for a moment before shaking her head. "Sending it is a good idea, but I don't want to expose anyone else to possible danger. I think I should take it myself."

"Danielle, you can send it over with a group of people or how about Fabrice and Francois? They'll be here for the party."

"I thought they were in Nice."

"Arrived back today."

It all sounded so simple. If the goons wanted the ring, she'd give it to them, no strings attached. And if the twins were willing to act as couriers, all the better. They were identical with their six-foot, two-hundred-twenty-pound builds, so were a good choice for the job. "Alright, I'll ask Fabrice and Francois to take the ring over. When will they get here? Should I call and ask them to come over early?"

"If they do not arrive at least an hour before everyone else, I will be very surprised."

Danny looked at her watch. "Okay. It's four thirty now, and they'll probably get here around five thirty or six. What say we take a walk and show Geremy our secret spot? He showed me his."

Danny saw the raised-eyebrow-look Philippe threw at Geremy. "Oh really?" he asked suggestively.

Geremy winked at him as Danny slugged her brother, who winced as if she'd really hurt him. "Really, Philippe. Sometimes you act like a fourteen-year-old. As I was saying, he showed me his spot so I thought I'd reciprocate."

Philippe laughed. "Some secret spot! There's a picture of it hanging on the wall!"

CHAPTER SIXTEEN

It was nearly four o'clock before Earling and McCafferty returned to the office and half past four when Earling finally read the message from Danny. "Damn!" He looked at the time that the message came in and then at his watch. "Damn!"

McCafferty stopped at the door, not knowing whether to go in or not. Earling looked up and, seeing him, motioned him in. "I know where Hansen and Maloney are, thanks to Ms. Davis." He walked around his desk and leaned against the edge of it, waving the message in front of him. "She called just after we left this morning to tell us that Hansen and Maloney are in Foix, watching her brother. She called to say that she is going to Foix to deliver the ring."

"Bloody hell."

"You've got his number. Call her so we can find out what's going on. Anybody around here speak French?"

"Emerson."

"Get him in here. We need to call the Foix police and ask them to pick Maloney and Hansen up for breaking and entering and kidnapping." McCafferty started to leave but then remembering why he had come to Earling's office, stopped and turned back to him.

"Just thought you'd like to know. I figured out what bothered me about Sanders's office. Pieces of furniture were missing. The carpet had indentations showing that furniture had recently been removed and the walls were very bare, also. Don't know exactly what that means, but it seemed odd to me, so I thought I'd pass it on."

"Cheers, Peter. Now go tell Emerson to get in here and then make that call to the Davis house."

"Right."

Danny, Geremy and Philippe filed out of the back door, over the cobbled courtyard, and through a wooden gate which set them on the path to Danny and Philippe's childhood hideaway. The path skirted a meadow which, after a day of full sun, was fragrant with meadow grass and late spring flowers. The path then cut into a copse of old hardwood trees, and Danny led them toward the middle of it. When she had nearly reached the center, she stopped and put her arm around a huge linden tree.

"We don't know who planted these trees or why, but we both felt it was a special spot the minute we discovered it."

Geremy noticed that the linden that Danny was leaning against was one of five that had been planted to create a natural perimeter for a small circular space in the center of the copse. The dense stand of trees on all sides acted as both a sight and sound barrier to the outside world, while the leaves on the trees greatly impeded the sunlight. The atmosphere was cool and carried the spicy scent of moss and decaying leaves.

Philippe walked to the center of the clearing and sat down on the carpet of old leaves. "We'd be out here all day playing games and camp out at night in the summers whenever we could. It was a great place to be a kid."

"One of the reasons Philippe hated to leave and move to San Francisco." Danny left the comfort of the linden and joined Philippe. Geremy continued to stand on the periphery.

"Yes, the big city held no fascination for me after my beautiful French countryside."

Silence descended as they each became lost in their memories.

Danny looked over at Geremy, standing quietly in the shadows. "Geremy?"

"Yes?"

"Do you still want to go look for the cave? Even though we're going to give the ring back, I mean."

"Yes, of course. It's the reason we came here. Giving the ring back hasn't dampened my curiosity about the whole thing."

"What 'whole thing' are you talking about? You never have told me what's so special about that ring."

Danny was aghast. "I haven't?"

He shook his head.

"Sorry," she said sheepishly as she took off the ring and handed it to her brother. "We've determined that the lines on the front," she dug her fingernail into the notch so that the stone would pop up, "and the back are a map depicting Pic de Maubermé, Mt. Valier, and Mt. Rouch, and that the diamond draws attention to the center of Mt. Valier."

Philippe held the ring closer, trying to read the script. "Rather odd that the writing is in Basque."

Danny looked at him in surprise. "I didn't know you knew Basque!"

"I know it well enough to recognize it and to ask for a beer, but I'm not conversant in it. What does it say?"

"According to the London Police it says, 'Three peaks guard the plain. In the heart of the middle, find the cave of the blue light, there but not there, in plain view but hidden, eternal haven to seekers of the flowering heart.' "

"That's cryptic."

Geremy pushed off from the tree against which he'd been leaning, came over, and sat down next to Philippe. "We know that the first part refers to the mountains and to some cave that supposedly exists in Valier, but we have no idea what the last part of the riddle means."

Danny took the ring as Philippe offered it back to her. "It sounds kind of weird, though, doesn't it? I wonder if it's a metaphor for something or maybe a lost civilization. Or maybe it's a wild mountain flower?" She looked at her brother. "What do you think?"

"Well, the mountain has its fair share of caves like all the mountains around here, and there's plenty of evidence to support the assertion that people have been living in the mountains since prehistoric times, so it could have something to do with a lost civilization. As for the flower, I don't recall having heard of a flower called a 'flowering heart,' but these mountains are covered with wildflowers, so I guess it's possible."

Geremy chuckled. "The image I get when I think of the line is of a group of really old people huddled in a cave praying to some primitive deity."

"That hardly sounds worth going to all the trouble those men went to for the ring, to lead them to a cave full of old people."

Philippe grinned at them. "Maybe it leads to the long-lost treasure horde of the Knights Templar."

Geremy nodded his head. "That's what Miles Jensen said."

Philippe laughed. "I was just kidding! If the Order ever hid treasure in these mountains, I'm sure it was recovered as soon as it was safe to move it. Another rumor you might consider is that the Nazi's secreted some of their plundered wealth in the Pyrenees. That seems more plausible to me."

"Well, we won't know unless we go take a look around."

"You're serious, aren't you? You're going to try to find this 'cave of the blue light'?"

Danny cast an inquiring look in Geremy's direction, and he nodded. She nodded to Philippe. "Affirmative."

"I don't know, Danielle. It sounds dangerous to me. If the ring was worth kidnapping you over, those guys may not think too kindly of you following its clues."

Danny stood up and extended her hands to both men at the same time. "I hear you, bro, but I can't stop now. It'll drive me crazy for the rest of my life if I don't at least go look at the area. But I promise that we'll be careful."

Standing between the two men, she hooked her arms through theirs and they made their way back to the house. They entered the kitchen just as Francois was reaching for a piece of cheese from a tray on the kitchen table.

—

Sebastian had not been in Jackie's room for five minutes when an unexpected knock came at the door. Jackie moved over to the door. "Oui?"

A man's voice, speaking English with a heavy French accent, responded. "I have a package for you from Danielle Davis."

Jackie looked over at Sebastian, who motioned for him to open the door. Jackie did so and found himself eye level with the chests of two large, young men. Without a word, one of them handed Jackie a small envelope and then both turned in unison and walked quickly to the stairs, just as they had been instructed. Jackie watched them retreat down the hall and then closed the door. Sebastian was beside him before he had even closed it, snatching the envelope from his hand. Without a word, Sebastian ripped the envelope open. The ring he'd been seeking for five years fell onto the floor.

For a moment, Sebastian and Jackie stood and looked at it, the overhead light making its dull, gold band gleam and the small diamond glimmer. Sebastian pounced on it and brought it closer so he could get a good look at it. "This is it! This is it!"

"That's what this is all about?" Jackie asked incredulously. "You wanted us to possibly kill someone *for that?*"

"Who's killing who for what?" Chas asked as he came into the room.

"Forget it, mate. The ring we were supposed to nick was just delivered, so we can get out of here."

Sebastian pocketed the ring. "That's right. Your services are no longer required here, but don't go back to London. As I suspected, the girl saw you and tipped off the police. They came by my office this morning asking about you. I suggest you clear out of here immediately. Your pay will be deposited to your accounts, so we do not need to see each other again." Jackie had already started throwing his clothes into his bag as Sebastian left the room.

All Sebastian could think about as he walked down the hall to the stairs was the ring that the fingers of his right hand caressed inside his coat pocket. He wanted to examine it in the privacy of his own room. As he approached the stairs, two French police officers emerged from the stairway. They looked at him closely and determined that he was not one of the two men they had been told to pick up. Although his stomach turned over when he saw them, he smiled at them and casually bent down as if to tie his shoe. He dallied just long enough to see that they went to Jackie's room and then he hurried down the stairs to his room on the second floor. He collected his still unopened bag and hurried down one flight of stairs to the reception desk where he paid for the room he had not slept in and left the hotel. He did not relax until he was safely in a room in a small hotel at the edge of town. Finally, in the privacy and quiet of the room, he pulled out the ring and a map of the Pyrenees and began to compare the lines.

As he surveyed the map, he fumed over the fact that the Davis woman had called the police. She probably expected to get the ring back after the police picked up Jackie and Chas. He froze as he considered the implications. If she wanted the ring back, she must have discovered its secret. He held the ring up and watched the small diamond wink at him as he determined what to do about Ms. Davis. "Things aren't going to be so easy for you, my dear," he murmured to himself. A cold look came over his face as he began to formulate a plan to make sure Danny Davis didn't cause him any more trouble.

CHAPTER SEVENTEEN

Danny stood next to the kitchen table waiting for Francois and Fabrice to return. She had given them very explicit instructions about delivering the ring and then coming back immediately. They had been gone nearly thirty minutes, and she became more tense with each passing minute. All the 'what ifs' started to crowd her brain. Then she heard them, laughing and talking as they strolled across the cobbled courtyard to the back door. Relief washed over her. She ran to the door and flung it open.

"Ca va?"

They stopped two feet in front of her and looked at her as if they didn't know what she was asking about. Then Fabrice smiled in comprehension. "Ah, oui, oui. Ca va! C'etait tres facile. J'ai donne l'envelope a l'homme dans la chambre et nous sommes partis. C'est tout." He shrugged then followed Francois past Danny and into the kitchen. Danny could still not quite believe that it had been so easy.

"Vraiment? Pas de problem?"

Fabrice kissed her on the cheek. "No, cherie. Very easy, no problem."

"Danielle?"

Danny turned to her brother. "Oui?"

"C'est le police de Londres au telephone."

She went to the phone. "Sergeant Earling?"

"No, Ms. Davis, it's Peter McCafferty. Sorry we weren't here when you called this morning. In fact, we did not get back to the office until an hour or so ago."

"Well, all's well that ends well."

"How do you mean?"

"The ring has been delivered to the two men. My cousins just returned from delivering it. I don't think they'll be bothering me anymore."

"Well, that is the truth. We contacted the Foix police, and they have assured us that they will pick the men up immediately."

"That's great! So I didn't even need to turn the ring over to them."

"Right. Well, the police there will probably ask you to positively identify the men, just to be sure."

"Okay, I can do that."

"We'll need to talk to you again when you get back to London. Do you know when that will be?"

"I'm not exactly sure. I may be here for a week or two."

"Hmmm. Well, we've got your statement, and if you go and positively identify them as the men who abducted you, we shouldn't need your presence here. Just call us when you get back."

"I'll do that. Thanks for calling." She hung up. Geremy found her, hand still on the phone, lost in thought.

"Earth to Danny."

She smiled at him. "I was just talking to P.C. McCafferty. He said the Foix police have agreed to pick up the two guys. I was thinking how I didn't need to send them the ring. He also said the police will probably want me to identify them. So I was also thinking that I should call the police and ask if they have picked the men up and, if so, can I come to the station right now, before the party, and get the identification out of the way."

"Makes sense. Want some company? I saw them, too, so I may be of assistance."

"That would be nice." She picked up the receiver. "Let me make sure that they are ready for me. Do me a favor? Go tell Philippe what we're up to."

The trip took longer than Danny had expected, so that when they returned to the house everyone was just sitting down to eat. A cacophony of voices erupted when Danny and Geremy walked into the dining room, everyone greeting her, asking where she had been, asking her to introduce her friend, telling both of them to sit down. The din was almost overwhelming. Geremy found himself commandeered by an older woman who identified herself as 'Tante Marie' and placed him in a chair next to her at the other end of the table from Danny and Philippe.

So much for the shields, Geremy thought to himself as he sat down.

Danny smiled sympathetically at him from her place at the table. She knew better than to even try to rescue Geremy from her aunt who could be very determined when she chose. This was the first man Danny had ever brought to this house, so he was quite an item for the aunt who thought Danny should have married long ago. Danny resigned herself to watch from a distance and resolved that if Geremy looked like he needed rescuing, she would come to his aid.

As it turned out, she needn't have worried. Early on, a burst of laughter from the other end of the table drew her attention, and she realized with amazement that Geremy was talking to her aunt and cousins in French. The laughter was because of a story *he* was telling *them*. Dinner was a long, leisurely affair, and before the party moved from the dining room table to the living room, Geremy was one of the family.

Danny cornered him before he left the dining room. "You didn't tell me you spoke French."

"You didn't ask," he said with a grin. "But I am most fortunate in that many in your family speak English because my French is far from fluent."

"Well you have certainly charmed my aunt, which is no small feat!"

"She is wonderful. Very direct. She wants to know when you and I plan to marry."

Danny blushed. "I'm sorry. She's afraid I'm getting old, and if I don't marry soon, I never will."

Geremy had a serious expression on his face as he said, "No need to apologize. I told her in six months."

Danny's mouth dropped open. "You what?" she gasped.

Geremy grinned and pointed a finger at her. "Got you again!"

Danny, realizing she'd been had, laughed. She grabbed his arm. "My day will come, maestro. In the meantime, shall we join the others?"

He gave her a slight bow. "Your servant, milady."

"You don't have any more surprises up your sleeve, do you?" she asked as they moved into the other room.

"If I told you, it wouldn't be a surprise, now would it?"

Danny started to question him, but didn't have an opportunity to pursue his meaning because they had entered the living room and Marie had immediately taken him away from Danny. As was typical with her family, a number of people had brought their musical instruments for some after-dinner entertainment.

After two songs, Fabrice put his guitar down, so Geremy leaned over and asked if he could use it. Everyone became quiet as he strummed the strings and listened to the guitar's tones. Finding it in tune, he looked up to find everyone looking at him in anticipation. While some were not familiar with the Mystic Celts, everyone was aware that he was a famous rock-and-roll star.

He grinned at them. "Any requests?"

Danny leaned forward. "I have one. 'Where Have You Gone?'
"

"Ah. An old favorite." He played a couple of chords before beginning the song, a poignant story about the bereaved Finn searching in vain for his beloved Saba, who had been enchanted and taken from him by an evil wizard. The group sat quietly listening to the beautiful song. While many did not always understand the words, everyone understood the sentiment. When he finished, they clapped heartily.

"Now, if you don't mind, I'd like to play something I've been working on recently. It doesn't have any words yet, but I call it 'L'esprit de Danielle'."

Danny looked at him and found his eyes on her. A look passed between them that everyone in the room caught; Tante Marie smiled. She'd seen that look before and thought they would be married sooner than the December date Geremy had given her. Then Geremy began to play, and Danny recognized the tune he had played the second evening at the cottage. He had made some changes and additions, but the refrain was the same and, to Danny, was one of the most beautiful tunes she had ever heard. As she watched him play and listened to him express his feelings for her through his music, a dam began to crumble inside of her, and the feelings she'd been holding at bay washed over her. At that moment, he looked up from the guitar at her and smiled.

—

Geremy stood in front of the open window wearing only his trousers, enjoying the feel of the cool, night breeze over his bare chest. It was just past midnight and the house was quiet, the last guest having left half an hour ago. He was dead tired, but he was too restless to sleep. He was leaning against the window frame, his head resting against his forearm, when he heard the creak of the opening door. He turned to see a figure in the doorway. The hallway was dark and the light in his room was dim, so the white nightshirt Danny was wearing was the only thing he saw at first. For an instant, he thought it was a ghost. Then, as his eyes adjusted, Danny's face came dimly into focus. He couldn't really see her eyes, but could feel them burning into him.

Danny couldn't move as she looked at him. She had seen him through the partially open door, standing at the window. She could feel the tension in his body and knew that he was thinking about her. She pushed against the door, knowing as she did so that there would be no turning back from the path that led to this man's arms. When he turned toward her, every fiber in her body knew that nothing could keep her from his arms.

The silence pounded against her ears as she stood there looking at him. She came into the room, her bare feet making no noise against the wooden floor. She took another step and a floorboard creaked beneath her foot. She paused, as if hearing a note of caution from the protesting floor.

Her cessation of movement brought Geremy to life. He strode across the room and, never taking his eyes off her, closed the door as if to block any escape. He came around to stand before her and hooked his finger under her chin, tilting her head up so he could look into her eyes. He had to see that she had no doubts. Her expression was calm, and he could find no lingering doubts shadowing her eyes. She, too, searched for the shadow she'd seen the day before and was relieved to see that it had been replaced by a sure and gentle expression of love.

They stood without speaking, neither willing to break the spell of silence that enveloped them. Geremy's hand gently caressed her face before he bent to kiss her eyes, her cheeks, and finally her lips. Drawing back from the kiss, he caught her hand in his and drew her to the bed. He began to undo the small buttons that ran down the front of her nightshirt, but after three buttons she stayed his hand. Danny stepped back from him and slowly pulled the nightshirt over her head, dropped it to the floor before reaching out to unfasten his trousers.

They stood for a moment, enjoying each others nakedness, before Geremy eased her onto the bed. Everything that touched her skin was a study in contrasts. The scratchy feel of the uncombed-cotton bedcover against her back, the soft, whispering touch of Geremy's lips and tongue on her breasts and stomach, the silky sweep of his hair against her inner thigh, and the rough texture of his calloused fingertips as they slid over her skin. She shivered with pleasure and then shuddered with release. Geremy moved slowly back up over her body, his lips, tongue, and teeth marking his progress.

She opened her eyes to see him looking down at her, a devilish smile playing about his lips. A slow smile spread over her lips as her fingers ran down his chest and caught his hard penis in her hand. He sucked in his breath as she caressed him. She released her hold and with a sweeping, upward motion ran her fingertips lightly over his stomach and chest. It was his turn to shiver with delight. Her hands went around his neck, and she pulled him down to a kiss.

Her lips were warm and soft and her breasts warm against his cool chest. His senses reeled, feeling her body beneath him, smelling her, hearing her moans of pleasure. He entered her slowly, trying to extend the exquisite sensation of their joining. She gasped with pleasure and began to move in rhythm with him. All notions of extending the moment were lost to him as he felt her responding to him. He felt the quickening in his loins and then the rush of release as Danny arched her back to meet his final thrust.

Geremy, still half asleep, reached over to touch Danny, but found an empty space instead. He rolled over just as she came through the door, wearing her nightshirt and carrying a tray.

He gave her a relieved though sleepy smile. "For a moment there I thought I had just had the most beautiful dream."

She set the tray down on the floor, jumped onto the bed, and rolled on top of him. "I had that same dream, maestro. What do you think it means?"

He wrapped his arms around her, rolled her over onto her back, and kissed her. He brushed some hair out of her eyes and kissed her again. "I think it means we should always sleep in the same bed since it results in such mutually satisfying dreams come true."

"Sounds good to me." She wiggled underneath him. "But, now release me so I can pour the coffee."

He rolled off her reluctantly, and she scooted off the bed. She poured two cups, handed one to Geremy, who was propped up with pillows, and sat cross-legged in front of him. "So, are you ready for the big adventure?"

Geremy gave her a smoldering look over the edge of his coffee cup. He brought the cup down and asked, "So soon?" He gave her a mischievous smile. "Oh, my mother did warn me about younger women." He ran a finger along the instep of her bare foot.

Danny grinned and nudged him with the foot. "The adventure to the mountains, silly."

He looked disappointed and his finger on her foot stopped moving. "Oh. That adventure. Now I remember. It was my *father* who warned me about younger women."

She nudged him again. "Sounds to me like I'm in a no-win situation. Damned if we stay, damned if we go."

He set his cup down on the nightstand, reached over and took her cup, and set it next to his. "I know of a lovely way to make this into win-win situation," he said as he leaned forward and started kissing her throat. "Stay a while, and then go," he murmured against her throat.

Danny reclined under the gentle pressure of his kisses. "Oh, I do enjoy these win-win situations," she said softly.

When they finally made their appearance downstairs, Philippe was ready to fix them breakfast and discuss the trip to the mountain. He told Danny where he had put the hiking and camping equipment and suggested she go through it while he made breakfast.

"Do you think I'll be warm enough in these shorts?" she asked her brother. Philippe nodded as he looked at the outfit of denim shorts and light sweater she had chosen. "Yes, I think you'll be alright. You might want to carry some slacks in your day pack, though. Just in case." She nodded and took Geremy, who was wearing regular jeans and a green, long-sleeve tee shirt, to the storage area to get day packs and any other equipment she thought they'd need.

When they returned to the kitchen, they each had a medium-sized day pack, a flashlight, and two water bottles. "Philippe, does Sophie have some wool socks and warm clothes I can borrow for a few days?"

"Yes. When you finish eating, we can go look through her clothes." He set two plates holding huge vegetable omelets down in front of them.

"You're not eating?"

Philippe shrugged. "I ate two hours ago."

Danny grinned back. "Oh."

Philippe brought a pot of coffee to the table and sat down. "Do you need any extra clothes, Geremy? Hiking socks, boots, or thermal wear?"

He chewed the bite he had just taken and swallowed. "No. I've got everything. Well, except for the hiking boots. I just planned to wear my tennis shoes. Great omelet, by the way. Thanks."

"Sure. And the tennis shoes should be alright. I believe that the trails on Valier are not difficult, and you two are not undertaking a major expedition. Just a day hike, right?" He directed the question to Danny.

"Yeah." She pointed at the road map with her fork as she chewed and swallowed a bite of omelet. "I've been looking over the map, and Siex looks like the best place to start. We'll find some place to stay for a night or two."

"Just remember to never underestimate the mountains. The weather can change for the worse in five minutes, and it can get dangerous. Enough people have been killed up there because they weren't paying attention or because they weren't properly prepared. Sorry, but I have to give that public service announcement."

Danny squeezed his arm. "Don't worry. I promise we'll be careful."

Philippe pulled the map over, his finger following a road route. "Good. Okay. I'd recommend that you take the D17 to Soulan and then cut south to Siex. It takes a little longer than taking the D117 by way of St. Girons, but it's a nicer drive."

"Thanks, bro. This is so helpful."

"Well, I still don't think this is a very good idea, but I know better than to try to talk you out of something once you've made up your mind." He looked her in the eye, his tone serious. "Just be careful, and keep your eyes open!"

"Yes, sir."

Philippe sat up straight and looked toward the sound of knocking that came from the front door. Danny put the last bite of omelet into her mouth as she stood up. "I'll get it."

A moment later, Philippe and Geremy heard scuffling in the front hall and Danny cry out in pain. They both jumped up from the table. When they reached the front hallway, they found Danny struggling in the arms of an unknown man.

"Stay back," he said coolly as he pointed a gun at them. When Danny saw the gun, she quit struggling. "I had hoped to get you away from the house unnoticed, but you are stronger than I expected, my dear. I'm glad, though, that you have a healthy respect for my gun."

Philippe and Geremy stopped a few feet away from him. Philippe held up his hands in a placating gesture. "Please, monsieur. Just put the gun down and calm down so that we can talk."

"I'm perfectly calm, monsieur. Sorry to interrupt your morning, but I need your sister for insurance."

"Insurance? What are you talking about?"

"The little scheme to send the ring and then recover it by having the police nick Jackie and Chas backfired, my dear," he said in Danny's ear, but loud enough for the men to hear.

"I don't know what you're talking about," she retorted hotly as she tried to loosen his arm from across her neck.

He jerked it harder causing her to gasp. "Stop squirming." She did as he said, and he loosened his arm a fraction of an inch. "I was there when the ring was delivered. I took it, and when I left the room, I passed the police on their way to Jackie's room. I figured you thought you'd get the ring back after they were picked up, but you didn't know that I would be there to take it. I saw you and your friend here go to the police station last night, only they didn't have the ring, did they?"

"I didn't even think to ask about the ring."

"Do you take me for a fool?"

"That ring is hardly worth all the trouble it's caused me."

Sebastian laughed. "Oh, that's where you are very wrong."

Philippe took a step toward them, and Sebastian aimed the gun at Danny's rib cage. "Don't move another inch or I'll hurt her." Danny winced when he tightened his arm across her throat.

Philippe stopped. "Alright, alright. Just take it easy. Listen, if you have the ring, what do you want with us?"

"I couldn't take any chances that you had figured out why the ring is worth all this trouble."

"And if I told you I don't have a clue, would you let me go?" Danny asked, her voice raspy.

"Too late for that now, my dear. You are going with me right now so I can be sure that I will have no more interference from you, your brother, or your boyfriend." He backed over to the door and used his foot to pull open the partially opened door. "If you interfere in any way, I will kill her." He pulled Danny out the door and, slipping his arm from her neck, grabbed her arm, jabbed the gun in her side, and walked her to his car. "Open the door and get in." She did as he commanded and sat on the passenger side of the front seat. "Slide over. You're driving."

Geremy and Philippe stood motionless as they watched Danny ease Sebastian's car out of the driveway and onto the quiet street. As soon as the car was out of sight, they sprang into action, running back into the house. In the kitchen, Philippe pulled the map across the table. "From what we've talked about, I think we have a good idea of their destination, but we don't know which route they're taking. I showed you the two main routes. I propose we split up, with you taking the D117, and I'll take the D17." With his finger, he traced the route on the map. "Just follow D117 to St. Girons and then go south. I think the sign is for Oust." He folded the map leaving the route to Siex visible and handed it to Geremy. "You get going. I'll stop at the police station and get some help." Geremy grabbed the keys to the rental car he and Danny had arrived in and was about to run out the back door when Philippe grabbed his arm. "Do you remember what his car looks like?"

Geremy nodded. "It's a maroon Renault sedan."

Philippe nodded. "Be careful, Geremy. He had a crazy look in his eye."

"I'll be very careful."

CHAPTER EIGHTEEN

Danny looked nervously at the gun that Sebastian still had pointed at her waist. "You need to tell me where we're going."

Sebastian kept his eyes straight ahead. "Take the D117 to St. Girons."

She made the necessary turns and was soon speeding down the D117, weaving around the Saturday-morning traffic. "Would you please put the gun down? It makes me nervous."

He laughed. "That's the idea," he said as he relaxed and rested his hand on his right thigh, the gun still pointing at her.

"Now that you've got me and we're on our way, you could at least introduce yourself."

His laughter was genuine as he nodded. "Of course. How could I have been so remiss? My name is Sebastian Sanders, Ms. Davis."

"Well, Mr. Sanders, now would you mind telling me what this is all about? What's so special about the ring?"

He took his eyes off the road and looked at her. His plans included killing her and then making it look like an accident, so he decided to humor her.

Danny had gazed over at him and felt a chill of fear sliver down her spine. A ruthless expression had passed momentarily over his features, and she saw a shadow of insanity behind the expression. She jerked her eyes back to the road and gripped the wheel until her knuckles were white while her mind raced over options for escape.

"The ring originally belonged to my grandfather. It was a memento of trip he took to these mountains in 1898. He went missing during a botanical expedition, but reappeared, seemingly out of nowhere, in 1903. Between some documents I discovered five years ago and the stories I recall about his adventures after he disappeared, I came to the conclusion that he had discovered a magnificent treasure horde." He paused for dramatic effect. "I believe he found some of the treasure that members of the Knights Templar hid in the mid-thirteenth century."

Danny gave a start and looked over at him, wondering if she, Geremy, and Philippe had actually stumbled onto the truth after all. He saw her expression of surprise and smiled.

"So you've heard the stories also."

"I've spent part of my life in Foix, so, of course, I've heard the legends. But locals believe it's just a fable."

"I thought the stories I'd heard as a child were fables, too. Then I found some correspondence from my grandfather. If he didn't find the treasure of the Knights, he did find somebody's treasure." The cold look returned to his eyes. "And I intend to claim it for my own."

"But how can you be sure it's still hidden? How do you know that someone besides your grandfather didn't find it? There was that priest in Rennes les Chateaux who was rumored to have found a treasure at the turn of this century."

He waved his hand as if to dismiss that rumor. "I read accounts of him. Documentation of his discovery focuses on written material, not a treasure of gold and jewels." He paused as if reviewing the information and then concluded, "No. It's still there. I can feel it." He said it quietly, but Danny could hear the conviction in his voice. She knew without a doubt that he was crazy.

People had been looking for that treasure for centuries, and now he was saying he knew where it was hidden. And if he was crazy enough to believe it was still there after seven hundred years, he was crazy enough to do her harm. She didn't want to follow that line of thinking too far, so she kept asking him questions. "If your grandfather found it, why didn't he keep it for himself?"

A look of consternation settled on Sebastian's face, and he pursed his lips. "I don't know. When he returned to England, he had more money than when he had disappeared. He gave my grandmother a fabulous emerald ring when they became engaged—the origins of which no one knew—which disappeared after she died. I'm of the opinion that he brought some of the treasure back with him and that he intended to return for the rest at a later date."

"Did he return?"

"No. He died en route to India in 1920. Then my father tried to find the treasure, but without success."

"Then it was your father who gave the ring to my mother?"

"Yes, but that was years later. Damn fool fell in love with her and gave her the ring. He planned to return for her and the ring, but he was killed before he was able to return, and the ring was forgotten by everyone. Forgotten, that is, until I stumbled upon the papers that reminded me of it."

"If you knew I had it, why didn't you just tell me? I would have given it back to you."

"I did try to buy it from you."

"When?" Even as she said it, the memory surfaced. She took a good look at him as he regarded her sardonically.

"Yes, now you remember!"

Danny's eyes grew wide as she went over in her mind the encounter with him in Seattle. This attractive, well-dressed, older man with a cultured English accent had approached her while she shopped at Pike Place Market. He just started chatting to her about nothing in particular and then started asking her about the ring. He had even offered to buy it right then and there. She had declined, in spite of his persistence—or even almost because of it. For no solid reason she could name, she felt uneasy about him. Then, a friend had hailed her from across the street, and she turned and waved. When she turned back to the strange man, he was gone. She was relieved that he had left, but the whole exchange had left her feeling apprehensive for days. Now she looked at him and asked, "Why on earth didn't you just tell me it was a family heirloom? I would have gladly returned it to you."

"No matter. I have it now."

"And a lot of unnecessary trouble along with it!"

Sebastian shrugged, indicating that now that the ring was in his possession and he was on his way to recovering the treasure, the trouble was of little import.

All talk ceased and both were left to their own thoughts. In the lull, Danny began to take more notice of her surroundings. Wild, red poppies mingled with blue cornflowers and golden grass that swayed in the wind like waves of color rolling over the countryside. Memories from her childhood flooded her mind of picnics to the ruins that dotted the area and berry-picking expeditions where she and Philippe managed to eat more than they saved. At the end of every outing, they always returned home with colorful, fragrant bouquets of poppy and lavender, buttercups and rosemary. The memories of her childhood in France were filled with sunshine and laughter. She found herself wondering why she stayed away for most of her adult life.

Her musings were cut short by the need to pay more attention to her driving. She reduced her speed as she neared the slowing traffic ahead of her. Campers had descended on the area for a weekend at one of the many local campsites. Sebastian swore. He had not anticipated the traffic.

Geremy was feeling equally frustrated at the slow pace of the traffic. He had passed cars twice, but both times had faced near head-on collisions. Now, the traffic was so constant in both directions that he had to content himself with the slow but steady crawl and the hope that the maroon Renault he'd seen half a mile ahead of him held Danny and her kidnapper.

Philippe slammed his hand against the wheel of his car. An accident involving a poultry truck and a caravan had brought traffic to a complete standstill on the D17. His car and the police car in front of him were hemmed in. The whine of the police siren died as the policeman turned it off, realizing that the cars in front of them had nowhere to go, so could not move out of the way. Everyone was stuck.

When they reached St. Girons, Sebastian instructed Danny to turn left, following the signs south.

"I know how to get to Siex." As soon as she said it, she realized her mistake and wanted to bite her tongue.

Sebastian turned a malevolent gaze on her. "So, you did figure out the puzzle. I'm glad I did not underestimate you. And that means that your boyfriend and brother know our ultimate destination, also." He considered his options in the face of the new information. "Yes, we are making for Siex, but there are a number of back roads in the area, so I am sure we will be able to elude them." He paused long enough to admire a woman sitting at an outdoor café. Then he finished his thought. "Because, you see, I know exactly which road we need to take, and they have no idea."

Sanders's unconcerned attitude about possible pursuit was unnerving. They headed south out of St. Girons, and Danny watched as the intermittent glimpses of the snow-capped Pyrenees became more regular. The traffic continued to be sluggish, and she was glad for the delay because she needed time to work out her options for escape. She sensed that arrival at their destination would not be good for her continued well-being. She hoped that Sanders did not know that she knew judo, but since he probably sent the Spanish thug to the flat, she had to assume that the Spaniard had relayed the information to his boss.

Much to her chagrin, traffic became lighter after they passed through Lacourt and, at Sanders's insistence, she picked up speed. In other, happier days, the green, rolling hills and the moist dirt of the freshly plowed fields would have made her heart sing. As a child, she had especially enjoyed the sight of the vineyards because she had always been amazed that anything could grow in such stony soil. Not only did the grapevines thrive, but she had been told that the stones soaked up the warmth of the sun all day and then released the warmth at night so the vines never got too cold. But today, as they neared Siex, she didn't have time to dwell on the timeworn beauty of the countryside.

They reached Siex at half past two. Sebastian directed her to a hard-packed, dirt road south of the village. After driving for twenty more minutes, the road became rougher with deep ruts and pot holes. Sebastian told her to pull the car off the road, pointing at some trees and bushes a few yards in front of them.

"Pull it in as far as you can, so the car is off the road completely." Doing as directed, Danny inched the car forward until the bumper nudged one of the trees. She looked over at him; the gun which was still pointed at her waist. "Hand me the keys and get out of the car slowly." When he was out of the car, he used the gun as a pointer. "Go stand in the road so that I can keep an eye on you."

She stepped into the road and surreptitiously took in her surroundings, weighing her chances if she tried to run for it.

Sanders's voice cut into her thoughts. "And don't be foolish enough to try to run away. I am an excellent shot and will not hesitate to shoot." She turned to him as he opened the trunk and extracted a backpack, which reminded her that she was completely unprepared for a mountain hike. She silently thanked Philippe for the filling breakfast. In spite of the memory, or perhaps because of it, her stomach growled.

Sanders motioned with the gun for her to walk ahead of him to a path that veered off the road and across a field. She took a few steps out from under the trees and into the field and saw what she supposed was Mt. Valier looming in front of her. Snow still lingered on its crest as well as on the peaks flanking it. Overhead, big, puffy clouds scattered across the deep-blue dome of the sky. The sun was warm, almost hot, on her bare head. She scanned the mountain in the hope of finding help from other hikers, but found none. Where were all the people they had seen on the roads? *Sitting in their comfortable campsites by a stream eating a leisurely midday meal,* she thought to herself. Sanders poked her in the back with the gun, and they began the hike up Mt. Valier.

They had been following a switchback trail across the face of the mountain for two hours when Sebastian told her to stop. The sun was well into its descent to the western horizon, so the lengthening shadows softened the beautiful, though rough, scenery around them. Blooming heather and early wildflowers grew in tufts on the ground and rocks of all sizes were scattered around the mountainside. Rising above it all were gnarled old pines and stunted bushes that dotted the mountainside, looking like groups of old men huddled against the weather. Danny looked back down the trail and noticed dark clouds building in the east. Philippe's words of warning about how quickly the weather could change in the mountains passed through her mind. As the sun moved behind the mountains, the cool breeze that had felt good earlier against her sweaty skin now left her chilled. She bent down to rub her throbbing right knee and thought again of how unprepared she was for a night on the mountain.

Sebastian had beads of sweat on his brow and was breathing hard from the hike when he told her to stop. He sat on a large rock next to the trail to catch his breath and drink some water. He removed a water bottle from his pack, took a long drink, and was returning it to the pack when Danny asked for a drink. He put it into the pack and looked up at her as she stood on the trail a couple of feet in front of him. A grim smile touched his lips. "That would be a waste of precious water, my dear."

"What's that supposed to mean?"

"It means that you have served your purpose and that I no longer have need of your company."

Danny tilted her head and regarded him with suspicion. "You're letting me go?"

He shook his head as he rose from the rock. "Not exactly." He pulled the gun into her line of vision.

Danny took a step back and held up her hands. "Wait a second. This is crazy. Why kill me? I don't give a damn about your treasure."

"Since you lied about knowing the secret of the ring, I feel safe in assuming that you are lying now."

"Good Lord! For some crazy reason, somebody was going to a lot of trouble to steal a ring that I thought had no particular monetary value. So I became curious. You can't kill me for being curious!"

He smiled, this time with genuine amusement. "On the contrary. The fact that you are so driven by your burning curiosity is all the more reason for me to get rid of you."

"But if you shoot me and someone finds my body, it will draw attention to you and this area."

Sebastian's eyebrows went up in surprise. "Thank you for pointing that out to me. I'll just have to make sure that your body is not discovered." He raised the gun, aiming it at her heart. Danny's mouth went dry as the thought struck home that she was about to die. Her mind protested that she wasn't ready to die and that it couldn't all end like this. The wind was picking up. Looking over Sebastian's shoulder, she saw that the storm clouds she'd notice earlier were rushing toward them. The air suddenly darkened, and as he began to pull the trigger, a deafening boom exploded over their heads and rebounded off the mountain.

Danny wasn't quite sure what had happened and expected to feel pain somewhere in her body. Then, as sheets of rain burst from the cloud, the realization sank in that Sebastian had not fired the gun because the clap of thunder had startled him. He took a quick look overhead. Danny, seeing her chance, spun on her right leg and threw a kick with her left foot that knocked the gun from his hand. As her foot made contact, her right knee, weakened from the hike, buckled, and she fell to the ground. Sebastian was on top of her in an instant, his hands closing about her throat. His grip was tightening when Danny jerked her left knee up with all her might. Sebastian grunted as the pain exploded in his groin, and his grip loosened for a split second. It was all she needed. She bucked and shoved him off her and slid away from him so that she could get to her feet. The muddy trail and her sore knee slowed her effort to stand. Just as she secured her footing and stood upright, Sebastian's fist blasted into her jaw. She had a momentary sense of falling backward and then lost consciousness as she tumbled off the trail, rolling and sliding down the side of the mountain.

Geremy came around a bend in the trail and, through the driving rain, he saw Danny tumble off the trail and roll down the mountain. Sebastian was hunched over as if in pain, but he was watching Danny fall. Geremy rushed Sebastian and jumped him, causing Sebastain to lose his footing in the slippery mud. Locked in mortal combat, the two men followed Danny down the side of the mountain.

When Danny came to, she tried to move, but a sharp pain shot through her right leg and her jaw. Then she remembered where she was and how she had gotten there, but had no idea how long she had been unconscious. The thought crossed her mind that the man on the trail might get his wish. She might die there, as she knew she would not be able to get out of this predicament by herself.

She was lying, a little twisted, with the side of her left leg in full contact with the ground and her right leg, slightly bent at the knee was on top of it. She could feel the bush or tree that had stopped her descent pressing against her back and supporting her head. A larger pine tree, bent by the wind, sheltered her from the rain. She tried to twist her body to get a look around, but the pain in her leg almost made her pass out again.

Dusk was falling and mist was swirling around her, but she couldn't tell where on the mountain she had come to a stop. The only things she could see plainly were some branches from the sheltering pine and, a few feet away, some rocks and boulders that marked the edge of an outcrop. The only things she could hear were the rain, wind, and an occasional thunder clap in the distance.

She wondered what had happened to Sanders and then felt tendrils of panic begin to uncoil inside as she realized that she might be alone on the mountain. She clenched her fist to quash the panic and began to check her body for damage.

Her arms, though scratched and muddy, were not hurt. Her right knee was seriously damaged and hurt like hell, the pain throbbing with her heartbeat. Her right foot was bare. From what she could ascertain, her left leg, aside from being scratched and muddy like her arms, was not broken or otherwise seriously hurt. Last but not least, she tested her back. The examination done, she rested against the tree, breathing hard, exhausted from the exertion.

She knew the greatest danger was from shock and was grateful for the tree's protection since it was keeping most of the cold rain off her. She relaxed against the tree and found that overall she was quite comfortable as long as she did not move. The drop ... drop ... drop of the now gentle rainfall was soothing. She had begun to drowse when a shower of rocks and mud came over the top of the rock outcropping.

"Danny?" she heard Geremy yell.

Her head jerked up and relief washed over her. "I dow here," was the best she could manage with her swollen jaw. Geremy and made his way around to the sheltered area at the base of the outcrop.

When they saw each other, both were shocked at the other's appearance. Of the two, Danny looked more frightful because the rain had not washed the blood and mud off her. A cut on her scalp had left a trail of blood smeared across her forehead, and her split lip had left her mouth and chin bloody. Mud and some twigs were tangled in her hair, and mud was smeared on her right cheek and covered most of the rest of her body. Geremy feared that she might be fatally injured, and the thought closed around his heart like a vice grip. "Danny?" he asked softly.

She looked up at him and whispered, "My gah, ou ook aful!" He was reaching down to her when she saw Sebastian loom up behind him, a big rock in his hands. She screamed a warning, but not before the rock came down on Geremy's head and he fell forward across her lap. The pain that shot up from her legs nearly made her pass out, but she fought to stay conscious.

Sebastian looked down at her, the big rock still clutched in one hand, a faint, eerie, blue light bathing his mud-spattered face and clothes. Oblivious to the light, Sebastian once again raised the rock. He moved in for the killing blow, but his movement caused the rain-soaked earth to shift and he was pulled off balance. In an effort to recover, he dropped the rock, narrowly missing Danny's head.

Danny watched in horror as he swayed, his arms waving like a windmill run amuck before he slowly pitched sideways and disappeared from sight. She heard him scream, but it faded as he went down the mountain. She felt a chill when it abruptly stopped. Only the sound of sliding rocks and dirt remained to mark his passage.

Danny shivered from shock and the chill evening air. Geremy lay unconscious, and she reached out to touch his head. A dark stain matted his blond hair, and she felt the blood, warm and sticky, against her fingertips. Tears filled her eyes.

"Geremy?" she quavered. Her left hand was feeling his neck for a pulse when she noticed a glowing light above and to her right. A cave opening, unnoticed until this moment, was emitting a soft, electric-blue light that was gradually becoming brighter. To her astonishment, a man stepped out of the cave and stood like a dark cut-out against the steady stream of blue light now spilling out from the small cave opening.

In dream-like fashion, the man and two others moved slowly toward her. Warmth and peace seeped into her body as they approached. The first man came and knelt beside her while the other two attended to Geremy. Geremy groaned as they gently lifted him, but Danny moaned in pain as his weight was removed. The man next to her laid a cool palm on her forehead, and all pain in her body disappeared. He lifted her effortlessly and as they moved into the light, Danny slipped into unconsciousness.

CHAPTER NINETEEN

The first thing that registered in Danny's brain as she woke up was how incredibly soft the sheets were against her bare skin. She took a deep breath and stretched her whole body. As her arms came out from under the covers, her hands touched the cool, stone wall behind her. She opened her eyes and felt immediately disoriented. She did not recognize the room. In fact, she didn't think she'd ever before seen a room quite like it. The room was oval in shape and the rock walls were smoothly polished and a warm golden-cinnamon color. The floor was flat, but the walls curved over her head. There were no corners, no sharp angles. A soft golden light bathed the room, but Danny couldn't see any light fixtures. The walls themselves seemed to be glowing.

She moved to sit up but froze when memories flooded through her brain. She waited for pain from her leg, but when none came, she panicked, fearing that amputation had been necessary. She threw back the covers and almost fell back with relief when she saw her leg still attached to her body. In fact, not only was it still there, it did not hurt at all. She clearly remembered that she had hurt it badly in the fall, but now her leg felt fine, and she could not see any bruises, cuts, or scrapes. She rubbed her jaw and found that it too was free from pain. Her hand then moved up to her hair, which felt soft and clean. "Wow," she said out loud. "Either I've just had the most vivid dream of my life or something very weird is going on here." She looked around the room. "And I bet it's going to fall into the very weird category."

Her eyes moved over the room. The lighting was soft but bright enough to enable her to see the simple furnishings of the room, which consisted of a bed, two chairs, and a table. She noticed that one of the chairs had a turquoise gown draped over it. She eased out of the bed and cautiously put weight on her right foot, fully expecting pain to shoot through her knee. When no pain materialized, she put her full weight on it and walked slowly over to get the gown. As it slid over her head she marveled at the feel of the fabric. Like the sheets, the gown's fabric was amazingly soft. "Gotta ask them which fabric softener they use," she said as her hands smoothed the fabric against her legs. Just then, the lighting grew brighter and the most beautiful woman Danny had ever seen stepped out of what she had thought was a shadow. She wore a green gown similar to Danny's, was tall, slender, and had long, golden-brown hair that seemed to shimmer with a light of its own. Her golden-brown eyes, which matched her hair, were shaped like almonds. Her oval face had delicate features and her skin was the color of creamed coffee.

"Hello. I am Mara. Will you please come with me?" The woman turned without waiting for an answer and disappeared into the shadow. The lights in the room dimmed with her exit.

Danny sprang after her into the shadow and discovered that it was just a darkened doorway. She saw Mara a few paces ahead of her in a hallway outside her room. "Hey! Wait a second! What the heck is going on here? Where's Geremy?"

Mara stopped when she heard the fear in Danny's voice, turned toward her, and smiled. Danny immediately felt calmness wash over her. "I take you now to the one who can answer your questions much better than I." She held her hand out to Danny. "Please have no fear. You are among friends."

Danny took her hand and felt another wave of calm wash over her. Mara, still holding Danny's hand, led her down the hall and into a large circular chamber. As they entered, the hidden lights brightened, and Danny gasped at the beauty of the room. The walls were the same smooth, cinnamon-colored stone, but the domed ceiling was covered with crystalline formations that sparkled in the soft light. She was reminded of a theater-in-the-round because of the plush chairs set in concentric circles in a floor that sloped gently down to the center of the room. She stared in amazement at the massive, magnificent grouping of crystals which dominated the room's center space. She turned to make a comment to Mara, but found that her guide had left her. "Oh brother, this is really weird."

Hesitant to move too far into the room, she leaned against the wall near the door and began to consciously register the sensual information she was picking up. The floor, although stone, was smooth like the walls and warm against her bare feet. The air temperature was perfect and had a slightly spicy scent, which she found pleasant. She walked along the wall of the chamber trying to identify the light source, but to no avail. The walls themselves seemed to be glowing. She was enjoying the feel of the wall's smooth surface when she saw movement out of the corner of her eye. She turned to see Geremy standing by the door with a very handsome man. Both wore trousers and tunics of deep, forest green.

Geremy took a step toward her. In an instant, she was in his arms, her feet off the ground as he lifted and held her in an embrace so tight that she thought he would crush her. Neither of them said a word as both remembered how the other had looked the last time they had seen each other.

Geremy finally set her down, took her face in his hands, and looked into her eyes. "My God, I was scared when I saw you lying under that tree."

She smiled up at him. "You didn't look too good yourself, maestro." She pulled his right hand over and kissed his palm and then pulled it away to look at what was now only a very faint scar. The scab had completely disappeared. "Hey! What happened to the cut?"

Geremy flexed his hand. "When I woke up, it was like this."

Danny nodded. "Me, too. For a second, when I didn't feel any pain in my leg, I thought it had been amputated," she said with a nervous laugh.

"We repaired your injuries after we brought you in from outside." Danny looked at the source of the beautifully timbered voice and was awed as she considered the man who owned it. He was around six feet tall and, like the woman, his beauty was almost beyond belief. He too had skin the color of creamed coffee and golden-brown hair, but unlike her very long tresses, his curls just touched his shoulders. In the soft light of the chamber, his eyes appeared to be green, through which he regarded her with such gentle kindness that she felt a rush of tenderness for him. As if reading her mind, he smiled at her and tilted his head to the side. As she looked at him, she found she could not even begin to guess his age and realized that she couldn't have given an age for Mara, either.

"You repaired our injuries?" she asked incredulously. "What exactly does that mean?"

"Actually, we just helped the body do its job." Danny started to ask another question when he held up a hand to stop her. "Please come and sit down, and I will do my best to answer your questions when we are all more comfortable." He motioned them to some seats in front of the crystal centerpiece, which began to glow softly as they approached it.

The base of the centerpiece was a beautiful gray and black rock that Danny guessed was about seven feet in circumference and two feet high. It thrust up from the chamber floor, and Danny had the sense that the room had been built around it. From the base rock, crystals shot out in all directions. The massive, clear center crystal had six sides, looked to be about five feet around, and stood about six feet above the base rock, reaching straight up toward the ceiling. The other crystals were significantly smaller and became more so the farther they were from the center to the edge, which was covered with small amethyst crystals. Every color of the spectrum appeared to be represented in crystal on the rock before them.

Geremy gazed, transfixed by the power and beauty of the centerpiece, while Danny walked slowly around it. "I've never seen anything like this. Is it natural?" she asked in a hushed voice.

"Yes. A gift from Mother Earth." He wordlessly invited them to sit in the front row and then addressed Danny as she sat down. "Now, what would you like to know?"

"Well, for starters, who are you?"

"I apologize. I am called Dario. I am a council leader and your appointed guide during your stay in Pangea."

"Pangea? That's the name of this place?"

"Yes."

She scanned the room. "Is this some kind of secret military installation or something?"

Dario smiled and his amusement infected his voice as he responded. "No, very far from it. Pangeans are more interested in constructive rather than destructive pursuits."

"Where are we?"

"Pangea is located within the heart of the Pyrenees."

"Within the Pyrenees," she repeated. She paused for a moment as she mulled over the statement and then asked, "Is this the cave of the blue light?"

"No. The cave of the blue light is one of the doorways to Pangea. We found you outside the cave, on our doorstep, as it were."

Danny remembered the outcropping of rocks and the tree that stood in front of it. The riddle had said that the cave was in the heart of the mountain, in plain view but hidden. She shook her head at the series of events that had brought them to the very spot they had been seeking.

Geremy broke in with a question of his own. "What happened to the other man?"

"We arrived too late to be of assistance to him," Dario said dispassionately.

Danny looked a Dario more closely. "You mean he's dead?"

"Yes, he is dead."

She rubbed her throat as she remembered the feel of his thumbs pressing against her windpipe. "Well, I hate to say it, but I'm glad. He was not a nice man."

"Greed has a way of turning the best of men away from their better nature." The voice came from behind them. As they turned to see who had spoken, Danny jumped up from her seat while Geremy rose more slowly from his.

"I thought you said he was dead," she said to Dario as the man came down the aisle toward them.

"The man who tried to harm you is dead. This is Albert Sanders."

Danny and Geremy looked from Dario to Albert, a puzzled expression on both their faces. Geremy, who'd only had a brief encounter with Sebastian, would have sworn they were the same man, but Danny had spent hours with him and could see the differences between the two men. Albert's eyes were a soft blue, not icy gray like Sebastian's, and Albert was shorter than Sebastian. Most of all, Albert *felt* different than Sebastian, who had radiated a tension that was missing from the man now standing in front of them. As he stood there, radiating a gentle charm, Danny took an immediate liking to him.

"Are you related to Sebastian Sanders?" Geremy asked.

Albert transferred his gaze to Dario, who nodded back at him. "Sebastian was my grandson."

Danny was dumbfounded. "Your grandson? That can't be possible! You look more like his younger brother."

"Be that as it may, he was my grandson," he said.

Feeling uneasy but unable to say why, she inched closer to Geremy who stood calmly regarding Albert Sanders and hoped that some of his calmness would rub off onto her. So far, her initial assessment that this experience was going to fall under the weird category was way off the mark. The experience fell more into the realm of the surreal.

Sensing her apprehension, Dario looked at Danny with compassion. "I can assure you that you have nothing to fear here."

As she returned his gaze, the wave of calm she'd felt earlier with Mara washed over her again. The apprehension melted away leaving her to wonder at their power to dispel anxiety.

Albert moved to her and took one of her hands. "I understand completely your feelings, my dear. I was just as bewildered when I arrived, but I can assure you there is no safer, more wonderful place on this planet then right here in Pangea." He released her hand and motioned for them to sit down while he and Dario remained standing.

Geremy looked skeptical. "I must confess I find it hard to believe that you are the grandfather to the man who abducted Danny. He looked to be around fifty years old, so you'd have to be at least eighty."

"In actual fact, I am one hundred and sixteen years old."

"That's impossible."

"You may rest assured that I speak the truth, though I admit the idea does take some getting used to." His hands moved back to rest on the rock behind him, and Danny leaned forward in her seat to get a better look at his left hand.

"The ring! You're wearing the ring!"

He pulled his hand forward and briefly scrutinized the ring before removing it and handing it over to Danny. "Sebastian was wearing it when we found him. Since it was originally mine, I removed it before he was buried."

Danny held the ring gingerly between her index finger and thumb and leaned back in her chair, every fiber in her body pulsing with fatigue as she tried to assimilate the information she was hearing. "Would someone please tell me what the hell is going on here?"

"That, Miss Davis, is exactly what we propose to do. If you will just sit back and relax, I will tell you how I first came to Pangea. Then we will both describe the chain of events that have resulted in your presence here now."

"Thank you, Mr. Sanders. Please proceed."

"Please call me Albert," he said with a gentle smile. "In 1898, I came to the Pyrenees as part of a botanical expedition. I was a student at Oxford and had been invited to participate in the expedition by one of my professors. The third day out, I wandered from the camp, walked off the trail, and ranged all over Mt. Valier. I was not paying attention to my route. When I looked up to get my bearings, I found I didn't have a clue as to where I was. I felt as if I had been sleepwalking, because I couldn't remember where I had been either. Darkness was descending and the wind had picked up, so I decided that, rather than get more lost and possibly injured stumbling around in the dark, I would spend the night in a cave I had discovered."

"Let me guess. The cave of the blue light?"

He nodded and continued. "I fell asleep, and the next thing I knew, a spark of blue light at the back of the cave wakened me. I sat, terrified and rooted to the ground, and watched as the light grew from a spark into a ball and finally into a doorway. In my fear, I passed out only to waken later in a warm, softly lit chamber. Like you, I was initially fearful and found what the Pangeans told me hard to swallow. But very soon, I saw that all they had told me of Pangea was true, and I came to bless the day I stumbled into that cave."

As he relayed the story, Albert became quite animated and his prowess as a storyteller took over. Danny was caught in the spell of his story and briefly forgot her fatigue and confusion. When he paused, she leaned forward, her face bright with curiosity. "If you liked it so much, why did you leave?"

He gave her a quizzical look. "How did you know I left?"

"Sebastian told me that his grandfather, you, disappeared in 1898 and then reappeared in 1903. He believed that you'd found a hidden treasure. Actually, he thought it was the legendary treasure of the Knights Templar and that it rightfully belonged to him."

"And he was using the map on the ring to find the treasure?"

"Yes." She rubbed her throat again. "And he nearly killed me in the process."

"It would appear that my love for telling a good story is at the root of your misadventure."

"How so?" Geremy asked.

Albert turned to Geremy. "I feel responsible because when my children, Henry and Amelia, were small, they loved stories, the more fanciful the better. One night, I told them about the secret cave, and before I realized what was going on in their imaginations, they had turned my simple cave with wise people into a gem-encrusted cavern filled with gold and silver and guarded by magical beings. Henry obviously passed that story onto Sebastian, and that's how he became fixated on finding the treasure."

"And all he found was death," Danny said softly.

Dario stepped forward from the centerpiece and said, "My friends, we must now stop for you need food and rest." He saw that Danny was about to ask another question and held up his hand. "You have a quick and inquisitive mind, Danny. You will learn much here, but for now you need rest."

Danny had to agree with him as she felt her stomach rumble. "Where do we go to get some food?"

"You may eat in the common area or you may eat in your room."

Danny wanted to get Geremy alone so that they could talk about what they had heard. "Do you mind if we eat in one of our rooms? I don't think I'm up for a social engagement."

"My room is bigger than yours, so we should eat there."

"Great." She paused. "How do you know how big my room is?"

He chucked her under the chin. "While you were sleeping, I was given a tour. I naturally wanted to know how you were, so that was the first place they took me."

"Can you find your way back to your room?" Dario asked Geremy.

"Yes, I believe so."

"Good. Your meal will be brought to you there."

"Thank you, Dario."

He bowed slightly. "Until our next session, then." They filed up the aisle and out the door with Dario being the last one out. As he passed through the door, the lights dimmed.

CHAPTER TWENTY

Danny and Geremy took a leisurely pace as they made their way back to Geremy's room. When they arrived, a meal of steamed vegetables, rice, freshly baked bread, fruit, and water was waiting for them.

They ate in silence for a few minutes, enjoying the delicate flavors of the food that worked so well to assuage their hunger. Both were also thinking about what they had just heard.

Danny laid her fork on her plate. "You seem incredibly unperturbed in the midst of this very weird experience. I don't know why, but this place feels kind of creepy to me. All these people living here, underground. Who are they?"

"I was uneasy when I first woke up and a little suspicious of Dario when he first arrived in my room, but after talking to him for a couple of hours, I came to trust him. Even after he told me where Pangeans come from."

"Ah! Please relieve my curiosity."

He ate another bite of food before speaking. "The answer may not make you feel any better. According to Dario, the people of Pangea are descended from a group of people who left Atlantis before the final earthquake that caused it to sink into the Atlantic."

"You're kidding!"

"That's what he told me."

"And you believe him?"

He paused for a moment and then said, "Yes, I believe him. I could not detect one ounce of subterfuge in the man, so it's either true or he is the most amazing liar I've ever met."

"Just because he believes his ancestors came from Atlantis doesn't necessarily make it true. But if he believes it, he can assert it without apparent dishonesty."

"True enough, but there certainly is something a little different going on here."

Danny gave a short laugh. "A little different? Major weird, is more like it. Take the lights, for example. I don't see any light fixtures, but there is light in here. It's like the walls are glowing. And there's no light switches as far as I can tell. The room gets lighter or darker, but I don't see any dimmer switches or even anyone touching anything to change the light level." Without thinking, she began to rub her knee as if to soothe an ache.

Watching her, Geremy asked, "Knee bothering you?"

She pulled her hand away and looked at her knee. She realized that the low-level ache she'd experienced ever since the car wreck was completely gone. "As a matter of fact, no. For the first time in years, it *doesn't* hurt. I guess the rubbing has just become a habit."

Silence once again reigned as, lost in thought, they finished their meal. Danny leaned back in her chair and sighed. "I didn't realize how hungry I was until Dario said 'food,' and now that I'm full, I'm ready for a nap."

He came around the table and held out his hand. "Come on. I could use a lie-down myself." They crawled into bed and lay in each others arms.

"Now if we could just figure out how to dim the lights," Danny murmured. The lights instantly dimmed. Her eyes opened wider, and she looked around. "Wow! Did you see that?"

"See what?" Geremy mumbled, his eyes closed.

"The lights! They dimmed when I told them to."

"That's good," he whispered before falling asleep. She nestled next to him under the sheet and pondered the lights for a moment until she too was fast asleep.

—

They were just finishing breakfast when Albert came into their room. Looking at Danny, he asked, "Now that you are rested and refreshed, would you like a tour of Pangea?"

"Is this an invitation for me or for us?" she responded.

"Geremy has already had the tour, so Dario has other plans for him." Albert's gaze moved to Geremy. "He asks that you meet him in the crystal theater."

Danny looked over at Geremy. "See you later?"

Geremy nodded and followed Albert and Danny out the door, turning to the left as they went to the right. As they walked away, Geremy could hear Danny asking Albert about the lights. He smiled as he walked off in the direction of the crystal theater. The hall he followed meandered like a river through the mountain, and as he walked, he enjoyed the feel of the smooth, warm stone against his bare feet. During the tour with Dario, he had been surprised to see that everyone he met was barefoot. He was in the company of kindred spirits.

He passed many rooms, most of which had darkened doorways, and other hallways leading to who-knows-where. The walk was visually stimulating and entertaining because of all the beautiful works of art exhibited everywhere. Colorful tapestries hung from the arched ceiling and moved with the air currents. Paintings hung from the walls and were interspersed with figurines and small sculptures on pedestals. Where hallways met, large sculptures anchored the center of the intersection.

He arrived at the crystal theater before Dario and found it dark. He entered and loudly said, "Lights up." The lights became very bright, and he squinted. "Far out!" With a self-satisfied smile, he proceeded down to the centerpiece.

Dario came into the theater and squinted at the brightness. He mentally pulsed for the lights to dim slightly and walked down to Geremy, who was touching and examining the crystal centerpiece. Geremy jumped back when it suddenly began to glow. Dario laughed. "Sorry. I thought you would find it more enjoyable if some light were emanating from it." He sat in a front row chair. "Go ahead. Put your hand on it, and tell me what you sense."

Geremy put his hand back on the blue crystal. "I feel a vibration that wasn't there a moment ago."

Dario nodded. "The greater the light, the stronger the vibration."

Geremy ran his hand along the smoky quartz crystal next to the blue one. "This one is warmer than it was a moment ago, but I don't feel any vibration."

"Each crystal vibrates at a different frequency, which we feel or sense in different ways. The molecules in the smoky crystal are moving, but at such a fast rate that it registers as heat to the touch."

"What about the center crystal?"

"Touch it."

He reached up tentatively and lightly ran his fingers across one of its six faces. He gave Dario an incredulous look as he pressed his whole palm to the surface. "I hear musical tones, almost like wind chimes!"

Dario stepped up and put his hand on the crystal. To Geremy, the tones became the music of flutes. He smiled as he 'listened.'

"Oh, my God. That's beautiful!"

Dario smiled at his obvious enjoyment. "Like everything in the universe, different crystals vibrate at different frequencies."

Geremy looked from Dario to the crystals and then back at Dario. "Before you arrived, the crystals were dormant. Are you making them do this?"

"The crystals respond to a thought frequency that I send, but each crystal receives the frequency to which it is attuned and then vibrates accordingly."

"Do you have ESP as well?"

"Yes."

"Then you can read my thoughts?"

"Yes. And yes, I will answer your questions about Atlantis," Dario said with a smile. He gestured toward the chairs. "Please sit down."

Geremy nodded and settled into the plush chair, his eyes watching as Dario chose to lean against the crystal base so that they were facing each other.

"Is reincarnation real?"

"Yes. And yes, you did live in Atlantis."

Geremy looked at him surprise.

Dario laughed at his expression. "Forgive me. Most of our communication here is telepathic, and it is sometimes difficult for me to shut out the thoughts of those who are not versed in telepathic communication."

"Then you know my next question?"

"Yes, but now I will close the door so that I will not see your thoughts. As for your question, yes you know Danny from your life in Atlantis."

"Can you tell me about my relationship with her then?"

A faraway look came to Dario's eyes as he stared at the far wall. His voice was subdued as he replied, "I can give you some information about that life." He fell silent for a moment. Then he cleared his throat and began to narrate.

"You and others that you know in this life lived in Atlantis. You were a famous actor, bringing stories of the past to life. Your plays were filled with magic, wizards, and heroic deeds, so people came from far and wide to see your performances."

"No wonder I've always been so enthralled by myths!"

"Yes, a mirror of sorts of your skills in that life. You were greatly admired for your skills as well as for your physical beauty. You were presented with choices in that life, and the paths you chose did little to broaden your emotional horizons, though you learned other lessons you had set for yourself."

"You can't tell me where I took the wrong turn, can you?"

"It was not a wrong turn. It was a choice. Every choice brings with it some form of illumination."

"What about Danny? Can you tell me about her?"

"Of course. Danny, or Layne as was her name in the other life, was an artist. In her youth, she possessed neither wealth nor beauty, but her heart was pure, and she was a talented painter. She eventually became one of the greatest and wealthiest painters Atlantis ever produced, perfecting a particular style that only two others were able to emulate. Only one of her paintings still exists. It hangs not far from here."

—

Danny paused to admire a painting hanging within a glass enclosure on the wall. The painting was a three-by-three-foot square, and when she first looked at it, she thought it was just an abstract pattern of very vibrant colors. But as she continued to stare at it, she had the impression that the colors were moving and began to see the face of a man take shape. She blinked a couple of times in disbelief before the paint stopped its movement, and she was looking into the eyes of a very handsome man.

His green eyes seemed to sparkle with humor as he looked out at her, his sensuous mouth curved into a rakish smile. His dark brown hair was pulled back from his face, but as she looked at the painting, she had an image of what it had looked like unbound and could almost feel the texture of it against her fingertips. She was disconcerted by how familiar the laughing eyes felt as she gazed into them.

Albert stood back from the painting and watched her as she watched the painting. "One of the finest painters Atlantis produced. The man in the portrait was a famous actor in his day."

"When was his day?"

"Ten thousand years ago."

"You're telling me that this portrait is ten thousand years old?"

Albert nodded as he steered her into a dimly lit cavern. The only light came from a narrow, soft-yellow band that glowed near the floor. Very little light carried up to the peaked ceiling where crystals twinkled like stars in the night sky.

"This is the night chamber."

"It's beautiful," she said softly, not wanting to disturb the hushed atmosphere in the cavern. After standing quietly for a few moments, they continued on their way. They came out into a narrow hallway that then lead them to a hallway of shops. One shop displayed works of art where Danny saw another painting.

"Why doesn't the paint in that painting move like the other one?"

"The medium used in the portrait is not paint as you and I know it. The artist used a medium that she discovered, some kind of liquid pigment that has magnetic properties. Only a couple of people were able to master the technique that was lost when Atlantis sank. The portrait you saw is the only known example of it in the world. The paint, for lack of a better word, reacts to the magnetic charge of the viewer. When we walked away, the paint became a random color sequence again, and it will stay that way until the next viewer arrives. Interestingly enough, since the paint reacts to the viewer, the portrait exhibits subtle differences from viewer to viewer."

"Who was the artist?"

"Her name was Layne."

"A woman?"

"Yes."

"But how can something that old still be around? Shouldn't it be dust about now?"

"On the outside it would be, but time does not pass in Pangea the way it does on the surface. That's why I don't look any older than I do."

Danny shook her head. "Is it something about the air or water? Is that why you haven't aged?"

Albert smiled. "No, Danny, it's not the air or the water. The best explanation I can give right now is that we simply live in the moment. When you live in the moment, time does not pass. All of your consciousness is in the moment *now*. Are my efforts to explain the concept helping you to understand?"

"Right now, no, but I'll let you know if a light bulb goes on."

They passed under an archway, and suddenly they were in a sunny park, complete with trees, birds, and a brook. "This is amazing!" They stopped at a fountain splashing clear, cold water and sat down. "Did you come back because you didn't want to grow old?"

"No. I came back because I yearned for the peace and openness I'd experienced here. I had returned to England, married, and had two children, but I was different from everyone else. I was not interested in the dramas that held others so enthralled. When the First World War ended and I'd seen so much death and destruction, I knew if I didn't return to Pangea, I'd die. When I left Pangea, Dario gave me the ring and he told me that I would return one day."

"Dario? The same Dario I met earlier?"

"The very same."

"How old is he?" Astonishment made her voice squeak.

"I don't really know. He was here when I arrived in 1898, looking much the same as he does now."

"Wow. That's amazing." She shook her head in wonder. "But wasn't he afraid that, once you were outside, you'd tell people about Pangea and reveal its secret location?"

Albert laughed. "This place is not a secret, Danny. The only reason its existence is not consciously acknowledged by more people is because of the narrow concept that most people hold of reality. For example, I did tell my brother about Pangea, but he could not accept what I told him. He thought I was suffering from a delusion and was very concerned about my mental health. I learned from his reaction that people would not be able to accept what I had to say. So I made up a simple, believable story about amnesia, and they accepted it." He bent over and swirled the cold water with his hand. "There have been visitors who've recounted what they experienced here and elsewhere, but they did it in fiction stories, songs, and music. The details change from story to story or song to song, but they are still about one community or another. These stories and songs plant possibilities in the minds of people." He gave her a mischievous smile as he shook the water from his hand. "You, in fact, may one day write about us."

"Me? What, in a music publication between articles about The Rolling Stones and Bon Jovi?" She shook her head. "Nah. Wouldn't fit the format."

He smiled. "You will not always confine yourself to music publications, Danny." He stood. "Come, let us continue our walk."

CHAPTER TWENTY ONE

Dario continued to lean casually against the crystal centerpiece. "Would you like to walk while we continue our conversation or would you prefer to remain here in the theater?"

"I'd rather stay in here. I like being near the crystals," Geremy replied.

"As you wish."

"So, your ancestors left Atlantis before it sank in order to preserve as much of their culture as possible?"

"Yes. A number of groups set out from Atlantis, each traveling to a different part of the world, and these groups became the seeds for the communities which exist today."

"Pangea is not the only place like this?"

"No. Other mountain communities exist, or have existed, in the Himalayas, the Andes, the Rockies, and the Scottish Highlands. Additionally, there is one community in the Australian Outback, one in central Africa, and one in Syria."

"Why those places? Is there something special about them?"

"They are outlets for the earth's energy. The groups were drawn by the high vibrational frequencies that permeate the areas. My ancestors were attracted to the spots in much the same way that people continue to be drawn to them. You, for example."

"I was just following Danny, and she was brought to the area by Sebastian."

Dario smiled. "People rarely recognize or acknowledge the pull. They can always find a rational explanation to account for their seemingly accidental arrival at Pangea, or at the other communities, for that matter." He straightened and slid his hand across the face of the clear, center crystal. "But I can assure you, Geremy, that no one arrives here by accident. Most are responding to the frequency alone. Albert falls into this category."

"What about Danny and me?"

"We invited you."

"What? You invited us? And how exactly did you do that?"

Dario thought for a moment before answering. "People vibrate in much the same way as these crystals. We sensed your vibration and felt you would benefit from a visit here."

"What about Sebastian? Was he invited?"

"No. Sebastian was following physical clues. Without the heart element, no one finds entrance to Pangea."

"Are you going to tell me why you invited us here?"

"Coupled with your higher vibration, both you and Danny have a great talent for communication. You've already proven your ability to communicate the higher frequency through your songs. Danny has yet to actualize her talent."

Geremy shrugged. "I just write what comes to me."

"Are you aware that much of the music you write consists of tones which induce a higher vibrational state in many of the people who hear it?"

"I don't think I ever thought of it that way. It seems to make both them and me feel good. That's all I ever noticed."

"Well, now you know why it makes them 'feel good.' They are experiencing the higher vibrational frequency that promotes a sense of cosmic union."

"I take it that you believe Danny is doing the same thing?"

"Yes, but in a different manner."

"If we're already doing it, then why did you 'invite' us here?"

Danny shook her head emphatically. "But I wasn't drawn here by any mystical power. Sebastian brought me here. He's the one who was drawn here, not me."

Albert laughed. "You would not believe how many times I have heard someone say that their arrival at Pangea was totally accidental, myself included. Sebastian was certainly drawn to this area, but for reasons that would not have brought him to the cave of the blue light. He would have wandered the mountains like his father before him and left in the same state of disappointment. You, on the other hand, would have found the cave because both you and Geremy were invited."

She stopped walking and shook her head as she looked at Albert. "Invited?"

"Let me explain the chain of events that brought you here." He coaxed her back into a stroll.

"That would be very helpful."

"When Henry gave the ring to your mother, Dario became specifically aware of her."

"Is the ring a transmitter or something?"

"Yes, it does carry a signature frequency. Through it, Dario was able to identify your mother's specific frequency, her own signature frequency, if you will."

"My mother had a signature frequency?"

"Yes, as do you. Everyone emits their own particular frequency. Dario and some other Pangeans have the ability to sense the frequencies as a mass, but they can also hone in on individual frequencies, the ones that stand out or rise above the others. Dario, in following the ring's signal, found your mother. He thought she would come to Pangea because she carried a strong, high-vibrational signal that would have found great resonance here. But she found a resonance in another person out there."

"Papa."

"Yes. Together, they were a very strong force. Dario maintained an awareness of them and through them, of you and your brother. Your parents shared a great love with each other and with their children. That love is the source of the high vibrational frequency, and the signal is strong in you."

"Now you're starting to sound like Obi-wan Kenobi in Star Wars." Her voice deepened. "Yes, the force is strong in my family."

Albert laughed. "Well, the concepts are synonymous. You can call the energy anything you like. We name it as frequency because that's how the Pangeans perceive it."

"We? Do you consider yourself a Pangean?"

"Yes."

"Do you think you'll ever go back? To England, I mean."

"No."

"Albert, will we be allowed to leave when we're ready?"

"Yes, of course, Danny. You and Geremy were not brought here under false pretenses. You may leave whenever you like."

"We won't get out there and find that five years have passed, will we?"

"That depends on when you decide you're ready to go. My experience is that most people find the idea of leaving difficult to contemplate. I know I did not relish it."

"Well, I guess I'm not going to leave until somebody tells me why I was 'invited' here in the first place."

Danny's attention was drawn to a small group of youngsters gathered around one of the doors leading into the crystal theater. She watched the group thin as the children filed into the theater.

Albert gestured toward the children. "Come on. I think you'll enjoy this."

They entered the theater behind the last child. Albert motioned her to follow him as he slid along the wall and away from the door. When he saw them enter, Geremy made his way to the back of the theater and stood beside Danny.

"Dario is about to give a lesson to the children on connecting with the crystal," Albert explained.

Ten children who looked to be around six years old stood in a semi-circle facing the crystal centerpiece. Dario stood at the far end of the line and faced the children. No one spoke, but a dull glow began to emanate from all the crystals on the centerpiece. The glow grew until the centerpiece was so bright it was hard to look at. It remained that bright for a couple of heartbeats and then gradually dimmed until it was once again dormant. Danny saw the look of wonder and pleasure on the faces of the children.

"Did they do that?" she asked Albert.

"No, that was Dario. He was showing them how to use the mind to connect with the crystals. Now it's their turn, but they will give a verbal command. Mental commands come later."

Each child, in turn, gave the crystal grouping a verbal command to glow. As each child tried, one and sometimes two of the smaller crystals would glow faintly.

"Dario wants the children to feel their individual power, but as you will see, he also wants them to understand that the group working as one is more powerful than the individual." After the last child had given his command, Dario instructed them to use the command as a group. When they did so, all of the small and medium-sized crystals began to glow.

Danny watched the expressions on the faces of the children as they focused on the crystals after verbalizing the command. She saw intense concentration that became more strained the longer the children concentrated. Dario told them to stop, and the crystal dimmed immediately.

As the lesson continued for the children, Danny leaned over to Geremy and whispered, "I think this means we have a first-grader's aptitude for environmental manipulation."

Geremy grinned and whispered back. "I bet they have already completely mastered the environmental lighting process so that probably puts us at the kindergarten level."

Danny tugged on Albert's sleeve. "Can they adjust the brightness of room lights with just thoughts or do they have to make verbal commands?"

Albert shook his head. "Lighting is very simple. They can manipulate the brightness before they begin to speak. The crystals require highly focused energy, so verbal commands are required at first."

Danny cast a discouraged look at Geremy. "Looks like our mental abilities rank lower than the six-month-old group."

"Guess we've got a lot of learning to do while we're here." They turned their attention back to the children. Their lesson completed, the children made their way back up the aisle toward the door. Albert nodded to Dario, turned to Danny, and gave her a slight bow. "I will escort the children, so I'll leave you with these two fortunate gentlemen." Stepping past Danny, he extended his hand to the last child in line. They left the theater hand in hand.

Geremy pulled on her arm. "Come here. I want to show you something." As he approached Dario, Geremy decided to try mental communication. *Dario?*

Dario turned and smiled. *Yes?* he pulsed back to Geremy.

Will you make the crystals glow for Danny?

The crystals began to glow faintly. Geremy took her hand and placed it on the center crystal, watching her expression as she heard the music.

"What do you hear?"

A look of wonder covered her face. "I hear a sound like woodwind instruments."

Geremy put his hand on the crystal and heard music that was different from the flutes he'd heard with Dario. The music still sounded like wind chimes, but now the tones were deeper. Dario then placed his hand on the crystal, and the tones became music that each of them experienced in their own way.

Geremy pulled his hand from the center crystal and pointed to the smoky one near Danny. "Try that one. Each one feels different."

She laid her hand first on the smoky crystal and felt its warmth and then brushed her fingertips across an amethyst cluster and felt a cool tingling in her fingers. "That's wonderful! How does it work?"

Dario laid his hand on a smoky crystal. "I have accelerated the molecules in the crystals, and each crystal reacts differently to the stimulus. If you put your hand on a light pink crystal, you will not consciously sense anything."

They did as he suggested and found he spoke the truth. "But when next you sleep, you will likely experience more vivid dreams because that crystal connects with your subconscious mind." He removed his hand from the smoky crystal, and the centerpiece slowly dimmed. "Now, I want to tell you why you are here. Would you care to sit while I explain?"

They claimed a pair of front row seats and waited for Dario to begin. He was staring at the center crystal, his back to them as if in communion with the crystals. After a moment, he turned to them.

"Atlantis was a great civilization. The people had a vast knowledge of science, healing, and the arts. They understood the mechanics of the universe and so created a civilization of unrivaled beauty and achievement. Sadly, wisdom did not keep pace with knowledge, and many of the people became arrogant toward other civilizations that they deemed were inferior to Atlantis. Atlanteans thus used their superior powers to subjugate the other cultures, which lead to the catastrophe that sank the continent of Atlantis. The people who established Pangea did not share the arrogant attitude of their brothers, and when they foresaw the impending changes, they decided to leave before the catastrophe struck. They were determined to guard the memories of humanity's birthright until humans were ready to reclaim it."

Danny tilted her head. "What 'birth right'?"

"The right to live free from fear, to experience the joy of each moment, to consciously create form from thought."

"Oh, yeah. *That* birthright." She settled back into her seat and tucked her legs up under her.

"Throughout the ages, we have guarded this treasure, helping any on the outside who seek a deeper understanding of their nature."

"Seekers of the flowering heart," Geremy said quietly.

"As I explained earlier, Geremy, every time you connect with the higher frequency, an energy exchange occurs. You not only access the signal, you also boost it. Then, through your music, you pass the frequency onto others."

He turned his penetrating gaze to Danny. "As for you, while you make regular forays into the ether, you have not yet found the medium through which to communicate what you have received. You are carrying a burden that blocks your expression."

Danny slid her feet out from under her and sat up. "What do you mean?" she asked cautiously.

"Both of you, in fact, carry the past into the present in a manner that inhibits further expansion."

"But I thought you said that Geremy was helping others to access the higher frequency through his music."

"He does, but he has reached a ceiling and, like you, will not be able to move beyond it until the past is released."

"And that's why you invited us here? To help us get in touch with our past?" Danny asked incredulously.

"We want to help you release the past, not just get in touch with it."

"But why? What's it to you?"

"Can it not simply be the joy of helping another human being to a higher potential?"

"It could, but then why not just anybody who happens to be hiking in the mountains rather than inviting certain people? And why not invite some world leaders? Seems to me, you'd have a more powerful impact on the world if you invited them."

"Danny, you and I have different definitions for the term 'world leaders.' As far as I am concerned, we do invite the world's leaders here."

"I write articles for music publications, for Pete's sake. My writing an article about Sting is not likely to change the world."

"You'd be surprised," Dario said with a smile. "The written word has toppled empires."

"They were not writing about rock-and-roll music."

"One point I feel I must reiterate, Danny, is that we do not randomly choose those whom we help. We simply become aware of those who are attuned to the frequency, whether they be king or fishmonger. And whoever comes to us, whether they are specifically invited like you or simply drawn to the signal, like Albert, receives help. We help them to expand beyond the capabilities they have when they arrive."

Geremy, who had been quietly listening to the discussion, stood and walked to the centerpiece. "First you tell me that I connect with this frequency that promotes cosmic union and that, through my music, I pass it onto my fans. Now you tell me that while I have been doing a pretty good job, I could be doing it better if I'd just release the past."

"Geremy, both you and Danny communicate a deep-felt love to the world around you. That you both use your life energy to bring your dearest dreams to life—or in current vernacular, that you are doing what you love most—increases the amount of love that you have to communicate. Love is the frequency that activates the flowering heart, and through your powers of communication, you both nurture the 'bud of love' in the hearts of the people who come in contact with you or your works.

"Within yourselves, the flower is coming into bloom, but the blooming process has been arrested because fear and bitterness about past events has restricted the frequency. The analogy is of the rose that begins to bloom, but slows its growth when the flow of water is restricted. I want to help you set your fear and bitterness aside so that the rose can come into full bloom."

"But why?" Danny asked insistently.

"It's really very simple. While we do realize great joy when we help others, the main reason is that each time another person becomes conscious of their connection to the frequency, the easier it becomes to reach even more people with the higher vibration. When enough people connect with the higher vibration, the harmonics of the planet will shift, and people will be ready to accept the treasure we have guarded through the ages."

"What past are you talking about, and how do you propose to help us release it?"

"In answering the first question, I will take the first step toward fulfilling the intent of the second question. The first step toward releasing a burden is to recognize its existence. For you, Danny, the great love you felt for your parents is slowly being eaten away by the bitterness you feel toward the man who caused their death. This bitterness will grow until it casts a shadow over the love you hold for your parents."

He paused as Geremy went back to his seat and sat down. "And Geremy, the great love you felt as a young man for a woman was initially a catalyst for accessing the higher frequency. The love has turned in on itself, and now it restricts your expansion." He paused long enough to let his words sink in. "Some find it difficult to contemplate the shadows within their soul, but illumination makes the shadows fade." His manner became more brisk as he faced them. "And now I must leave to attend to other matters."

"That's it? You're going to leave us with that?" Danny was dumbfounded.

Dario smiled shrewdly. "A wise teacher encourages the students to discover a portion of the lesson on their own. After you have considered what I have said, we will talk again." He gave a small bow and walked up the aisle to the door.

For a while, neither one of them spoke as they thought about what Dario had said. Danny felt the truth behind his words, but she didn't know how to get past the anger she felt toward the man who'd caused the wreck. She then thought about what Dario had said to Geremy.

"Are you still in love with her?" she asked, breaking into his thoughts.

Geremy did not respond immediately. He was leaning forward in his chair, his elbows resting on his spread knees as he examined the scar on his palm. He ran his index finger over it a few times before speaking. "I don't know. It's been a long time, but her memory still haunts me. I've never been free of the feeling of loss I experienced when she disappeared."

"Had you known her long?"

Geremy got up, walked to the crystals, turned, and leaned against them as he told Danny about Maggie.

"Not quite a year. I met her about four months before the release of our first album. She was the friend of a friend of Miles's. The Celts were playing a gig in Birmingham, and she came with the friend to see us. When we met, it was love at first sight. It was the most amazing feeling. We were crazy about each other. We saw each other at every possible opportunity, which wasn't as much as either of us would have liked because the band was finishing work on the album.

"Well, that album was released, and the Celts became instant celebrities. Four months after the release, we were booked for a world tour, ten months on the road. Before I left, I asked her to marry me when the tour was over, and she said yes. When she saw me off at the airport, she said that she loved me and would be waiting for me when I returned.

"For the first two months of the tour, we were in steady contact. Then, she told me that she was planning a trip to France and that she'd call me when she returned. That was the last time I spoke to her. When I didn't hear from her, I called her flat and was told that the line had been disconnected. I didn't know what to do. Finally, I hired a private detective to find her. He discovered that she had booked passage on a ferry that had capsized in the channel. Twelve of the passengers drowned and four of them were never found. Since she was listed as a passenger and her body was not recovered, the authorities listed her as a casualty of the disaster."

He fell silent. Danny recognized the faraway look on his face, only this time the look reflected the pain he felt as he thought about the past. He pulled himself back to the present and looked at Danny, sadness in his eyes. "Her ghost has haunted me ever since."

"The love songs, like 'Where Have You Gone?' are about her." Danny could feel her insides tightening.

He gave a pained laugh. "Yes. The myths were a perfect way for me to express myself without the world knowing that it was I who was searching for his lost love. The irony was that the songs were tremendously successful and made me very wealthy, but I was empty on the inside.

"For the first few years, I was in the twilight zone. I was still so much in love and longed so for her that I poured my heart into the songs. More tremendous success, more money, but still empty."

"Then the band took the break and you 'wandered'?"

He nodded. " I had resolved to forget her and entered my disastrous marriage in the mid-seventies. After the divorce, I had a number of relationships, but realized that I was trying to find someone who could excite the same feelings I had for Maggie. I went from woman to woman trying to find what I'd lost, but all I found was disappointment." He sat down in his chair and took Danny's hand. "Then I just gave up. Thought I'd had the big one, and that was it. I figured love like that doesn't happen twice in one lifetime."

Danny turned her head away and tried to pull her hand from his grip. He held tight, using his other hand to turn her face back to him so that he could look into her eyes. "Then I turned around one day and saw you standing in a doorway. The heart that I thought was dead began to beat again." She blinked and a tear fell on his hand.

"How can you still be in love with a woman who died over twenty-five years ago?"

"I don't know. For years, she just didn't feel dead to me." He sighed. "Since they never found her body, I kept hoping— believing—that one day she'd reappear." He examined the scar on his palm once again before saying quietly, "But she never did." He stood up. "I need to walk. Will you come with me? We can find out if we received the same tour."

They followed the route that Albert had taken with Danny as they continued to talk.

"Philippe told me a little more about the accident, how scared he was when he saw you all bandaged up. Will you tell me about it?"

She nodded. "I came to and saw Philippe before he saw that I was awake. His face was the color of ash. Then when he looked at me, I knew my parents were dead. I was doped up for a few weeks until I asked for the doctor to lay off the drugs because I hated feeling so out of it. The physical pain was excruciating, but the grief I felt for my parents was even more terrible. It was made worse by the fact that I couldn't move. I couldn't walk or run or swim or throw things or do anything physical that might have helped me get it out of my system. Before the wreck, whenever something was on my mind or if I was depressed, I would run, sometimes for hours. The physical activity helped me work through things. But after the wreck, I couldn't do anything, and the scene leading up to the wreck just kept going through my mind over and over again until I thought I would go insane. I wanted so badly, as I lay there reliving it, to tell Papa to take a left turn or stop at a shop or something to avoid the wreck. But I couldn't do anything." She stopped talking. They continued to walk in silence for a few minutes before she resumed.

"Philippe knew what I was going through, so one day he brought a word processor into my room. That's when I re-discovered how much I loved to write. I don't even remember what I wrote about. All I know is that, whatever it was, it released me from the mental prison I was in. It was hard at first because my right arm was broken in two places, so I was typing with just my left hand, but the challenge of figuring out how to do it took my mind off the wreck and my pain. Then physical therapy started, and I was completely absorbed by that. The doctors were not optimistic about my recovery, so I set out to prove them wrong. It was so grand to be able to move even if it did hurt like hell. The sheer exhaustion I felt at the end of each day helped me set my grief aside long enough to get a new grip on life." She fell quiet again and looked over at him. "You know, I've never really told anyone about that time. It feels good to talk about it."

They had been walking aimlessly when Danny realized that they were near the entrance to the night chamber.

"Did Dario take you into the night chamber?"

"No."

She steered him toward the door, and they were presently within the cool, quiet chamber of the night. No one else was there, so they wandered to a dark corner and sat down in a reclining chair made to hold two people and watched the 'stars.'

Lost in their own thoughts, neither spoke for a while. Both were enjoying the soothing affect of cool air and the twinkling crystals in the dim light. Feeling chilled, Danny snuggled close to Geremy. He raised his arm and put it around her, drawing her to him so that her head rested on his chest.

"You said you set your grief aside. Did you ever work it out of your system?" he asked, his voice soft and low.

She thought about the dream and the overwhelming feeling of drowning she'd experienced when she tried to process her grief soon after the wreck. "No, I don't think so. It was easier to set the grief aside. I thought it would fade away if I didn't pay attention to it."

The silence that followed was soon interrupted by a growling noise coming from Danny's stomach. Geremy laughed. "Your stomach is most insistent when it wants to be fed."

She chuckled, glad for the diversion from her past. "It's true. I love to eat."

He slid out of the chair and held his hand out to her. "Come along, milady. We don't want to keep your stomach waiting."

Food was on the table when they arrived back at Geremy's room. He shook his head in amazement. "I could really get used to this place. Everything appears when you're ready for it."

Danny sat down and helped herself to some rice. "Yeah. It's kind of like life, isn't it? Things come to you when you're ready for them."

He sat down and helped himself to the food. "What else did you see with Albert?"

"He took me to a sunny park with a fountain. The sun felt so nice. Then he took me by a painting that was quite amazing."

"How so?"

"The paint is a random series of colors until someone looks at it. The paint then moves into a portrait of a man." She thought back to the painting and how familiar the man seemed. "It was odd, but I felt like I recognized him. He must resemble someone I know or have seen before."

"I did ask Dario if I'd lived in Atlantis in another life."

She grinned at him. "Oh, yeah? What did he say?"

"He told me that I had. And so had you. That we knew each other and that you were a well-known artist."

"What were you?"

"I was some sort of actor. Quite good and well-known, of course."

"Of course."

"And quite handsome, too."

"So you were a man in that incarnation, also?"

"Yes. And you were a woman."

"A woman? And an artist?"

"Yes. What's the matter?"

Danny stopped eating and stood up. "Come with me. I want you to see the painting I was telling you about." She was out the door with Geremy close on her heels.

Geremy was equally impressed as he watched the paint begin to move when he stepped in front of it. When it stopped, he was looking into the same green eyes that Danny had seen earlier. But the humor was gone from the eyes and the mouth no longer curved into the rakish grin she'd seen. Instead, the expression on the man's face was wistful, the eyes sad, and just a hint of a smile graced his mouth. Danny felt the twinge near her heart as she looked into the eyes.

Geremy didn't say anything. He just stared at the portrait. Then he looked down at the bottom of the painting and saw the name of the artist.

"Danny, you were Layne."

"And that's a portrait of you as you were then." She spoke with conviction, knowing without a doubt that she was right. "Let's walk away and come back, only this time I'll stand in front of it." They did as she suggested, and the paint moved into the expression she'd seen earlier.

"That's amazing!"

Danny looked for a moment more and then turned away, unable to identify the strange mix of feelings which filled her as she gazed at his face. She felt tired as she moved away from the painting. "I'm ready to go back to the room."

She took a few steps and then stopped. "Did Dario tell you about us? What we were to each other then?"

"No. Just that we knew each other. No details."

They walked in silence, and when they arrived back at the room, Danny realized that she'd lost her appetite. The swirl of emotions she was feeling made the food she had eaten sit uneasily in her stomach.

"Are you alright?" Geremy asked, his voice tinged with concern.

"No, actually. I don't feel very well."

He took her by the hand and led her to the bed. "Come on. Let's have a lie-down." She waited by the bed as he pulled the cover back. She slid in as he moved to the other side of the bed and got in beside her. She moved easily into his arms.

"Lights dim," he said softly, and they were left in semi-darkness. Geremy savored the silky softness of Danny's hair as she lay quietly in his arms. He began to hum the tune he'd been composing for her and soon felt her steady breathing. He let himself relax and fell into a restless sleep.

He found himself running, trying to catch up with the woman who walked in front of him, her long, blond hair flowing and moving as she walked. He had to catch her, it was very important, even though he couldn't remember why. He ran and ran, but never seemed to get any closer. His lungs felt as if they would burst from his efforts. But then he realized that he was gaining on her. He reached out to touch her on the shoulder, and she began to turn around.

He was jolted awake by a cry that came from Danny, who was sitting up next to him on the bed. He sat up and touched her arm, and she turned to him. Her face was damp with perspiration, causing her hair to mat and stick to her forehead and temples. Alarmed, Geremy brushed the hair off her forehead and pulled her down and back into his arms. He could feel her heart pounding and her irregular breathing. She shuddered. He held her more tightly, saying, "Shhh. It's alright. It was just a dream." He remembered that he had been having a vivid dream, but couldn't remember what it had been about. Then he remembered what Dario had told them about the pink crystal they had touched. "Damn crystal," he muttered. He kept brushing Danny's hair back from her forehead and temples. "Want to tell me about it?" he asked gently.

Danny lay still for a moment before speaking. "It's a recurring dream I've had for years. Only this time, it seemed more real than before."

"Remember the pink crystal we touched? Dario said it would make the next dreams we had more vivid."

"Great timing," she said sarcastically.

"So, what was the dream about?"

In the warmth and comfort of his arms, she felt safe bringing the dream that was already fading back to the surface. "It's of the accident. I am with my parents and we are driving down the road. Suddenly, I know what's coming, and I try to tell them, asking Papa to stop or to turn around. In the other dreams, they don't or can't hear me, and they keep right on going. This time, Maman turns to me, smiles, and says they know, and it will be alright. I beg her and Papa to stop, *plead* with them to stop. The car keeps moving forward, only everything is now going in slow motion. We approach the intersection. I can see the other car coming, still in slow motion. It comes closer, and I can see the face of the man driving, see the sun glinting off his car as it approaches, feel the terror at what's about to happen and knowing I cannot stop it. It's never felt that real." She shivered.

Geremy kissed her temple, tasting the salt that lingered there, and felt an overwhelming need to protect her. He propped himself up on one elbow as he began to kiss her cheek and then her lips. Desire swept through him as she responded to his kiss while she slid her hand under the tunic he still wore.

He sat up and pulled the tunic off and then helped her slip out of her gown. She then helped him pull off his trousers. He hadn't even been thinking of making love when he first kissed her temple, but when he bent to kiss her face and tasted the lingering salt from her tears, an urgency to have her, to join with her, overtook him. Danny responded passionately, needing to immerse herself in life and to fully express the love she felt for him. Like the fire that burns hot and is quickly reduced to embers, their lovemaking was passionate, but soon after they fell into a deep, dreamless sleep.

CHAPTER TWENTY TWO

Albert was concerned and he said as much to Dario, who was sitting before him on a wide, rock ledge enjoying the last rays of sun that streamed into the outdoor garden. It was one of many spread throughout Pangea and was situated at the bottom of a wide crevice between two crags in the mountainside. The Pangeans kept an optical illusion in place that prevented outsiders from seeing the openings, seeing sheer, rocky mountain walls instead.

"Excuse me for questioning your pace, Dario, but do you think it's wise to present them with so much information so quickly?"

"You are a sensitive man, Albert, and your insights are valued and appreciated. You know that I share your concerns." The sun slipped behind a peak, and bluish-purple shadows engulfed the two men. "But they are both open to the information, else they would not be here. As to the pace, well, I believe they will not be with us much longer, so I stepped up the pace for them. And, yes, I believe they can handle it." Dario turned his head to the right and looked at the entrance to the park. A moment later, Danny stepped through it and into the garden.

"Hello, Danny. How did you know we were here?"

"I didn't. I just let my feet bring me to you."

Dario smiled in comprehension. He was sorry she would not be with them for much longer for he felt her psychic abilities would increase dramatically were she to stay.

"I have to talk to you, Dario."

Albert, understanding that she wanted to be alone with Dario, gave them each a slight bow and retreated from the garden. Dario patted the space beside him on the ledge. "Please. Come sit down." As with Geremy, he had shut her thoughts out of his psychic abilities, but her expression was troubled and aura was dull. "How can I help you?" he asked as she slid onto the ledge.

"Please tell me about Layne and the actor."

"What would you like to know?"

"What was between them? When I look at the portrait of him, I feel a jumble of emotions, one of which is apprehension. I sometimes get the same feeling when I look into Geremy's eyes."

Dario took her hand and sandwiched it between his warm ones. Danny felt the calm she came to associate with him fill her. He released her hand, and she relaxed back against the black stone wall that was still warm from the sun.

"The feelings you are experiencing relate to some unresolved issues between Layne and Kester, the man in the portrait. Those unresolved feelings and events in this life are both present to help you learn forgiveness."

"Kester must have done something low to Layne. Can you tell me what it was?"

"I will not tell you the details of the drama as it unfolded in that life because it may affect the lesson in this life. You must trust that what I hold back is for the best."

"If I have to forgive Kester and Geremy was Kester, does that mean that Geremy will do something low to me in order for me to forgive him in this life?"

"I do not know the answer to that question, Danny."

Danny sat quietly, letting his words sink in. The sadness she felt as she contemplated the possibility that Geremy might do something that would require forgiveness from her left her hollow inside.

Dario interrupted her thoughts. "I can tell you that the most pressing opportunity to learn forgiveness has been provided by the man who caused the wreck. You must release the bitterness you feel toward this man."

All thoughts of Geremy disappeared as a picture of the man's face flashed into her mind, and she felt a wave of bitterness wash through her. "Dario, I don't know if I can release it. He was staggering drunk when he killed my parents and shattered my life. His life wasn't shattered because of his thoughtlessness, but mine was. How can I forgive him?"

Dario's compassionate gaze rested on Danny as he tried to determine the best way to tell her what he had to say. "I do not know how much of this you will understand, but I want you to at least consider what I tell you." He paused, waiting for her to acknowledge his request. She gave a slight nod.

"Regardless of how the incident came to pass, you must forgive this man. He has his own burdens to bear with regard to the accident. You only hurt yourself by holding onto this bitterness. The anger you feel does not allow for release of your grief."

Dario could tell that his words were not getting through to her. He tried another approach. "I ask you to look beyond your immediate reaction to occurrences and understand that there are many, many other forces at play and that, while something may be painful to experience, you must allow yourself to experience *all* your feelings, not just the bitterness and anger."

He took her hand again. "I feel in you a deep reservoir of tears that seek to spill forth, and yet you keep that reservoir capped with a lid of anger. The reservoir has been growing steadily, and unless you release it consciously, it will erupt though a subconscious outlet, such as through illness. Do not fear to open the reservoir, Danny. You will not drown, I promise. You are a strong swimmer."

His kind smile and gentle gaze filled Danny with the sense that she could do anything he asked of her. "Love your parents, feel grief at their passage, forgive them for dying, and most of all, forgive yourself for living. Finally, forgive the man who caused the accident. When you do this, you will discover and accept the deep love you seek, for the two are connected."

Danny sat quietly and felt a single tear slip from her eye. She knew that Dario was right. Since the first day of consciousness from the accident, she had never cried for her parents. She hadn't even been able to attend their funeral. The reservoir of tears was indeed inside of her, but she didn't know how to release them. After so many years, the lid appeared to have rusted shut. She didn't know what to say, so she said nothing. Dario seemed to have said all that he had to say, so they sat in silence in the mountain twilight. Presently, Dario slid off the ledge. "Come. Geremy has awakened and seeks you." When she stood up, he took her hand and tucked it into the crook of his arm. They strolled back toward Geremy's room.

Geremy felt weighed down as he walked through the halls of Pangea. The power of the pink crystal had filled his dreams with images of Maggie. The longing and sadness that had been in the far recesses of his mind now filled him completely. It was as if he had just received the news of her death.

The Celts had nearly completed the tour when the private detective notified him that she had been listed as a casualty of a ferry accident in the channel. As he sat in the hotel in stunned silence, he realized how little he knew of her. Did she have a family? He knew she'd come from Canada a month before they'd met, but he didn't even know from where in Canada or if her family, if she had one, was there.

He had very little memory of the last gigs of the tour because of his grief, but everyone who had seen the concerts told him that they were some of the best performances of his career. Their one live album had a number of cuts from those last dates. Inspired, is what they'd all said. He had wondered more than once at the irony of it all.

He had felt her presence so strongly for so many years after her death that he was convinced she was still alive. He had waited for her to come back to him and tell him it had all been a terrible mistake. Now, when it seemed that he had finally put her to rest, her memory was stronger than it had been in years. He could even remember the scent she always wore and could have sworn it lingered in the air when he woke from the dreams. He felt as if he were going crazy.

Without thinking of where he was going, he walked until he found himself outside the crystal theater. He opened the door slowly and peered into the dimly lit chamber, relieved to discover that no one was inside. He slipped through the partial opening. The door closed quietly behind him as he made his way to the centerpiece. He stood in front of it for a moment before resting his hand on the clear, center crystal, enjoying the cool feel of it against his palm. He wanted to press his cheek or forehead against it in the hopes that its cool, smooth surface would drain all the sadness from him, but the crystal was too far away for that. He had to be content with resting his palm against it. He heard the door open behind him and turned to see Dario and Danny enter the theater.

As Dario approached him, Geremy asked the question that plagued him. "She is alive, isn't she?"

Dario took a deep breath before answering. "Yes. She is alive and is in England, though that has not always been the case."

"Where has she been all these years?"

Dario shook his head. "That is a question you will have to ask her, if you see her."

"If I see her? Of course I'll see her!"

"She is in England temporarily. If your paths are to cross, you must leave Pangea very soon."

"Why?"

"Because, as I have said, she is in England temporarily. If she leaves before you return, it is likely that your paths will not cross again."

Danny had been standing back listening to their exchange, the meaning of their words finally sinking in. Maggie was alive, and Geremy had to leave Pangea to find her. She watched the emotions play over his face as he considered the real possibility of finding Maggie. She felt a lead weight begin to grow in her stomach. Her throat was dry; she tried to swallow, but without success.

"Why can't you tell me where she's been all these years?"

"It is for her to tell you, and she may not want you to know. And I must tell you that, even if you leave Pangea right now, the possibility exists that your paths will not cross. But if you do not leave soon, I am close to certain that the opportunity to see her again will not occur. The choice is yours."

Geremy looked at Danny for the first time since she and Dario had arrived. The wary expression on her pale face made him flinch. The implications of his choice bore down on him. "I have to go," he said softly, his voice barely audible, a pained expression on his face.

She nodded as her mouth formed the words "I know," though her voice failed her. Without a sound, she turned and left the theater and made her way back to the garden. She needed time to sort through her feelings and calm her troubled thoughts.

She sat in the cool, night air and breathed the crisp mountain fragrance deeply into her lungs. She hoped that the clarity of the air would help to clear her mind and discover what course to take. Part of her wanted to stay in Pangea and hide away from the painful possibilities that could unfold on the outside. Albert's words that most people found the prospect of leaving Pangea difficult rang through her mind, and she understood what he meant. She could stay here and learn how the Pangeans help the body heal and how to communicate telepathically. Calm washed through her as she thought about staying in this peaceful haven. She stared up at the stars that sparkled brightly against the midnight-blue sky and silently asked for help with this decision.

Memories of her childhood began to stream through her mind. She saw sunshine and laughter and felt the love that she'd taken for granted all her life. She smiled as a memory of Philippe, grinning proudly as he showed off one of his first paintings, came to mind. Her smile faded as that image was replaced with his ashen face as he tried to tell her that their parents were dead. She couldn't just disappear, leaving Philippe to wonder what had happened to her. She had to go back, if only to let him know she was alright.

Then she thought of Geremy, and the intensity of the love she felt for him made her tremble. She went over what Dario had said about Kester and that she and Geremy had some lessons to learn. But a deep memory told her that his learning process could be painful for her. She took another deep breath and slid off the rock ledge. In spite of that very real possibility, she knew she had to return to London with Geremy and find out about Maggie. Her decision made, she retraced her steps to the theater.

When she did not find Dario or Geremy there, she went to the room that she and Geremy had been sharing, only to find that it too was empty. She approached the bed and saw the clothes she'd been wearing when she arrived in a neat pile looking as new as the day she'd bought them. She knew they had been torn and muddy from her fall down the mountain; now, it was as if the fall had never happened. She was once again amazed at the power of the Pangeans, not only that the clothes had been cleaned and repaired, but that they had been returned to her. Dario probably knew her decision before she did.

She had changed her clothes and was trying to eat an apple from the fruit bowl on the table when Geremy came into the room. He was dressed in the jeans and tee shirt he'd been wearing when they arrived, showing that he was ready to leave Pangea. He came over to the table and sat down across from her.

"Are you alright? You dashed out of the theater so quickly I was a little concerned."

"I needed to be alone to think." Her tone was cool as she retreated into her protective shell.

He nodded knowingly and then noticed her outfit. "Are you leaving, too?"

"Yes, of course I'm leaving. In case you haven't noticed, I'm a part of this thing, too."

He reached a hand over and covered hers. "I know you're a part of this, but everybody gets to make choices in this game, or so says Dario. I thought you might choose to stay here."

"I did consider it. But I couldn't do that to Philippe."

"Right." He pulled his hand away and then stood, went over to the bed, and sat down. He needed to distance himself from the chill he felt from her.

"Danny, please don't shut me out. I'm just as confused by all this as you."

"You may be confused, but you stand to win whatever the outcome. While you're riding into the sunset with the woman of your dreams, I get to stand by and wave you off." Her old ally anger began to take hold. She felt some comfort in it. Anger was so much easier to handle than fear and sorrow.

"You sound as if you know the outcome of this thing, and you're throwing in the towel." Her anger infected him and he gave it free reign. "I never would have pegged you as a quitter."

"Oh, would it suit your male ego more if I fought for you? Told you that I can't live without you? Begged you to choose me?" She stood up and stepped away from the table, adding to the distance between them. "Sorry. That's not my style."

"Not your style! My God! We're not talking about a business negotiation here, Danny. We're talking about a relationship. Has it even crossed your mind that you may be the woman of my dreams?" He stood and took a step toward her but then stopped. "No, probably not. It's so much easier to push me away, to be an island unto yourself. Much easier than possibly admitting that you care for me." He knew he was pushing her, but he needed to hear her say it. He needed to hear her say that she loved him, to admit that it mattered to her what happened out there.

Danny stood motionless across the room from him, an incredulous look on her face. "Admit that I *care* for you? Do you think I'd be this scared if I merely *cared* for you?"

Geremy came over to her and gripped her shoulders. "Then say it! Say it out loud. I want to hear you say it."

She looked up into his eyes and said quietly, "I love you, Geremy Hawker, with all my heart and soul." She looked away. "Are you satisfied?"

His grip loosened. She stepped away from him, her eyes still averted. Dario came into the room and found them standing apart. The tension in the air hit him like a wall and filled him with concern. He did not know how things would turn out for them for he saw many possibilities, but only one path would lead them past the karma he had told Danny about earlier. He wanted them to choose that path more than he'd wanted anything in a long time.

Danny looked at him in surprise. "You are dressed as if you are going out with us."

"I will lead you back to the trail and perhaps walk with you for a while, unless you do not wish my company."

Danny's mood lifted a little. "I would be most happy for your company." She had not been looking forward to the long walk back to the car with Geremy. So much still needed to be said, but the energy that had fueled their angry outburst was gone, and neither of them had any reserves left over to resume the conversation. She hoped Dario's calm presence would ease the strain between them.

When they arrived at the door that would lead them to the outside, they found Albert waiting for them. He approached her, his hand outstretched.

"I want you to have this."

Danny looked down at his open palm and was astonished to see the ring. He extended his hand a little further, encouraging her to take it.

"Go ahead, take it. I won't be needing it."

She took it while looking at him, her eyes questioning. "Are you sure?"

"Absolutely. I want you to have a reminder, like I did, that this was not a dream. Believe me, there will be moments when you will wonder if it was."

Tears filled her eyes, and she hugged him. "Thank you, Albert. I hope I'll meet you again someday."

"Anything is possible," he replied with a knowing smile. He then turned to Geremy and held out his hand. "It's been a pleasure talking to you. Keep up the good work."

Geremy took his hand. "I'll do my best. May you continue to find peace during your sojourn here."

"We must go," Dario reminded them. He stood silently in front of the stone door for a moment and then a small hole appeared in the middle. The hole slowly grew bigger, like the aperture of a camera lens, until nothing of the stone door was visible to the eye. A fresh, cool breeze blew in smelling of moist earth; Danny breathed deeply of the pungent odor. Dario was the first through the opening with Geremy close behind him. Danny followed them into the cave, pausing long enough to look back at the opening that was already beginning to close. For some reason, the light shining through from Pangea maintained a steady blue tint, which made the cave walls look blue while the door was open. She now knew why it was called the cave of the blue light. Then the opening closed completely, and she made her way through the darkness to the front of the cave and the early morning light.

Dario led them over the rough terrain of the mountain until they reached the trail. Once on it, he led them in single file down the mountain. They walked in silence. Dario did not have to read their thoughts to know that both of his companions were pondering the future and the unknown events which lay ahead of them. Half a mile from the cars, he stopped and turned to them.

"This is where I must bid you farewell." He took Danny's hands in his and leaned down and kissed her on each cheek. "I am glad you came to us. Remember that you do not need to be here to learn the lessons. Just trust your inner voice, and follow your heart."

Dario then turned his attention to Geremy. "Do not despair over these developments, my friend. You must follow the course to its completion and, if you remain honest with yourself, you will discover the happiness you seek." With that, he left them, turning only once to wave before continuing his climb back to the cave.

CHAPTER TWENTY THREE

Danny looked out at the clouds that floated beneath the plane that was carrying them back to London. Geremy was asleep beside her. She looked at him and felt a little envious. She couldn't remember ever feeling as exhausted as she did at that moment, but her brain was too full of the events from the past few days for her to sleep. Dario had told them that they would experience some disorientation with regard to time for a day or two and that accounted for some of the fatigue she felt. All she wanted to do was crawl into bed, forget everything for a while, and go to sleep.

Her fingers brushed over the onyx ring on her index finger. She looked down at it with a wistful smile. To think that such a small thing could have such a big secret hidden within it. She shook her head in amazement that only half a day had passed since they'd left Pangea. She wondered how long they had really been in Pangea. Somewhere between one night and a lifetime was the closest approximation she could make. However long it was, she was now having a hard time remembering what day it was.

They had come down the mountain and into a near mob scene by the cars. Philippe, the police, and locals were assembled and preparing to scour the mountains for her, Sebastian, and Geremy. When she and Geremy appeared, Philippe had just about crushed her in an embrace that told her how fearful he had been that he might not see her alive again. When she asked in a whisper what day it was, he gave her a perplexed look. When he told her it was

Sunday morning, it was her turn to look perplexed. They had been gone only one night.

She then explained to him and the curious people standing around them that Sebastian had died in a fall down the mountain and that she and Geremy had spent the night in a small cave. When she mentioned the cave, Philippe gave a start, but before he could say anything, her eyes pleaded with him to keep silent.

As the group disbanded, the police took charge of Sebastian's rental car while she rode back to Foix with Philippe, giving her time to tell him what had really happened. Geremy followed them in his rental car. Upon arrival back at the house, Danny and Geremy made arrangements to catch the next flight back to London. Four hours later, they were in the air.

"Danny?"

When she looked at Geremy, her heart went out to him. He looked so tired and out-of-sorts. The shocking information that Maggie was alive and well had left its mark on him. "Some great adventure, huh?" she asked with a sad smile. "Next time, say no."

His hand came up and touched her cheek with his fingertips. "I love you, Danny." His eyes were so sad when he said it that she knew what was coming next. His hand came down and took hers. "But I have to find her. I have to find out what happened."

Danny's throat felt tight and dry as tears began to fill her eyes. "I know." She swallowed and blinked the tears back, refusing to cry. "I've been thinking about things. I think it would be best if we chilled out until you find out about Maggie and I finish this job assignment." She took a deep breath and, by the mere act of making a decision, could feel a measure of calm returning. "I'm just glad that I've already written a preliminary story based on the stuff you and Miles have told me because my brain power feels very reduced right now."

"Right. The day before we left for France, I left messages with both Neil and John, telling them that you hoped to interview them for the piece." He gave a slight grin. "Since I was the sacrificial lamb for the interview, it was my job to check you out before they would agree to meet with you." Disbelief flickered across his face. "Good

God, I hadn't a clue what I was walking into when I entered that flat last week." His eyes traveled over her face. "Is it really possible that it's only been a week since we met?" He shook his head and then quietly said, "I've lived a lifetime in a week."

She could feel the calm slipping away as she looked into his eyes and felt the familiar twinge in her heart. She struggled to hold onto the calm because it kept the tears at bay, and she wasn't ready to open the floodgates just yet. The grief for her parents that she had kept down for so long was now just under the surface, and the turmoil she felt because of Geremy threatened to act as a valve for that reservoir of tears. Dario had told her that she needed to let the tears flow and drain the reservoir, but not yet! Stick to business.

"Now that all the excitement has passed, I'll go back to Jasmine's to stay, but I'd like to swing by the house to get my briefcase and camera case. Then can you take me to Jasmine's?"

"I'd rather not."

She looked at him in confusion.

"I'd rather that you stay at the house," he said in all seriousness.

She raised her eyebrows as she looked at him. "Geremy, I need to distance myself from you so that I can get my job done and so I don't have to watch you search for Maggie. No, I'm going back to Jasmine's." She looked down at her hands and noticed that they were locked in a tight grip. She loosened the grip and rubbed her fingers.

"I understand that. But call me paranoid if you like, I'm just afraid that if I let you out of my sight, you'll disappear or return to Seattle, and I'll find out that Maggie ... well, I don't know what I'll find out." He tilted her head up so that he could see into her eyes. "Just promise me that you won't disappear. That if you decide for whatever reason to go away, you'll tell me first."

She felt tears prick her eyes as she looked into his eyes. "I won't go anywhere unless you discover that Maggie is everything you've always dreamt of. But if that happens, I doubt I'll discuss my travel plans with you. I'll probably just go."

Geremy's eyes ran over her face, saw the determined set of her jaw, and knew she would do just that. "Just promise me that you won't do anything rash. I may not find her, she may not want to be found, and until we know the score, promise me you won't disappear."

"I'll do my best not to disappear. But you must promise me that you'll be honest with me. If you decide that Maggie is all you've dreamt of, tell me straightaway so that I can get on with my life."

Danny saw his eyes flicker as if he'd felt pain. "Let you go? At this exact moment, I cannot begin to conceive what would induce me to make that decision." He paused and swallowed, not taking his eyes off her face. "But if it should come to that, I will tell you straightaway."

"Thank you," she whispered, her throat again dry.

He leaned over and lightly kissed her on the corner of her mouth. "In answer to your original question, of course we can go by the house to get your things before going to Jasmine's."

The stewardess's voice came over the intercom to inform them that the jet was making its final approach into Gatwick. Danny tightened her seat belt and mentally prepared herself for the other part of flying she did not like: landings.

By the time they had made it back to the house, they were laughing and joking about bizarre traveling experiences. Danny was relieved that some of the tension had lifted and that she had been able to keep the lid on the tears that were now so close to the surface.

Geremy opened the door to the house and proceeded up the stairs to the second floor living room. "Didn't you leave your things in here?" He walked through the archway and into the living room where he suddenly came to a halt. Danny, following close behind, bumped into him, but the bulk of his frame screened the sight that had caused him to stop. She laughed and pushed him. "We've got to quit running into each other like ... this."

Geremy looked as if he were seeing a ghost as he stared at the beautiful, well-dressed, blonde who had risen from her chair. Danny knew she was seeing the ghost that was no longer a ghost.

Maggie and Geremy stood staring, not saying a word. Danny felt her insides tighten as she saw the expressions on both their faces, but it was the expression of joy that shined on Geremy's face that tied her stomach in knots. Feeling like a voyeur, Danny knew she had to get out of there. She could feel the tears welling up inside of her and didn't want to be there when they spilled over. She took a step back. Her movement seemed to set the long-parted lovers into motion. They wordlessly came together in a hug as Danny backed out onto the stairway landing. She wasn't ready for introductions just yet. As she quickly turned and ran down the steps, she didn't see Miles as he came down from the third floor. All he heard was the sound of the front door slamming.

When Danny got outside, she was relieved to see that the taxi they'd arrived in was still in front of the house. The tears were falling in a steady stream down her face as she jumped into the taxi. The startled cabbie turned to her, and she gave him the Cornwall Gardens address.

He looked at her with concern. "You alright, miss?"

She looked back at him, tears streaming down her face. "No, not really, but if you drive me to Cornwall Gardens, I'll be better than I am now."

He nodded, turned back to the wheel, and set the car in motion. It wasn't until they had gone a few blocks that Danny remembered that her things were still in the house, but she had her suitcase and purse so she'd be able to get into Jasmine's. She'd worry about her briefcase and camera case later.

When she got into the flat, she closed the door behind her and leaned against it, wondering if she could make it to the couch. The exhaustion was back in full force and her body felt like it was made out of lead. She continued to lean against the door and, as she looked around the flat, memories of Geremy flooded her brain. Geremy turning to her on that first day. Geremy holding her after the knife attack. Geremy straightening the furniture. The tears fell unrestrained. She stumbled to the couch and fell on it, sobs wracking her body. After some time, the sobbing subsided, and she fell asleep only to have anxiety-fraught dreams about wandering through cinnamon-colored hallways, looking for the train she knew she had to catch, but unable to find the platform.

The flat's overhead light came on. Danny struggled out of the dream, feeling disoriented as she squinted at the light. Startled by a noise to her left, she sat up and looked over the back of the couch only to find Jasmine staring back at her.

"Danny? What are you doing in the dark?" Jasmine put her bags down and, coming toward Danny, noticed her puffy, red eyes. She came around and sat down next to Danny. "What's wrong?"

Danny's eyes began to fill with tears. Jasmine put her arms around her friend, pulling her head down to her shoulder. "Oh, honey, what's happened?"

Danny sat up and tried to wipe the tears from her face, but fresh ones just replaced the ones she wiped away. "My parents are dead."

Jasmine was a little confused. "I thought your parents died years ago."

Danny nodded and sniffed. "They did, but a very wise man just brought it to my attention that I had never properly grieved for them. And then something happened that kind of triggered the tears."

Jasmine, wise in the signs of a broken heart asked, "Did you and Stephen have a fight?"

Danny gave a strangled laugh. "God, I wish it was that easy." She stood up from the couch and began to pace, the flow of tears momentarily stopped. "No. I managed to fall in love with someone else." She looked at Jasmine in grim amusement.

"But, who? You've only been here for a … Oh no." Her hazel eyes became big as saucers. "Not … Geremy Hawker?"

A pained look came over Danny's face. When she nodded, two tears fell onto her cheeks."

Jasmine got up from the couch and went to Danny, who had stopped pacing, and put her hand on Danny's arm. "I am so sorry. I wanted to warn you when you told me you were going to interview him, but I don't like to gossip. Besides, your relationship with Stephen seemed so strong."

Danny's tears dried, and she sniffed as she gave Jasmine a perplexed look. "What gossip are you talking about?"

Jasmine went to the bathroom and came back with a tissue that she handed to Danny. "Well, Geremy has quite a reputation as a lady's man. You know, the love-'em-and-leave-'em sort. He's broken quite a few hearts."

Danny gave a heavy sigh. "Jasmine, I have had one hell of a week."

Jasmine nodded. "I know just what you need," she said as she walked to the kitchen.

Danny gave a small laugh. "Let me guess. A nice cup of tea?"

Jasmine grinned. "The English cure for all ills."

Danny walked up to Jasmine and gave her a hug. "Thanks for coming home." Then she backed away and looked at her as if she'd just realized that Jasmine was in London. "Wait a second. What are you doing here? I thought you were going to be in Seattle for two weeks?" She scanned Jasmine's face. "Everything okay?"

"Everything is just fine. Well, with me everything is fine, but one of the members of the band I was working with has a drug problem, so the project was put on hold until he gets out of rehab." She placed the pitcher of water on the heating pad and pressed the button, activating the heating element below the pitcher. "Damn heroin," she said to the pitcher. She then asked it, "Why do such talented people think they have to use that shit? It's a killer." She sighed and looked from the pitcher to Danny. "So, I'm fine and, if I'm free, I'll go back when they're ready. Now, tell me about the crazy week you've just had." She snapped her fingers. "Oh yeah, before you get started. The police still don't have a clue as to who broke into your house, but to be honest, I don't think they've given it very high priority since nothing was taken."

Danny sat on one of the bar stools and began the story as Jasmine pulled out two cups, honey, and biscuits and put them on the bar in front of Danny. When the water boiled, she made a pot of chamomile tea, set it next to the other things, and joined Danny on the other side of the bar.

For two hours they sat while Danny told her story with Jasmine interrupting from time to time with questions. The one that made Danny laugh was when Jasmine asked if Dario was married, adding that he sounded like too much of a dish not to be. She had to honestly say that the question had never crossed her mind.

When she had finished, Jasmine sat shaking her head. "Blimey. And I thought I had a tough week!" She tried to take a sip of tea, but found that her cup was empty and so was the pot. She carried the cup and pot to the sink, came back to the bar, and faced Danny. "Well, what are you going to do?"

"About what?"

"Danny! About Stephen. About Geremy. What are you going to do?"

Danny ran her hands over her face and through her hair. "What time is it anyway? I lost my watch in the mountains."

"I don't know. Around midnight, I guess. So? What are you going to do?"

"I don't know." She got off the stool. "Yes, I do. I'm going to bed. I'm beat. I'll think about it tomorrow."

"Yes, 'Tomorrow is another day' as Ms. Scarlett would say," Jasmine murmured thoughtfully as Danny walked to her bedroom.

When Jasmine came out to the kitchen the next morning, Danny was already pouring herself a cup of tea. Jasmine shook her head. "Excuse me for saying so, love, but you look like shit."

Danny gave her a tired smile. "Thanks, Jasmine. You're a pal. I didn't sleep very well, as you may have guessed."

"Thinking about the muddle?" She poured herself a cup of tea.

"Yes."

"Made any decisions?"

"Yep. I'm going to call the police like I told them I would when I returned to London. Then I'm going to finish the job I came to do."

"No decisions about the men, ay?"

"I do have to call Geremy because some of my things are still over there, and I need to pick them up."

"Good! Get back there and fight for him!"

"Jasmine, he has just been reunited with the woman that he has been in love with and dreamt about for twenty-five years. He's known me for one week. I don't like the odds."

"A lot can change in twenty-five years, especially if two people haven't seen each other in all that time."

"Or they could still connect on that deep level and just pick up where they left off. I'll go get my stuff, but I'm not going to hang around and watch them make goo-goo eyes at each other. It practically killed me yesterday. I don't think it'll be any easier to take today. Geremy can sort out his feelings without my being there. When he does, he'll let me know."

"And what about Stephen? I met him when I was over there. He seems like a nice bloke. Are you just going to leave him hanging while Geremy sorts out his feelings? Seems to me that he has an interest in all this, too."

"Well, I don't have to make a decision on that today, do I? A day or two won't matter."

Jasmine's brow creased as she looked at Danny. She was not one to interfere, but she just might have to make an exception today.

"I'm going to take a shower. That alright with you?" Danny asked as she walked toward the bathroom.

"Sure, that's fine. Help yourself to whatever you need." Jasmine was pulling her personal phone book out of her purse when she heard the shower begin to flow. She found and dialed the Seattle number, happy that she had written it down in her book. She had just realized that it was one in the morning in Seattle when Stephen answered the phone, his voice thick with sleep.

Danny came out of the bathroom wearing one of Jasmine's robes, drying her hair with a towel. "Jasmine, I've decided to go to Grosvenor House while I finish this assignment."

"What? But why? I don't mind your being here. In fact, I'm enjoying your company."

"I like to be alone when I'm working on a project. I work better and faster."

"I'll be very quiet and promise not to bother you."

Danny laughed. "You're starting to sound like Stephen. No. You're a dear, but it's best for me if I go to Grosvenor's."

"But it's very hard to get a room there on such short notice."

"Now you're starting to sound like Geremy," she said as she walked back into the bathroom.

Jasmine followed her and sat down on the toilet while they talked. "What are your plans for the day?"

Danny began to work a comb through her damp hair. "First, I'm going to call the bands' Richmond house to see if anyone is there and to find out if we can finish the interview this afternoon. In any case I have to go over there to get my briefcase and camera. After I get that sorted out, I'll call the police and find out if they need me to come by and, if so, when. And at some point I need to check into Grosvenor's." She finished combing her hair and went to her room to put on the same dress she'd worn the day before. She came back out and found Jasmine in the kitchen. "What are you doing today?"

"Since I'm still supposed to be in Seattle, I have no plans."

Danny held her arms away from her body and looked down at the pink cotton dress she had worn back from France. "I need some retail therapy. Want to go with?"

Jasmine's eye lit up. "Retail therapy? I'd love to."

Danny smiled at her friend. "Great. I'll make the calls right now and find out when we can go."

"Do you want some breakfast? I'm making."

"No thanks. My stomach doesn't feel like it would appreciate food just yet."

Danny dialed the number for the band's house and felt progressively more nervous with each ring. Finally, the phone was answered, and she braced herself for his voice. But it wasn't Geremy. She took a deep breath, almost in relief.

"Hello. This is Danny Davis..."

"Hello! I'm so glad you called!"

"Who is this?"

"Oh, I'm sorry. This is John Dearing. Geremy called me at home yesterday and asked if I was available for an interview today or tomorrow."

"Do you know if I'll have a chance to talk to Neil?"

"He should be here late this morning or early this afternoon."

"Would it be possible for us to meet this afternoon?"

"Not only possible, but preferable. We both have other engagements tomorrow."

"Will Miles or Geremy be there today?" she asked half-hoping, half-dreading that the answer would be yes.

"I don't think so. I don't really know where Miles is, but Geremy has gone off with a friend of his. Said he'd done his share of the interview, so I don't think he'll be here."

Danny's stomach tightened into a little ball. She was glad she hadn't eaten anything. "Yes, he's done his share of the interview." She bit her lip. "Right. Since I have to come by to pick up my things, we can just do the interview there if that's all right with you."

"That would be marvelous. How about if you come over around two? I'm sure that Neil will be here by then."

"Great. I'll see you at two."

"Right. Looking forward to it. Cheers."

Danny heard the line disconnect before she returned the handset to its base.

When she looked up, she found Jasmine watching her as she munched a piece of toast. "Will he be there?"

Danny gave her a wry grin. "Appears not. He says he's already done his share of the interview."

"Bastard."

"Right. Well, now I'll call the police and see what they have to say."

"You still plan to go to the Grosvenor House?"

"Yes," Danny said as she picked up the handset. "I'll call them after I call the police to make sure I can get in. If so, I'll go after I talk to John Dearing and Neil Fairgraves." She dialed Earling's number. "Hello, Sergeant Earling! It's Danny Davis, and I'm not calling to report a goon attack."

Earling laughed. "I'm glad to hear it. Are you back in London, then?"

"Yes. I told P.C. McCafferty that I would call when I returned in case you needed me to come down to make a statement, or whatever you call it."

"When can you come in?"

"I think I can come in tomorrow afternoon."

"Alright. We've had some interesting developments that I'd like to run by you."

"I'm intrigued! I may have some interesting news for you, too."

"Oh, really? Now I'm intrigued. See you tomorrow then."

"Yes. I'll call and let you know what time."

"Cheers. Bye now."

Danny pressed the disconnect button and went to find her phone book. She dialed the number for her friend at the Grosvenor House. As she expected, it was no trouble getting a suite. Her father and the CEO of the board of directors had been great friends, so she always had a place to stay if she needed it. She rarely imposed on the open invitation, so when she called, they made sure to take care of her.

"Jasmine?"

A muffled "Yes?" came from the bedroom.

"I'm set for the Grosvenor House. And the morning is wide open for shopping. Still want to go?"

Jasmine came out to the living room with a big smile on her face. "Oh, yes! Retail therapy works best when you do it first thing in the morning!"

Danny laughed. "You like to go shopping any time of day."

"Yes, that's true. But it's morning now, so now is always the best time!"

****

Danny felt tense as she got out of the taxi in front of the band's house. She didn't know if Geremy would be present during the session with John Dearing and Neil Fairgraves, so she felt uneasy at the possibility of seeing him. She didn't think her fragile emotions could handle it.

She looked down at the new emerald-green mini-skirt, white blouse, green and black bolero jacket, and black shoes she'd bought and knew that, even if she felt a little scattered, she looked great. She didn't usually think too much about the clothes she wore when she went on interviews, but today, with the emotional ups and downs she'd been experiencing, she needed all the help she could get, even if it was just some new clothes.

The 'retail therapy' had done the trick and had helped her step away from herself long enough for her to regain some of her equilibrium. Geremy's presence would sorely test that newfound equilibrium, and she didn't feel like being tested right now. She just wanted to get through the interview and finish the job. As she walked toward the front door, she recited the litany about the dangers of getting involved with an interview subject. She decided she had chosen a dangerous profession. She reached the door, took a deep breath, and knocked.

A few seconds passed before she heard footsteps on the tile floor and the door was flung open. A slender man with penetrating blue-gray eyes stared out at her. She recognized John Dearing immediately. His angular face was clean-shaven and his shoulder-length, black-and-silver hair was pulled back into a short ponytail. He wore his trademark black cotton shirt buttoned to the collar and black jeans, but today he also sported a vest covered with brightly colored embroidery. His boots were black and the tips were covered with silver. He held out his hand. "Hello, Miss Davis. Please come in."

She took his hand as she came into the house. "Thank you and please, call me Danny."

"With pleasure." He took her elbow and guided her into the living room. "It is such a pleasure to see you again after all these years. I know it's been a while, but I still feel grief at the death of your father."

"Yes. Me, too."

"I never met your mother. You always think you have time, don't you? And then one day, you hear that the one you thought you had time to get to know is no longer there."

Danny felt a lump forming in her throat. *Oh, brother,* she thought to herself. She swallowed and cleared her throat. "Yes. Well, I think we're supposed to use those realizations to make sure we make the most of the time we have with other people."

"Well said."

She needed to change the subject, so she got right down to business. "I left my briefcase and camera case here. Have you seen them?"

"Yes. Follow me. I believe they are upstairs." They went up to the second floor. "Is this them?" he asked as he pointed at her things against the far wall.

She followed the direction of his pointing finger. "Yep. That's them."

"Good. I'll go see what's keeping Neil." He ran upstairs, leaving Danny to collect herself.

She took a deep breath, relieved that she had a moment to get a grip on her feelings. She couldn't believe that he had homed right in on one of the two subjects that could knock her off-center. She rationalized that it stood to reason since he and her father were acquainted, but she hadn't seen it coming. She hoped there would be no more surprises.

She moved her things to the dining room table, so was out of sight when John and Neil came downstairs. They were in the midst of a conversation. When she realized what they were talking about, she stopped what she was doing and listened.

"So neither Geremy nor Miles will be here?" Neil asked.

"I guess not. The three of them left soon after I got here last night."

"And you're sure it was Maggie Matthieson who was with them?"

"Yes, without a doubt. I'd have recognized her anywhere. Besides, Geremy introduced her as Maggie."

"I don't get it. What was all that stuff about her dying in that ferry accident? Where has she been?"

"I don't know. I didn't really get much information before they left. It was all kind of strange actually. There was some tension, as you may imagine, and Geremy certainly wasn't himself, but she looked absolutely wonderful. Wherever she's been, it's agreed with her."

"All these years, he's insisted that she wasn't dead, and he was right. Kind of makes you wonder, doesn't it?"

The knot in Danny's stomach was starting to grow into a softball. She decided that she'd heard enough and went back into the living room.

"Excuse me, but I'd like to get started if you're ready?"

Neil came over to her. "How do you do, Miss Davis? I'm Neil Fairgraves," he said as he stuck out his hand.

She smiled at his very formal tone and took his hand in a brief shake. "I do very well, Mr. Fairgraves, but please call me Danny."

"Yes, of course. And you must call me Neil." She was least familiar with Neil, so she quickly scanned him. He was her height and had very straight, dark brown hair that was also pulled back into a ponytail. To her, he looked like a Mexican bandit with his dark brown eyes, olive skin and full, though neatly trimmed, mustache. He was wearing blue jeans and a Mystic Celts tee shirt. She suddenly had an image of him with his nose buried in a romance novel and suppressed the urge to giggle, managing a big smile instead. He returned her smile. She saw why so many women considered him the most attractive member of the band. When he smiled, his face lit up and his eyes turned into the sexiest pair of bedroom eyes she'd ever seen.

"It's a pleasure to meet you, Neil." She looked past him, her eyes scanning the room. "Now. While we've got some good light in here, I'd like to get some pictures of you two. As you know, I've already interviewed Miles and Geremy and have gotten some pictures of them. I wish I could have talked to all of you together, but we take what we can get."

For three hours, she talked to them and took pictures. By the time she left, she was so engrossed in thoughts about the technical aspects of the article that she was able to forget about her other problems. When she arrived at Grosvenor House, they had a suite ready for her. After settling in, she got to work.

CHAPTER TWENTY FOUR

The glow of the computer screen was the only light in the dark room when Danny looked up. She reached over and turned on the desk lamp, stood up, stretched, and rubbed her eyes, wondering what time it was. She went to the bedroom to look at the clock as she absently thought that she'd have to buy a new watch since she'd lost her old one in the mountains. She was a little surprised to see that it was nine thirty. She'd been working for three hours without a break, and her stomach was empty and complaining. The light lunch she had taken with Jasmine had disappeared long ago, so she picked up the phone, rang room service, and ordered an omelet, a fruit plate, and some toast.

She hung up and went to the window to look out at the streetlights and the darkness of Hyde Park beyond. As she stood there, it came to her that she was alone for the first time in over a week. She welcomed the quiet and felt that, as she had immersed herself in writing the article, her jumbled nerves had settled down. She felt like herself again, quiet and calm, and knew she was ready to look objectively at the events of the past week.

Like Geremy, she could hardly believe that only a week had passed since she'd found him standing in the middle of Jasmine's wrecked flat. Starting with that memory, she began to move through the events and feelings of the past week. She wanted to understand where they had brought her and where she could go with the lessons she hoped she had learned. She was so deep into her thoughts that she had completely forgotten about the omelet, so the knock on the door gave her a start. She had been thinking about the first time she and Geremy had made love so, for an instant, she thought he was at the door. When she saw that the caller was room service with her dinner, she didn't know if she was relieved or disappointed.

She finished eating her dinner around ten thirty and then spent the next four hours either working on the article or thinking about her parents, Geremy, and what Dario had said about letting go of the past. As she wrote, she found that the theme of releasing the past became the theme for the article. In covering the history of the band and its continued success through the years, she was able to weave an underlying message about the importance of acknowledging the past while at the same time releasing it in order to make room for the future. She used the musical changes that the band had gone through over the years as an analogy for the changes and releases that everyone must manage in day-to-day life. She concluded that the band and the fans had changed together and that, in keeping with that process of change, the fans could rest assured that this concert tour would combine the old with the new in a way sure to please their fans, both old and new.

She saved what she'd typed, turned the computer off, and turned off the desk lamp. She sat in the dark thinking about her parents and the man who had run into the car. Tears trickled down her cheeks as her heart swelled with love for her parents. She pictured them in her mind's eye as she first hugged her mother and then her father as she bid them farewell.

She knew that releasing the bitterness toward Pembroke would take a little more time, but she knew she would eventually do it. She also knew that she would not take him to court to make him do the five hundred hours of community service. It was time to let it all go. She felt as if a wall of ice were melting inside of her and, as it melted, her tears dried. When she went to bed, she felt light with relief and fell into a deep and restful sleep.

—

Danny woke up at seven fifty eight, refreshed and relieved that most of the fatigue that had dogged her for two days was gone. She was out of bed by eight ten and back at the computer to check her work from the night before. She remembered thinking that it was very good at two in the morning; she just hoped that it looked as good in the cold light of day.

She sat down with a cup of tea and reviewed the piece. Aside from a few spelling errors, she thought it was good enough to run a copy by Dennis Eckhart, the Mystic Celts' manager. As she sat with cup in hand, she made a mental note of the other errands she wanted to run while she was out, one of which was to take the only roll of print film she'd shot to get it developed. The other rolls she'd used were slides, so she'd just FED-X them, the processed photos, and a floppy disk to the magazine. If everything went smoothly, she might be able to wrap this job up by Friday.

Feeling the best she had in days and wanting to keep the mood, she decided to pamper herself for her day around London. She pulled one of her new dresses out of the closet and laid it on the bed. It had short, capped-sleeves, and a snug bodice with five gold buttons down the front. The bodice loosened at the waist into a flaring, thigh-length skirt that moved beautifully when she walked. Danny's favorite thing about the dress though was its color: brilliant red. She had modeled it for Jasmine, who had guaranteed her it was a showstopper. She pulled out some black panty hose and the new black heels she had worn the day before and set them next to the dress. In keeping with her taste, the outfit was a simple but chic. She looked it over, nodded in approval, and went to get her bath ready.

She took a leisurely lavender-scented bath and then smoothed lavender-scented lotion all over her body. She carefully applied some make-up before getting dressed. When all her ministrations were done, she looked at her reflection in the mirror with approval. As she turned in front of the mirror, she decided that Jasmine was right: definitely a showstopper. When she went down to the lobby and made her way to the door, every single person who saw her turned to watch her pass. She walked out onto Park Lane and hailed a taxi, a large smile decorating her face.

The shop where she dropped the roll of print film was near Earl's Court, so she decided to see if Sergeant Earling was available, even though she'd forgotten to call him first. When she arrived at the Earl's Court police station and stated her business, the constable behind the desk asked her to take a seat while she rang Earling. A few minutes later, Earling appeared and showed her to one of the small consultation rooms on the first floor.

"You are looking very well, Miss Davis. France seems to have agreed with you."

Danny shrugged and smiled. "It was an interesting experience, I'll say that much for it." She sat down in the chair he indicated. "Sorry I didn't call before coming. I was in the neighborhood, so I thought I'd take my chances."

He shook his head. "Quite all right. This shouldn't take long. We identified a connection between the men who were causing you trouble. They all worked for a company called Sanders Enterprises."

"Sebastian Sanders?"

"Yes. Do you know Mr. Sanders?"

A wry grin creased Danny's face. "I met him France."

"In France? He must have gone over soon after we had our little chat with him. Anyway, he told us that Hansen, Maloney, and Ortega—that's the man who pulled the knife on you—all worked in his warehouse in Esher. He said that he had fired all three for not showing up for work and that he didn't know anything about why they would be interested in you."

Danny laughed. "He was the mastermind behind it all!"

"What exactly happened in France?"

"If you don't mind, I'd rather tell you after I hear what you found out." Seeing the look of doubt on Earling's face, Danny was quick to reassure him. "I think if you tell me what you know, I'll be able to make better sense of what I discovered. I promise, I'll tell you everything."

"Fair enough. After we had our chat, McCafferty did a little digging into the activities of Mr. Sanders and Sanders Enterprises. It seems that Mr. Sanders sold a fake porcelain figurine as authentic to an American buyer. He claimed he had been completely fooled by the piece, so no charges were brought, but he lost credibility with his upper-crust clientele. In short, he was financially in dire straights and his creditors were beginning to feel nervous about his ability to repay his debts."

"Well, that was the piece to the puzzle I was looking for. Depending on how you look at it, his creditors will either be relieved or disappointed to know that he's dead."

"What?"

"He died on Mt. Valier last Saturday while he was attempting to kill me and Geremy Hawker."

"Please. Start from the beginning, and tell me what happened."

Danny relayed the events of the weekend, without revealing the detour into Pangea. She told Earling that she and Geremy had managed to escape with only a few cuts and scrapes, but that Sebastian had plunged down the mountain and that, as far as she knew, his body had not been recovered.

"He wanted the ring because he thought it led to a hidden treasure?"

Danny laughed. "Can you believe it?" she asked with feigned incredulity. "Hidden treasure stories abound in the Pyrenees, for some reason. Probably because of all the caves and the romantic aura of the area."

"What happened to the ring?"

Danny felt it, warm against her breast, as she shrugged. "I'd say it's where it won't cause any more trouble."

"With Sebastian?"

"Possibly. He had it on when he went down the mountain."

"How can you be sure he's dead?"

"I'm very sure. It was an awful fall. No one could have survived it. Now, Sergeant, what about Hansen and Maloney?"

"As a matter of fact, the French police are detaining our boys so that they may ascertain whether they were responsible for some burglaries in Toulouse. Of course, Hansen and Maloney claim their innocence, but the police want to make sure before they send them home. If possible, I'll need you to come back in about two weeks so we can wrap this up. Will you still be in England?"

"I think so. I plan to take a holiday at a cottage in the Cotswalds. If my plans change, I'll let you know."

He stood up and led her to the door. "Thank you for your cooperation, Miss Davis. I think we can bring this affair to a close very quickly."

"Thank you for your help. Good day, Sergeant."

The day was going very well, and Danny returned to the hotel with the smile still on her face. She had completed all her errands and even managed to go by Annie's store for an hour-long visit. But the spring in her step and her smile faded as she walked through the entrance hall toward the elevators and reception. When she was sure she was not mistaken, she called out to the man near the reception desk. "Stephen?"

He turned around and looked at her like a starving man seeing a luscious meal. "Danny!" He put his bag and coat down, took her in his arms, and gave her a big hug. Then he pulled back and looked at her for a brief moment before giving her a long, hungry kiss.

Geremy had been sitting in the hotel's lounge when he saw Danny go by. He quickly settled his account and tried to catch up with her. As he came around the corner and into the large reception area, he saw her from behind, in the arms of a well-dressed man. He backed up a few steps and watched them from a distance, knowing that the man must be Stephen from Seattle. Geremy couldn't believe how beautiful Danny looked, and he felt a stab of jealousy when he saw how Stephen looked at her and how he kept his arm possessively around her. He continued to watch as they walked with arms around each other to the elevator. Geremy didn't move until the elevator doors closed. He left the hotel, sure in the belief that in the two days since he'd seen her, Danny had decided to reunite with Stephen.

"Stephen, what are you doing here?" Danny asked as they entered her room.

His eyes looked her over from head to foot as he tossed his rain coat over the back of one of the chairs. "You look beautiful."

"Thank you. Now, please tell me what you're doing here."

"Jasmine called me …"

"Jasmine Baker?" she interrupted.

He nodded. "Jasmine called and told me that you were having a hard time and that I should come over for a visit. Cheer you up, take you out, spend some time with you." He held his arms out from his sides and smiled. "So here I am."

Danny was dumbfounded. "I can't believe Jasmine called you." She made a mental note to give Jasmine a good talking to.

Stephen arms fell back to his sides, but the smile remained. "So what's the problem? Why are you having a hard time?"

She went over to the sofa and sat down. She looked up at Stephen and patted the cushion next to her. "You better sit down because I don't think you're going to like what I have to say." She suddenly felt very tired and was wondering if feeling was such a great thing after all.

The smile left his face as he moved slowly over to the sofa, sure from her tone and expression that he was not going to like what she had to tell him. As soon as he sat down, Danny got up and began to pace back and forth, her right hand held firmly by her left. She stopped in front of him, started to say something, and released her hands as if loosening them would help her speak. But when she looked at him and saw his curious expression, words escaped her. She took a few more steps before turning to him.

"I'm sorry, Stephen. I can't figure out where to begin."

He stood up, took her hands in his, and bent down so he could see into her eyes. "Danny, what is going on? Either start at the beginning or start at the end, but tell me what the problem is."

She looked into his eyes, took a deep breath, and started at the end. "I'm in love with someone else and cannot marry you. " The words tumbled out of her mouth.

Stephen dropped her hands and took a step back. "What?" he whispered.

She stood not speaking as she looked at him. She felt relieved after telling him the truth, but the relief was mingled with sorrow as she saw the pain in his eyes. She went to him. "I'm so sorry, Stephen. I swear this has taken me as much by surprise as anyone."

"Who is it?"

"It's not really important is it?"

"I want to know!"

"His name is Geremy Hawker."

"Someone you work with?" he asked, not recognizing the name.

"He's the lead singer for the band I came here to interview."

He gave her a look of incomprehension. "Wait a second! How long have you known this guy?"

"Eight days," is what she said, but *all my life*, is what she thought.

"*Eight days*?!" he asked incredulously. "You say we're through because of a man you've known for *eight* days?"

"I don't expect you to understand..."

"Oh, I think I understand very well. This is a recurring pattern for you, isn't it?" he asked heatedly. "Whenever a relationship starts getting too serious or a man asks you for a commitment, you bolt. You always have a very good reason for going, but you go."

"I'm telling you how I feel."

"So you get involved with this guy, and as soon as he wants to commit, you move on again?"

"I don't know if we will get involved. He's with someone else."

"Oh? This gets better every minute," he said sarcastically. "You've fallen for the unattainable man. You're tossing off our relationship for a man who's not available. If that's not classic fear of commitment, I don't know what is."

"And you would certainly know, wouldn't you?" she asked, her own anger beginning to rise. "You, who went from woman to woman, practically changing them with the seasons. But now, the great Stephen Sorensen, most eligible bachelor in Seattle, has decided he wants to settle down. Only the woman he has chosen doesn't want to marry him so *she* must have a problem with commitment." She walked away from him, wanting to cool off before she said something that she'd regret. She turned and came back to him, only slightly cooled down. "And where do you get off psychoanalyzing me and my feelings? I'm telling you that I'm experiencing feelings that I've never felt before. The fact that I'm feeling them for a man who is involved with someone else does not reduce their intensity.

The feelings are just there, and I'm trying to be honest with you about them." She sat down on the sofa, the anger draining out of her and, with it, most of her energy. "Stephen, I just can't continue with our relationship when I feel this way about somebody else. It wouldn't be honest or fair," she said quietly, sounding as tired as she suddenly felt.

Stephen stood stiffly in the middle of the room, his face reflecting the blue, early evening light coming in through the window behind Danny. He stared out the window, letting the silence grow until it felt like a heavy, wet blanket weighing down the air between them. Finally, he pulled his eyes from the scene outside and looked down at Danny. "So this is it? I leave here, and we don't see each other anymore?"

Danny's body felt like lead again. She wanted to go to him, but she couldn't seem to get her limbs to cooperate. "I'm sorry, Stephen."

He pulled his coat off the chair and picked up the bag he had left by the door. He opened the door before turning back to her. "Goodbye, Danny." He left. The door closed softly behind him.

"Good-bye."

CHAPTER TWENTY FIVE

Danny rolled over and looked at the clock while she wondered who could be calling her in the middle of the night. She groaned when she saw that it was nine o'clock in the morning. That she had slept so late after going to bed at nine the night before told her the fatigue had returned. She still had her doubts about letting her feelings run free, especially if it meant she would sleep for twelve hours every time she had an emotional confrontation. She picked up the receiver and gave a groggy, "Hello?"

"Miss Davis?" came the cheery response from an unknown English man.

"Yes?"

"This is Dennis Eckhart, Miss Davis."

She rubbed one eye and sat up in bed. "Who?" she asked sleepily.

"Dennis Eckhart." When she did not respond he added, "Manager of the Mystic Celts."

"Oh, yes. Yes, sorry."

"I apologize if I woke you up …" He waited for her to politely let him know he had done no such thing.

"It's no problem. I should have been up by now." She stifled a yawn. "Did you get a chance to read the article?"

"Yes. I'm calling to say it's very good and that you can print it as is."

"Great. Thanks for calling me back so quickly." She let the next yawn run its course.

"My pleasure, Miss Davis. I hope we'll be able to work together again in the future."

"That would be great." She paused before asking, "Mr. Eckhart, why did you ask for me to do this article?"

"Ask for you?"

"Yes. My editor said that you specifically requested that I do this article on the Celts."

He paused for a moment before responding. "I didn't make any special requests for you to write this piece. Though now that I've seen the finished product, I probably will do so in the future."

"You didn't ask the magazine to send me?" Danny was more than a little bewildered.

"No, I'm sorry, I didn't. But, as I said, I will in the future. This piece was well done."

"Thank you very much. Good-bye." Her hand moved slowly through the air as she returned the receiver to its cradle. "Wow. That's weird." She pushed the covers back, got out of bed, and walked to the bathroom as she reviewed the conversation she'd had with her editor in May. She could have sworn that he told her that the Celts had specifically asked for her. And Geremy told her that the their manager had made all the arrangements. She looked at herself in the bathroom mirror and shook her head. "Very weird."

The call from Eckhart reminded her that she needed to pick up the film she had put in for processing. She took a quick shower and put on a pair of blue jeans and a blouse. She smiled at the black heels and red dress as she pulled her running shoes out of the closet. The other outfit was a showstopper, but she opted for low-key comfort this morning.

She waited for the clerk to pull her photographs, anxious to see how many of them would be good enough to go with the article. She hadn't taken very many of Geremy and Miles, so she was a little concerned at the reduced options that entailed. The clerk handed her the photo envelope and, as he rang up the purchase, she began to look at them. She was flipping through the pictures fairly quickly when her hands stopped as she came to the first of the four she had taken of Geremy as he sat at the desk in the house. She laid all four out on the counter and felt a chill when she saw the expression on Geremy's face as he looked back at her from the photograph.

The light for the picture was coming from the left and a little behind him, so his right cheek was shadowed, but his hair shone like gold, and he had a soft violet-and-gold halo around his head. Technically, with the lighting and the halo, it was a beautiful picture, but it was his expression that held her attention. He had a slight smile that barely reached his eyes, but they had such a soft, warm expression that she felt a rush of emotion as she looked into them. Regardless of what happened with Maggie, she knew how Geremy felt about her. She had caught it on film. She put the photographs back into the envelope, paid for them, and made her way back to the hotel so that she could look at the pictures in a more leisurely fashion.

Danny sat on the sofa with Geremy's photographs laying next to her. She had slowly reviewed the other photographs and was happy to see that many were good enough to go with the article. She put the photos she wanted to submit back into the envelope, but left the four photos of Geremy out on the sofa. She extracted the corresponding negatives and placed them along with the photos on the coffee table

She picked up the photograph of Geremy and looked at it for the umpteenth time. If she'd had any doubts before she saw this picture about his feelings for her, she had no doubts now. She also knew that it was possible that he was still in love with Maggie. The fact that she had not heard a word from him led her to believe that he and Maggie had gone away to get reacquainted and had not yet returned. She couldn't help but draw a further conclusion that, if they were still away together, they must have found that they were still in love. She remembered the look on his face when he saw Maggie in the den, and she felt such a pang of sadness that tears welled in her eyes. She blinked them back, wishing she knew why Maggie had not come back into his life until a week after she and Geremy had met. One week earlier, things may have been very different. A knock at the door startled her. She had to think for a second if she had ordered room service.

She found Miles Jensen standing in the hall when she opened the door. "Miles!"

"Hello, Danny. May I come in?"

She stepped back and motioned him in. "Yes, of course." He stepped in, and as she closed the door she added, "You are nearly the last person I expected to see when I opened the door."

"I hope I'm not disturbing you?" he asked as he looked around the suite.

"No, not at all. I was just doing some wrap-up work on the article."

He grinned. "Got it done in spite of all the excitement?"

"Yes. I have a few of the photographs I took the night you, Geremy, and I talked. Care to see them?"

"Absolutely."

"There are only a few. Most are slides and I haven't seen them, but the photos turned out quite well. Your female fan-following is sure to increase after the article is published." She pointed to the sofa. "They're over here." He sat down on the sofa and pulled the photos out of the envelope she'd handed him.

Danny sat in one of the chairs and watched as he nodded at some and laughed at others, but she could tell he had something on his mind. When he finished, he found her questioning eyes on him. "What's on your mind?" she asked.

He screwed up his face as he thought about his answer. He decided on the direct approach. "It's probably none of my business, but I have a good reason for asking." He paused and looked at her. She gave him an encouraging nod. "What's going on with you and Geremy?"

"Why are you asking me? Why don't you ask him?"

"Because I can't find him."

She crossed her legs and watched her hand as it smoothed the denim fabric against her thigh. "Have you checked with Maggie?"

"I know he's not with her."

Her head came up at the finality of the statement and his tone. She saw concern on his face. Looking back down at her hand, she said, "I haven't seen Geremy since Sunday."

Miles suddenly stood up as if he could no longer bear being still. "Have you had lunch?"

She shook her head as she realized that she was hungry.

"Let's go get some lunch, and I'll tell you why I came over here today. Maybe we can share notes?"

"Why are you concerned?"

"Lunch?"

"Okay." She went to the bedroom to grab her purse and was back in a flash. "I'm ready."

At Danny's recommendation, they took a table at the restaurant on the ground floor of the hotel. After they placed their orders, the waitress brought the drinks and told them the food would arrive in a few minutes. Miles took a long drink of his beer and gave a sigh of satisfaction before speaking.

"You say you haven't seen Geremy since Sunday?"

"No. Not since we got back from France. We went by the house so that I could pick up my briefcase and camera, and when we got there, Maggie was in the living room."

"Right. I brought her to the house."

"You?"

He nodded.

"Well, we went in, and when Geremy saw her, I'm afraid it was a little too much for me. We had been through an emotional wringer in France, so I was not in the best shape to meet the love of his life. When I saw how he looked at her, I couldn't take it, so I just turned around and left."

He nodded. "I was just coming downstairs when I heard the door close. Then I walked into the living room and saw Geremy hugging Maggie. I put two and two together and figured it was you that I heard leaving." He took another long pull on his stout and resumed his story. "So there I stood looking at them, only they didn't notice me at all, so I cleared my throat. Geremy turned and saw me, but kept looking around, I presumed, for you. I told him you'd left, and he ran downstairs after you."

Silence reigned as the waitress set lunch on the table. Miles handed his empty pint glass to her, asking for a refill. They both ate in silence for a few minutes before Miles continued his story in between bites.

"Geremy came back and, as might be expected, he was in a bit of a funk. I explained that Maggie had called me and that I had invited her to come to the house. Then John arrived, and we all talked for a minute, but I could tell that Geremy was distracted. After about ten minutes, he asked Maggie if they could go somewhere to talk. She said yes and they left. I didn't see him again until yesterday afternoon. He looked terrible, like he hadn't slept since Sunday. I was worried, so I asked him if he was alright. He gave me a very strange look and said that in resolving his past, he had lost his future. I asked him what had happened with Maggie and he said, still with that strange look on his face, 'Nothing.' The phone started ringing. I left to answer it and came right back, phone in hand, but he was gone. As I thought about what he'd said and how he looked, I became more and more concerned, so I've been trying to find him—with no luck. His housekeeper says he hasn't been home and there's no answer at the cottage. That's when I decided to check with you."

"No. I haven't seen or heard from him since Sunday. I thought that he and Maggie were off somewhere getting reacquainted." She sipped on her lager.

"Will you please tell me what happened in France?"

"Geremy didn't tell you?"

"No. He and Maggie went off together, so not only did I not hear what happened in France, I also did not find out where the hell Maggie's been for the past twenty-five years." She could hear the frustration in his voice.

"France was unreal. After we got to my brother's, we decided to send the ring to the men who where watching the house, hoping that they would take it and leave us alone. We knew where the maps led and had a copy of the script, so we figured we could give the ring back and still try to find the cave." She fell quiet, her half-eaten lunch totally forgotten as she remembered the hike. She shook her head slowly and resumed the story. "Only, we didn't count on the fact that the guy who wanted the ring in the first place was crazy. He barged into my brother's house, took me hostage, and made him drive him to Mt. Valier." She took a sip of beer and laughed. "Turns out you were right, Miles. He was convinced that the map would lead him to the long lost Templar treasure."

"No!"

"Yes!"

"Well, who was he? How did he know about the ring?"

"His father was the man who gave the ring to my mother."

"Blimey."

She laughed. "Blimey is right. But wait. It gets better. We get to the mountain and are climbing when he decides it's time to kill me.

"What?"

"He just wanted me long enough to make sure that Geremy or Philippe didn't cause any trouble. He figured he was almost to the cave, so he could dispose of me and make it look like an accident. To make a long story short, we fought, and I went down the side of the mountain and landed amongst a big pile of rocks. I was pretty banged up."

"Good Lord!" Miles, too, had forgotten about his lunch as he listened to the story.

"The funny part of the story is that the pile of rocks and the tree that had arrested my fall obscured the entrance to the cave of the blue light."

"I don't believe it!"

"Believe me when I say that so many strange things have happened since this whole thing began that I now believe that anything is possible and that there is no such thing as coincidence."

"So? What happened next?"

"I regained consciousness and, a few minutes later, Geremy found me. I thought everything was going to be okay. Only the man, Sebastian Sanders, was right behind him and hit him over the head with a rock. He was about to hit me when he lost his balance and fell to his death."

"Blimey." Miles shook his head in disbelief. "And what about the cave? How did you reach it?"

Danny gave a chuckle as she thought about the strange turn her story was about to take. She took a deep breath and continued. "Three people came out of the cave, lifted us up, and carried us to the cave." Miles eyebrows went up, but he kept silent as Danny went on. "Geremy was already unconscious, and I passed out, too, when I was lifted. But we were soon to discover that the cave was merely the entryway to the real wonder spot." Miles started to interrupt her, but she held up a finger, and he closed his mouth.

"When I came to the second time, I was in a soft bed in a dimly lit room and no longer had any injuries. I had awakened in Pangea." She felt a thrill when she said the name.

"Pangea?"

"It's the name of the place on the other side of the cave." She took another sip of her beer. "We saw some pretty amazing things. People have been living in Pangea since just after Atlantis sank."

"*Since Atlantis sank?* You mean there really was an Atlantis?"

"So it would seem."

"But how could they exist for so long without us knowing about them?"

"I'm not really sure. I came out of there with more questions than I went in with, that's for sure. Our guide, Dario, said that Pangeans help to maintain some kind of high vibrational wave that some people can tune into. I guess it raises their consciousness? He said that Geremy picks up the wave and that, through his music, he communicates the wave to the general population."

"That is heavy!"

"Tell me about it!" she said with a laugh. "You should have been there."

"I wish I had been," he said earnestly.

"Dario went on to tell us that we both had some work to do if we wanted to free ourselves up to reach the wave more regularly."

"What kind of work?"

She let out a big sigh. "Dario told Geremy that Maggie was alive and that he had to come to terms with his feelings for her. As for me, he told me that I had to release the bitterness that I've been holding toward the man who killed my parents."

Miles sat back against the booth seat and looked thoughtfully at Danny. "No small accounting bills there." He paused, and a speculative look came to his face. "How interesting that Maggie popped back into our lives just when Geremy was supposed to deal with his feelings for her."

"Yes, and that Geremy and I were rushed out of Pangea and arrived at just the right moment to find her at the house."

"The news about Maggie must have come as quite a shock," he said quietly.

"That is an understatement. Like I said, we'd been through the wringer by time we got back to London."

"And how are you doing, Miss Davis?" he watched her closely as she responded.

"I've been up and down more times in the last week than a yo-yo, but I think I'll be alright."

"What about you and Geremy?"

"What do you mean?"

He leaned forward and looked at her long and hard, the usual expression of humor gone from his face. "I've known Geremy for a long time. As a matter of fact, I was kind of responsible for him meeting Maggie." He looked down at his nearly empty glass and rolled it between his palms as he tried to determine how to say what he wanted to say. He knew how Geremy felt about Danny, but he hadn't been able to get a sense of Danny's feelings for Geremy. A firm believer that the eyes are the mirrors of the soul, he looked into hers to see what they told him about her. He felt power and honesty flowing from them and decided he could be frank with her.

"Geremy feels things more deeply than anyone I've ever met. I guess that's fairly obvious since he's carried this torch for Maggie for so long. It's just that he was so in love with her, he didn't hold anything back when he fell for her. Then when she disappeared, it was like a part of him disappeared with her. He was devastated when he heard that she was counted among the dead of that ferry accident. If it hadn't been for his music, he probably would have gone crazy. He was so filled with grief over her death even though he maintained for years that she wasn't dead." Miles's eyes were sad, but his lips curved slightly into a tight smile. "Interesting, yes?"

She gave a slight nod.

"He had a haunted look in his eyes for years. In the past few years, I was happy to see the look fade. He seemed to be finally putting her and his feelings for her behind him." He paused long enough to drain his glass and looked into her eyes again. "I'm telling you all this for two reasons. The first is that last week I saw a look on his face that I haven't seen since he was with Maggie. Only this time, the look was because of you. The second reason is that when I saw him yesterday, the haunted look had returned. What I don't know is why. I was hoping you could tell me."

"I don't know. Like I said, I haven't seen him since Sunday. On the plane back from France, we had agreed that we would chill out while he went to find Maggie. Then, when he found her, he was supposed to contact me and tell me where we stood. But you're telling me that it didn't work out with Maggie. I haven't heard from him, so I don't know what's going on."

"So you do care for him?"

"Care for him?" she repeated softly. She gave a small laugh as she looked back at him. "I've been in love with him since I was eight years old."

CHAPTER TWENTY SIX

Geremy lay on the grass in the middle of the island clearing. Twilight was falling around him and he lay watching and waiting for the first stars to appear. He had watched the clear sky turn from the sharp blue of midday to the soft teal-blue of late afternoon as he lay there contemplating the mysteries of love. His guitar was leaning against the big rock behind him, untouched since he'd put it there. He was not really conscious of the passage of time as he lay there, but he was conscious of the feeling of peace that seeped into him as he watched the changing colors of the sky.

He had spent the afternoon thinking about Maggie, saying good-bye to the woman he had known and loved for twenty-five years, a woman who he now knew no longer existed except in his memory. He had been in love with a dream, and it had taken a dose of reality to make him realize it. He had learned more about her in the three hours they had talked after leaving the house than he had known about her after a year of being together. Mostly, he had learned that the real Maggie could never measure up to the dream he had built around her. Nor could the love that he thought he'd felt for her in the past measure up to the love he felt for Danny in the present. He now knew why events had unfolded as they had. He needed Danny so that he could see Maggie clearly, and he needed Maggie so that he could see Danny clearly. He now saw everything clearly.

The rental car slid to a stop on the gravel as Danny parked it next to Geremy's Jaguar. She got out of the car and almost kissed the Jaguar because it told her he was here. She ran into the house, but knew immediately from the stillness that he was not inside. She went out the back door and walked to the river path where she began to run to the island. She was breathing fast when she reached the small beach that served as the boat launch. Looking across the water, she saw the boat on the island and without another thought, she waded into the cold water. She remembered that the river current had carried the boat to within a few feet of the island, so she let it carry her rather than trying to swim across it. The current was swift, but the river was deep enough so she didn't worry about hitting her knees on rocks. She was just about even with the island beach when she began to swim. The current released her, and she glided up to the beach.

Geremy smiled as he lay on the grass. He felt her before he heard her and heard her before he saw her. He stood up as she walked toward him, looking like a water nymph just emerged from the river. He took two steps, and she was in his arms. "I knew you would come."

His hug pulled her feet off the ground. As he made to swing her around, his foot caught on something, and they fell down laughing. Danny found herself on top of him, so she took advantage of the situation. Straddling his stomach, she leaned over him and pinned his hands to the ground near his head. "So you knew I would come, huh?"

He grinned up at her. "Yes, I did."

"And what made you so sure?"

"I was projecting my thoughts of love out to you," he said matter-of-factly, still grinning. "Besides, you said you'd rented the cottage, so I knew you would get here eventually."

"I see. You were just going to let me wonder, possibly anguish, over what had happened between you and Maggie?" Her strong thighs tightened around his middle.

"Ouch!"

"So what did happen?" Her thighs loosened.

"Nothing." He bucked, rolled over, and laid on top of her. "Which is what I came to tell you when I went to the Grosvenor House yesterday. I must say, I felt a scare when I saw you with Stephen in the lobby, though."

"You were at the Grosvenor?"

"Yes. I came to tell you that I had wakened from my dream of Maggie, but when I got there, you were in his arms and then you went upstairs together. I thought you had decided to stick with him."

"If you would have stayed in the lobby for thirty more minutes, you would have seen him leave."

He shook his head. "I ran straightaway, feeling quite muddled as I tried to work through everything that had happened."

"Did Maggie tell you where she'd been all these years?"

A shadow passed over his face. "Yes." He rolled off and lay next to her as he looked up at the sky. Danny propped herself up on her elbow and looked at him.

"Well?"

"It was really very simple. She met someone else, a man with whom she worked. He was offered a very nice job in Australia, so he asked her to go with him. They married and had three children, but he died last year.

"She came to England for a holiday, but also with the idea to look me up. For weeks, she'd had a strong impulse to call me, but didn't know how to get ahold of me. Plus, she didn't know what my situation was, if I'd want to see her. Then, a week before she was set to return to Australia, she ran into the person who had brought her to the gig where we first met. The woman gave her Miles's telephone number and also told her that I was not involved with anyone. Hearing that, she thought that we might be able to pick up where we left off. So she called Miles, and he invited her to the house."

"The way you looked at her last Sunday, I thought you would get back together."

Geremy shook his head. "It was great to see her, and for that first moment, time fell away, and we were young again. But when I turned and saw that you had left, I felt panic. I ran to catch you, but you were already gone. I went back into the house to get Maggie so that we could go somewhere to talk." He was silent for a moment as he recalled their conversation. "As we sat in the restaurant, all I could think about was you, how very calm and peaceful I felt when I was with you. I remembered that I had never felt peaceful with Maggie. She was so wild and unpredictable. It was good to see her and put the ghost to rest, but I knew I wanted to be with you. So we talked for a few hours and then we parted. She went back home."

"She's gone back to Australia?"

"Yes. She left yesterday."

"What about the ferry accident? Did she tell you about it?"

He nodded. "She was on the ferry, ready for a trip to France, when her future husband came aboard and asked her to go with him to Australia. She simply got off the ferry, went to the airport with him, and they flew to Sydney. No one knew."

"How could she do that to you? Leave and not tell you? Let you think that she had died?"

"She didn't know about the ferry accident and that she had been listed as dead until years later. As for leaving without telling me, she said she couldn't face me. She said that I loved her too much and that she couldn't take it. So she ran off with a man who made lots of money and who, as she put it, didn't cramp her style."

"Didn't her family miss her?"

"She was from Canada and had just come to England when we met, as a matter of fact. Her family was in Canada, and she was not in close communication with them. They thought that she had died and didn't know otherwise until she called them a couple of years later to tell them that she was in Australia. That's when she found out she'd been listed as dead. She said she thought about calling me, but kept putting it off because she didn't know what to say."

" 'I'm alive' would have been good for starters." Danny shook her head. "If you don't mind my asking, why did you fall so in love with her?"

He smiled up at her. "No, I don't mind you asking a question I've been asking myself. It's hard for me to say now exactly why because I don't think I remember her so much for how she was as much as how I wanted her to be. As you may have seen, she is quite beautiful and, as I said, a bit on the wild side. I had just come from a very stuffy, proper household, and she was like the wind, wild and carefree." His voice became a bit more animated. "She was also very exciting in bed. She was only the second woman I'd been with, so her experience and enthusiasm went right to my head, if you'll excuse the pun." He became quiet for a moment. "After she and I talked we went our separate ways and I was feeling so confused. Nothing was as it seemed. Then when I saw you with Stephen I felt very muddled. So I came here to sort things out."

"So, everything's sorted out?"

He knocked out her elbow support and rolled back on top of her. He leaned down and kissed her with tenderness and desire, and felt her response that mirrored his. "Yes, milady. I do believe everything is sorted out," he said, his voice husky.

Danny could only sigh in response as he began to unbutton her blouse and kiss her in a new spot as each button was released. When she opened her eyes, she smiled as she saw the first stars of the night shining in the dusky sky.

The End of the Beginning